P9-CFU-036

THE AWFUL GRACE OF GOD

The
DECEIVERS

FORGE BOOKS
BY HAROLD ROBBINS

The Betrayers (with Junius Podrug)
Blood Royal (with Junius Podrug)
The Deceivers (with Junius Podrug)
The Devil to Pay (with Junius Podrug)
Heat of Passion
The Looters (with Junius Podrug)
Never Enough
Never Leave Me
The Predators
The Secret
Sin City

HAROLD ROBBINS'

The DECEIVERS

JUNIUS PODRUG

A TOM DOHERTY ASSOCIATES BOOK
NEW YORK

THE DECEIVERS

A Forge Book
Published by Tom Doherty Associates, LLC
175 Fifth Avenue
New York, NY 10010

www.tor-forge.com

Forge® is a registered trademark of Tom Doherty Associates, LLC.

ISBN-13: 978-0-7653-1830-5
ISBN-10: 0-7653-1830-X

First Edition: September 2008

Printed in the United States of America

0 9 8 7 6 5 4 3 2 1

For
Matt Cimber

❖

Acknowledgments

Many people helped bring this book to fruition. They include: Jann Robbins, Hildegard Krische, Robert Gleason, Eric Raab, Melissa Frain, Elizabeth Winick, and Nancy Wiesenfeld.

Harold Robbins

left behind a rich heritage of novel ideas and works in progress when he passed away in 1997. Harold Robbins' estate and his editor worked with a carefully selected writer to organize and complete Harold Robbins' ideas to create this novel, inspired by his storytelling brilliance, in a manner faithful to the Robbins style.

A darkness will settle on the people of Cambodia. There will be houses, but no people in them, roads but no travelers; the land will be ruled by barbarians with no religion; blood will run so deep as to touch the belly of the elephant. Only the deaf and the mute will survive.

—ANCIENT CAMBODIAN PROPHECY (NIC DUNLOP, *THE LOST EXECUTIONER: A JOURNEY TO THE HEART OF THE KILLING FIELDS*)

The
DECEIVERS

1

❖

Phnom Penh, Cambodia

My name's Madison Dupre, people call me Maddy, but *Your name is Mud* pounded in my head like a bad rap beat. I hadn't heard the taunt since I was a little girl. It came back now as I sloshed in dirty water above my ankles down a dark street, worrying over the fact that I just killed someone.

I was in a strange city, one that made the list of the world's most dangerous places. No one would believe me if I told them I had only fought back. The thought of dealing with the police just added to my fears. In this small, poor country, police were not here to "protect and serve." They had a gun in one hand and held the other out for a bribe. And I didn't have the money to buy my way out of a murder charge.

Hell of a day, Mud. You sure know how to have fun.

If I was at home in New York sitting on a couch with a glass of Merlot, I would have had a lot of different emotions spiking through me like electric shocks. After all, I never killed anyone before. But cohesive thoughts about what I'd done didn't gel. I just kept pushing them to the back of my mind. The man was a pig, for sure. Someone tough like Tony Soprano would have said he got what he deserved. But I'm not tough.

Why me, Lord?

❖

Things went to hell at a place I never should have been, but desperation makes you do crazy things. We all have that panic button in us, a point where even the most timid of us will explode with fear and strike back.

I was scared. And wet. Really scared, really wet. Rain didn't drizzle and pour in Cambodia—it exploded from the sky. I was grateful that it washed the blood off my poncho and let me hide under it. Right now I needed that anonymity. For sure, I'd be spotted as a Westerner from the color of my skin, but Phnom Penh—*pa-nom-pen* is how I pronounced it—had a regular colony of free-living, free-loving, free-drugging young Westerners from places like Phoenix, Sydney, and London hanging about. When you leave your own country to live in a foreign one, they called you an "expat" for expatriate. Freewheeling Cambodia, where any kind of sex can be bought, called them "sexpats."

That's what the bastard was who I killed, a sexpat who preyed on children.

I'm a thirty-something businesswoman, an expert on antiquities from New York, in town on business. Dirty business, though not of my making. I'd been sent undercover to get information on criminals who looted antiquity sites even though I'm not a cop or even a detective—just an art expert who ended up in a city that was a pit stop before hell because I was too broke to turn down a dangerous job.

It wasn't long ago that I'd had it all—a high-paying job, a Manhattan penthouse with a closet full of Jimmy Choo shoes and Versace dresses, jewels from Harry Winston's on Fifth Avenue. Then I'd lost it all. That's why I was walking in the rain in *pa-nom-pen* with blood on my hands . . .

They say you should never shop for food when you're hungry because you'll pick up things on impulse. The same thing could be said about taking a dangerous job when you were broke.

I came to the Cambodian capital to resurrect my life, to get back to where I was before I fell from grace with the haughty world of priceless antiquities, to redeem my reputation—and bank account—with a feat that would stop antiquity looting from this small, poor third world country in the Far East.

But all my good intentions won't buy me out of a murder charge.

My feet kept moving faster than my mind as I sloshed in the dirty water. When it rained like this, the gutters overflowed and brought garbage and other foul things onto the sidewalks. And there was plenty of stuff in the gutters to float out. It was a tough town, a dirty, sullied one, not user-friendly, with a history of violence few cities could equal.

The most lasting impression of the city was illicit sex—it came in all varieties here, from two-dollar whores past their prime at twenty, to thirteen-year-olds who supplemented family income by spreading their legs for tourists who came halfway around the world to stick their cocks in places they'd do twenty-to-life for Stateside.

The city sported old-fashioned whorehouses, go-go bars with pole dancers, "date" bars with lap dancers, blow job bars with knee dancing, and a city dump where the scavenger families were so poor, a certain type of man could buy a child to do things considered unimaginable by sane people.

Like I said, Phnom Penh wasn't a nice place.

The whole region was also a mass of startling conflicts: Indochina—countries like Cambodia, Thailand, and Vietnam—had some of the world's most conservative social customs. It included a tradition that women wear conventional clothing, appear modest and demure, with a taboo on showing romantic affection between the sexes in public.

But those old-fashioned traditions were combined with some of the most beautiful women on the planet being available for hire for almost any imaginable sex act, involving any bodily orifice, usually for an amount of money most Americans called chump change and Cambodians called salvation.

While America had abandoned cowboys for astronauts as heroes after *Star Wars,* the Old West was hot stuff here where go-go bars often had names like Dodge City and Roundup Club, and featured thong-wearing pole dancers with cowboy boots who were able to shoot Ping-Pong balls out of their vaginas.

Buddhism's Noble Eightfold Path to enlightenment—right views, right intention, right speech, right action, right livelihood, right effort, right-mindedness, and right contemplation—was practiced Cambodian style side by side with banditry, lawlessness, civil war, and endless varieties of illicit sex, some of which involved young girls who should have been in classrooms rather than back rooms.

With the endless varieties of sex available, household pets probably even got into the act.

❖

Violence and political turbulence were also not strangers to the city. It wasn't uncommon to see men in battle dress, packing AK47s, swagger out of two-dollar whorehouses as serene Buddhist monks carrying begging bowls flowed by in their red- and saffron-colored robes.

AHEAD, TWO CITY POLICEMEN huddled under a portico as they smoked and jabbered with prostitutes. I tried not to look away, but kept my chin up and eyes straight ahead. The thought of being locked up in a Cambodian jail terrified me. If the city was a pit stop before hell, a prison here must be frightening enough to raise the hair on my soul. I began trembling despite the warmth of the monsoon rain.

A moto driver rolled by me with a passenger. Motos were a modern version of a rickshaw—they looked like a wheelchair being pushed by a small motorcycle. He stopped in front of a hostess bar and let off his passenger.

As I approached, the driver asked me, "Cowboy, you want girl for boom-boom?"

I pulled back the poncho hood enough so he could see I was a woman. "No boom-boom. I need a ride." I climbed into the passenger chair.

"Where you go?" he asked.

"Take me to the quay."

The river quay was a five-minute ride halfway to my hotel. It would give me a chance to think. I needed a plane ticket out of this nightmare, but I couldn't get on a plane without a passport and it was back at my hotel.

I didn't feel safe going directly back to the hotel because it was the first place the police would go if they were looking for me. The quay was the restaurant and tourist nightlife area of the city. I could slip into a restroom there and clean up any blood left on me. Then drive by the hotel in a regular taxi and see if a police car was outside. If it was clear, I could dash in and get my passport from the front desk and make a run for the airport. I wouldn't even go to my room to pack. Just leave it.

Jesus. My mind wasn't geared up to deal with this. It all sounded so complicated. And scary. What would I do if the police were already at my hotel? I had no place to go, nowhere to hide.

One foot in front of the other. That was how I took tough times; I just kept moving forward, putting one foot in front of the other, not looking back for fear the hounds of hell were yapping at my heels. My biggest regret whenever I felt miserable was not being rich—the rich weren't any happier than the rest of us, but at least they could afford to choose their miseries. Or buy their way out of them.

Police cars ahead had parked sideways in the street, creating a roadblock. All traffic was being stopped.

They found the body?

"Pull over, I'm getting off." I had to tell the driver twice before he understood.

He started yapping about the fare. I pulled dollar bills out of my pocket and gave them to him and hurried away. American dollars were more welcome than Cambodian currency.

Another police car came down the street behind me.

I was in front of a boom-boom joint with large plate-glass windows that showcased provocatively dressed women and girls lounging on couches. A pulsating lipstick red sign flashed "La Petite Khmer." Khmer was the ancient name of the Cambodian people.

I took a deep breath and stepped into the whorehouse.

2

❖

I was immediately assaulted by the warm scent of sweet tropical fruit—apparently the perfume of choice.

Brightly lit, the room had flashy neon signs of palm trees, coconuts, and posters of hula girls on the walls. How the Hawaiian posters made it from Honolulu to the wall of a whorehouse in Phnom Penh surely was a tale to be told.

The walls were stark white and so were the couches—when the sun was up, you'd need sunglasses to navigate the room. I'm sure no one thought about the fact that white was the color of purity.

Petite young women wearing bright pastel shorts and tops glittering with red sequin trim lounged on the snow white couches and looked like Christmas ornaments from an "Adults Only" store.

My movie perception of what a house of prostitution should look like included crystal chandeliers, round red velvet couches, and erotic women in elegant evening dresses. This place was a faked orgasm—stark commercialism under racks of white lights that exposed its dark heart, cheap sex, and not a few roaches.

The "girls"—a generic word for prostitutes of any age—were all chips off the same block. None looked over thirty to me and most appeared to be in their late teens to early twenties. Some wore short-shorts with bras and spiked heels; others, cowboy boots and light cotton skirts that barely covered their crotch area.

I instantly felt sorry for them. When I saw people who were down-trodden for reasons out of their control, a phrase my mother often used would come to me: *But for the Grace of God go any of us.*

A matron with a big cheesy smile as sincere as a time-share salesman welcomed me.

"Come, come, come, everyone welcome. Have beautiful partner for you."

She made a grand, sweeping hand gesture at the roomful of young women who stared at me with limp eyes and professional smiles.

"Boom-boom for short time, boom-boom for long time, very good boom-boom—"

"No boom-boom." I nodded at a sign that advertised massages. "A massage, I want a massage."

"Good massage." She gestured at a girl dressed in bra and shorts with lacy frill and black patent spike heels. "Boom-boom for short—"

"A massage. I'm in a hurry."

What I wanted was out of the bright room with its large windows facing the street and into a back room where I could hide.

The matron waved us toward a door down the hallway. "Good massage. Boom-boom, too."

Her English was obviously limited to what was necessary for the business at hand.

I followed the girl down a hallway and into a room that was low budget basic: a double bed, a Chinese screen with a towel tossed over it, a small wood basin with a pitcher of water beside it. Too bare and plain even for a Motel 6.

A curtained window faced the street. I pushed the drape apart just enough to get a look outside. Two police officers on foot, maybe the ones I'd seen earlier, stood by a police car stopped in the middle of the street and were talking to the driver.

I hoped I wasn't the subject of their conversation.

I turned around and found the girl had removed her bra to expose small, erect mounds of breasts.

She couldn't have been more than eighteen or nineteen. No doubt a "mature woman" in her occupation considering that the country was notorious for having prostitutes in their early teens.

She stared at me, uneasy, her features passive, but her eyes wondering. I wasn't acting like a typical customer. Besides men, straight and lesbian women also came to Phnom Penh looking for action, paying for sex when they failed to hook up with other tourists who were birds of a feather, but their body language didn't have the hunted animal look that I had.

"Boom-boom" with a woman may have just been another paying customer in a day's work for this girl.

"Boom-boom?" the girl asked.

I shook my head and made like I was rubbing myself. "Massage."

The girl pointed at the white towel draped over a Chinese screen. I needed to get the massage or the girl would get suspicious. I stepped behind the screen and disrobed and wrapped the towel around me. The towel was thin but looked reasonably clean.

Knowing I needed to keep the girl on my side since I was acting strange, I took a twenty-dollar bill out of my handbag and gave it to her.

"Good massage," I said.

She nodded at a sign on the wall and rattled off something in Cambodian. It had the word "massage" in big letters and words in smaller print underneath. I gave it a quick glance but my first concern was the sheet on the bed. It looked reasonably clean, no stains that hinted at recent activity. I still didn't like the idea of lying on it but it was better than going back outside.

Lying facedown, I left the towel draped over my bottom half and kept my handbag beside me.

I twisted to tell her to go ahead and found she'd taken off her shoes and was slipping out of her shorts, leaving only a thin thong that barely covered her pubic area.

"We have a communications problem," I said.

She gave me another puzzled look.

I rubbed my side. "Just massage. No boom-boom."

She nodded but I had no idea if she understood. I wondered if she knew how to give a therapeutic massage . . . or only the kind that men got off on.

❖

I raised up enough to pantomime again, rubbing myself. "You understand, massage."

The girl nodded vigorously and said something again that I didn't understand. She gestured at the sign on the wall again.

"Yes, good massage," I said.

I forced myself to lie still, resisting the urge to run to the window and peek out or stick my head out the door to see if the police were coming down the hallway. As her hands touched my skin, my tense muscles contracted with spasms.

Relaxing wasn't an option, but I tried to smother my panic and think about what I'd say if the police suddenly barged in and started questioning me in Cambodian. Do they rape women in Cambodian jails, I wondered. In a country where human life counted for so little and young girls supported families by spreading their legs, it didn't seem likely that these cops would respect a woman's body.

Would they understand if I asked for the American embassy? Would they care even if they understood?

Jesus.

The girl applied a light coat of warm oil as her hands glided over me. The oil had the same tropical fruit smell as the lobby, but it wasn't an unpleasant scent. The warm, gentle touch felt good. Rather than kneading my back, her fingers danced, delicate strokes on my naked skin.

Surprised and relieved that she could actually do a massage, I closed my eyes and tried to relax. If the police came in, maybe I'd just act sleepy. Yeah, that would fool them. Just keep my eyes shut as they jerked me off the bed and did whatever they do to a woman who just killed a man.

The girl's hands were really quite wonderful, moving smoothly from my shoulders down to the small of my back and up again, barely touching my skin even when applying oil. The spasms stopped as the tension in my back faded, but my jaws were still tight as I listened for sounds of police boots in the corridor.

How do I get myself into these things?

This wasn't the first time in my life that I found myself in a foreign country and in danger . . . but it never should have happened again. Fool me once, shame on you, fool me twice . . . *shame on me*. I walked into it with both eyes wide closed. It was my fault, no one else's. Bait was put out and I jumped for it. I should be home in my Manhattan apartment with my feet up, watching the evening news, not making the news in a small, poor, corrupt country on the other side of the world.

The country still had millions of land mines left over from decades of war and I felt as if I'd stepped on one.

The girl pulled the towel off of me as she worked my tush with a little more firmness. Some people didn't like having their bodies touched, but I loved massages. When I was in the money, I had several a week. The soothing rhythmic kneading always helped me relax and think; besides, getting my rear end and thighs worked was serious business as cellulite built up and things started a southern drift.

The girl's hands moved to the inside of my thighs and flowed down below my knees to the soles of my feet. I gave a little sigh as she worked her thumbs into the bottom of my feet. Reflexology on the feet and hands was supposed to relieve stress and promote healing to other areas of the body.

She said something in Cambodian and signaled me with her hand to turn over and I rolled to lie faceup.

Her thong was gone, exposing a neatly trimmed sheath of fine pubic hair, as shiny as the coat of a black cat. She was completely naked now.

"Just massage," I warned her.

The girl bobbed her head and pointed at the sign as she spoke. Again I only caught the word "massage," but I hoped she understood. It was hot and humid in the room, not surprising since it was a tropical country. Maybe taking off her clothes was her way to cool off.

I closed my eyes again and tried to tune out my fears that the police were going to kick open the door at any moment.

Each passing minute gave me a little more hope that I wasn't going to be arrested, that the only thing between me and safety was a taxi ride to my hotel to pick up my passport before the cabbie dropped me at the airport and I took the next flight that went anywhere out of Cambodia.

She applied oil to my face, gently caressing my forehead and temples, moving down to my cheeks, working the tension in my jaw area with the delicate tips of her fingers before she moved down to my neck. The fluid strokes were comforting, but didn't calm my brain. You don't soothe away death with a gentle caress.

❖

Art and money . . . the sources of all my troubles. A love of art and the desire to have material things. Art was number one in my heart. Whether artists created their works yesterday or a thousand years ago, they imbued it with an essence from their own human spirit. That spirit shined and touched our hearts and minds when we viewed it. I've never stood in the Louvre and gazed at the *Venus de Milo* without getting goose bumps. That feeling wouldn't come if it was just a piece of cold, dead marble. I got that same feeling when I looked at other exquisite works of art.

Artifacts from ancient times were wonders to me, cultural treasures that had to be protected from the ravages of time and people. Protecting them wasn't always easy. Because of their priceless rarity, they not only roused greed in people, but a desire bordering on lust, sometimes powerful enough to incite murder. I know from personal experience how many of the seven deadly sins these priceless objects wrought.

At times like this I wondered why I hadn't become a lawyer or doctor, even a nun—anything to have kept from getting involved in the international game of art where billionaires called the shots and the only rule was that *anything* went when they wanted a museum piece.

I really screwed up my life. If there was only one pile of poop in the world, I'd find it and step in it. And there'd be a land mine under it.

The girl's fingers trickled down the outside of my thighs while her other hand danced on my abdomen. It felt good . . .

Her palm gracefully slid over my genitals at the same time she squeezed my breast. I froze. My eyes snapped open.

She used that massage phrase again and bobbed her head at the sign she'd indicated earlier. I followed her gaze. The sign was a mishmash of languages. Besides the Cambodian one, I recognized French, English, and German.

The English version said a massage was $5. Under it in small print: "Exotic Massage $10."

I had paid twice over for an exotic massage. I didn't need a translation to realize what "exotic" meant.

The girl caressed the tip of my nipple and it immediately got hard.

Her other hand cradled my pubic area, her fingers stroking the erogenous zone in an up-and-down fluid motion, brushing over my clit.

I'd read somewhere that straight women didn't have the same

prejudice about having sex with other women that straight men did about having sex with other men . . . it's just that in general women preferred men for cultural and reproduction reasons.

It sounded like something a man had thought up—probably one who got off watching two women making love.

Good Lord—here I was in a foreign country, on the run from the police, getting stroked by a teenage prostitute in a whorehouse.

And my nipples got hard.

I am truly a damaged person.

Two Weeks Earlier

3

❖

Rainy days and Mondays always get me down played in my head as I came out of a grocery store and into a downpour. The Carpenters's song summed up my feelings. Rainy days made me melancholy even though the city always smelled cleaner afterward, a layer of urban rot washed away. But now that I was back to struggling for basics after ten years of hard work and success, rain made me a little glum and dispirited. Maybe because it forced me to stay in my little postage-stamp apartment and stare at the four walls most of the time.

I thought about that attitude as I came out of the store and found the sprinkle that had been coming down when I went in was now a downpour. *Nothing negative in my life*, was my new mantra. Rain or shine, I was going to have a positive attitude. I wasn't going to let anything keep me down; not the rain, the song, or the bitter turns my life had taken. *I'm not down, I'm just on my way up from scraping bottom . . .*

But broke and out of work were understatements. Crash and burn better described my situation. I had been the head curator for a small, very rich museum. I lost my big paying job, my park-view penthouse, and all the social-economic accoutrements of having "made it" when I innocently got swept into a crooked art purchase for the museum.

Being "not guilty" didn't count after I paid over fifty million dollars for a Babylonian piece that turned out to have been looted during the sack of the Baghdad museum when American forces entered the city. The dead bodies that started popping up in the wake of the purchase didn't help, either.

I made it once and I'd be back on top again. I'd have to work even harder than I did the first time, but I wasn't afraid of hard work. When opportunity arose, I'd grab it. My father used to say that a great lesson in life was never to be a standing target but to roll with the punches life threw. That's what I was doing now—rolling with the punches so I could get back on my feet.

"I can take it!" I told the rain. That was my expression of the power of positive thinking. I could make things happen, but I had to keep myself in a good place.

Despite my positive thoughts and the good luck crystal I'd bought in a Chinese herb shop, things were still pretty shitty. Broke and desperate were words I wanted to drop from my internal résumé.

The grocery store was four blocks from my house, but New York blocks could be as long as football fields—and they stretched out twice as long when it was cold, windy, or wet. Just what I needed when I'd been ecologically conscious, choosing paper over plastic. Not a good choice for walking in the rain—a paper bag became biodegradable real fast when it got soaking wet.

As I struggled against wind, rain, and the wrath of the gods I'd offended—I was so beaten down, it had to be from divine retribution—I tried to keep my groceries from slipping out of the disintegrating bag.

Besides thinking positive about getting back what I'd lost, I'd been thinking green lately, too, trying to do something for the planet. I guess the wake-up call for me were the stories of seals and polar bears starving and drowning because arctic ice was melting from global warming—while "global warming deniers" were racking in huge fees from polluters. So I'd bought nonfat organic milk in a glass bottle rather than plastic, but now its weight threatened to carry it through the bottom of the wet bag and break at my feet, taking with it my seven-grain bread, turkey bacon, and free-range eggs.

❖

Strapped for money, I still bought high-end food for breakfast. I figured it balanced out the cheap fast food I had for dinner and the crackers and cheese I had for lunch. I hated cooking—for one. Cooking was only fun when I had a man and a bottle of wine to share it with.

When I fell from grace with the haughty world of New York art, none of my friends or associates threw me a lifeline, but I guess that said more about me than them. On gloom and doom rainy days I sat in my apartment and wondered how things would be now if I had just done things a little bit different . . . and told myself to learn from my mistakes because soon I would be right up there again.

I wore a lightweight, hooded raincoat rather than carry an umbrella. That left the paper bag exposed, so I hurried, passing street vendors who were frantically covering books, hot dogs, and hot—as in pirated—fashion jeans, CDs, and DVDs.

The mixture of races, clashes of cultures, and street people hawking everything from designer brand purses—knockoffs, of course—to peanuts and hot pretzels gave some New York neighborhoods an exotic third world ambiance. Close your eyes, listen to raised voices speaking a Babel of tongues and the angry honking of car horns, and you could imagine yourself in Beirut. Sadly, the sounds of emergency sirens and threats of terrorist bombs sometimes also gave the great city the feel of Beirut.

As usual, every taxi that went by had their roof emblem off, signaling that they were occupied or off-duty. In New York you could step off almost any curb and taxis fought for you . . . unless it was raining. Then the mysterious happened and taxis were more likely to run you down than stop—or they simply vanished from the streets.

Maybe it had something to do with quantum physics or that stuff called dark matter that astronomers now say we're all swimming in. Not that I had to worry about it. These days my transportation were my feet and the subway, a far cry from a few months ago when I paid more for parking my car each month than I do for rent on my current studio walk-up.

By the time I reached my building, I had the bottle of milk in one coat pocket, eggs in another, and everything else in the wet bag clutched to my chest.

My landlord came down the front steps to the street as I hurried up. He gave me a smirk that said things could be better for me if I was "nicer" to him. I gave him a small, polite smile. He didn't bother turning back to open the building door for me. *Bastard.*

I had already bounced a rent check with him and I'd only had the place for three months. Not a clever move.

Vaguely southern Mediterranean in looks, he had the bald head, thick neck, and petroleum-barrel torso of a professional wrestler on one of those TV shows where men brutalized each other in a ring while the crowd roared for more blood. He didn't need to pump up on steroids because he was naturally a big, hairy ape.

He looked at me as if I were a piece of meat to pound with his dick.

That image came as I scrambled to cover the bounced check, hocking a wristwatch for $900 that had cost me $11,000.

Now I was desperately short of things to hock. Which created another perverse thought: How many weeks—days?—of apartment occupancy could I "buy" if I gave him a blow job?

Jesus—what a repulsive thought, but it popped into my head as I climbed the interior stairs to my apartment. It wasn't the sort of thing that a man would think about. And I'd gulp down Drano before I did anything like that—at least I hoped I would.

But whichever way I went, bleeding wrists or lying down with a swine, I wouldn't be the first woman who did something repulsive in desperation. Or the first man, for that matter, though it was easier for a man in one respect: A bed at the homeless shelter for him doesn't come with a fear of getting raped.

Think positive . . .

I put away the groceries and stood by my window, staring down at the street below, not really seeing anything, just watching the hypnotic rain glide down, trying not to think about the mistakes I'd made and the wrong turns I'd taken.

Another line from that Carpenters's song played in my head: *Feelin' like I don't belong . . .*

I didn't belong to anyone; no husband, lover, significant other. No family, not even a job where I could relate to others for eight hours a day. Twists and turns and bumps, losing control and going into a spin around dangerous curves, that's what my life seemed to have become the last few months. Just about everything had changed.

I wasn't just broke, I was lonely and broke. I hadn't had a date for so long, the battery had run down in my vibrator. I sighed just thinking about the money I used to spend, the things I used to have, the lovers I once enjoyed . . .

Just keep thinking positive and roll with the punches.

My cell phone rang. I started to hit receive and stopped because I didn't recognize the calling number. Better that it went into voice mail. I had a new address and new phone number, but I was still getting hassled by bill collectors. The CIA could learn things from these people. I had to dodge one coming into my building yesterday. The woman had called me a "deadbeat" loud enough to be heard in the Bronx. I rushed into the building, embarrassed. There were some things I could confront and control with as much courage as a 125-pound woman could muster . . . but knowing I owed debts that I couldn't pay wasn't one of them.

I had scribbled "Deceased—Return to Sender" on collection notice envelopes now for weeks, but it hadn't fooled anyone.

I checked voice mail and my suspicion was right. A Mrs. Garcia wanted me to give her a call so she could arrange a special repayment plan for my Saks bill. She made it sound like I was getting in on the ground floor of a golden opportunity. The woman should be selling penny stocks.

I already knew from experience that the tenor of the calls got nastier as time went on.

Those TV ads where the bankruptcy lawyer with the shiny polyester suit and toothy crocodile smile says he can get the hounds off your back were beginning to look better every day.

Being a deadbeat hadn't been my plan and wasn't the way I thought of myself. Things had just gone to hell for me in the proverbial handbasket. Real fast. Like slipping down the side of a glacier into a smoking volcano.

I'd come to the big city out of college full of dreams and drive and had spent a decade working myself up from a fifth-floor studio walk-up to a penthouse in the Museum Mile area on the haughty Upper East Side.

Now I was back in a small apartment. Smaller than my last bedroom. Gone were my designer-furnished penthouse with a view of Central

Park, my $85,000 Jaguar, and my walk-in closets full of designer labels. Hell, I lived in a walk-in closet.

Gone was my black American Express Card, too. You got one by invitation only. I'd heard that the card was usually offered only to people charging $150,000 or more a year. To me, the card was my diploma from the School of Hard Knocks that said I had made it. I felt worse about losing it than my sports car.

Materialistic? Sure. And not "green" of me. It was only a piece of plastic and plastic was the nonbiodegradable bane of the world, the stuff that would still be around choking the environment ten thousand years from now, indestructible "artifacts" revealing our artificial souls to archaeologists who have computer chips for hearts and brains.

I was really in a confused mental state, vacillating between wanting to save the world for baby seals to wishing I still had a credit card that permitted a person to buy a ridiculously priced sealskin purse . . .

Christ, sometimes it felt like my thoughts were ricocheting in my head, one minute desperate to do anything to be back on top, the next worrying about the health of the planet. I was still suffering aftershocks from the collapse of my career. It didn't just come to an end—a Category Five hurricane roared through my life.

Still, I couldn't walk away from antiquities. These fragile remnants from past civilizations, often the only remembrances of millions of people who had lived and loved and created great works of beauty, were a part of me, in my blood even before college. When I was a little girl I had a stack of books next to my bed on the history of art from my father's personal collection. I leafed through those books, staring at the gold, marble, bronze, and jade works created by people dead a millennium.

Working with antiquities wasn't something I could walk away from, but I needed to reinvent myself because no one would hire me.

I went freelance, opening up my own business: *Madison Dupre, Art Inquiries*. That and my cell phone number were all my business cards said.

Art Inquiries. I liked the sound of it. It had a snooty British ring to it that gave my business a bit of class.

I deliberately made the name vague because I wanted to be open for any kind of work—tracking down art for buyers, appraising it, investigating ownership history, authenticating pieces, negotiating prices. My phone number had to go on, but I didn't dare put my address on the cards for fear a prospective client would know where I lived. People with money wanted to deal with people who had money . . . at least enough of it to infer that they were successful.

If a meeting was necessary, I planned to go to the client's place or meet for lunch. Just in case I absolutely needed a mailing address, I rented a mail-drop box in the Financial District. The address left the impression I had an office in a prestigious building, but that facade hadn't been necessary yet because I had no clients.

I mailed business cards to everyone I could think of—people who knew me and I hoped trusted me, people I'd met through the museums, major collectors, and galleries I'd dealt with over the years. I even wore out shoe leather going from gallery to gallery to drop off my card.

The commission from just one of the art buys and sales I used to handle on a regular basis would keep me on my feet as I got my new career rolling. But so far my phone hadn't rung yet. At least not from someone who wanted to *give* me money.

Plenty of wealthy art collectors could have used my help buying or selling art, but none were calling. The only "collectors" calling were the ones who dealt in past due bills.

After a month, I became worried. Two months and I was scared. Now I was just plain desperate. I couldn't hold out much longer. Soon I'd have to go to plan B—which I didn't have at the moment.

Where was my twenty-twenty hindsight a year ago? Putting nothing in a savings account was mind-blowing. My theory had been that after you paid for the essentials, anything left over was free money. You earn it, you spend it. Simple as that. But I hadn't planned on a thermonuclear meltdown of my life.

I lay back on my couch, telling myself to keep thinking positive. It wasn't long before my eyes closed and I fantasized about being on a beach with crystal-clear blue water and bright sunny skies. I was naked and walking toward a tanned, gorgeous-looking man . . . he was naked, too. We lay on the sand, our bodies coming together with the warm wet surf teasing my bare skin . . .

Then trouble knocked.

❖

If a thing's worth having, it's worth cheating for.

—W. C. FIELDS TO MAE WEST

4

❖

I jerked awake to a persistent knocking at my door.

I wasn't expecting anyone and I knew the neighbors on my floor had not gotten home from work because I hadn't heard feet on the stairs and slamming doors. That left undesirable candidates—a bill collector or my horny landlord.

I looked through the peephole in the door and got a surprise: My Thai restaurant deliveryman grinned at the peephole.

I'd become a regular customer at the restaurant down the street and was a good tipper despite my poverty. My favorite dish was a noodle and vegetable combo with chicken and spicy peanut sauce.

I hadn't buzzed him in, but he could have slipped in with someone coming or going or made a delivery to another apartment in the building. I unlocked the door and opened it, but left the chain attached and my foot against the door. He looked pretty harmless, but this was New York.

He had a brown paper bag in hand and a big smile.

"Hello, miss," he said. His accent was thick.

"Hi, Sammy." I couldn't pronounce his name so I called him something that sounded similar in English. I raised my eyebrows. "I didn't order anything."

"No pad thai. Something better." He held up the bag. "From Thailand. Art for sale."

My mood immediately picked up.

"Come in."

He knew I was in the art business because my name tag on the buzzer pad at the front door downstairs said "Art Inquiries."

Sammy seemed a bit edgy and nervous; not the way he usually acted. That put me on my guard.

"What do you have?"

"For you, very nice."

He took out of the bag a sandstone panel a couple inches thick and about the size of a car license plate.

My eyes lit up: a sandstone bas-relief with the venerable, aged look of a genuine antiquity.

Bas-relief figures were carved in the stone so the figures stood out from the background, as opposed to being etched in like an engraving. Creating raised figures wasn't easy. It required much more talent and time than simply etching figures, especially in hard materials like marble and sandstone.

The relief had three dancing goddesses called Apsarases, seductive women of Hindu mythology. Beautiful water and forest nymphs who played music and danced for the gods, they held a place in Asian myths similar to the Muses of Western mythology.

Far Eastern art wasn't my forte but I knew the dancers were a common motif in the artistic creations of temples in India and Southeast Asia.

Said to be able to change their shapes at will, the beauty of an Apsaras was beyond human description. Wives of the Gandharvas, court servants of Indra, the god of thunder and rain, the women danced to the music made by their husbands in the palaces of gods.

The instant question was whether I was looking at a bona fide artifact or a tourist reproduction.

I took the piece to examine the workmanship. Each female had struck a different dancing pose and had an elaborate headdress. Barebreasted with jewelry on various parts of their body—necks, arms, ankles, even some fingers—all had scant clothing below their neckline.

The fine detail was outstanding and no two dancers had the same clothes, jewelry, or expression.

Experts could usually tell just by looking at a piece whether it was genuine. They looked at the quality and workmanship, even its rarity. But a good copy sometimes was hard to tell from a real artifact and scientific tests were needed.

Some artifacts were made from materials that lent themselves to being duplicated later. Cast gold and bronze were easier to fake than hard stone materials like sandstone, limestone, and marble that required more skill.

The outer appearance was important. The patina, a covering that develops gradually on an object, over centuries for many antiquities, was often simulated to make it look old, and that was often where the forger failed.

The patina on this relief had the aged appearance consistent with the inferred age of a piece a thousand years old.

Another tip-off for forgery was the use of modern tools that left telltale marks.

I examined the relief closely with my magnifying glass, looking for anything on the sandstone that showed it was made with modern electric tools like sanders, grinders, or saws, but saw nothing that revealed it was a fake.

The only odd thing I saw under magnification was a tiny mark in the background. The mark was almost a half-moon with the flat line on top slightly concave.

Because the mark could have been an imprint of a tool the artist used, or created when something pressed against the piece since it had been made, it didn't help me in determining if the relief was authentic.

As a professional, I would never have authenticated a big ticket item like this without putting it through scientific tests. But you can't make it in the art business without having radar in your gut—and my instincts were screaming that I was looking at a thousand-year-old piece.

I knew infinitely less about Far Eastern artifacts than Mediterranean pieces, but Sammy's piece struck me as Khmer art. The Khmers flourished as a powerful empire about a thousand years ago in Cambodia and left behind temple complexes that became choked by jungle over the ages.

Angkor Wat was the most prominent of the temple complexes. A magnificent edifice that ranks as a wonder of all time, many art critics consider it even more inspired than the monuments of ancient Egypt and Greece. But Angkor Wat had also been unmercifully looted over the centuries, with most of the stolen pieces making their way to Japan and the West through Thailand, along with most of the heroin that got pushed our way.

I could hardly breathe. My God . . . what I held in my hands was worth a small fortune.

"You like?"

"Yes. Uh, Sammy, where did you get this?"

He grinned. "Grandmother's attic."

"Uh huh." I smiled at him. I'm sure my lips were trembling as much as my knees. "You could make a lot more money if there were more of these."

He grinned and nodded. "Plenty more."

"I need to have the piece tested to help me authenticate it. You understand?"

He was already shaking his head *no*. "How much worth?"

"That's why I need to have it tested. Scientific tests are the only way we can see if it's real or a fake."

"No fake. How much worth?"

"I agree that it doesn't look like a fake, but I need to be sure. I need to take it to be examined by experts."

"Take pictures, tell me how much worth."

"Okay."

I grabbed my camera and started taking pictures. A piece couldn't be authenticated by a picture, but I was stalling for time. I didn't know if he brought it to me to buy or just to find out how much it was worth in order to sell it.

If it was real, museums would want it. So would a horde of collectors. Asian art was the rage among Americans and Japanese. A museum-quality piece like this had to be worth hundreds of thousands, maybe more, even with a suspect ownership history.

I tried to control my excitement. I was holding my salvation. A ticket back to the good life. I could probably buy it from Sammy for a fraction of its worth and resell it for enough money to restart my life. It meant not only getting an apartment bigger than a shoe box, but return of my credibility as an art—

His cell phone rang. It broke the spell. A sudden dose of reality washed over me as he answered the call.

Museums and collectors did not lay out megabucks for artifacts without knowing their previous ownership history. For at least the last hundred years most countries have had laws prohibiting the export of national cultural treasures. As a rule of thumb, most of the items acquired during the twentieth century were subject to claims from the countries of origin that the antiquities had been taken out of the country illegally.

Each year demands came from Italy, Greece, Iraq, Egypt, and other countries with archaeological sites rich in cultural treasures for return of illegally exported pieces. The demands were made on major museums. Many of them, including the Metropolitan Museum of Art—the Met—and the Getty, two world-class icons, had not only returned antiquities that could only be described as "priceless," but were still under pressure to return many more.

Knowing the ownership history was crucial when buying a work of art or artifact. The art trade calls ownership history the piece's "provenance." With antiquities, the word referred both to the place of origin—an archaeological site in Egypt, Greece, or wherever—and to the chain of ownership that established that the piece had left the country of origin legally and that the current seller had good title to it.

I was staring at an antiquity that probably had been looted in the Far East and smuggled into America. I didn't know how many years in prison that added up to, but just the thought of being in jail was enough for me.

After taking the pictures I had to sit down before my knees folded. I collapsed on a chair and stared at the artifact sitting on my lap as Sammy jabbered in high-pitched Thai with an ever increasing tempo.

Jesus, what was I thinking? The sandstone Apsaras piece wasn't a ticket to the good life but a free pass to jail. Obviously, it had been smuggled out of Cambodia and smuggled into the States . . . in a carton of rice noodles for all I knew.

What kind of ownership history could it have when it arrived in a brown paper bag that smelled of succulent Thai spices? I already had one long, hard, crushing fall from grace with the art world and the law because of a piece with a bad provenance.

Even more important, what I held in my hands was part of the cultural history of a small, poor nation, a treasure of its people that had been stolen, looted by thieves who often destroyed more than they hauled away . . . with the looted antiquities ending up in the collection of rich people who didn't give a damn about—

Sammy suddenly shouted. Almost a cry of pain. He took the cell phone away from his ear and stared at it wide-eyed as if it had suddenly come alive.

"Give me!" He grabbed the piece from me.

"Wait!"

He fled with the piece, out my door with me right behind grabbing at his shirt.

"Wait—I'll give you money!"

He knocked my hand away and flew down the stairs. I stood at the landing and watched him disappear.

With my salvation.

Or maybe he saved me from myself.

❖

5

❖

As I watched the street below from my window, Sammy shot out of the building and ran down the street as if all the hounds of hell were snapping at his heels. Maybe they were. A noodle deliveryman with an incredibly valuable piece of ancient artwork—obviously there were some tangled webs about the piece. For all I knew, the restaurant was a den of art thieves. Right off it sounded like a great front for smuggling art in from the Far East.

The first scenario that jumped at me was no honor among thieves—he was supposed to deliver it somewhere and decided to sell it himself. And the person on the phone had given him a preview of what was going to happen to him if he didn't return the item real fast.

Whatever the caller said had put a fire under him. And I didn't think it was the Thai restaurant cook chewing him out for being late for a delivery. Sammy was really scared.

Alarm bells were going off in my head, the kind that ring between my ears when I'm doing something stupid that I know is stupid. I should pick up the phone and call the police.

My phone rang and I nearly jumped out of my skin.

❖

I stared down at the number. It was that Mrs. Garcia who wanted me to pony up the Saks's bill.

I ignored the call and paced. This wasn't the first time Sammy had brought artwork to me. A month ago he had shown me two small bronze statues. Because they were cast rather than carved, bronze objects were especially easy to reproduce with an appearance of being ancient. As many as 90 percent of bronzes for sale are fakes or copies.

I noticed the poor workmanship immediately, though to a tourist in a souvenir shop they would have looked authentic enough.

He hadn't seemed surprised when I told him they were fakes. He just wrinkled his brown eyes and smiled at me.

Now I realized he had been testing my skills as an appraiser because he had something more significant he planned to show me.

To get his hands on a piece as valuable as the Apsarases, Sammy had to be connected to very big-time art smugglers. Or art thieves. For all I knew, the piece had been stolen from a collector, gallery, or museum here in the States, but that premise immediately sounded unrealistic to me. The contraband art trade was so widespread in poor Asian countries it would be infinitely easier to obtain antiquities there and smuggle them in rather than steal a piece here and have the theft publicized not only in the news media but posted on Internet art loss sites.

Sammy said there were more pieces. Considering the value of the Apsaras relief he showed me, if there were more pieces, the inventory would be worth millions.

I wondered if he really knew what a valuable item he had. I suspected he didn't. The value of stolen works escalated from very little to very much as the piece made its way up the art theft food chain. And Sammy would definitely be a bottom feeder in that chain.

Even if he didn't know the value, he wasn't stupid. He had to know it wasn't a tourist souvenir but a genuine work of art.

For sure, there was money to be made, one way or another . . . hopefully honestly. I didn't want to spend my life running from creditors or stick my nose into something that left me running from criminals.

I couldn't let this thing drop. I was pulled too many ways by too many emotions, from feelings of a mother hen in protecting the piece from people like Sammy who didn't respect its priceless cultural value, to figuring out a way to make money on it . . . without going to jail.

❖

My thinking wasn't straight, but neither was my life. I had to admit that my fall from economic grace had caused me to do some serious thinking about who I was, where I came from, and where I was going. Like people who only pray when there's hell to pay, I had thoughts about a simpler life . . . a little house with a white picket fence, rug rats crawling around while I prepared a Sunday pot roast for that man in my life . . .

A few months ago I would have howled with laughter from the image. But like a scary medical diagnosis, the free fall that left me financially crippled and my reputation roadkill had put the fear of the Lord in me. They say there are no atheists in the foxhole and right now I was crouching down in a battlefield with the slings and arrows of creditors flying at me. So I watched my cussing, my drinking, and my impure thoughts. At least, I tried.

Besides desperation, the fall from grace had brought one definite change in me: I now knew I wanted life beyond my career, not just the material accoutrements from having an income that rated a black credit card, but I had to find the right man or there would be no one to cut the lawn and take out the garbage.

I wasn't really that cynical about love. I talked facetiously about sex because I'd never found the right person to share my life with. And I was running scared that I might never experience that deep, passionate, soul-satisfying eternal love that books and movies say we need. I avoided permanent entanglements because I wanted to make sure I had all my "wants" satisfied so I wouldn't end up like my parents with an "I wish I had" attitude that followed them to the grave.

My dad, a community college art teacher, had wanted to be an archaeologist exploring ancient sites around the world. My mother had dreamed of being a dancer but became a homemaker and librarian.

What they accomplished should have been enough for anyone, but for inexplicable reasons probably relating back to their own upbringings, it wasn't. They wanted more and expressed vague feelings of discontent to me about the directions their lives had taken.

I believed that my parents were great successes. But both of them had conveyed to me a melancholy desire about what might have been instead of them being satisfied with their accomplishments. I always wondered if their discontentment was connected to their relationship with each other rather than their careers; whether something was missing between them.

They had died in a car accident about the time I was getting out of college and I missed them dearly.

I picked up from my parents a free-floating dissatisfaction with where and what I was, a feeling that there was always one more step to take, one more hurtle to leap. I knew I should be satisfied with myself . . . bookstores were filled with psychobabble books to guide people who thought like me. But it was a lot easier to figure out what made you tick than to change the behavior.

Now what? My parents weren't here to help me, I was divorced ten years ago, and the few friends I had acted like I'd give them a computer virus if they answered my phone calls or e-mails.

What did a woman do when she was too educated and too experienced to get an ordinary job? Who was going to hire me to work a cash register at Wal-Mart when my last job paid twenty times more? And I worried about an employer doing a background check. Was there a database of people like me who were arrested but never charged? Not that they'd need it—I was as infamous in the New York art trade as Kenneth Lay was to members of the financial community.

It used to be a matter of pride to me that I was so single-minded about art. Now I was paying for it. I kept asking myself what I would do if I couldn't get something going in the art world and my answer was to shake my head and pray that lightning struck.

There was an expression to describe people who were inescapably drawn to a disaster: fatal flaw. And I had it.

Everything I owned was in this one room. A wooden table with two chairs served as both my desk and kitchen table. I found them at a flea market for thirty dollars. By adding two coats of paint and new foam cushions to the chairs, they were good as new.

Even though my apartment was tiny, the high ceiling and two windows made it appear less claustrophobic. Painting the walls a bright white helped, too. I had a large walk-in closet; one thing I liked about the place. All the other studios either had a tiny closet or none at all.

Besides my table/desk and two chairs and the love seat sofa I sat on, I had a double-size bed with a backboard I made myself from a piece of wood covered with fabric, one wicker nightstand, an old trunk suitcase for a coffee table, and some bookshelves that I put on the wall myself. The open kitchen was tiny, just enough room to stand in, but I wasn't much of a cook anyway. Besides, fast food often cost less than home cooking, especially for someone like me who didn't have the condiments.

As a student, I had lived in a fifth-floor studio walkup in Chelsea and now gravitated back into lower Manhattan because the area had a certain energy to it and was affordable. Only this time I found a place on the cusp of Soho, Little Italy, and Chinatown. I was back to living with "working people," back to being part of the anonymous masses that limos and ecology-raping SUVs splashed water on as they pulled up to curbs on wet days.

The street life here was much richer and more diverse than the sterile Upper East Side along the park. Worker tenements shouldered ten-million-dollar "lofts"; the sign at a postage-stamp-size parking lot on Mulberry Street in Little Italy read "Mafia Only"; and if you looked like a tourist, you couldn't move ten feet in Chinatown without someone edging close and whispering, "Handbags?" Of course, the bags were knockoffs of high-end designer labels.

The building I lived in needed a paint job on the outside and the inside lobby needed a serious makeover, but the rent was cheap. No elevator again, so my legs got a workout taking the stairs up to the third floor.

The tenants were ordinary decent people, just trying to make a living and raising their families. They went to their jobs five days a week, whether they liked it or not, had little left over after paying bills, enjoyed their two days a week off, and went back to work again. On weekends when the sun was out they took their kids to a park. Same routine week after week until they retired or died.

These people worked for essentials—food, shelter, clothes—as I did when I was struggling through college and launching a career. When I was on top, I could have lived on a fraction of what I made. Instead, I had worked to enjoy a life of luxury: hiring an interior decorator to do my penthouse, sleeping on the finest silk sheets, dining in restaurants without menu prices, driving a car that turned heads.

I wish I could say that life beside simple people who worked hard for a living was the best thing that ever happened to me; that like

Jimmy Stewart in *It's a Wonderful Life*, a near-death experience had brought new meaning to the simple joys of life . . . but dragging myself up long flights of stairs to a cubbyhole apartment with the smells of spicy jerk chicken and Spanish language TV soap operas blaring through doors was no match for a snooty Upper East Side penthouse in a building where the doorman parked my Jag and the reception area had handwoven Persian rugs tossed on plush carpeting.

Sure, my poor-but-honest working-class neighbors were a lot friendlier; they smiled more and unlike that shit of a landlord would wait and hold the door open when you met them coming or going, but like any good New Yorker, I didn't know my neighbors well enough to pick them out of a police lineup.

Sighing, I forced myself away from the window, hoping my melancholy would fade. *Think positive*.

I got into a comfy position on the sofa and stared vacantly at the rain slashing against the window. The heat in the room made me drowsy. Usually I could control the steam radiator heat but the handle was broken . . . again. I jotted down a note to myself to tell the landlord to fix it—again.

I'd been sitting for an hour, trying to figure out what way I should turn, when the phone rang. I didn't recognize the number, but it wasn't Mrs. Garcia's number so I answered it.

"Maddy, it's Bolger."

I couldn't have heard a better name or voice to help with my predicament. Bolger was a top-notch art expert who opened a one-man, one-room bookstore that sold new and used art books after he retired from the Met. He occasionally hired himself out as an art authenticator, examining pieces to separate the fakes from the bona fides, but the field was mostly dominated by laboratories with high-tech equipment.

We'd worked together at the Met when I was a young intern learning the world of museums and he was an old pro in the unit that performed tests to determine the authenticity of pieces that the museum wanted to acquire.

Bolger had an encyclopedic knowledge of antiquities, but after leaving the museum, the march of technology had relegated him to the status of an anachronism—a person who belonged in another time.

❖

"I'm obsolete," he told me years ago. "I weigh two hundred pounds and a computer chip that weighs a thousandth of that can store infinitely more knowledge."

When I was still head curator at the Piedmont, I sent him artifacts to authenticate. I had more faith in his instincts than a laboratory full of high-tech machines.

"I have a referral for you," he said. "More accurately, I gave your name and phone number along with a high recommendation to a very rich and serious collector. Hopefully he will be calling."

"Great. I need the business. I'm glad you called. We haven't talked in ages."

He was on the list of people I'd sent business cards to after I'd decided to launch my business. So far he was the only one who had called me.

"How you doing?" he asked.

"Well, as you know, I started my own business and things are a little . . . ah . . ."

"Slow?"

"Uh huh."

"Tough?

"Uh huh."

"I know, I've been there. Something will happen soon. Send me a batch of your business cards and I'll give them out to everyone from book buyers to the mail carrier. Your luck will turn around."

Bolger knew about the Semiramis scandal, but he was too much of a gentleman to say anything, which was fine with me—I was tired of explaining myself and proclaiming my innocence.

"Maybe it has. Something really weird happened that I need your opinion on. Are you busy right now?"

"I haven't sold a book in two days, but that's okay, I like my books and hate to part with them. What's up?"

"I just saw a piece of art and it's blown my mind. You won't believe it when I tell you."

"You said weird. Is this going to be one of those scenarios in which someone puts out five bucks at a yard sale for a painting that's been in grandma's attic for fifty years . . . and it turns out to be a Matisse?"

"You're a mind reader. But do grandmas have attics in Thailand?"

"Only bamboo ones that monkeys swing in."

"Somebody showed me a sandstone Apsaras relief a little while ago that looks real."

"It might be. There are looted pieces around. The creators of Angkor's Khmer art used an enormous amount of sandstone in its wonders and the dancers are a common subject. So right off my first inclination, sight unseen, is that it's a Khmer piece."

"My thought, too. I have a picture of it."

"I haven't heard anything about an Apsaras panel on the contraband lists, but I'll check. Com'on over, you've got me intrigued."

"I'm on my way."

❖

6

❖

Bolger's place was on the west side of Chelsea a couple blocks from the Hudson River. Back in the days when I was struggling to get a career going, my place in Chelsea wasn't far from where Bolger was located now.

The rain had stopped by the time I stepped out of the subway station three blocks from his place, close enough to hoof it the rest of the way. Not a glamorous neighborhood, some of the apartments and stores looked a little seedy, but the streets were clean.

I got an odd feeling that someone was following me and I turned to look over my shoulder. I was being followed all right, by dozens of people, none of whom appeared to know I existed. As in any big metro area, few people smiled or even made eye contact at passersby. Too many people, too many nuts.

Bolger's small bookstore was on the bottom of a two-story brick building that he owned. The apartment living room was the actual store. The only furnishings in it were a dog-eared recliner that needed recovering and a TV that was perpetually on. I never saw him look at the TV and I suspect it was more "companionship" than entertainment.

The two-bedroom apartment upstairs was rented out to a middle-aged couple with no children, like most of his previous tenants. He didn't dislike kids; what he didn't like was the pitter-patter of running feet above him when he was engrossed in one of his art books or examining a work of art.

Unlike me who had focused on the works of the great Mediterranean civilizations, he had a wide range of knowledge. The Met was an eclectic museum that housed pieces from most of the great antiquity sites of the world. Working there for over thirty years, he developed a profound mental database of the key elements to look for on a particular piece—and it didn't matter whether it was a Greek sculpture, a Mayan pictograph, or a clay pot from the Gobi Desert, he had seen it sometime in his career.

I didn't know if he still was doing authentications for fees. People like me who knew him from the old days could call him up to pick his brain.

A very small sign outside on the wrought-iron railing said "Bolger's." Nothing about being a bookstore. Probably wasn't permitted to have a business in the building, but it wasn't much of a business, anyway. The fact that he hadn't sold a book for days wasn't news—he hated to sell his beloved books and was more likely to encourage customers to browse the book or even borrow it rather than part with it.

I'd never seen the rest of his apartment but if the bookstore was any indication, it was probably overcrowded and disorganized. In the store part, books overflowed boxes, were stacked in leaning, wobbly-looking piles, and crammed into shelves. The place looked ready to collapse with a good sneeze.

How he kept track of what-was-where I didn't know; yet if you asked him for a particular book he knew exactly where it was located.

Besides books, he had antiquity pieces in nooks and crannies and on high shelves around the room. The pieces were an eclectic lot, some real though not priceless, some extremely good fakes, including several he obtained after he exposed them as reproductions to a disappointed owner.

Bolger was in his early seventies and a bachelor. His first name was Charles, but I never heard him called anything but Bolger even back at the Met.

He wasn't a small-talk person. I knew nothing about his personal life other than the part about art. And he could be crotchety at times. I once asked him why he never married and got an irritated "Too damn busy" as a response. "None of your business" probably was what he meant.

His tenure at the Met had ended abruptly and he went into retirement a couple years after I left the museum. Rumors in the art trade had swirled after he left, ranging from being fired for telling off a supervisor to taking something home that belonged to the museum. I never really believed that he stole from the museum, but if he did, he wouldn't be the first art lover who couldn't control an irresistible impulse and pocketed something he loved.

Art addiction can affect people like drug compulsion. Art lovers have cut priceless paintings out of museum frames, used razor knives to cut old maps out of books, pocketed small antiquities on display in museums and galleries, and committed a thousand other crimes against the thing they loved the most.

I'd stopped at a drugstore on the way to Bolger's and had my digital pictures printed in an enlarged format. I couldn't afford a printer right now and probably couldn't figure out how to connect it up if I had one.

Bolger was talking to a customer when I entered the bookstore. I waved hello and walked over to a stack of books on the floor and starting flipping through the pages until the person left. Morty, his cat, was usually wandering about talking to everyone but I hadn't seen him yet. Bolger named the handsome cat after Mortimer Brewster, the character played by debonair Cary Grant in the 1940s classic comedy *Arsenic and Old Lace*.

"Finally got a customer?" I asked after the woman left.

"The woman's after my body, not my books. She pretends to have an interest in art but she doesn't know farts from Warhol."

"From the looks of the dust and cobwebs in this place, she only needs to know the difference between a mop and a broom."

"Dust and clutter adds to the artsy-fartsy ambiance I deliberately cultivate to prove that I'm an intellectual."

"Where's Morty?"

"Asleep in his bed."

"A perfect day for it." The rain had let up but it was still damp and wet outside.

"Yeah, he has the life of Riley. Let's go in the back and I'll put on the teapot and you can tell me what's going on."

❖

He put a "Shut" sign on the door.

He walked with a cane for support because his arthritic hip had gotten worse over the years. I think the pain was one of the main reasons for his grouchiness.

His kitchen was a pleasant surprise.

"Neat and tidy," he said, grinning. "Not at all what you expected after seeing heaps of books in the other room. I only keep the store a mess so people can't find what they're looking for and take away my precious books.

"So business is not so good, huh?" he asked as he got the teapot going.

"Worse than yours—no one even wants my body, unless you count my pig of a landlord who looks like he'd lust after anything that walked on two—or four—legs."

I laid the pictures out on the table.

He grunted as he picked up his magnifying glass. "I could tell a helluva lot more if I had the actual piece instead of a picture. Can I see it?"

"I'm working on that." I told him about Sammy bringing it to my place. "I had it in my hands for maybe one minute."

His eyes grew wide. "You opened your door and a Thai deliveryman was standing there with a piece of Khmer art in a paper bag? You're damn right about it being weird—it's the strangest art story I've heard."

"He showed up unexpected, got a phone call, and flew out of my place in real fright. Which makes me wonder who called him and what was said, though I have some guesses that the caller described some unpleasant things that would happen to Sammy if he didn't return the piece."

"Doesn't sound like it's something you'd want to get involved in. I suggest we shred the pictures and you go on with your life without looking over your shoulder."

"I'm trying to see this as an opportunity rather than a threat. I can think of lots of reasons why a restaurant delivery guy would be walking around with—"

We ended the sentence with a laugh.

"Okay, it's probably hot, so let's just do this as an academic question. Do you think it's the real McCoy?"

He grunted again. "Your pictures are pretty good. The piece certainly has the look of the real thing. But there are damn good fakes on the market today, though Khmer sandstone works don't top the lists. Sculpturing hard stone is too hard and takes incredible talent. Casting bronze and baking pottery is much easier to deal with if you're going to make a fake. With some antique Chinese porcelain pieces going for tens of millions of dollars, the rewards can be pretty incredible."

"I have a feeling it's the real thing. When I held it in my hands, I felt the touch of the ancient artist who created it."

That got a *humph!* instead of a grunt from Bolger. "You could make a fortune opening a psychic art evaluation service. But back to reality: The first instinct is always to identify Khmer pieces only with the Angkor temple complex, especially Angkor Wat. That's where the empire was centered and the distinctive Khmer style was perfected, but there are hundreds of lesser temple sites scattered in the jungles of Cambodia, some of them still undiscovered."

He looked up at me. "Hundreds of temples, thousands of pieces, over a century of looting, no cataloging of the artifacts, all a recipe for disaster for the wondrous complex. You know better than me what a terrible tragedy the looting of the Iraqi museum was. It's been compared to the loss of the great library of Alexandria that held much of the knowledge of antiquity during the time of Julius Caesar and Cleopatra. But you don't hear that sense of loss when people talk about thousands of pieces of Khmer art being stolen by tomb robbers each year."

He shook his head in disgust. "Do you know that Angkor Wat was left off a modern list of the so-called wonders of the world? The list was voted on by millions of people who have no idea of where the hell Cambodia is, never heard of Khmer art, and are ignorant of the wonders of Angkor.

"It's that extensive? The looting?"

"You have to assume that any piece of Khmer art without a clear record of legal ownership for the last century has been looted. And since the West has only had a high interest in Khmer art for the past few decades, that means most of the stuff on the market, in collections, and displayed at museums don't have valid provenances. In fact, a lot of Khmer stuff is sold specifically without provenances of any kind."

Even before talking to Bolger I had already pretty well concluded that the Apsaras piece was looted, but that wasn't the end of the story for me. I was too desperate to let it go without getting to the bottom of it.

"What's even worse," he said, "is that for every piece they take out, the temple robbers destroy many more. To get this little section of Apsarases, the looters would have broken off a much larger piece, destroying much of it and just salvaging a small part. They do the same thing with statues. They usually won't take a whole statue because it's too hard to conceal crossing border checkpoints. Instead they cut off the head because it's the most valuable part and leave the body."

To maliciously damage a piece of art that had survived centuries or even millenniums was a real sin. I told him I wished now that I'd gotten deeper into the art of the Far East.

"You're not alone. Our art is focused on the great Mediterranean civilizations because they're linked to our heritage. There's a diminishing number of pieces on the market because it's been collected for so long. Now collectors have woken up to the Far East and the fact that Khmer art is among the most splendid on the planet. And that means trouble for the sites in Cambodia, especially the Angkor site. One of the highest achievements of man's artistic talents is being destroyed to satisfy the greed of collectors."

I gave a big sigh. "Thanks, Bolger, just what I needed when everything has gone to hell in my life. Now I can agonize over the loss of irreplaceable cultural treasures. Please tell me what you think about its authenticity before I cut my wrists."

He pointed at the pictures. "How do you expect me to tell you anything from pictures?"

"Because you're a genius."

"Now you've pressed the right button, girl."

"Just give me your gut reaction."

He went back to examining the pictures.

I knew his gut reaction was usually as good as most scientific tests. The cost of tests ran into the thousands and often Bolger could study an object with the naked eye and be right most of the time. A lot of people who worked with art could do the same, including me, but since he had worked for decades authenticating pieces at one of the major museums of the world, his frame of reference was infinitely greater than most of us.

He studied the pictures closely for several more minutes before he said anything. "It looks right . . . I can see why you think it could be real but are cautious. Faking has become such a fine art nowadays. Even if I had it in front of me, I'd need to study it."

"What's your gut saying?"

"The same as yours—it pings as genuine. Even the broken edges appear to be what you'd expect from a piece looted from a temple. But unless you have the actual piece and can put it through the paces, you can be easily fooled, especially by a photograph. Excuse the pun, but the art of faking has turned into a real art with modern techniques."

I pursed my lips and nodded. "I read that there are sculptors in Greece, the Middle East, and the Far East who are able to create ancient-looking art that's difficult to distinguish from the real stuff. Even governments are getting into the picture. The museum in Cambodia's capital has a workshop that's turning out realistic-looking fakes for the tourist market."

"We both know that it's usually easy to spot a fake," Bolger said, "but once in a while a piece shows up that is so good, it's really hard to tell whether it was created for Julius Caesar or for someone last week."

"If it's a fake, wouldn't scientific tests show that the sandstone doesn't match Angkor antiquities?"

He shook his head. "Forgers get blocks of sandstone from the actual quarries used to build Khmer temples. They paint it with chemical solutions and bury it in Cambodian soil for months. It's very convincing. As you know, you can't scientifically age-date a stonework, anyway. Radiocarbon dating only applies to materials like wood which was once living."

The kettle whistled on the stove signaling that the water was ready.

"Why don't you fix us some tea while I grab a couple of my books."

He talked as we leafed through books.

"Since you've expressed an ignorance about Khmer art, we'll start with the name. Cambodia is the name of the country, but the people are mostly of an ethnic heritage called Khmer. A thousand years ago, when Europe was coming out of the Dark Ages, the Khmer Empire had its center at Angkor in what is now central Cambodia. Its kings created the world's largest religious compound, probably as tributes to themselves as living gods, much like the Egyptian pharaohs did.

"Their religion was an adaptation of Buddhism from India and in that region a Buddhist temple is called a wat. The most famous temple complex is Angkor Wat built in the early twelfth century under King Suryavarman II."

"So Cambodians are Khmers, Angkor is where they expressed their art in the grandest way, and a wat is a temple."

I knew generally most of what he related but would never have gotten the king's name right.

"That's the big picture. Angkor Wat is also famous for having the longest bas-relief panels in the world. Most of the sandstone carvings were once painted and gilded. They depict historical episodes in the life of King Suryavarman, scenes from Hindu epics, the *Ramayana* and the *Mahabharata*, the exploits of the Hindu gods Siva and Vishnu with celestial nymphs known as Apsarases, and scenes from the daily life of the Khmer people at the time the complex was built."

That was a mouthful. Like I said, his knowledge was encyclopedic.

He tapped a picture. "Tell me more about the workmanship on the piece you saw."

"I wish I had a camera that did micro close-ups because the detail was striking. The faces were really well defined and the dancers wore intricate jewelry. I didn't find any major cracks or repairs in the stone. The surface coloring was in splotches of red, brown, and orange hues."

He nodded. "Khmer pieces from Cambodia frequently have this mottled, variegated surface coloring. The colors actually leach from both the inside of the sandstone and minerals from the area where it was removed. But like I said, the stone is easy for a forger to get."

As I talked, he quickly flipped through a book.

"Ah, here it is. Look at this. A piece from an Angkor Wat temple wall."

The image was of three Apsarases. The women portrayed in the book resembled the bas-relief that Sammy had shown me, but I immediately saw tiny differences, which was to be expected: Artists who did the carvings gave their own interpretations of Apsarases, but kept faithful to the mythology that they were exotic dancing girls.

"Similar, but not the same."

I slowly leafed through the book as he went back to examining my pictures with his magnifying glass. Pictures of the dancers had only slight differences in pose and jewelry from Sammy's piece and the others in the book, but I could spot subtle differences that indicated different artists had created them.

"Obviously all the Apsaras pieces bear similarities," I said, "but I don't see a match close enough to suggest that Sammy's piece was a copy."

He finally set down the magnifying glass and pictures. "I need to see the piece. Even at that, it's so good, tests would have to be run on it. You realize it's extremely valuable even if it's a fake."

I nodded. "Far Eastern art is hot on the market."

"Especially Khmer art now that the Chinese have not only cracked down on contraband art, handing out death penalties for infractions, but Chinese billionaires are buying up the stuff in foreign hands and taking it back home. The antiquities black market is worth billions of dollars. You even have poor countries tolerating the illegal export of art objects because corrupt government officials are on the take.

"Even countries in Western Europe like Italy and Greece which have the money to protect their cultural heritages are plagued by tomb raiders. The professional tomb robbers like those they call *tombaroli* in Italy are murdering their own cultural history, but at least the Italian government fights the thieves. That's not always the case in the poor countries of Southeast Asia, Latin America, and the Near East. There's wholesale looting."

Mortimer suddenly jumped on my lap and rubbed his body against me. "Hello, Morty." As I petted him he purred and kneaded his claws into my thigh. A little painful to take, but cats think we love it.

"Tell me more about Angkor Wat art," I said. "How many of these Apsarases are there?"

"Twenty-six, each representing a distinct aspect of the performing arts, similar to how the ancient Greeks thought of their Muses. A couple of thousand images of them are carved in sandstone at Angkor Wat. That's why they're so identified with the site."

"Have you been to Angkor?"

"A couple times. Long ago. The damage to the site is obvious and a lot of it happened during our lifetimes, especially during the seventies and eighties. You've heard of the Khmer Rouge?"

"Some kind of political thing?"

He nodded his head. "Some kind of political insanity. Khmer Rouge means Red Khmers, as in communist red. They took over the country back in the mid-seventies and banned all institutions—stores, banks, hospitals, schools, religion, even families. They set up an unworkable agrarian utopian society instead.

"Everyone was forced to work twelve to fourteen hours a day, every day. Children were separated from their parents to work in mobile groups or serve as soldiers. People were fed a watery bowl of soup with a few grains of rice thrown in. A horrible time in history," he said, shaking his head. "Babies, children, adults, the elderly were killed en masse."

I grimaced.

"The Killing Fields is what they came to call it," he said.

I'd heard the expression. "Wasn't that a Vietnam War thing?"

"The years following it. The Killing Fields were sites in Cambodia where large numbers of people were killed and buried by the Khmer Rouge. A good movie was made about it."

"How many people actually died?"

"One out of every three or four people in a pretty small country, to the tune of maybe a couple million. The commies killed people if they didn't like them, if they didn't work hard enough, if they were educated, if they came from different ethnic groups, if they showed any sympathy when their family members were taken away to be killed—"

"Jesus, who didn't they kill?"

"They weren't discriminatory, for sure. Everyone had to pledge total allegiance to the government. It was a campaign based on instilling constant fear and keeping their victims off balance. It was a bloody, brutal reign of terror."

I smiled at him. "Is there a moral in this horror story for me?"

"Absolutely. You start flirting with contraband Khmer art, you'll find yourself running with tigers and sharks that make the Mafia look like schoolboys."

"Sammy's Thai, not Cambodian."

"Same difference, right next door. The Thais run the criminal syndicates in Indochina because they have more international contacts than any of the other groups."

He leaned forward, locking eyes, staring at me, hard. "Walk away from this, Maddy. It means nothing but trouble for you. Things are a little tough, but I still get authentication work. I'll start subbing the assignments out to you."

"Thanks. Let me think about it."

I needed to change the subject and talk more about Khmer art instead of the sick bastards who killed people—and the dangers to me. Bolger didn't understand how desperate I was.

Morty stopped kneading and got himself in a comfortable position on my lap.

"Getting back to Khmer art, what do you look for in differentiating between an authentic piece and a forgery?" I asked.

"Sandstone is a good substance for creating frauds because it's not subject to most tests that determine authenticity. While none of the tests tell us how old the piece is, we can examine the corrosive coating on the stone to see if the chemical, biological, and mineralogical composition of patina conforms to the conditions where it was supposed to have been for centuries. A forged antiquity has to appear properly aged, so the forger has to make it look a thousand years old in a matter of weeks or months. That's where many stone forgers trip up—the artists can't get that thin coating on the piece exactly right. At least in terms of coloring, we can see your piece has the right look."

"Was there anything you saw in the pictures that suggested it wasn't created with ancient tools?"

"The artist could have used iron tools not much different than the ones used for eons."

I knew there were no obvious signs of modern tools but I was still picking his brain. "So basically, if it turns out the sandstone itself is from a quarry where it should have originated from, and the workmanship is on par with the craftsmen of the Khmer Empire, then the patina is what we should concentrate on."

"But even that's not a sure bet. Weathering causes an erosion layer at the surface that can vary from less than a millimeter up to several centimeters deep. Sometimes the environment deletes layers rather than adds them. It gets even more complicated because tomb looters sometimes clean pieces, wiping away a couple thousand years of aging, because they're under the erroneous impression that a piece is more valuable clean than in its natural state."

❖

He was seeing me out when I noticed several small art pieces on a high shelf—a bronze of the monkey general Hanuman who rescued Rama's wife, a sandstone Buddha sitting on a wide-back chair made of a coiled cobra with fanning head, and a sandstone linga, a phallic symbol of fertility often identified with the god Siva.

"The linga's Indian," he said, "but the monkey general and the Buddha on the naga, the cobra, are Khmer, based on Hindu mythology. Reproductions, but I wish they were real. A foolish collector paid ten thousand for the monkey king in Hong Kong. It took me about thirty seconds to tell him it was a fake. The patina came off on my fingers when I wet it and rubbed it. He left in disgust and didn't pay me. I guess he thought leaving an expensive fraud was payment enough."

"I just remembered something. There was some kind of marking on the back of the Apsaras relief."

"What kind of marking?"

"I'm not positive, but it looked a little like a half-moon."

Bolger stared at me.

"Have you seen the mark before?" I asked.

"No, of course not. It could be anything. Are you going to take my advice and walk away from this thing?"

"I don't know what I'm going to do. I'm thinking about going to that café where Sammy works."

He shook his head. "You didn't listen to anything I said about how ruthless these people are. There's no guarantee your friend Sammy even still has the piece. Hell, Maddy, there's no guarantee Sammy is still breathing. They call double-crossers like Sammy 'fish food' in the Far East. That's what they become after they're chopped up and the pieces are tossed into the sea."

"I know, I know. To be honest, I feel like I'm spinning in circles. I can't stand the idea of Sammy and a gang of antiquity thugs smashing works of the ages. And I'm wondering if there isn't something in it for me." I smiled. "Maybe the gods were telling me something when they sent Sammy to my door."

"And maybe they were testing your naïveté. Wasn't your experience with Iraqi looters enough for you? Look what it cost you. This time it may be your life."

"That's not fair. I lost my job because I wouldn't stand by and let a cultural treasure be lost to the Iraqi people."

"It's your life. Just watch yourself."

"I'll be careful."

Famous last words.

7

❖

Bangkok, Thailand, a week earlier

Taksin moved through the Thieves Market in the darkness with ease after having done it hundreds of times. The stalls were closed but when the marketplace awoke in the morning, it would be buzzing with customers, many of them tourists looking for a bargain. The marketplace got its name from the practice of thieves unloading their ill-gotten gains there. That was all supposed to be in the past because the thievery practiced today in the market was mostly just separating tourists from their money.

Taksin thought of himself as an artist, not a thief . . . though some might say that he was both an artist and a thief. He didn't take money with sleight of hand like a pickpocket or with a gun like a robber, but by creating reproductions of great works of antiquity. Because of his incredible skills, more often than not the works were sold as bona fide antiquities.

He didn't consider his works fakes, nor thought of them as fraud when they were sold as antiquities. He created what he had the ability to craft and if others believed the pieces were something besides the works of Taksin of Bangkok . . . well, people could believe what they wanted. Besides, Taksin never got involved in selling his creations to collectors. He sold to dealers who in turn marked his pieces up a thousand percent and resold them.

About thirty years old, he had been raised by Buddhist monks but left the order in his teens. He wasn't certain of his exact age because he had been a foundling left on the steps of a temple. The monks gave him the name of a famed, eighteenth-century general king because he was found on the great man's birthday.

His talent for carving and sculpturing was recognized early. At first he made small wood objects that he "gave away" for no more than an extra bowl of rice because he wasn't permitted to sell the pieces. From wood he graduated to carving soapstone for inexpensive tourist souvenirs. His early life was spent in a temple near the Cambodian border and he was drawn to Khmer art.

When he was in his late teens, antique dealers noticed that Taksin's inexpensive soapstone reproductions of Buddhist religious objects often looked as good as the authentic pieces he was copying. Dealers began having him make custom pieces from sandstone that they then passed off to buyers as authentic antiquities.

He gave up his bright saffron robe and begging bowl for a more earthly existence reproducing works of art and experiencing a more worldly existence than his life in the temple.

The progression from making souvenirs to making works of art was evolutionary and inevitable because Taksin was simply a genius. A Renaissance master for his own time and place, he possessed the eye, touch, and patience of Khmer masters dead a millennium.

He began a work by buying a piece of sandstone. To make it appear authentically Khmer, rather than freshly quarried stone, he bought temple rubble—chunks of building material from Angkor and other Cambodian sites.

Taksin didn't know that sandstone had a "fingerprint" in that it could be tested for its mineral and chemical content to establish whether the stone actually came from the claimed antiquity site.

He chose the temple rubble because in his own mind the stone from religious sites was imbued with a spirit that made his finished piece of art even more desirable. The debris was inexpensive and easy to obtain.

Taksin worked his pieces with just a mallet and a variety of iron chisels. Dealers who wanted him to produce pieces quicker urged him to use some modern tools to speed up the process. Modern steel chisels had a different cutting edge than the iron ones used by Khmer craftsmen a thousand years ago; much sharper, they would have made his work easier and faster, but he insisted upon using iron ones, refusing to use steel even in the early shaping of the piece.

Electric tools would have speeded up the work even more; it was common to use electric tools in the production of faked artifacts, with the telltale marks covered up by sanding and chiseling later. But Taksin made his pieces slowly and laboriously because he believed that was the only way he could really walk in the shoes of ancient craftsmen.

Once he had the stone sculptured into the final shape, the last step was to re-create a realistic surface coating, the patina. This, again, was a step where fakes were frequently exposed. The surface coating that gave an authentic Khmer antiquity its aged appearance came from sun and rain, jungle foliage, dirt, river water, or whatever other environmental forces the piece had been subjected to since it had been created a thousand years before.

It was easy to "age" the piece by creating a coating that made it look old. Every Thai artist had their own technique for aging, but just burying it in a muddy pig's pen for a few months could give the piece an aged look. Bronze pieces especially "aged" well, adding centuries over a short period of time.

To pass more than cursory scrutiny—simply having an aged look wasn't good enough—the piece had to look exactly like artifacts from the site where it was supposed to have been obtained. More important, if it was to be sold at a high price, scientific tests would usually be done, so the corroded coating of the piece had to have a chemical fingerprint like those found at Cambodian antiquity sites.

In creating the patina, Taksin again had acted intuitively rather than from knowledge of scientific tests. He chose only rubble that had not been fully buried, thus didn't have an impact from leaves, tree roots, and organic matters contained in soil that would have made it easier for tests to determine exactly where the piece was supposed to have come from—and thus easier to expose as a fraud by comparing it to authentic pieces.

After carefully removing the outer coating from other pieces of rubble, he liquefied the mixture and let the piece ferment in the concoction for months in a warm clay oven.

Nothing was foolproof but each step he took made it more difficult for experts to detect that his works were fake.

In Taksin's mind, he wasn't trying to fool anyone. He was simply recreating the piece exactly like the masters of old had done.

The most common "fingerprint" left by the master artists of antiquity was their workmanship. And Taksin had been kissed by the gods when it came to creating with stone. His work played well when put up against masterpieces of ancient Khmer art . . . and that was the most telling test of all and the most difficult for an artist to fake.

Because he had a sense of his own worth and an ego, he "signed" each work with a mark that was visible only with a magnifying glass. The lopsided half-moon shape symbolized the object that had been most connected with him during his years as a monk: a begging bowl.

He had progressed from a teenager creating for the tourist trade, to a young man making pieces for the art trade in antiquities. Now he had reached a higher dimension: fine art for the rich. Pieces so good they couldn't be differentiated from genuine artifacts . . . and that sold for millions of dollars because they were "authentic."

A year ago he thought he had reached the height of success when he got a thousand American dollars for his pieces. But he transcended even that plateau when he was approached by Cambodians and offered twenty times that.

Earlier in the day he finished a thousand-dollar piece and had delivered it to a dealer at the central market. It had been promised long ago and was the last one he would do at that price. Never again would he make what he had come to think of as "small pieces." Now he would devote himself to "big pieces." Not big in size, but in price.

His change in life coincided with the city's Songkran celebration, the water festival that was a time for cleansing and renewal. A friend, Phitsanu, was coming over so they could go out together to wash away his old life and bless the new, richer one he had embarked upon.

ENTERING THE TWO-ROOM HUT that served as his home and workshop, Taksin hid in a secret hole in the floor less than half the money he received from the dealer. He kept out the rest for the night's activities—it was going to be an expensive evening and he would have to pay for both Phitsanu and himself.

After Phitsanu arrived, they drank a bottle of rice wine and then stood by the river in the dark and masturbated. They were going to be with prostitutes later, and prepped themselves so they would not ejaculate quickly when they were paying for sex. "More bang for the buck," Taksin said, quoting a line from an American movie he'd seen.

Afterward, they made their way through the playful, noisy, and ruckus crowds of the Songkran Festival.

The rituals of the festival were observed by people bathing monks and religious objects and then each other. It went from a serious rite to fun as people sprayed water on whoever they could. Water came flying from people on the street, passing cars and trucks, and from balconies overhead. Buckets and bowls of water, water balloons and water guns, and even an occasional garden hose was put into action.

All of it was done with good humor—getting splashed was the objective, not something to avoid. The water renewed the spirit by washing away bad luck.

Homes were cleaned thoroughly at festival time because it was believed that throwing away things that were old and useless kept them from bringing bad luck to the owner.

Taksin and Phitsanu stopped at a street vendor's cart for a meal of spicy squid on a stick and green curry chicken served on a banana leaf. They squatted behind a counter to eat in order to keep from being targets for water throwers.

After eating, they went to a bar for the first step of Taksin's celebration of his new life of affluence and satisfying his dreams and desires: a cobra-blood cocktail.

The drinks were expensive. For the king cobra concoction Taksin would pay the equivalent of two hundred dollars each for him and his friend.

Live snakes in glass cases lined a shelf behind the bar. Taksin and his friend didn't just walk in and order the famed cocktails—there was a ritual to be observed. They sipped ordinary rice wine and looked over the snakes from their positions at the bar, evaluating their size and color, talking to other men who were also bellied up to the bar, getting the opinion of the bartender, as they debated which snake they would choose. It was not unlike selecting a lobster from a glass tank in a restaurant.

The snake cocktail was prized among Thai men because it was believed to be an aphrodisiac that gave men powerful loins and made them irresistible lovers.

The bar served other drinks that were reputed to increase a man's sexual prowess—above the cages with live snakes to be used for blood cocktails were jars of rice wine flavored with Chinese herbs. Each jar contained a creature from the jungles of the country—coiled vipers, cobras, and green snakes, scorpions as long as a hand, the balls and penis of sheep and oxen.

The creatures were pickled in the wine for several years before the concoction was considered aged enough to drink. No wine was served before its time . . .

The wine didn't absorb the poison of the snake, making the liquid drinkable—for those who could stomach it. And a surprising number of men were willing to drink anything to increase their sexual potency.

When it came time to order, Taksin pointed out the snake he wanted. The bartender opened the lid and stuck a pair of metal clamps in the cage, seizing the snake just below its head. He raised its head out of the box with the clamps enough to grab it with his free hand. Bringing it to the bar, he slammed its head against the counter until the snake was dead.

It wasn't a technique that a bartender blotched more than once.

Spreading the creature out with its pale belly up, the bartender slit it along the belly with a knife and drained the blood into a container. He poured rice wine with a high alcohol content into the container, then added the snake's heart and other innards. He shook the whole batch up and used a strainer as he poured the liquid into a glass.

The bartender set the glass in front of Taksin and tossed the meaty innards from the strainer into a pan to be heated and served as a side dish to the blood cocktail.

Nervous but laughing at the egging on he was getting from his bar mates, Taksin got up the courage and jerked down the drink. The snake cocktail burned like liquid fire going down his throat.

Phitsanu followed suit and downed his cocktail.

❖

A bit tipsy, Taksin and Phitsanu left for their next stop: a house of prostitution. They had not bothered to get condoms. The cobra cocktails were reputed not only to drive up their sexual performance, but to prevent AIDS.

That medical fact was verified by the bartender and confirmed by a man at the bar who said it saved him twice from the dreaded disease.

The district Taksin chose for their next adventure was a section popular with *farangs*—foreigners, mostly Americans, British, Canadians, Aussies, New Zealanders, and Japanese. Because of the tourist prices, locals—except for the very rich—avoided the entertainment centers that attracted foreigners.

Taksin knew the girls would rather fuck foreigners because the tips were bigger. But the girls, in general, were well mannered, genteel creatures no matter who hired them—they were just a little more receptive if they knew they were being paid well. Taksin was generous at these times, reasoning that the more money he flashed, the more a girl would make him feel as if he were a prince among men . . .

The two friends went to Soi Cowboy, "Cowboy Lane," a short street with several dozen clubs that mostly catered to foreigners. He'd heard it was named after an American ex-GI who wore a cowboy hat and ran a bar in the area during the Vietnam War era.

The street was a circus—elephant rides, handlers selling elephant food to tourists, street girls, pickpockets, and kids of all sizes and shapes, some of them learning to be a pickpocket. A neon jungle, it was much smaller but even flashier than the pictures he'd seen of the Las Vegas Strip.

They walked by a café with an outside patio that featured the traditional form of Thai fighting called *Muay Thai* in which eight human "weapons"—hands, elbows, knees, and feet—were used.

Called the Science of Eight Limbs, there were eight different ways to strike as opposed to the Western tradition of using two fists in a boxing ring and the four points—two fists, two feet—in most martial arts.

Taksin enjoyed watching the fights, but not tonight, and not at tourist prices.

As they went by a nightclub that offered Ping-Pong shows—women shooting Ping-Pong balls from most orifices of their bodies, including the one between their legs—Phitsanu grabbed his arm.

"I want to see them do it."

Taksin shook off the grip and kept going. "For tourists."

Men lured in by the macabre act often found their drink bill surprisingly more than they expected . . . and bouncers who were not friendly to those who objected too loudly.

Taksin led his friend to a club where he'd paid for sex before. His passion was for a *katoey*, a male to female transgender that was commonly called a ladyboy. Ladyboys ranged from simply cross-dressers to those who were completely castrated and had reconstructive sex organ surgery and hormone treatments.

The preference for men to be women was not considered an evil. Thais believed that being a ladyboy was the person's karmic destiny and that they were helpless to alter it.

Some faithful Buddhists went further and believed that being a ladyboy was the result of wrongdoing in a past life, thus the person was not responsible for his present sexual preference. Either way, there was a great deal of tolerance even among people who otherwise rejected sexual deviation.

Taksin's own personal choice for sex was a male to female transgender who had been physically altered and now appeared completely female. Perhaps his upbringing and training as a monk had left him more comfortable around men, yet still with the sexual desire for a woman . . .

He had first encountered his ladyboy in a blow job club in the Nana district, another red-light venue in the city. The ladyboy had moved over to Soi Cowboy when a go-go bar opened up that offered the services of katoeys exclusively.

Taksin paid an admission price at the door that included a drink and entered. Ladyboys who had already been selected by customers were at tables. Six who were waiting to be selected held on to aluminum poles as they stood on top of the bar counter.

The dress code ranged from the skimpiest thongs to more modest shorts and bras. Spiked heels and cowboy boots were the favored footwear. For the ones wearing thongs, it was easy for a customer to tell which ones hadn't been altered by looking for a bulge in the crotch.

❖

Taksin spotted his ladyboy on the bar counter and signaled her. She wore a red thong, a glittering red bra, and shiny red patent leather cowboy boots.

Her long black hair had a sheen and glittering stars, her eyebrows sketched high above their natural location had a heavy dose of blue eye shadow. Ruby red lipstick and the tattoo of a green parrot on her right shoulder completed the bar-girl ensemble.

She joined Taksin after he argued with a bartender over the amount of the "bar fine" before agreeing to pay the Thai baht equivalent of fourteen dollars. The payment got him two hours with the ladyboy. He would have to "tip" the ladyboy an equal amount. He paid the same amount for his friend's selection.

The ladyboys slipped on simple pullover dresses and followed the two men outside.

Keenly aware that every second wasted was a moment of pleasure lost with the ladyboy, Taksin hurried the group to the hotel where he had stopped earlier to arrange for rooms.

Once inside the room, Taksin became clumsy and nervous as he undressed. This was only the third time he had had sex and each time was with this ladyboy. Raised by monks, he knew little about women because monks were more insulated from women than even religious figures in the West. Women were discouraged to physically touch a monk. If a woman wanted to give something to a monk, she was to lay it within his reach.

All he knew about sex with a woman was to stick his penis in and pump. He'd heard that prostitutes were dry but he didn't know why. He followed the advice of friends and brought oil to rub on the head of his penis. He used no protection except the cobra blood drink to protect him from diseases and the ladyboy didn't insist upon any. Both had a sense of fatalism that certain things were out of the hands of mere mortals.

After the ladyboy stripped in front of him, Taksin cautiously reached out and touched her small breasts. As always, he was both extra courteous to women and curious about the female form.

"Lie down," the ladyboy told him.

After checking his penis for sores, she tore open a packaged handwipe and washed his organ with it. He was not circumcised and that was the norm for men of his background.

With his erect penis resting on his belly, she glided the palm of her hand up and down the hard stalk, from the tip of the penis to his testicles. He shuddered with glee.

Then she stroked and licked his penis.

Suspecting he may come quickly, and that she'd get paid more if he ejaculated in her, she mounted him and used her leg muscles to squeeze his cock and give him more pleasure . . .

Two hours later Taksin and his friend were back on the street, heading home, still tipsy from the liquor consumed earlier.

"I have rice wine at my hut," Taksin told Phitsanu. He wasn't sleepy and didn't want the celebration to end.

He had already stepped into the dark hut before he realized two men were inside and two more were behind him and Phitsanu.

He knew they were not Thai, but Cambodian, except for one man who was a light-haired foreigner.

Rather than showing panic or anger, Taksin's instinctual reaction from his training as a monk was to remain calm and give a traditional Thai greeting—the *wai*, hands placed together and raised toward the face with the head lowered in a small bow.

He kept his face impassive.

"Why have you come to my house?" he asked the foreigner.

The man hit him.

As Phitsanu leaped forward to defend his friend, a Cambodian grabbed him by the hair, jerked his head back, and slid the cutting edge of a long knife across his throat.

❖

8

❖

New York

Another fine mess I'd gotten myself into.

Bolger's warnings stayed with me as I walked back to the subway station. It drove up my paranoia. I stopped and pretended to look at merchandise in a clothing store window to see if anyone was following me. In my mind, the candidates would be movie-style Asian martial arts experts—young, gravely intense, slender, kickboxing-karate-looking dudes in black clothes. Once again I saw nothing to fuel my fears.

My head was buzzing again with a million conflicting thoughts, most of which could get me into trouble, a circumstance I seemed to gravitate to with little encouragement from the rest of the world. Being broke just aggravated my own inherent propensity to get in over my head. Worse, nothing was simple. Messing with a gang of art thieves could prove deadly, a fact I knew from personal experience.

I mulled my next move while I sat in a crowded subway car and stared blankly at a printed public service warning about family preparedness for terrorist attacks.

I had two choices: call the police or go to the Thai restaurant where Sammy was employed.

❖

If I called the police, I would be out of it, period. My chances of making any money would be nil and there was no guarantee they would be able to recover the Apsaras piece or anything else.

Worse, considering my previous experience with art theft and art cops, it would probably put me under suspicion because the cops would assume it was a falling out of thieves and I'd gone to the police for revenge. Or, as they say on the evening news, I'd be a "person of interest" in an art fraud. Not something my already tarnished reputation could absorb.

If I went to the restaurant and talked to Sammy and whoever else was involved, who knows what would happen, but like Bolger, I could think of some very dicey scenarios, none of them good for me.

For all I knew, the Apsara piece was a very good reproduction. If so . . . well, that might not be the worst of all worlds. Far East art was hot and there was a limited supply. The piece didn't even have to be represented as authentic. There were plenty of rich collectors who would buy a good fake just to show it off to friends, boasting of course that they paid half a million for it instead of fifty thousand.

Before I called the police, I'd call the Cambodian embassy in Washington and find out if they paid "finder's fees" for recovery of their country's art.

When a valuable piece of art was stolen, the owner or insurance company often offered a payment for its recovery. That commonly translated into ten percent of the value of the piece. As bizarre as it sounded, it was not unusual for thieves to steal something worth millions just so an accomplice could negotiate a finder's fee for its return.

If I could prove to the Cambodians that I not only knew where the Apsarsa piece was, but that there was a whole hoard of them, I might work out a fee that got me out of desperate straits. And get the pieces back to where they belonged.

To get a finder's fee, I had to make sure it was an actual antiquity.

The first obvious step meant walking into a restaurant that was probably a den of smugglers; a place where the staff spoke a language I didn't understand; and who might stand in front of me smiling while they discussed in Thai different ways to murder me and slice me up for chicken-on-a-stick while I stood there looking stupid.

I didn't kid myself—on the one hand, returning it was going to be like how Indiana Jones operated, battling temple looters so the antiquities rightfully went to a museum. But as Bolger got across so adamantly, the violence in the real world of art smuggling wasn't done with movie magic.

I wasn't even sure the people in the restaurant were involved, but it seemed highly likely.

Going to the Thai restaurant was the scariest idea I could think of . . . but absolutely necessary.

I had to go to that restaurant. My feet were already taking me there.

THREE BLOCKS FROM MY apartment, the restaurant was a rice bowl and pad thai place—inexpensive food, reasonably healthy, and with good-sized portions. It was my kind of dining experience now that I was one step from a homeless shelter.

I thought hard about how I would approach Sammy when I got to the restaurant. Thought hard and came up with exactly nothing. The last time I saw Sammy he was panicking over something being said over the phone. For all I knew, he was now being served up to customers as Siamese spicy beef.

Still pondering what I would say by the time I made it to the restaurant, I said the hell with it and walked in.

The place was warm and smelled of succulent Thai spices. Busy, too. Most of the tables were occupied. A waiter tried to seat me and I said, "Takeout."

I'd never been in a Thai or Chinese restaurant where the servers didn't speak pidgin English with a heavy accent. I'm sure the same was true across America. While I should be humbled by the fact that at least they spoke a foreign language, it made me wonder if they didn't cultivate the accent for effect, like American actors cultivate British accents. After all, who wanted to eat in an Asian restaurant where the waiters spoke perfect English?

I had this irrelevant thought as I stood by the cash register and pretended to look at a take-out menu. Sammy wasn't in sight.

I asked the young woman behind the counter, "Sammy, the deliveryman, is he around?"

"Sam—me?"

"You know, Sammy, delivers food." What the hell was his Thai name?

She gave me a blank look.

"Delivery, the deliveryman. Takeout. Deliver to apartments. You know, Sammy."

"No, no Sammy." She shook her head and smiled.

Why did I think she was lying? A waiter came out of the kitchen, the door swinging shut behind him. We both looked in that direction. When I turned back, she avoided my eye and pretended to look at a receipt.

I went for the kitchen door—fast—with an exclamation from the hostess behind me. Pushing through the door I almost ran right into Sammy. He gave a startled yell and fled toward the back of the kitchen.

"Sammy! Wait!"

As I started after him, a short, squat man with a butcher knife suddenly stepped in front of me. He waved the big knife and shouted. I caught one word in English: "Out!"

"I need to talk to—"

"Out! Out!"

He waved the butcher knife and I backed up, walking quickly through the restaurant and out the front door, smiling and pretending that I hadn't just been threatened by a cook with a large knife.

Once outside, I picked up my pace and hurried down the street. There was more than one way to skin a dog or cat or whatever that saying was that my father used to say when I was a kid. An alley ran in back of the restaurant and I headed for it, going down the street and around the corner to enter it.

The back door to the restaurant was a hundred feet from the corner. As I hurried past the Dumpsters posted behind the businesses and approached the back of the restaurant, I saw smoke coming from the other side of its Dumpster.

A cigarette came flying into the alley. Sammy followed it, yawning and stretching. Obviously a man with little on his mind except the next noodle order.

He saw me and gaped.

"Sammy! I need to talk to you!"

He froze in place and gawked. Something akin to panic spread across his face.

"Sammy, I need to see that piece. Don't worry, I'll help you. It might be extremely—"

I suddenly realized that he wasn't looking at me. He was staring at something behind me. I swung around.

Holy shit.

A man dressed in black, Thai I guessed, with a white shirt and a black tie, walked toward us.

I stared at the gun in his hand, fascinated and petrified at the same time.

I could hear Sammy's footsteps retreating behind me but I was too stunned to turn and look or even start running myself.

The man made eye contact with me and raised the gun to fire.

I stood still, rooted. My feet wouldn't move. I just stared open-mouthed at the man. It wasn't registering. A man was coming at me with a gun in his hand and was about to shoot me.

He looked beyond me and pointed the gun. I unfroze enough to see that he was pointing it at Sammy who was running like hell up the alley. I screamed and dropped to my knees as a big black SUV came around the corner and into the alley with screeching tires.

The man with the gun swung around to face the SUV. He seemed to be unsure of what to do as the SUV came at him and another one entered from the other end of the alley.

He made up his mind and put his hands up in the air, still holding the gun until men and women in body armor leaped out of the SUV with one of them shouting for him to drop his weapon.

NYPD was printed on their vests.

❖

9

❖

"I was in the wrong place at the wrong time," I said.

The man sitting across from me wasn't buying it. He was a police detective, with the dour, cynical view of life that big-city cops get.

"You're in deep shit."

It was the second time he had characterized my situation that way.

I was in an interrogation room in a police station on Centre Street. In police custody. Not of my own volition but under suspicion of a large number of vague charges. The fact that saving me from being murdered had blown a police surveillance particularly incensed him.

This wasn't the first time I'd been told by an art theft cop that I was in deep trouble. I should have taken being arrested again as just rolling with another punch, but beneath my brave smile my heart hammered and my knees shook. Emotionally I was torn between breaking out in sobs . . . and flying across the table to strangle my tormentor.

"I have so many charges to file against you, it's going to look like an indictment of the whole Soprano mob."

Michelangelo was the name of my interrogator. He was actually Detective Michael Anthony, but the news media called him Michelangelo because he was a painter and his real name was vaguely similar to the great artist.

He was in charge of Art Theft Detail in the Special Investigations Division of the NYPD.

I'd never seen any of his art, but had read an article about him in the paper last year. A gallery owner who had seen his work told me that the detective's painting skills were in the range of the couple hundred-dollar landscapes displayed for sale on the walls of the corner coffee-house rather than the stuff of millionaire's mansions. But that was nothing to sniff at—my own artistic skills were in the paint-by-number range.

I sighed. And tried to keep a happy face even though I wanted to throttle the sarcastic bastard. “I haven't done anything . . . illegal.”

That was my line of defense—I hadn't done anything. I still didn't even know if the Apsaras piece Sammy showed me was real or fake, but regardless of what it was, I hadn't done anything with it. I was just trying to track it down and see if I could make some money from it. Or as I told the detective, so I could make sure it got back to its original owner if it had been stolen.

He hadn't seemed captured by the notion that I was innocent, so I kept coming up with theories in the hopes that one would connect.

“I was just in the wrong place at the [illegible].”

“You keep saying that but you have a history of dealing in contraband art.”

“That's a lie! There were never any charges filed against me.”

He pretended to read off a list like an indictment from God. “Trafficking in looted Iraqi artifacts—”

“A mistake. I bought into a fraudulent provenance.” I spread my hands on the table between us. “Look, Detective, I've been through this before with cops—”

“The FBI.”

“As tough and suspicious as you—and that's not intended as a compliment,” I smiled sweetly and said very slowly, “I haven't done an . . . nee . . . thing. Nothing.”

“You were in an alley trying to make a deal with a Thai smuggler when we saved your ass.”

That was a matter of interpretation. Mine was that the man with the gun in the alley was going to kill Sammy, not me. But I wasn't really sure.

"Why don't you help yourself out by telling the truth. Come clean and there are things I can do for you with the D.A. and judge."

"Here's the truth—*again*." At least a decent proximity thereof, I could have added. I had to stick to enough of the truth to be credible and not be caught in a lie, because I knew from past experience that even breathing around contraband art could be incriminating. "Sammy the deliveryman brought a sandstone relief of Apsarases to my apartment. He knew I was in the art business. I had no idea—"

"How did he know you were in the art business?"

"It's on the name plate outside my apartment building entrance," I said sweetly. "And we'd joked about it."

"So he just shows up at your place without an invite with a priceless—"

"I didn't know it was real, I thought it was just a decent-looking *fake*. I was hoping he'd have a warehouse full of the *fakes* because there's a market for good *fakes*." Fakes, fakes, fakes. That was the key. There was no law against fakes unless you represented them as the real thing. And I hadn't represented anything to anybody.

I found that the more I lied, the more I could do it with a straight face. I should have been a lawyer. Or a politician.

Detective Anthony shook his head with feigned sympathy and sadness. "You know what I think? You can't resist getting your hands on artifacts with dirt on them. It's in your blood. Like a heroin addict, once you've tasted the forbidden fruit, you're hooked."

"You know what I think, Detective? I think you've been dealing with crooks for so long, you no longer can tell the difference between good and bad people." I stood up. "I want a lawyer."

"Sit down and shut up."

"You have no right—"

"You're going to be given an opportunity assignment."

That stopped me. "A what?"

"A way to clear yourself."

"I haven't done anything—"

"And make money."

He had my attention. I sat down.

❖

The door opened and a man entered. He was Southeast Asian, perhaps Thai, I wasn't sure. Handsome, maybe forties, early fifties. Well moneyed. His Salvatore Ferragamo briefcase rang up in my mind as equivalent to two months' rent on my walk-up studio. His Canali suit was food on my table for a year.

He had a commanding presence, the suave arrogance that comes with culture and money . . . the kind you were born with. You can't work a job and make big bucks and have the haughtiness that old money conveyed.

"Prince Ranar, Madison Dupre." Detective Anthony nodded at me and at the prince. "Your salvation. If you play it right," he said to me.

"Ms. Dupre. I am Deputy Minister for Security of Cultural Heritage for Cambodia. I am well aware of your credentials in the art world. With the permission of you and Detective Anthony"—he gave the detective a nod and turned back to me with a golden smile—"I ask for your help in a matter of great importance to my country."

I brushed back a piece of hair off my forehead. "Of course."

Ranar took a seat at the end of the table. "First, I must apologize for the circumstances under which we meet."

"She's lucky we're not meeting in a cell at Riker's Island."

Such a charmer. The prince looked a little puzzled at the detective's remark. "The city's most notorious jail," I said.

I brushed more hair off my forehead and gave the prince a brilliant smile. "I'm not sure what's going on, but you should know up front that I am here because I was at the wrong place at the wrong time, not because I'm a criminal."

Detective Anthony snickered. "That's only because she hasn't been caught red-handed . . . yet."

Prince Ranar held up a hand as if he were calling time out with children. "Please. This is a very serious matter for my country."

"What do you want from me?" I asked.

"Has Ms. Dupre been informed about the situation?" Ranar asked.

"I hadn't gotten around to that. Go ahead and fill her in. I'm going to get a cup of java. Anyone want one?"

"I'll have water," I said. "Bottled."

No sane person drank the stuff from the city taps.

I must have said something funny because he left laughing.

❖

Ranar met my eyes with his warm almond ones. "I understand that you were once . . . what do you call it? A major player in the city's art scene?"

His voice was soft and soothing. I could get to like this man. He oozed with money, charm, and sex appeal.

"Yes. But I'm afraid I've been in the wrong place and time on at least one other occasion."

"Let me assure you that you aren't the first curator to buy an artifact with a bad provenance. The collections in museums all over the world contain such items."

"It was a small museum, a big price tag, and a very high profile heist. Uh, what do you want from me?"

"May I ask you a question first? What is your opinion of the Khmer piece you examined? The Apsarases."

I hesitated. Having watched cop shows on TV, I knew the conversation was probably being recorded, perhaps even videotaped. And it struck me that Detective Anthony had chosen an unusual moment to walk out. Were they playing good-cop, bad-cop?

"I didn't really *examine* it. I just got a quick glance at it before Sammy, the man who showed it to me, grabbed it back and ran. But it looked like an antiquity, it had the right color of patina and the wear and tear that sandstone gets from a thousand years of sun, rain, and wind . . . but one thing did strike me."

"Yes?"

"The artistry was exceptional. I'm sure you know that when an expert examines an antiquity, they're not just gauging how old it is, but looking at the artistic workmanship. A poorly made Khmer piece is worth a hundred times less than one with exceptional workmanship even if both are centuries old. This piece had some very fine details, especially the dancers' jewelry. It was exceptionally well defined."

I took a deep breath. I was telling the truth. It just sort of burst out of me and I kept going. I paused and locked eyes with him. Not even Bolger had come up with the conclusion I was about to drop on the Cambodian prince.

"It's a fake," I said. "That's my conclusion without being able to get a more thorough examination and scientific study. And I base that on the eyes in my gut because the ones in my head scream it's genuine."

❖

"A fake because it's too exquisite?"

I spread my hands on the table. "In a manner of speaking, yes. If this artist had done this fine a piece in ancient times, we would see more of his work because he would have been in great demand. This piece is also broken off a longer relief. If the rest of it was out there, it would be noticeable because it is done so well." I shrugged. "That's it. The exceptional detail was the tip-off. It's made by a master, there's no more of his work known, so the odds are that it's a fake."

He raised his eyebrows. "Two experts, a curator from the Met and the head of the largest gallery in the country specializing in Khmer art, examined the piece this afternoon and validated it as authentic. Made about nine hundred years ago."

I shrugged. "It's not the first time I've been wrong."

"But you're not wrong. *It is fake*. An exceptional one done by an exceptional artist. We know that for a certainty."

"Okay . . . so why quiz me about it?"

"To test you."

"Test me? I'm being held in a—"

Anthony entered and I shut up. He sat a coffee cup down in front of me. "Sorry. The only water is from the New York City pipes that feed the water cooler out in the corridor. The one with the green slime and ugly brown gook around the spout."

The beige mug had a red lipstick stain. I smiled at the detective and raised my eyebrows, pointing at the mug. "Your shade?"

Ranar smothered a grin. He took an unopened bottle of water from his briefcase and set it on the table.

I ignored the water and stood up. "I appreciate the courtesy, but I'm finished here."

Detective Anthony frowned at me. "Where do you think you're going?"

"Home. I'm hungry, thirsty, tired, and angry. I've had it with you and your arrogant attitude and rudeness. You're a policeman, not the Gestapo. And as this nice gentleman said, the piece is a fake—just as I thought. And I don't think there's any law about fakes." I suppose there was a law for just about everything under the sun, but I was hoping I was right about fakes.

❖

“Please.” Prince Ranar held up his hand again to calm the children in the playground. “My limo is outside. I suggest we all retire to a restaurant of Ms. Dupre’s choice and discuss this matter in a civilized manner over a meal and fine wine.”

“Nobu’s,” I said.

❖

10

❖

At the restaurant I tried not to appear famished as I devoured a lobster salad. Ah, lobster. Sex on a plate.

I felt like I was back on top with a penthouse, an expense account, and a reputation. I'd done this scene a hundred times, sitting in an upscale restaurant sipping wine and talking art. Though not with a cop and a prince.

On the way over, we chatted about the difference in the weather between New York and Cambodia. Cambodia was tropical year round while New York went from steamy August to frigid January. Not the most fascinating subject, but Prince Ranar brought up the subject, obviously to talk about something entirely neutral.

Sitting close to both of them in the Mercedes limo, Detective Anthony smelled of male aftershave with a tinge of workout sweat while the prince's cologne had the sweet smell of money. Even though the detective annoyed me, his masculine scent was more of a turn-on to me than the prince's expensive fragrance.

While Prince Ranar reeked of money and culture, Anthony was probably the kind of guy who watched football games with his pals at a sports bar, came home with booze on his breath and lipstick on his collar, and made passionate love with his significant other after a knock-down, drag-out fight about what an inconsiderate bastard he was; the kind of guy I'd met too often in my life and had been attracted to. When it came to men, I had beer tastes when it should have been champagne.

I wondered what kind of prince Ranar was. Having dealt with "princes" and "princesses" a couple of times when I worked at a big auction house, I knew that the title oftentimes had only vague connections to royalty. Mostly it was a centuries-old empty title passed down long after the last king had lost his head. I discovered Cambodia still indeed had a king when Ranar mentioned that the king was in town to address the United Nations.

I didn't want to get into a discussion about his country and expose that I knew little about it other than the brief art history lesson—and political horror story—Bolger had told me. With a proposition being hinted at that meant money for me, exposing my ignorance didn't seem too clever. I was curious about the proposition, but didn't press for details because I didn't want to appear too eager.

The chitchat about nothing continued through another glass of wine and a dessert that included coconut sorbet and Jasmine ice cream. Wine and ice cream topped my list of favorite foods . . . next to chocolate, of course, which I ordered as a second dessert along with what I hoped was a ladylike smile to take the edge off of what they thought of my appetite. I didn't want to leave the impression—the correct impression—that I had been subsisting on fast food and hadn't had a high-end dinner in months.

I had inhaled my first glass of wine and ate as slow and ladylike as I could manage with a growling stomach urging me on. The wine hit me almost immediately, giving me a buzz because I drank it before food came. And I ordered another. One good thing about living in Manhattan even if I didn't have limo service home—I didn't have to worry about driving and drinking because I'd go home in a cab or subway.

Ranar finally broached the subject of Cambodian art over coffee drinks and more wine at the end of the meal.

"As I'm sure you know, Cambodia is one of the areas in the world where antiquities are being looted and destroyed on a daily basis. The pillaging is as blatant and ubiquitous as what happened to Iraq following the American invasion. Organized gangs that Detective Anthony calls a Thai-Cambodian mafia have a network that extends from stealing antiquities to smuggling them out of Cambodia and into the West and Japan, often with a stopover in Hong Kong."

Detective Anthony said, "Police agencies internationally have banded together to exchange information about the problem. The FBI, Sûreté and Interpol in Paris, the Art Theft unit in London, NYPD, and LAPD are all cooperating."

"Is that what Sammy is, some kind of mafia?" I asked the detective.

"Sammy's a deliveryman with a gambling problem. He was supposed to take that Apsaras piece to a gallery, but thought about selling it to you because the gamblers he owed money to were going to cut him off at the knees. When he didn't show up at the gallery, a phone call went out from the restaurant to find out what happened to him. He was with you, of course. The gunman in the alley was from the gamblers."

I gave him one of my brilliant smiles but wanted to stab him in the heart with my fork. "So you knew all the time that he came to my place on impulse, but still put me through the third degree."

"Actually, I didn't know if you two had conspired about bringing it to you. I'm still working on that angle."

What a bastard.

He gave me a malicious grin. "Don't think you did us any favors by making us come in to save your ass in that alley. I planned to have a surveillance go for weeks and net some big fish, but we had to break our cover because you blundered in."

"I'm sure Ms. Dupre's motives were pure," Prince Ranar said. "The police in my own country are, of course, fully cooperating with the international effort to stop this savage looting of Khmer treasures."

I had the feeling that Ranar's comment was directed at the detective. I detected friction between the two. From what Bolger said about the chaotic situation in Cambodia, I had a suspicion that the NYPD detective was not happy with the performance of his Cambodian counterparts.

"I'm confused," I said. "You say the Apsaras piece is a fake, a really good one at that. But there's widespread looting. Why bother making a fake if authentic pieces can be stolen so easily?"

"Money," Detective Anthony said. "The demand is greater than the supply. The market for Asian art has skyrocketed while the supply is shrinking as the international art community gets more educated about the damage being done to Khmer art. And as you said, the piece was exceptional. It wouldn't be sold as a fake."

So he had eavesdropped after he stepped out of the room.

The detective grinned, realizing he had slipped up. "The fact there's no meaningful catalog of Khmer art on the market means that an exceptional fake can be passed off as the real thing. The art gallery chosen to move the piece in New York may not have known it was a fake . . . or wouldn't care if they knew. For sure, the buyer wouldn't know and in some cases also wouldn't care. Because of its artistic appeal, the piece would have sold for many times the average Khmer artifact."

"What a businessman would call diversification has happened," Prince Ranar said. "With less exceptional pieces on the market, gangs of criminals have started pushing exceptional fakes."

"Must be real money in it," I said. I was dying to know how much.

Detective Anthony pulled a four-by-six picture from an inside pocket of his coat. "Art crimes rank third after drug trafficking and illegal arms sales in the financial impact of crime. This is why."

He handed me the picture.

"A Siva," I said.

Siva was one of the main gods of Hinduism, the paramount lord in the pantheon of gods in some sects. A very complicated deity, the Hindus considered him both a destroyer and a restorer, a wrathful avenger yet sensual and a herdsman of souls.

The sandstone statue in the photograph was typical of how Siva was portrayed in works of art: It had four arms and three eyes, one of them giving him inner vision but capable of fiery destruction when focused outward. His necklace was a serpent threaded through skulls. He sat in the lotus position, with legs intertwined, left foot over right thigh, the right foot over the left thigh.

One arm was broken off at the elbow and a hand was missing at the wrist. Limbs were the first to go on stone figures as war and mishandling occurred over the ages, which was why bronze was a more typical material for this type of complicated piece. But the price of a truly fine piece of art wasn't much affected by broken limbs. The *Venus de Milo*, with one arm broken off at the shoulder and the other above the elbow, was proof of that.

❖

"An exquisite piece," I said. "How large is it?"

"About a foot," Detective Anthony said. "It was sold to a private party for twenty-two million."

"It's fake?"

"How could you tell it's fake?"

"That was a question, not an opinion. I can't tell from a picture, but we were talking about fakes. It certainly looks real, but so did the Apsarases."

"It's a fake," Prince Ranar said. "Another excellent piece. Detective Anthony believes it's by the same artist who did the Apsaras piece."

"The only reason why it got exposed as a fake is because the buyer, a woman who runs a home goods company and has a weekly TV show on decorating, decided to show it off when she did a segment on her new apartment here in Manhattan. Someone from the Cambodian embassy spotted the piece. A quick check with the National Museum in Cambodia confirmed that the original was still there."

"Did the same people who smuggled in the Apsaras piece bring in this one?"

Detective Anthony shook his head. "Actually, this one came through Hong Kong. It was owned by a Russian, one of those ex-KGB thug types who got rich in the nineties after the Soviet Union collapsed. Oil, I think. Great system. Pay off politicians and suddenly you're an oil billionaire. He may have bought it legitimately, thinking it was authentic."

"How did he get the piece?"

"I don't know and he's not talking."

"Can't the police—"

"He's dead."

"Oh . . . because of the Siva?"

"We don't think so. He was gunned down in a nightclub in Hong Kong, apparently by other ex-KGB types to whom he wasn't paying enough protection. His girlfriend, a model, is still in Hong Kong. She's the one who put the piece on the market. We think she's sitting on more, but she's not talking, either. And there's not much we can do about it. Hong Kong's the gateway for much of the contraband art coming out of Asia."

Asian mafia. Ex-KGB billionaires. Murder. A Hong Kong model sitting on a hoard of fake art. Where did I fit into this? I asked the question and the detective answered.

"We're never going to stop the smuggling of contraband art, looted or faked, until we get to the source. The police in Thailand, Cambodia, and the Hong Kong territory of China are not always helpful."

"We are a poor country," Prince Ranar said, "the poorest of the three mentioned. We have more land mines left over from wars than people to step on them. We've had revolutions that crippled us and even today there is an uneasy truce among political factions. Our police are overwhelmed with struggles against drug trafficking and prostitution that destroy the lives of young girls. The looting of our antiquities is the third arm of this trinity of evils. Unfortunately, these evils are rampant because Westerners feed the corruption with money. They buy drugs, sex, and stolen art.

"Our cultural heritage is being vandalized, but we lack resources to deal with it. There are thousands of antiquity sites, many of them still covered by jungle, making it an impossible task to police with our limited resources. In our opinion, the best alternative is to increase the criminal sanctions against the wealthy Americans, Europeans, and Japanese who finance the crimes by paying enormous prices for unlawful goods."

The detective shook his head. "That isn't practical. People have the right to buy art and rely on provenances."

I suddenly realized the role they wanted me to play. "You want me to act as an antiquities buyer."

"That is what Detective Anthony had in mind," Ranar said.

"An undercover thing," I said. "Pretend to be in the market for stolen art."

"You've got it," Detective Anthony said.

I thought about it. Probably dangerous because the criminals wouldn't be happy when they found out I set them up. I wasn't about to get myself killed for the love of art. But I could set up perimeters as to how far I was willing to go—like never meeting with the devils except in a safe place with a lot of police surrounding me. Of course, the most important thing after safety was my commission. So I asked and Detective Anthony gave me the answer.

❖

"All expenses . . . and a big bonus if you get us a bona fide lead."

"How big a bonus?"

He nodded at Ranar. "Get the name of the head of the operations and the Cambodian government will pay you a fee of fifty thousand."

Almost chump change when I was a high roller in the art trade, but it sounded like a fortune to me now. But I shook my head. Never take the first offer was a rule of my chosen profession.

"I want a hundred thousand and all anticipated expenses up-front."

Detective Anthony looked to Ranar and raised his eyebrows. "You said a hundred thousand. Still willing to pay it?"

Ranar nodded. "Yes."

Damn. I should have asked for more. He had tricked me by low-balling the offer.

"Okay. When do I start?"

"Can you expedite getting her a visa?" Detective Anthony asked.

"A visa? What do I need a visa for?"

"You can't get into Cambodia without one."

"*Cambodia?* Are you insane? I'm not going to Cambodia."

11

❖

Jungles. Temple looting. Revolutions. Drug trafficking and prostitution practiced openly. People stepping on land mines—when they weren't stepping on poisonous snakes or being eaten by crocodiles . . . That was how Ranar had described his country—and I had the impression that he was deliberately downplaying the country's problems.

In the best light that Ranar gave it, the country sounded like a disaster in the making for me. The sort of place that news stories report, "An American was reported missing today in . . ." before the story just falls off the radar until a couple years later when they find the decomposing body in the jungle.

Now that was a pleasant thought.

I lay in bed the next morning and considered the proposition. A cop called Michelangelo wanted me to go to Cambodia. Find out who was running the Thai-Cambodian mafia or whatever it was. Come back and collect a hundred thousand. If I was still alive.

Refusing to commit, I left the offer on the table, literally, and fled in a taxi to home and bed. I should have said no, but instead I said I had to think about it. It wasn't just money being offered, it was my salvation. If I helped break a big smuggling ring, I might even generate publicity that would cleanse my name in the art world. Of course, the same caveat kept coming back at me: It wasn't worth it unless I was alive to collect.

Leaving my apartment, I headed around the corner along Canal to Mulberry and down to Bayard Street in Chinatown. I needed two things to help me think—an ice cream cone from the Chinatown Ice Cream Factory and a Chinese foot rub.

Both the ice cream and the rub were soul-soothing. At a time in my life when Thai takeout was my idea of splurging on dinner, little things like a foot rub took the place of jumping into a plane on impulse for a weekend at a five-star spa hotel in Bermuda.

I had to admit, living where Chinatown, Little Italy, and Soho bumped into each other was never dull because of the energy that constantly flowed on the streets: a babble of languages everywhere, ethnic restaurants, trendy and funky boutiques along places that sold used clothes, designer stores, art galleries, dozens of tourist shops, street vendors hawking their wares . . . It was all around me, alive and teeming with energy.

Chinatown was a city within a city, like a piece of old town Shanghai had been transported here. Locals crowded into the vendor shops each day to select their vegetables, fruit, spices, fresh fish, and meat. The freshest fish was still flapping when you bought it. I had found a dim sum restaurant that was cheap and good, right across the street from an ice cream factory that made the best homemade ice cream. My favorite flavor was Zen Butter made with peanut butter and toasted sesame seeds.

As I licked my cone and dodged people on the crowded sidewalk, I wondered why Detective Anthony had been more gung ho than Ranar to send me undercover to Cambodia. I could tell from Ranar's body language that he wasn't enthused about the idea. I didn't know whether it was because I was a foreigner who could get hurt . . . or he didn't want any more of the dirty underbelly of his country exposed. I had a feeling that my life rated rather less than national face.

One thing I was sure of . . . Detective Anthony wasn't going to force me to go undercover in some godforsaken place under threat of arrest. He had nothing on me or he would have pressed charges. I had deduced that all by myself. Figuring out cops was something I was getting good at . . . no doubt a talent linked to my experience narrowly escaping criminal charges.

I called Bolger before I stepped into the foot rub parlor. After giving him an overview of my adventures in the alley and under police interrogation—his cold silence signaling "I told you so"—I asked for a favor.

"Can you check the Internet and tell me anything about a Prince Ranar."

"What kind of prince is he?"

"Cambodian. Deputy minister for cultural security, something like that."

"You know, you really should get into the Internet yourself."

"I know, I will, but then I wouldn't have the fun of bugging you."

"What are you getting yourself into now? Do you plan to give your Thai mafia friends another chance to kill you?"

"I'll be careful."

I hung up in the middle of his loud, unpleasant burst of laughter.

WITH MY HEAD BACK and my eyes closed, I tried to shut down my mind and just listen to the petite Chinese woman's birdlike humming as she massaged my feet. I really missed the days when I got a full massage three times a week. And didn't have to worry about risking my life to earn a living.

My quiet moment was shattered by my cell phone ringing. I'd forgotten to turn it off. The Chinese lady didn't miss a beat in her song or the pressure points on the bottom of my feet. I thought it was going to be Bolger already, but I didn't recognize the number and hesitated answering, wondering if it could be a bill collector. I let it go into voice mail and checked it—Michelangelo the cop.

"Call me." That was it. Charming bastard. But sexy.

He answered my call with a "Yeah?"

"You called me," I said.

"Yeah. Have you told his highness yet that you're going to take his offer?"

"Detective Anthony, I am still considering all the national and international ramifications of—"

"Your bill collectors?"

Bastard. "When I finally come to a decision, I'll be sure and let you know . . . when and if I get around to it."

"Listen, Dupre, I'm cutting you some slack here. There's a federal agent who called and said he'd love to kick the chair out from under your feet if I could put a rope around your neck."

That was an understatement. I could guess who called him. The FBI agent had tried to lynch me over the Babylonian mask. "And why are you being so gracious?"

"Well, first of all, I'm a sucker for a good-looking woman."

He paused to let that comment tickle my ego for a moment—which it did.

"And I don't like crooks messing around with art. Drugs, whores, gambling, that's where crooks should keep their noses. But art, that's culture. It's not a place for thugs and punks."

"Your feelings about art endear you to me . . . almost. If we could just add some manners and a little grace to that ax murderer personality of yours, you would be almost likable. As it is you're . . ."

He stood in the doorway grinning at me, the phone still to his ear.

"What are you doing here?" I asked.

"Taking you to lunch."

I waited until I'd left the foot massage place before I made an accusation. "You've had me followed. Otherwise you wouldn't have known where I was."

He shook his head. "You overrate your importance. In a world where terrorism takes number one priority, camel-jockey cabdrivers take precedent over mafia dons at being tailed. I was on my way to drop off a painting at a Soho art gallery when I saw you go into the foot rub joint."

"Something you painted?"

"Yeah. Wanna see it? It's in my car."

His unmarked car was parked in front of a fire hydrant. He opened the trunk and removed a bedsheet wrapped around the painting.

"Self-portrait," he said.

It was indeed. But the swirling, chaotic brushstrokes and intense colors—his blond hair was almost orange on the canvas—was more Van Gogh than his namesake Michelangelo. And it wasn't very good. I wouldn't have recognized it as a self-portrait.

"Very nice," I lied.

"You really think so?" He wrapped it back up. "Better not tell you where it's gonna hang. Considering your habits, you might steal it."

So much for my compliment. "You did leave out one thing."

"What?"

"Your horns."

"I guess I deserve that. And you deserve lunch. There's a dim sum and then some place down the street. Best Shanghai dumplings on the planet."

THE RESTAURANT TURNED OUT to be one of my favorites. I poured myself hot tea, he ordered a Tsingtao Chinese beer—no glass.

He toasted me with the bottle. "May you reach heaven an hour before the devil knows you're dead."

"Old Irish toast?"

He looked at me, surprised.

"Exactly. Told to me by a priest. I was a choirboy, you know. Before I grew horns." He took a swig. "I guess you think I'm riding you."

"Why should I think that? Just because you're coercing me to go to one of the most dangerous places on the planet to rat out murderous criminals? No, I don't think you're riding me, I think I did something to you in a past life and now you're going to pay me back by getting me killed."

He gave me a charming boyish grin. "I see that your brief interaction with Far Eastern art has given you karmic spirituality by osmosis. But getting you killed is an overstatement. It's not quite that bad. Cambodia has quite a tourist trade and—"

"A million land mines and smugglers robbing temples."

"That, too, but you're not going to be Angelina Jolie fighting tomb raiders. Phnom Penh, the capital, is civilized—more or less. You can have a great vacation, stay in a first-class hotel, hop over and see Angkor Wat, which I saw last year and loved . . ." He grinned. "And all you have to do is put out the word that you're in the market for museum-quality pieces."

"Wouldn't it make more sense to send a cop over?"

"We did, but they cut off her ears and nose and sent them back to us."

He howled at the look on my face.

"Just kidding, Maddy."

"Bastard."

He got serious. "I'm going to tell you why you're a perfect fit for the job, it's going to get you pissed, but you already know it."

He didn't have to spell it out.

"I come with the right credentials, that's what you're saying? I made one mistake in my entire life—"

"Fifty-five million worth. You're famous in the world of art for having handled a world-class piece of art loot. The temple looters in Cambodia will flock to you."

"You have an overworked imagination and are highly delusional if you think I'm a crook who will attract other crooks." I smiled, sweetly. "In case you haven't noticed, despite the best efforts of you and the FBI, I'm not wearing prison stripes. If you had any real evidence against me, instead of idle threats, you would have charged me. Instead, you malign my pristine reputation with baseless, malicious accusations."

"Will you sleep with me?"

"Ah . . . now isn't that a romantic approach. I'm touched. You didn't even use the word 'fuck.' And Detective Anthony, Michelangelo, whatever your name is, I admit I was attracted to you . . . for a very short time, right up to the point where you tried to pin a crime on me that I didn't commit and realized you want to get me killed in a foreign country. I have this strange aversion to men who give me a choice between a cell at Riker's Island or getting my nose or whatever cut off."

"You're right."

"About what? Give me a list."

"My approach wasn't romantic. And fucking was exactly what I had in mind, as opposed to candles and sweet nothings. I like to get right down to basics with women. And I'm willing to concede that you weren't conspiring with the delivery guy. But that's not what's important right now."

"It is to me."

"You love art, much more than a guy like me who only dabbles in it.

It's your life. Even after you got knocked off your feet, you jumped right back into it. From what I'd heard, when you found out that fifty-five-mil piece was a cultural treasure that had been looted, you set out with the wrath of God to redeem it."

"I see. You've found out that you can't control me with threats, so you'll try a little honey."

"I'm just doing my job. What am I supposed to believe after you'd been handling a contraband Khmer piece shortly before I find you chasing a smuggler in an alley? I don't recall hearing that you called 911 when you realized it was contraband?"

"All right, I love art. It's the most important thing in my life." I brushed hair off my forehead. "It's my only love because I've never found a man yet that's excited me as much as a good piece of art—pun intended. Let's cut to the chase. You want me to go to Cambodia. You said you've been there?"

"Briefly. Saw Angkor. Phnom Penh's just a smaller version of Bangkok. The Thais just hide the dirt better than the Cambodians. It's safe enough."

"I get the impression that Prince Ranar isn't as enthused about me going to Cambodia as you are."

"Ranar is afraid of stirring up the pot. His country's already got a black eye in the international community for not cracking down on the looting of the country's Khmer art. Far Eastern art is hot. And he walks a tightrope. There are people in high places in his country who are on the take and don't want the trade to stop."

"And you want me to step into this snake pit?"

"I want you to help put a stop to the destruction of the cultural heritage of a small, poor nation. A thousand years ago people worked pieces of stone into shapes of gods and kings. Sometimes they spent years, decades, on a single piece. In seconds, a tomb raider with a hammer and chisel breaks off a piece and destroys much more. They cut off the heads of statues and sell the heads."

He put his hand on my knee. "The only way we can stop this destruction is do what the tomb raiders do to statues—cut off heads. The heads of the looters. We need to find out who's behind it and stop them. We're not going after the villager who makes a hundred dollars. It's a year's wages for them. That hundred-dollar piece sells for a thousand to a dealer in Bangkok. Ten thousand when it hits Hong Kong. And a hundred thousand when it's sold in New York, London, or Tokyo."

The hand under the table found my warm spot.

12

❖

We were going up the steps to my apartment when my cell phone went off and I recognized Bolger's number.

"Ranar has a vague, long-distant relationship to the Cambodian royal family," he said.

I kept going up, Detective Anthony beside me, pawing and trying to kiss me as I tried to keep my voice neutral for Bolger. I hoped none of my neighbors stepped out of their apartments and caught the action.

"A bunch of people call themselves princes and princesses over there," Bolger said. "Ranar's made speeches at UNESCO and other cultural heritage conferences about the destruction of the cultural treasures of third world countries. Since Cambodia is right up there with post-invasion Iraq in terms of wholesale looting of antiquity sites, he no doubt qualifies as an expert on the subject.

"He's half French, half Cambodian. His mother was French, an old plantation family, his father a big shot in the government until the commies took over and he was executed. Spent a bunch of years in Paris. Probably more cosmopolitan than most Cambodians."

"Why the French connection?"

"Cambodia was a French colony, part of French Indochina until the

1950s. Had rich French rubber and other plantation owners. Some of the French stuck around even after the country became independent. The country still has a cultural connection to France. Ranar's education in Paris is typical of rich Cambodians even today.

"By the way, I took a look at news reports of the present political situation in Cambodia. The stability is measured by how dominant the current dictator is. It's a typical third world country with the usual problems of corruption, violence, and poverty."

I thanked Bolger and hung up as I opened the apartment door with Anthony still pawing me. He was trying to take off my dress. Not a good idea in my hallway. He had all the subtle romantic finesse of a horny sixteen-year-old.

What was wrong with me? I was a thirty-something, sophisticated woman of the world, educated, ambitious, successful—before I fell from grace. And I loved being pawed by this guy who drank beer straight from the bottle, parked in front of fire hydrants, and had artistic credentials not far beyond paint-by-numbers.

What happened to that woman who expected champagne and diamonds before falling into bed with a man?

"Who were you talkin' to?" he asked.

"Friend."

He started to pick me up, and I stopped him and pointed at the bed.

"Small apartment," I said.

"I have something big for you."

Oh, God, what a dumb line.

He bent down and grabbed my dress and pulled it up over my head. My slip went off next. I was down to panties and bra and platform heels.

No class, I thought. Pure animal instincts. Why would a woman with class and worldly experience put up with this base sexual play? I could get as much relief from a vibrator. But not as much action. A vibrator just didn't feel the same as a throbbing cock.

I'm a weak person, I thought as I helped him strip off the last of my clothes.

My detective lover left in the middle of the night. I slept for a couple hours, then woke up and stared up at the darkness, my mind racing. I always had a problem sleeping, even before my life started unraveling. I did my best thinking at night, working out problems that didn't seem to have a solution in the light of day. Like instant replay with videotape, I also ran the mistakes I'd made back over in my mind, agonizing over them, wishing I could erase the tape and start over.

I slept until nearly noon and then called Bolger.

"I'm going to Cambodia," I said.

"Are you insane? Must I look up the latest statistics on murder, rape, and pillage in the country?"

What could I say? I was being asked to save the world.

The world of art, at least.

❖

U.S. Department of State
Bureau of Consular Affairs
Washington, D.C. 20520

Consular Information Sheet: **CAMBODIA**

CRIME: The Diplomatic Security Service rates the overall crime threat in Cambodia as critical. Street crime remains a serious concern in Cambodia. Military weapons and explosives remain readily available to criminals despite efforts by authorities to collect and destroy such weapons. Armed robberies occur frequently in Phnom Penh, and while not specifically targeted, foreign residents and visitors are among the victims. Victims of armed robberies are reminded that they should not resist and should surrender their valuables as any perceived resistance may be met with physical violence, including lethal force. Local police rarely investigate reports of crime against tourists and travelers should not expect to recover stolen items.

The U.S. Embassy advises its personnel who travel to the provinces to exercise extreme caution outside the provincial towns during the day and everywhere at night. Many rural parts of the country remain without effective policing. Individuals should avoid walking alone after dusk anywhere in Sihanoukville, and especially along the waterfront. Some of the beaches are secluded, and post has received reports in the past of women being attacked along the Sihanoukville waterfront during the evening hours. These security precautions should also be taken when visiting the Siem Reap (Angkor Wat) area.

Pickpockets and beggars are also present in the markets and at the tourist sites. Persons visiting Cambodia should practice sound personal security awareness by varying their routes and routines, maintaining a low profile, not carrying or displaying large amounts of cash, not wearing flashy or expensive jewelry, and not walking the streets alone after dark. Travelers should be particularly vigilant at tourist sites in Phnom Penh, Siem Reap, and Sihanoukville, where there have been a marked increase in motorcycle "snatch and grab" thefts of bags and purses. In addition, we recommend that Americans travel by automobile and not use local moto-taxies or cyclos for transportation. These vehicles are more vulnerable to armed robberies and offer no protection against injury when involved in traffic accidents.

[Consular Information Sheets can be accessed at *http://travel.state.gov/travel*]

13

❖

Phnom Penh

Pa-nom-pen. With a guidebook open in my lap, I practiced the pronunciation of the city's name silently to myself during my flight to the capital of Cambodia.

After having spent sixteen hours on the plane from New York to Hong Kong, then adding on another twelve hours for the time change, by the time I arrived in Hong Kong I was in a haze. The long flight exhausted me. Since I couldn't afford the luxury of first class or even business class anymore I was stuck in the cramped coach section. It was bad news all the way around. The plane was full, so no empty seats were available to stretch out on.

God . . . I'd forgotten what it was like to be squashed in a center seat with elbows on both sides, my knees almost up to my chin while I breathed recycled air. I'm certain I saw Ebola and other nasty things crawling out of the vents.

The food was edible only because I was trapped in a plane. The clever person to my right in the prized aisle seat—that my last-minute, Internet economy ticket didn't entitle me to—had brought a deep dish pepperoni and cheese pizza aboard. As I stared at my airplane food, something called Chicken Milano, wondering if the chicken had come from an egg or a test tube while the smell of pizza made me delirious, I was tempted to beg for a piece of the pizza.

I'd gotten an advance for expenses from Ranar and that included a business-class airplane ticket, but after I did some quick calculating I realized I could pay two months' rent from the excess if I flew coach both ways.

I took my usual antihistamine pill an hour before my flight because of my allergies, but halfway through the flight I had to take another one because my ears were starting to get that familiar stabbing pain. I didn't travel anywhere without what I called the three A's: aspirin, antihistamine, and antacid.

Now I could add aggravation to the list.

When I finally got off the plane in Hong Kong and checked into my room that afternoon, I took two aspirin, fell asleep, and didn't wake up until the following morning. Normally when I arrive at a new place I'm eager to go out and check the area but this time I just wanted to crawl in a warm bed and go to sleep. To be sure I didn't miss my flight to Phnom Penh the next morning I asked for a wake-up call from the front desk clerk.

The five-hour trip to Cambodia was a vast improvement. I flew Cathay Pacific to Saigon and thirty minutes later boarded a Vietnam Airlines plane and an aisle seat for the hop to the Cambodian capital.

I wish I could have taken at least a quick taxi ride into Ho Chi Minh City. It used to be called Saigon and Ho himself was called the devil incarnate . . . at least that's what Americans were told back during the Vietnam War. Now tourists flocked to the city.

The guidebook I picked up at JFK revealed that Cambodia was a different type of tourist destination. Definitely for more adventurous travelers with a reward of seeing one of the great wonders of the world—Angkor Wat. The antiquity site was an hour's plane ride away from the capital of . . . *pa-nom-pen.*

"Nom pen," a male voice across the aisle from me said.

"Excuse me?"

I stared at him for a moment, my weary brain scrambling to remember if I had spoken the name out loud. Either the man had very good hearing or he was trying to strike up a conversation. He hadn't said a single word during the flight but he did stare at me a couple of times, a look that gave me the creeps.

"It's pronounced both ways, with and without the *pa*, but most of us expats hanging around the city try to slur the name to sound like we're locals, so we pronounce it *nom-pen*." He shifted in his seat and extended his hand across the aisle. "Emmet Bullock."

I shook his hand. "Madison Dupre."

Even though the cabin temperature was a little cool, his hand felt warm and sticky. I felt like using an antibacterial wipe to clean my hand but decided to do it later when he wasn't watching. He had a weak handshake, a trait I always considered to be a character defect.

He nodded at my guidebook. "I saw you reading the book. First time to Cambodia?"

"I'm afraid I'm a first-timer when it comes to the Far East," I said.

Bullock was middle-aged, heavyset, with pale, unhealthy-looking skin and drooping jowls. Seated, gravity had bunched up much of his excess bulk around his midsection. The man needed to lose a good fifty pounds. Maybe more. He wore a wrinkled white linen suit, a Panama hat, and a hot pink shirt with black necktie. Other than old movies, the last time I had seen anyone wear a Panama hat was years ago on a trip to Aruba.

"Going to Nom Pen on business or pleasure?"

"Pleasure. Mainly as the staging area for a trip to the Angkor site." I wasn't in the mood for conversation but I didn't want to be rude. "Is there much to see in, uh . . . the city?" I decided not to try the abbreviated name. It didn't sound right to me and I'd already memorized the one from the guidebook.

"Plenty to see . . . a regular Disneyland in a way. One designed by the Marquis de Sade," he said with a throaty laugh.

A strange analogy. The marquis was a nineteenth-century French writer famous for his erotic and scandalous writing. He spent much of his life in prison and insane asylums for his perversions, but managed to etch out a place in history nonetheless.

"It sounds a little . . . offbeat."

"Offbeat. That's a good one, I hadn't heard that before. Strange, bizarre, La-La Land, I've heard those descriptions. No question, it's fascinating for some people and repulsive to others. A marvelous place to examine all the carnal sins . . . and a few even the Bible doesn't mention. Everything that's ugly on the planet can be found in Cambodia and it's nicely gathered in a central section of Nom Pen." He leaned a little closer and smirked. "You can satisfy any appetite . . . if you know what I mean . . ."

He didn't have to explain. I knew exactly what he meant. And he looked like the type with a big appetite for creepy things.

I cringed in my seat and signaled him with a look that maybe we shouldn't be talking too loud about the horrors of the country in a plane loaded with Cambodians. He obviously didn't care or was oblivious to it.

Ugly American, I thought, the sixties term connoting arrogant, rude, and thoughtless behavior by travelers in poor countries. He spoke loud enough to be heard by others. I got the sense that he was doing it deliberately. Either he liked attracting attention to himself or had utter contempt for the sensibilities of other people.

In other words, he was a shit.

His tropical white linen suit reminded me of actor Sydney Greenstreet's cultured villainous style of dress during the Golden Age of Hollywood, but that's where the similarity ended. Sydney Greenstreet only *acted* as if he was a high-class crook. Bullock desperately tried to look classy and fell way short. A greasy food stain on his lapel didn't help.

I took an instant dislike to him.

"You've heard of the Killing Fields, haven't you?" He asked the question with the sort of arrogance that guaranteed he would play one-upmanship regardless of the answer.

"Wasn't that a movie?" I played dumb. I never did watch the movie that Bolger suggested.

"More like a real-life horror story. After breaking away from France's colonial empire in the fifties, Cambodia became a violent extension of the Vietnam War. We bombed the hell out of it. But the real nightmare began in the mid-seventies when a communist group called the Khmer Rouge took control in the country and set out to take it back to the Stone Age. Pol Pot became the head honcho despite the fact his family had royal connections.

"It was the crazies taking over the asylum, so to speak These nuts tried to completely redesign society by first getting rid of the existing people, the businesses, even the economy. The regime was so naïve and inept, they outlawed money. They thought they could rearrange the economy so money wasn't used. Can you imagine that?"

He stopped and looked at me for some kind of response.

"No," I muttered. Two passengers looked back at me and I was sure they understood what he was saying.

"They drove people out of the cities and forced the entire country back to an agricultural level. I guess they figured the system wouldn't work if the people had any brains, so they set out to kill anybody with any sort of education. Can you imagine that?"

I shook my head back and forth.

"They murdered about one out of every four or five people in the country of seven or eight million. Can you imagine—"

"No."

Bolger had told me the same thing. I did a quick calculation and realized if that happened in the United States, the figure would amount to some sixty or seventy million people.

"Of course, Pol Pot's dead now and his regime is out of power, but the old Khmer Rouge warlords still rule large areas of the country and the corruption is ubiquitous at all levels of government. It's damn crazy. People are poor, the police are corrupt, fourteen-year-old prostitutes are common, and murder can be hired rather easily. Can you imagine that?"

The only thing I could imagine was this guy on the other side of the aisle splattering blood as he whacked people with a chain saw on a busy street. Through gritted teeth, I said, "No."

He leaned closer, the lewd look appearing in his eyes again. "If your personal tastes run toward birds of a feather, I'm sure the girls there won't mind as long as you tip them well."

The guy got on my nerves up to the point of no return. I tried to come back with some clever remark but nothing hit me. What I really wanted to tell him is what a jerk he was but I thought . . . what for? He had no meaning in my life and after I got off the plane I'd never see him again. "Thanks for the advice," was all I said.

Hearing a description of the country again was an eye-opener. It had been depressing when Bolger talked about it, but I heard it thousands of miles away. Now I was about to be knee-deep in a country with a scary past and an uncertain future. A poor, traumatized, corrupt third world country with bloodthirsty warlords and hungry crocodiles wasn't exactly where I wanted to be.

I looked back down at the guidebook, staring at nothing, hoping he would take the hint and stop talking but no such luck.

"I hang out at Nom Pen for business and pleasure. I'm in the art business. Buy, sell, appraise, import, export, you name it. I do it all. Let me know if there's anything I can help you with."

I don't think so, I told myself.

"Here's my business card."

"Thanks." I gave him a feeble smile and took his card, then closed my eyes to shut him out.

The more I thought about it, the more uncomfortable I felt about him. He claimed to be in the art business. Now wasn't that a coincidence. Here I'm on my way to investigate an art theft ring and this sleazy guy who's in the art business strikes up a conversation with me on the plane. I didn't buy it.

A list of questions swirled in my head. Was this character involved? Was there a leak in Ranar's operation? Someone knew I was coming and had told the criminals? Was Bullock really in the art business?

I put the creepy guy out of my mind, determined that win, lose, or draw, going to Cambodia at the very least meant I was going to see one of the great man-made wonders of the world.

Thinking about Angkor Wat made me feel a little sad because it brought back memories of my father. His lifelong dream had been to go there and help restore the ancient site. I always remembered him saying he would go when the time was right. Of course, the time never came. What he didn't realize was that sometimes you just have to bite the bullet and do it. You don't wait around, otherwise you'll always find an excuse not to go.

He missed out on seeing one of the top wonders of the world—for some art lovers it was number one on their list.

I wondered if all those times he talked about the wonders of Angkor wasn't the reason I avoided Far Eastern art in my studies and career, whether his disappointment in not realizing his dream had made me avoid it.

Had he known that modern tomb robbers with electric diamond-edged saws and trucks were taking out large statues, even temple walls, and selling them to waiting customers?

If there was an opportunity for a crime in this world, it seemed like someone was always around to step in and commit it, even if it meant the destruction of cultural treasures thousands of years old.

I dozed off with a mental image of Bullock ripping up an Angkor Wat stone temple with a screeching chain saw. I was there too, only I just stood, my feet frozen in place. I wanted to move but I couldn't. I tried yelling at him but nothing came out of my mouth. He saw me and starting laughing, then continued cutting away like a frantic lumberjack.

I woke up with a start. Bullock's hand was nudging my shoulder and I stared at him.

"Looks like you were having a bad dream or something. Your body was twitching."

"More like a nightmare."

"Well, it's a good thing I woke you up then. By the way, we're landing in thirty minutes." He had a smug look on his face as if he knew something I didn't.

"Thanks."

I got up and went to the back of the plane just before the fasten seat belt sign came on. I had to use the toilet but I also needed some water to take two aspirin because I felt the tension starting to build in my neck area. This man really got to me.

Just my luck to be seated across from a scumbag instead of a tall, dark, and handsome stranger.

Horror Story: When the Crazies Take Over the Asylum

U.S. Department of State
Bureau of East Asian and Pacific Affairs

The Khmer Rouge turned Cambodia into a land of horror. Immediately after its victory, the new regime ordered the evacuation of all cities and towns, sending the entire urban population out into the countryside to till the land. Thousands starved or died of disease during the evacuation.

Many of those forced to evacuate the cities were resettled in new villages, which lacked food, agricultural implements, and medical care. Many starved before the first harvest, and hunger and malnutrition—bordering on starvation—were constant during those years.

Those who resisted or who questioned orders were immediately executed, as were most military and civilian leaders of the former regime who failed to disguise their pasts.

The new government sought to restructure Cambodian society completely. Remnants of the old society were abolished, and Buddhism suppressed.

Agriculture was collectivized, and the surviving part of the industrial base was abandoned or placed under state control. Cambodia had neither a currency nor a banking system. The regime controlled every aspect of life and reduced everyone to the level of abject obedience through terror. Torture centers were established, and detailed records were kept of the thousands murdered there. Public executions of those considered unreliable or with links to the previous government were common. Few succeeded in escaping the military patrols and fleeing the country.

Hundreds of thousands were brutally executed by the regime. Hundreds of thousands more died of starvation and disease.

Estimates of the dead range from 1.7 million to 3 million, out of a 1975 population estimated at 7.3 million.

[More information about Cambodia can be accessed at *www.state.gov*]

14

❖

During the plane's descent, Bullock offered me a ride in the private car waiting for him, speaking loud enough for everyone nearby to hear that taxis were dirty and that he was being picked up in an air-conditioned, chauffeured limo.

I turned him down with the simple excuse that some friends were meeting me. Imaginary friends were a safer bet than riding with this rude bore who raised the hackles on my paranoia.

After his limo left, I waited in line for the next available taxi at the taxi stand. The heat was stifling and naturally the taxi had no air-conditioning. Opening a window was opening an oven door.

My game plan was to visit antique stores and leave my name and hotel phone number after subtly letting them know I was in the market for high-quality antiquities. Not stolen ones, of course. I hoped that part would be assumed. The trade in antiquities was secretive and cut-throat, tending to attract dealers who could have marketed the haul of Ali Baba and his forty thieves. I was sure that word about an American with big money to spend would make the rounds to dealers with goods under the table.

I stared numbly at the disorder that grew the closer we came to the heart of the city. Phnom Penh is not a huge city by today's standards, about a million people, but right off I realized it ranked high on the chaos scale. The sidewalks were pressed with people and street vendors. Streets were choked with bicycles, cars, and motorcycles, the latter two spitting out black smoke while legions of bicycle riders had bags attached to their backs and wore hats and scarves as protection from the hot sun.

I'd never seen so many motorcycles and bikes. Unlike the big street motorcycles that Americans drove, these were smaller and lighter, more like dirt bikes. Many of the motorized and pedaled bikes were a type of rickshaw with a passenger chair in the back; others pushed a chair in front.

I was surprised at how poor and undeveloped the city appeared. I'd read about it but it was still astonishing when I saw it in person. The roads were in bad repair and pockmarked with potholes. Open sewers ran down gutters and litter was strewn on sidewalks and streets. Most of the streets off the main thoroughfare appeared to be unpaved and dusty. Tenements looked ready to crumble in a minor earthquake. Sadly, most of the children I saw were barefoot, some naked, and some in ragged clothing.

Contrasting this state of poverty was an ambiance of refinement to the city. French influence in architecture combined with traditional Cambodian styles added a certain exotic elegance to some of the buildings. The city was both ugly and quaint.

I felt as if I had stepped onto another planet and I had: *Welcome to the Third World.*

I always wondered what that expression meant other than it connoted an industrially underdeveloped country. If this was the third world, was the U.S. and other rich countries the first world? Who was the second world? I made a mental note to ask Bolger when I had a chance.

Taking out several one-dollar bills, I stuffed them into my pocket so I wouldn't have to fumble with my purse to pay the taxi and the hotel porters when I got to the hotel. Both Prince Ranar and my guidebook said that U.S. dollars were a common currency in Cambodia, along with the Cambodian riel. It took about four thousand riel to equal one dollar, so it was much easier for me to deal in terms of U.S. dollars than trying to convert riels into dollars. Dollars were so ubiquitous, prices were often listed in both riels and dollars.

When the taxi pulled into the long, wide, circular driveway of the Raffles Le Royale hotel, things started looking up. The hotel was located in the heart of the city and about twenty minutes from the Pochentong International Airport. Lush greenery everywhere added a tropical atmosphere to the place.

I was immediately greeted by hotel personnel and swept into an air-conditioned marble lobby with tall round arches and a French colonial ambiance. The lobby had tropical plants, art deco furnishings, and Cambodian objets d'art. Definitely old world charm.

A cool, damp towel and a cold fruit drink with an alcohol kick was in my hand by the time I reached the front desk to register. Somewhere off the lobby, I heard the soothing and peaceful sound of a violin. I knew right off I was going to like this place.

The hotel had three interconnecting wings and I chose to stay in the main building because I had read it had been restored a few years ago to its original architectural style. The establishment had been around since 1925 and frequented by an international clientele of royalty, dignitaries, writers, journalists, and adventurers.

My room overlooked the garden in the courtyard. Although small, it was cozy and less expensive than the other rooms available. Again, I was thinking about what I could save from my per diem to survive on back home if I didn't hit a jackpot in Cambodia.

My room wasn't luxurious but it still had a certain quaintness created by Cambodian art. I flopped onto the bed, spread my arms and legs, and sighed. I felt in the chips again. Then I dragged myself off the bed. I had work to do.

I sorted out my things, hung up some clothes, took a shower, got dressed, and set out to see the city. I wasn't ready to fake it in antique shops. I wanted to scope out things first.

When I got down to the lobby, Pho, the concierge, advised me to take a regular taxi rather than the motorized chairs.

"A taxi is much better for you," he said with a big smile.

"Those rickshaw things look interesting."

He explained that a tuk-tuk was a motorcycle pulling a small cart with seats, motos were motorcycles pushing a wheelchair-looking seat, and cyclos were pedaled bikes pushing a similar seat.

Too much to remember. Rickshaws were good enough for me. "Are they safe?"

He shrugged. "Not as safe as regular taxi."

I thanked him and told him the rickshaw looked like fun.

He was scratching his head when I looked back over my shoulder. Another crazy tourist who could afford to ride a taxi and used poor people transportation because it was "more fun."

The hotel was close to Monivong, a major street that flowed down to the National Museum and other tourist attractions, so I didn't mind walking the short distance. Even though I was a single woman, I felt there was safety in numbers—the streets were packed with people.

Now that it was late afternoon, I figured it would be a little cooler when I stepped outside but I was wrong. The temperature felt the same as before. Wet, steaming hot.

Coming onto Monivong Boulevard after leaving the hotel's sanctuary, the pounding third world hit me with a vengeance. Drivers of the motorized and pedaled rickshaws chattered away in a mixture of broken pidgin English and Cambodian as I walked along the crowded street.

"Hey, lady, cheap for you."

"You ride. Good price."

I shook my head and continued walking. I didn't get far before I had beggar boys and girls at my heels pleading for money. There were too many to deal with and too many to ignore. I threw dollar bills behind me and the swarm of boys descended on the money like a pack of hungry young wolves. I almost ran to get away. It was a dichotomous scene: poor children begging on the sidewalk while expensive foreign cars drove by on the street.

As I moved closer to the curb to avoid a legless man holding a sign written in French and English that said "Land Mine," a young man on a motorcycle suddenly pulled up to the curb and grabbed my handbag, pulling me down as he jerked it away from me. It happened so fast I didn't have time to think, but my adrenaline immediately kicked in and I started up right after him.

"Hey!" I yelled.

❖

He barely got going before a man ran into the street and smacked him in the face with his elbow, sending the thief flying backward off the bike. The man yelled something to the driver in Cambodian and picked up my bag. He handed it back to me as the driver got up, blood on his face from a bleeding nose. He pushed his motorcycle to get the engine going and left with a screech of tires and a cloud of black smoke.

"This belongs to you."

My rescuer handed me my purse. His accent struck me as Scandinavian.

"Thank you."

"I saw him eyeing you and knew what was coming."

I shook my head. "Does this happen a lot?"

He grinned. "It happens most often to foreign women who walk close to the curb and don't pay attention to where they're going. Didn't you read the section in your guidebook about crime in the city?"

"I guess I forgot that part. Shouldn't we call the police?"

The thief had disappeared into the heavy street traffic.

"Not unless you want to spend hours at a police station filling out meaningless forms in a language you don't speak. Getting mugged in Phnom Penh is just one of the less touristy things that happen here to foreigners. You soon learn that you stay away from the curb when you walk and carry your belongings on the building side."

"I'll remember that. I don't know how to thank you."

"I do. You can have a drink with me." He smiled and put out his hand. "Kirk Carlson."

"Madison Dupre."

I gave him a firm handshake and got one back.

He didn't have handsome Hollywood looks, but he certainly had a masculine and sensuous appeal. Short, blond, almost white hair, and a deep tan, he reminded me of Rutger Hauer, a Nordic type who played the killer android in *Blade Runner*, an old Harrison Ford movie that I had watched with my dad. But there was something quirky about his face. Looking close, I realized his face looked too perfect—like it had been wiped clean and put back on with plastic surgery.

I must have been staring at him because he grinned and said, "Explosion. I was on a military bomb squad with NATO peacekeeping forces in Bosnia and I got too close to one of the bombs."

"Sorry, I didn't mean to stare."

"I'm used to it. It happens a lot. But I have to confess, I was much uglier before the slate got wiped clean."

His accent was tinged with a touch of foreign intrigue.

"You're lucky. The effect is sexy, if a bit menacing."

"Sexy and menacing. That's the best description I've gotten. I think I'm going to like you."

I started walking with him beside me. "Amazing city. Very exotic, very dirty and crowded, but exciting."

I was about to step off a curb when he quickly pulled me back as a car shot by.

"Wow, that's twice in the same day. Three's a charm."

"Three's a charm?"

"An old saying, three's a charm, things happen in threes. I've had two already, so now . . ." I knew I was babbling, a little embarrassed for being so careless. "Never mind."

He shook a finger at me. "Pedestrians don't have the right of way here, so don't assume cars will stop. They won't."

"So I've found out."

"Another piece of advice: If you have to cross and there's traffic coming, wait and cross with a monk."

"A monk?"

He nodded at three monks in red robes crossing the street. Traffic had stopped for them. Each had a black umbrella and a sack thrown over one shoulder.

"Okay . . . but what if there are no monks around?"

"They're almost always around. Forget about crossing if you can't find one." He grinned as he took a firm hold on my arm and guided me to a motorized rickshaw. "You look hot, jet-lagged, and a little bruised. I'm buying you a cool drink."

He took me to a restaurant in a renovated colonial building across from the river quay. The heat was still oppressive and stepping into the cool, dark bar was a godsend.

I read aloud the name on the building. "The Foreign Correspondents' Club. I love it. Sounds like a place Humphrey Bogart would have started if he'd come here instead of Casablanca."

"It was called the 'F' by reporters and diplomats who made the place their watering hole after the Khmer Rouge fell out of power and Nom Pen became only relatively dangerous instead of a killing zone. Now it's a favorite place for expats and, more recently, tourists."

He pronounced the name of the city the same way as Bullock.

We went up to the second-floor terrace for a river view.

"The city's at the confluence of three rivers, with the Mekong being the King Kong of them. The Mekong flows all the way from the icy Roof of the World in Tibet to the South China Sea. As hot as it gets here, you would never think that the Mekong started out as melted snow."

He suggested a Tonle Sap Breezer, a drink he said was named after the biggest lake in the country. One of the three rivers coming into the city flowed from the lake.

"What's in it?"

"Vodka, cranberry juice, and grapefruit juice."

"Sounds good. I'll try it." I admired the view for a few moments, then asked, "So, what do you do for a living?"

"I'm a bounty hunter."

"For criminals who jumped bail?"

"For land mines and bombs."

"Interesting . . . and why do you search for such nasty things?"

He grinned. "There are hundreds of thousands, probably millions, of land mines all over the country, a result of decades of civil war and foreign invasions. The country got hit with a million bombs, too, and a whole bunch of them didn't explode and are out there waiting for someone to stumble over. I came here with a humanitarian group about ten years ago to clear the mines and ordnances. As I told you, I've had a bit of experience with bombs. After a couple of years, the group ran out of money and now I hunt down the explosives for a bounty paid by the government." He stopped and took a sip of his drink. "Your turn now. What do you do?"

"Nothing as noteworthy as you I'm afraid. I'm in the art business, buying, selling, appraising, that sort of thing. Cambodia has one of the world's greatest art treasures, so I thought I'd check it out."

"So you're going to Angkor Wat?"

"Yes. I have reservations on a flight in a couple days."

"Then let me introduce you to someone." He led me to a group standing on the other side of the terrace and gave a friendly peck on the cheek to a woman who appeared to be in her thirties. "Chantrea Son, this is Madison Dupre."

We shook hands as he spoke.

"You two are on different ends of the same business. Madison is an art dealer from New York. Chantrea is a deputy director of Apsara, the government agency that administers Angkor Wat."

Meeting a woman in the top echelon of management for the Angkor site was a piece of luck I hadn't counted on. Prince Ranar had offered to set me up with people to contact but I turned him down. I could hardly go around pretending to be on the make for looted antiquities if I came with a recommendation from the country's antiquities security chief.

"I'm sure you can find some nice pieces here in the city," she said, speaking perfect English. "Of course, you don't want to touch anything that's prohibited from export."

"I'm in the market for any piece with resale value, but I stop at robbing cultural treasures." I obviously didn't want to give her the impression that I was here to buy looted pieces.

"Good. You'd be surprised how many foreigners come here with the idea they can slip a few dollars to a customs official and take home a museum piece. Unfortunately, sometimes even the locals get involved." She asked Kirk, "Did you hear Hardy got arrested?"

"Yes. Two days ago, I understand, just before I left Siem Reap. For smuggling antiquities."

My eyes perked up with interest. "What happened?"

"Hardy owns a bar close to Angkor Wat. They found some pieces when they searched his bar, but there's a rumor that it was a setup."

"Was it?" I asked.

"Siem Reap is the main town near Angkor," Chantrea explained. "Hardy's bar has been very successful. In fact, he's taking business away from the other bars. Getting accused of dealing in illegal antiquities is a good way to get rid of the competition."

Kirk made a slicing motion across his throat. "You can get the death penalty for smuggling antiquities. They're especially hard on foreigners."

Oh, wonderful. Something to look forward to—getting my head cut off or hanged or whatever they do to foreigners.

A man approached us and I cursed a silent *oh shit*. Of all people, why did it have to be him.

❖

“Emmet Bullock, this is Madison Dupre.

His eyebrows shot up. “Not *the* Madison Dupre.”

“Are you someone famous?” Chantrea’s eyes lit up.

“Not at all,” I said, shaking my head. “We met on the plane.”

“She’s just being modest. She’s very famous in New York art circles. She was the head curator at the Piedmont Museum before all that nasty stuff about buying stolen antiquities from the Baghdad museum came out.”

I forced a smile at the sleazy, arrogant bastard. Now I knew the reason for his smug look on the plane. “Yes, I accidentally bought one of the fifteen thousand or so pieces stolen from the museum when it was looted as American forces entered Baghdad. It cost me my job and a lot more.”

“I’m surprised you didn’t mention on the plane that you were also in the art business, but it’s a cutthroat business, isn’t it. I imagine you’re hot after a particular piece.” He gave me a wink.

“Just on vacation.” I was tempted to tell him I didn’t mention anything personal because he gave me the creeps but I held my tongue out of respect for Kirk and Chantrea.

He gave me a belly laugh. “Sure. Art is like perversion, it’s a 24/7 preoccupation. I’m here in Nom Pen to buy. Why else would anyone come to this shit hole? Here’s a tip: If you’re looking for pieces that can be exported, check out Sinn’s shop at the Russian Market. There’s always a few things left after the better stuff has been picked over.”

Chantrea cleared her throat. “Excuse me, gentlemen, but I’m stealing Madison away for a bit. There’s someone I think she should meet.” She took my arm and led me away.

“Charming bastard,” I said, once we were out of earshot.

“He’s rather disgusting, isn’t he? Comes over from San Francisco for months at a time. He likes to brag about the big-game hunting he does.” She rolled her eyes upward in a distasteful look. “He went to one of the so-called shooting ranches outside of town and paid a couple hundred dollars for the privilege of shooting a staked-out water buffalo with a machine gun.”

“That’s real sportsmanship.”

“It gets worse. If I told you what he was really famous for, you’d shove your cocktail pick in his heart.”

I already wanted to stick it in his eye. I was about to ask Chantrea what Bullock was notorious for when Kirk came up behind us.

"Sorry about that, Madison, but he did give you some good advice. The Russian Market is a good place to start if you want to pick up Cambodian art pieces. Not antiquities, of course, those come with a death sentence, but there are plenty of reproductions, some of them quite good. Sinn is spelled with two n's and it has some good pieces."

"Why do they call it the Russian Market?" I asked. "Was it started by a Russian?"

Chantrea shook her head. "Back in the eighties when the Vietnamese invaded and broke the power of the Khmer Rouge, they occupied Phnom Penh. The Vietnamese had a close relationship with the Russians and a lot of Soviet bloc goods were sold in the marketplace."

"You can buy just about anything there," Kirk added, "from shoes and handbags to fake thousand-year-old Buddhas and fresh marijuana and opium."

"My guidebook said drugs aren't legal anymore in the country."

"They're illegal, but they're openly sold."

He saw the question on my face.

"Cambodia is like the Roman god Janus—everything has two faces. Take prostitution. It's illegal, but you can easily buy an hour with a teenage prostitute for the price of a pack of cigarettes in the States."

"Really." A pack cost somewhere between five and six dollars.

"We also have some very nice aspects of the city," Chantrea chimed in, smiling. "It's not a big city. You can see the most important things in just a couple of days. This area has a lot of popular bars and restaurants frequented by foreigners and across the street is a strip of park that runs along the river. You'll like the esplanade. It comes alive after the sun goes down and people come out for a breath of air."

"A carnival atmosphere," Kirk said. "You can even ride on an elephant."

"We have the National Museum which is a stone's throw from here, and the Royal Palace, silver Pagoda, and emerald Buddha are not much farther. They give tours of the palace even though the king still lives there. You really should see the gardens, they're beautiful, and nearly as dazzling as the colorful tiles of the palace roof."

"I'll skip the elephant, but I would like to see the museum."

"Good. I'll be glad to show it to you. I have a meeting tomorrow, but if we start early, I can give you a tour of it. I'm not on the museum staff, but my position with Apsara gives me access to just about everything."

"Okay, I'd love that."

Kirk escorted me back to the Le Royal Hotel in one of the motorized rickshaws. "Don't let Chantrea's Pollyanna view of the city make you drop your guard. If you make a list of all the bad things in the world—heroin, teenage prostitution, rampant AIDS, illegal arms, money laundering, police corruption—you'll find it here in the city, in spades. If you don't believe me, take a look at the local English language papers—you'll find ads in it from outfits that will negotiate with kidnappers."

I believed him. "Why don't you tell me more about it over a drink I still owe you?"

"You don't owe me anything."

"Yes, I do. You came to my rescue."

I found out he was actually staying at the hotel attached to the Foreign Correspondents' Club and had been in my neighborhood on business.

We went into the Elephant Bar, an ensemble of old world Cambodian elegance and charm. He ordered an Angkor beer.

"They have a popular drink here called the Femme Fatale. It's a mixture of cognac and champagne. They supposedly created it for Jackie Kennedy. Want to try it?"

"Sounds too potent to me right now. Maybe some other time. I'll just take purified water." I wasn't in the mood for liquor.

After listening to him talk about the ills of a country plagued by land mines and unexploded bombs for half an hour, I started to yawn.

"I'm boring you, aren't I?"

I smiled. "No, you're not. I don't know why but my eyes are suddenly tired." I couldn't avoid another yawn. "Sorry."

"I can take a hint. You need your beauty sleep."

"I guess I'm still bummed out from jet lag."

"I'll walk you to your room."

"That's not necessary."

"No, I insist. That way I know you're safe and sound."

He made it sound like my life was in danger.

My room was close to the elevator. "Okay, here we are . . . thanks for the escort and for helping me today . . . good night."

❖

We shook hands but after several seconds he still hadn't let go of my hand. He looked in my eyes for a minute. Was he hoping I would change my mind and invite him inside? I was attracted to him, but I didn't want him to think I hopped into bed on short notice.

"Good night." He started to leave, but then turned around. "I'm glad we met today."

"Me, too."

He gave me a quick kiss on the cheek and left.

A real gentleman, I thought. Not at all like Detective Anthony.

I sighed. Of course, it would have been nice to spend the night in the arms of a man.

WHEN I LOOKED AT the clock, it was close to midnight. Even though I was ready to hit the sack, I had to do one thing before I went to bed. With the time difference involved I figured it was nine o'clock in the morning in San Francisco, a good time to catch an old art school classmate who worked at the National History Museum in Golden Gate Park.

"Oh, yes," Hailey Phillips said when I mentioned Bullock's name. "Everyone in the Bay Area art world has heard of Emmet Bullock."

"Major dealer?"

"Major prick . . . and you can add thief and pervert. His specialty is arranging for third world dealers to be victims of robberies."

It didn't surprise me that Bullock was involved in a scam. Phony robberies was an old trick. Dealers couldn't just smuggle well-known antiquities out of the country. When the pieces showed up in an auction catalog in New York or London, the cat was out of the bag. So a "robbery" was arranged. And it didn't get reported to the police until the "thief" was safely out of the country and through customs with a phony bill of sale listing the items as reproductions.

If the antiquities were ever tracked to an auction, the antique dealer back in the country of origin just shrugged his shoulders and told the police the thieves must have smuggled the pieces out of the country and sold them with a phony provenance.

"Yeah, he didn't have a good reputation to begin with, and ripping off museum pieces from poor countries hasn't helped him."

"Where does the pervert part come in?"

"I hear there's a warrant out for him. He had his computer repaired and the tech found a slew of child porn stuff on his hard drive."

"I thought that only happened to priests and politicians."

She was still laughing as I hung up the phone.

❖

The National Museum of Arts in Phnom Penh . . . has a very rich collection of Khmer art. . . . [I]t lacks the most basic things, including security, locks, telephone lines, resources, etc.; as well as poor displays. On one occasion an exceptional statue was returned to Cambodia and then stolen again. Since then it has completely disappeared from view, most probably into somebody's collection.

—MASHA LAFONT, *PILLAGING CAMBODIA: THE ILLICIT TRAFFIC IN KHMER ART*

15

❖

I met Chantrea for breakfast early the next morning. It was only seven yet the streets were alive and crowded, the noodle restaurants in full swing. On the smaller side streets people sat on squat stools and chatted as they ate their morning meal.

"The city wakes up early," she explained, "stays open until midday, shuts down for the heat of the afternoon, and then continues working until early evening."

Carts loaded with roasted peanuts, chicken and beef teriyaki sticks, and steamed dumplings lined the streets. Big blocks of ice were being dumped onto the sidewalk for food vendors to break up and keep their food from spoiling.

I followed Chantrea's lead and ordered spicy Shanghai noodles. "Is this the same theory as Mexican food—hot and spicy dishes keep you cooler?"

"Nothing keeps you cool except air-conditioning and an evening breeze. I'm sure they serve an American breakfast of bacon and eggs at the hotel, but I thought you might want to try the local food."

"Great. I love Cambodian cuisine." A small lie. I had actually never tried Cambodian food, but glancing around the other tables, I could see the food looked similar to the Thai and Chinese dishes I was used to eating.

"It's very good," I said. The clear soup with noodles, bean sprouts, strips of shredded chicken, scallions, mint, and red peppers was hot and delicious.

"I thought you'd like it. Rice and fish are the main staples for the Cambodian diet but noodle dishes are very popular."

We left the restaurant on foot and Chantrea hailed a motorized rickshaw. The National Museum faced the Tonle Sab River north of the Royal Palace.

When we got off near the museum, an old woman approached me with a bird in a small cage.

"What's she saying?" I asked.

"She wants you to buy the bird so you can release it. Our people believe that freeing a bird brings you happiness and a long life."

I bought the bird and set it free. "With my present state of luck, I should set a whole flock of birds free. Kirk said everything in the country had two faces. What's the other face of the bird legend?"

Chantrea laughed. "Some say that the birds are trained to fly back to the women who sell them."

"Recycled fortune. Just my luck."

The National Museum was built in Khmer architectural style with a brownish-red tone of terra-cotta. Exotic and graceful with multiple tiers of roofs gliding up to a tall spire, it reminded me more of a temple than a museum. Whimsical swirls at the edge of the roofs left an impression that the building could take magic flight.

The building was ancient and venerable, serene, and even exotic. It was hard to believe it was a twentieth-century creation, opening in 1920. In America, the facades of modern museums were often ordinary concrete because the fine craftsmanship needed to make them individualistic was lost. Here in the Far East the art of exotic building remained true.

As we went through the museum gateway, a uniformed man handed both of us a flower.

"The flowers are given in the hope you'll place a donation in the bowl that's in front of a Buddha." Chantrea smiled. "We're a shockingly poor, politically corrupt country . . . but you can find Buddhist temples with donated money lying around in plain sight and no one will touch it."

Off to our right as we approached the museum entrance a life-size bronze of an elephant peered at us from bushes. At first glance it appeared to be a whole elephant, but when I stopped and took a good look I realized it was an illusion—only the head, tusks, front legs, and feet were shown. An outstanding piece, it conveyed the majestic quality of the great beast that is so symbolic of Asian culture.

Khmer versions of fierce Chinese fu lions, the mythical protectors of temples and palaces, stood guard at the stairway leading up to the main entrance.

A souvenir shop was on the right as we entered and guides to be hired on the left. We immediately came face-to-face with an unusual creature. Terrifying in an almost comical way.

"Garuda," Chantrea said.

The huge, elephantinelike bird in front of the elaborate metal railing to a stairwell must have weighed a ton. It had human form, along with wings, beak, tail, and talons.

"In Hindu mythology, Garuda was the bird that Vishnu rode across the sky. He carried Vishnu after he lost a bet with the god. Sometimes he's identified with the sun itself. Right now he's pointing the way into the exhibits. We have galleries for sandstone, bronze, ceramics, and one devoted mostly to Angkor Wat and Bayon styles."

Chantrea introduced me to Rim Nol, a curator, before going off to her meeting. She told Nol that I was an art expert from New York new to Khmer art, which was essentially what I had told her.

"Nol is the assistant curator in charge of the finest Khmer pieces in the museum," she said.

I assumed Chantrea had given his name in the Cambodian fashion in that Rim was his family name and Nol his given name.

The curator had white hair and the grave, stoic mannerisms of a scientist-philosopher.

"The museum contains items dating back two thousand years," Nol said. "Especially significant are pieces from the golden age of the Khmer empires. Are you familiar with Hindu mythology?"

"Only vaguely. My training is in European and Mediterranean art."

"You Westerners rather accurately called this region of Cambodia, Vietnam, Thailand, so forth . . . Indochina. We not only physically lie between India and China, but our art and culture has been influenced by both."

I knew that most Khmer art was based upon Hindu mythology as well as influenced by Chinese art, but like dealing with Bolger, I felt it was more polite to let the curator guide me through.

"Khmer culture assimilated several religious traditions of Hinduism and Buddhism to create its own unique beliefs. Each of our ancient kings associated himself with a particular god and built a temple dedicated to his patron divinity to solidify his symbolic relationship with that god. Each king also constructed at least one temple dedicated to his ancestors to ensure the continuation of the royal line. Some further emphasized their power by constructing *barays,* or reservoirs, to symbolize their glory.

"Many of the pieces in our museum come from Angkor. Angkor Wat is the greatest and certainly the most famous of all the temples in the Angkor complex. Built by perhaps a million slaves, it is a Hindu structure whose main temples were constructed to mimic the universe. Water flowing in the surrounding hillsides represents the Ganges River in India and you can see hundreds of relief friezes depicting scenes from Hindu mythology like the Apsaras that adorn the temple. Virtually every surface is covered with carvings depicting characters and episodes from Hindu legends."

We paused in front of a pinkish sandstone head with piercing eyes and lethal fangs.

"A yaksha," Nol said. "An evil-tempered demigod. They were cruel, violent giants who caused troubles for the gods."

It was amazing how someone chiseling hard stone could bring out the ugly soul of a mythical character.

I let him show me other pieces, including a bas-relief battle scene from the great Hindu epic *Mahabharata* before I made a beeline for the original Siva that had been copied and sold at a New York auction. It was a lovely piece, old and fragile yet a survivor of centuries of political upheaval, war, storms, and neglect.

I nodded at the Siva. "I understand there are significant problems with faking Khmer antiquities and selling them as authentic pieces."

"Yes, a big problem."

"This is the one that was copied, wasn't it?"

"That is what I am told."

I thought he would tell me more about it but he didn't.

Nol's face remained impassive, but I sensed a subtle shift in his posture. Since I had been at auctions where millions of dollars are at stake with the flick of a bidder's paddle, I had to be aware of what poker players call the "tells," almost imperceptible changes in body language. A Persian rug dealer once told me he knew if a buyer wanted a particular carpet just by watching the person's eyes—the pupils would widen when they were shown a rug that caught their eye.

In this case Nol's pupils narrowed when I mentioned fake art. It reminded me of temple doors closing shut to keep secrets from escaping. It set off alarm bells for me.

As we walked around the museum, I asked questions about the different pieces in an attempt to get him to open up more. My impression was that this gentle, intelligent curator, who loved museum pieces like parents love their children, could not be involved with art fraud, yet I was sure he wanted to tell me something but was too rigid, perhaps too frightened, to speak up.

I'd been in other third world countries like the Middle East and Africa so I knew better than to put someone on the spot with a subject matter that could get him into trouble with the police.

As I examined another thousand-year-old Siva piece, this one a beautiful sandstone in which the powerful god was holding a smaller version of his consort, the mother goddess Uma, I caught Nol staring at me, as if he was about to say something. Whatever it was, the impulse passed and he moved away.

"Chantrea didn't mention it, but I was also once a museum curator," I said. "We specialized in Mesopotamian art."

He nodded. "The land between the rivers. The cradle of Western civilization. Certainly a worthy area of study for a curator."

"I screwed up. Royally."

He stared at me.

I smiled and shrugged. "In American terminology, I made a huge mistake. I bought a Babylonian piece that had been looted."

"Yes, I understand. The museum in Baghdad was extensively looted when law and order broke down as American troops entered the city. You must have felt bad to have purchased one of the stolen pieces, but I understand thousands were lost during the looting."

"Close to fifteen thousand. But I felt more than bad. I lost my job because I had paid a lot for the piece, relying on a phony provenance."

He stared around, as if he worried that our suddenly intense conversation was being watched.

"Let me show you the courtyards," he said.

I followed him into a lovely area where a statue of what I first took to be a Buddha was surrounded by a small pond.

"The Leper King," Nol said.

"Is there a legend about him?"

"We call him Dharmaraja, but it's most likely he's based on the Hindu god of death, Yama. Some people say he's called the Leper King only because of the discoloration from moss and fungus growing on him, but there were two Cambodian kings who suffered from leprosy." He gave me a sympathetic look. "I know the story of the Babylonian piece."

I nodded. "That doesn't surprise me. The entire universe of museum antiquities isn't that large. Besides, nothing can be hidden from the Internet."

"The story was carried in a French journal of art. I didn't recognize your name when Chantrea spoke it, but I do now that you have refreshed my memory."

"I have a great sympathy for your situation here in Cambodia. Your looting has been going on for decades."

"Many of the finest pieces of our national heritage are in museums and collections in other countries."

"I don't know what that article you read about me said, but the Babylonian piece ultimately went back to where it belonged."

A woman who had come out of the building spoke to him in Cambodian.

"I'm sorry," he told me, "my superior has a question I must respond to."

"Perhaps we can talk later?"

He shook his head. "Not today. I will be attending a staff meeting most of the afternoon."

"Perhaps tomorrow—"

"I will not be here. I volunteer one day a week at Choeung Ek. Have you been there?"

"No. I haven't heard of it."

"The Killing Fields exhibit."

"Oh, yes."

"I will be there all day tomorrow. If you decide to come, I will show you around the exhibits and explain this saddest period in our history."

I wandered back into the museum to get another look at the Siva that had been duplicated by the world-class forger. Rim Nol had left me with the feeling that the invite to the genocide exhibit was more than just a polite invitation to get a guided tour. I had deliberately brought up the story of my own connection to the rescue of a cultural treasure of a small, poor country in the hopes of striking a cord with him and I think I had.

I just wished we could meet and talk about the Cambodian art scene over a cold drink rather than going out to the notorious site. The grisly display was mentioned in the guidebook as a must-see, but it wasn't on my list.

I studied the Siva. It was an extraordinary piece, but after seeing what the forger could do with Apsarases, making a perfect imitation of the small statue was certainly within his abilities.

What had drawn me back to the Siva was a question that had been gnawing at me probably from the time I found myself in an interrogation room with Detective Anthony and Prince Ranar.

Why was the Siva chosen to be duplicated? It was a museum piece. Well known to experts on Khmer art. A catalogued museum piece. Its sale in New York would have set off alarm bells throughout the world of Far Eastern art. At least I would have thought so. But it didn't. It took a nationally televised display to raise questions and then it turned out it was only a reproduction.

Why choose a museum piece to duplicate? Why not start from scratch and make a quality piece and pass it off with a false provenance with the implications that it's a looted piece that no one would be able to trace? A much safer way to go than duplicating a museum piece.

Maybe the Siva was chosen because the forger didn't have the ability to create a masterpiece from scratch—there is a paradox that art students can copy a great work of art almost perfectly but can't themselves create a masterpiece.

If Sammy's Apsarases was an original creation, as opposed to being a copy of an existing sandstone, the artist certainly could do the quality work necessary to duplicate the Siva.

I realized that if I came up with the answer to the mystery of why a prominent museum piece like the Siva was chosen to be duplicated, more pieces to the puzzle would fall into place, maybe all of them.

At the moment trying to put together pieces to a puzzle gave me a headache.

16

❖

My head was still throbbing as I went past the fu lions and down the steps of the museum. What had Kirk said about Cambodia? That everything in the country had two faces? I was beginning to wonder if that wasn't an understatement.

Another word that came to mind: *chaotic*. I was a product of a society where things were orderly and could be anticipated. There were stoplights at intersections and even if an intersection didn't have a light, the law that said you stopped for pedestrians was usually obeyed. If there were rules in Cambodia, no one obeyed them.

I was experiencing the impact of a culture that was new to me—the exotic Far East, a small, traumatized country that had endured a decades-long nightmare, and an awakening third world country whose top echelon were making a greedy grab for luxury while young girls spread their legs for the price of a pack of cigarettes . . . yet there was also that really nice curator at the museum, the people at the hotel, the friendly, smiling people on the streets who were sincere and guileless . . .

It was all too much for me. I couldn't wait to get back to New York where the chaos was managed and only appeared on the six o'clock news.

❖

A surprise was waiting for me as I came out the gate to the taxi line—Prince Ranar standing by a sports car.

He opened the door for me and did a sweeping gesture with his arm. "Let me take you back to your hotel in my carriage."

I got in and sighed as a blast of air-conditioning hit me.

As he pulled into traffic, he asked, "What do you think of my country so far?"

"Beautiful, exotic, a little much for an innocent abroad like me."

I didn't mention I was mugged by a moto driver within a couple of hours of arriving, that creeps like Bullock shot water buffaloes with machine guns while the rest of the country seemed to be up to its neck in anything-goes-sex-for-sale and antiquities smuggling when they weren't stepping on land mines. Not to mention that the Cambodian people and the rest of the world was waiting for the government to punish the Khmer Rouge murderers guilty of genocide decades ago.

"Have you made any progress with your investigation?"

The question of the day. And nothing I felt confident about sharing with Ranar. He was technically my employer, but I was dealing with something more important than money for my rent—human beings. In a country where corruption was as common as rice, I had to wonder what would happen if I made unproved allegations about people. If I said that I'd spoken to a museum curator who seemed to want to share some information with me, would he be questioned? Or even treated much worse? How about Kirk and Chantrea? What kind of trouble would I get them into just mentioning their names?

I just didn't know and didn't want to risk it, but I needed to tell him something.

"I'm onto a couple leads I want to explore further." God—did that sound like a politician hemming and hawing. "There's an American named Emmet Bullock who has a very dirty reputation in the U.S. art world."

Bringing Bullock's name into it was inspired. If he was tortured and dismembered, it wouldn't hurt my feelings at all. I went on with my indictment.

"I checked with contacts in the States. Bullock's been known to conspire with art dealers in foreign countries to set up phony robberies so the dealer can smuggle antiquities out."

"You think he's involved in smuggling Khmer art?"

"I don't have the evidence at this point, just my gut reaction to the man. He oozes slime and has a track record of dealing in contraband art in other countries. There's a shop at the Russian Market that he has a connection to. I'm going to check it out." I actually had intended to do that.

"Did you find out anything from the curator at the museum?"

How did he know that? Obviously, someone had reported my movements to him very quickly. I thought of Rim Nol's quiet smile and warm, soft eyes. I didn't want to risk Nol's career by saying anything that would cause Ranar to focus on him.

"No, only that the museum has a marvelous collection of Khmer art and that sadly even more pieces are in foreign museums. Something did occur to me that I find puzzling."

"Which is?"

"Why would the forger choose a museum piece like the Siva to duplicate? He obviously ran a high risk of exposure."

Ranar shrugged. "Not really. The piece is not internationally known and there are literally thousands of Siva pieces in collections around the world."

"I suppose so. But I also wondered how it could be duplicated without the forger having the Siva in hand to closely examine it for an extended period of time. It's hard to believe that a museum piece can be duplicated without the artist having the original to work from."

I was certain it couldn't be done with photographs.

"You are operating off of false premises. The problem is not in the museum. We know that. The personnel and collection have been thoroughly examined." He shot me a look. "It won't be necessary for you to go back to the museum. Your presence there may start rumors that affect my own investigation."

"I see."

"The problem is that a very clever forger is making Khmer art good enough to pass for genuine pieces. You are probably wasting your time here. The forger and the smuggling ring are in Bangkok. And probably Hong Kong."

Ranar weaved in and out of traffic with as much respect for law as the rest of the drivers. He said, "I've heard that the girlfriend of the dead Russian billionaire is planning to sell another piece at auction. This time the sale will be held in Hong Kong. She lives there and it's a convenient venue for marketing stolen art. I would like to see some action before my country's reputation is embarrassed again."

I could have told him his country's reputation for not protecting its art was already black.

"Do you know the name of the dealer in Hong Kong?"

He shrugged. "No, but it should be easy to find out. Don't you have sources in the art trade for that kind of information?"

"I have a source." I could call Bolger in New York and he could get it off the Internet from the auction company site.

I pursed my lips. "I might need to make a trip to Hong Kong. See if I can follow the money. But I don't think I'm wasting my time here. It's Cambodian art that's being looted and duplicated. It stands to reason that at some point somebody in Cambodia got money from the model or her husband before he got whacked."

"Whacked?"

I grinned and made a slicing motion across my throat to indicate he'd been killed. "I guess I've seen too many crime shows."

He pulled up in the front of the hotel. "I'm having a gathering at my place early this evening." He put his hand on the top of my thigh. "I'll send a car for you."

I took his hand off my leg. "I've already made other plans."

Stupid, stupid, stupid. I'm attracted to a guy who hunts bombs for a living and turn down a chance to hook up with a real prince who could help my career.

Ranar was not happy with me. I didn't know whether it was because I'd not made progress . . . or if it went back to my feeling that he didn't want me here in the first place. Maybe both.

My session with Prince Ranar had left me with a free-floating sense of anxiety. Nothing he said made me uneasy, but . . .

I realized it was what he *hadn't* said. I told him my suspicions about Bullock. Ranar is head of security for the nation's antiquities. Shouldn't he have asked more questions about Bullock? I threw him the name of a foreigner with a reputation for illegally smuggling art and he hadn't been interested.

Maybe he already knew about Bullock's existence. That was possible.

❖

But wouldn't he have volunteered something like you're on the right track or we've already checked him out and he's nothing but a pedophile?

He didn't ask me who else I'd met or where I'd been. If he had asked, I would have been forced to tell him I'd met Kirk and Chantrea.

It occurred to me that that bit about everything having two faces could also apply to Prince Ranar. How many levels of deception was he playing? Anyone that rich and good-looking who could call himself a prince was too good to be true.

I wondered about Chantrea, too. Did she report my activities to Prince Ranar? That notion hit home. She works for the antiquities administration; he's the country's head of antiquities security. If she had, it wouldn't have surprised me. Cambodia was a place where survival wasn't a God-given right. And if she wasn't already reporting to Ranar, he may know by now that she was the one who took me to the museum. It was likely he would order her to report my activities to him.

In a country like Cambodia, it's a sure thing she'd report to Ranar regardless of what she thought of me. It also bothered me that she made contact with me at the Foreign Correspondents' Club within hours of my arrival. And maybe Kirk hired that mugger to—

Christ, my imagination was running wild. I no longer knew who was up to what. I was seeing a huge conspiracy surrounding me.

I got a cold facecloth for my forehead.

As I patted my face, something else occurred to me.

Ranar had been pushing me toward Hong Kong. And Bangkok.

Anywhere but Cambodia.

He didn't want me to come in the first place. I'd hardly begun my investigation and I was already persona non grata to the man paying the bill and calling the shots.

17

❖

The front desk called and relayed an earlier message from Kirk that he wanted to take me to dinner and would pick me up at eight. He said that I had no choice but to say yes. That was fine with me. It gave me plenty of time to rest, take a leisurely bath, and get ready.

He took me to a place called Tiger Moon. The restaurant was in a rather run-down French colonial building that looked like it hadn't been repaired since the French withdrew half a century ago and the decades of war that followed.

Deviously attractive women in provocative dresses, sure to arouse the carnal desires of any red-blooded male, were sitting at the bar. When we walked in, a bar girl wearing a dress barely covering her crotch approached us and held up three fingers.

Kirk shook his head.

"What was that all about?" I asked.

"She wanted to know if we wanted to make it a threesome. Sometimes couples come to Nom Pen to double their pleasure. Interested?"

"Sure. If we can find a cute young stud built like Jet Li who would do both of us."

That got a laugh out of him. But I was only kidding—watching Kirk making it with another man didn't appeal to me even if I was supposed to double my own pleasure by getting it from both ends.

I told him about my visit to the museum with Chantrea and then taking a tour of the Royal Palace. I came close to telling him about my suspicion that Nol wanted to tell me something, but caught myself. What did I really know about Kirk? In my mind he was what they used to call a "soldier of fortune," a person who seeks fortune and adventure in faraway places. I couldn't think of any other way to describe a man who hunted land mines in the jungles of Cambodia for a living.

But that didn't mean that he was reliable or even honest.

As men came in and teamed up with the underdressed, overly made-up women at the bar, I raised my eyebrows at Kirk.

He grinned. "Okay, it's a hostess bar, but low-key. Nothing overt. Some bars have girls who come and sit on a guy's lap . . . even before the man sits down. But that's just a starter. Tiger Moon lets you pretend you're having a real date instead of store-bought love. I come here because the food's good and cheap. Best hamburgers and fries in Nom Pen."

"Hamburgers? I came halfway around the world to an exotic city and you take me out for a hamburger?"

"You haven't tasted anything like this before. The hamburgers on this side of the planet have peanut sauce and the fries are sweet potatoes mixed with hot peppers. You're going to love them."

He was right. Maybe I was just hungry, but everything tasted delicious.

After dinner we went to the Foreign Correspondents' Club and watched a boat parade from the upper level. Chantrea was also there. I wasn't surprised to see her and wondered if anything was going on between her and Kirk. If there was, why was he putting the make on me?

"It's a river festival," Chantrea said as a boat shaped like a dragon breathed fire into the night while it floated down the river. "To celebrate the Tonle Sab River reversing its flow and flooding back down its course, bringing water for the rice crop and plentiful fish. The boat that's coming now has dancers whose performance tells the story of the Mermaid and the Monkey."

"That's an unlikely pair," I said.

She laughed. "It's a love story."

❖

"With a happy ending," Kirk said.

"Kirk's right. After a princess is kidnapped, a monkey general is ordered to rescue her. He has to build a bridge across the ocean to do the rescue, but each time his men set large stones in the water, a mermaid carries them away.

"First the monkey general and the mermaid battle and neither is able to conquer the other, but out of conflict comes love. When they fall in love, peace is made, the bridge is built, and the princess is rescued."

"Love conquers all," I said. "What I like about the Khmer myths is the effort taken to preserve them forever by recording them in stone."

"You'll see wonderful tales of Khmer mythology when you visit Angkor," Chantrea said.

"I can't wait."

"Speaking of Angkor," Kirk asked, "when are you planning to go there?"

"Sometime in the next couple of days. The flights are pretty frequent."

"That's because they have to keep planes moving in the hopes one of them will make it." He grinned. "Just joking, but they don't have the same safety record as the commercial airliners in industrialized countries. Like most poor countries, a highly technical skill like airplane mechanics isn't always practiced as a fine art. Personally, my feet never leave higher than the floorboard of a car unless flying is the only option."

"What about taking a boat up the river and across that big lake called Tonle Sap? Doesn't the Tonle Sab River come from there?"

"Yes, but it's not a pleasant trip," Chantrea said, shaking her head.

"The old ferries are more *African Queen* than Caribbean cruise," Kirk said, "and the new ones can still get stuck on sand barges and let you bake in a hot tin boat. Besides, all you get to see is dirty water and green riverbanks."

"So what's the best way to get to Angkor?"

"Driving," he said. "And that doesn't mean you rent a car and head out, it's not a road for the uninitiated. You need pros who know the roads like Chantrea and I do. As a matter of fact, I'm leaving early tomorrow morning for Angkor. I'd invite you along but I need to take care of a land mine along the way."

❖

Chantrea said, "I'm leaving in two days and meeting up with Kirk halfway to Angkor so we can caravan. The road's mostly safe and caravanning makes it even safer. Why don't you come along with me? I could use the company."

"There's one thing driving will give you that a one-hour flight at twenty thousand feet won't," Kirk said.

"What?" I asked.

"An adventure that lets you see the real Cambodia, jungle and farmland, much of which hasn't changed in eons."

"I like that part, but I usually find that adventures are fun memories only after I survived them in one piece. What are the dangers?"

He shrugged. "The usual warlords, bandits, land mines, two hundred miles of oxen wandering out onto the roadway, and buses that don't stay on their side of the road. But you only live once."

"That's the point," I said.

"Okay, I'm exaggerating, but there are a few adventures en route. To be honest, it wasn't that long ago the area was a hot bed of Khmer Rouge and just plain bandits. But the government has it pretty well cleaned up."

"It's safe," Chantrea said. "The most common hazards are pigs and oxen that think they own the road. I make the trip every couple of months and the worst I've run into were tire blowouts and getting stuck in the mud when I hit a rainstorm. I wouldn't make the trip unless it was safe. I'll be driving an official car and Kirk's SUV is known everywhere in the country. No one wants to mess with the great land mine hunter . . . he's needed too often. Besides, he's known to be armed and dangerous."

I didn't want to be a chicken. And the idea of flying on a third world airline wasn't appealing. "I'm game for it. If you don't mind—"

"I'd love to have you along," Chantrea said again. "I'll explain everything you want to know about Khmer art along the way. We'll even see some sites."

"Great. I'd love to see the art in its natural environment."

Chantrea smiled and shook her head. "Some people would say that the natural environment of our art has become the back of a smuggler's truck. The market for stolen antiquities is so hot that men who once smuggled heroin now use power saws to slice off pieces of our national heritage as if they're cutting cords of wood."

The nightmare image of Bullock sawing away at a temple suddenly came back in my head.

WHEN KIRK ESCORTED ME back to my hotel, again at his insistence, I didn't resist. I had watched him and Chantrea together that evening and couldn't see any lovey-dovey glances or secret gestures so I assumed nothing was going on between the two of them but I still wasn't totally convinced.

As we got off the elevator I said, "Chantrea is very nice."

"Yes, she is."

"How long have you two known each other?"

"Not that long."

"Does she have a man in her life?"

"I honestly don't know. Why all the questions about Chantrea?"

"Just curious. She seems to like you."

"I like her, too." He suddenly stopped and put his hand on my arm. "Wait a minute, do you think her and I have something going on?"

"Well, I wasn't sure. I didn't want to butt in if . . ."

"No, we're just friends, that's all."

"Okay, that's good to know."

When we got to my door, he took me in his arms and said in a low voice, "Are you going to invite me in tonight?"

A whiff of musky aftershave lotion filled my nostrils as he nuzzled my ear. It sent goose bumps down my back. "I promise not to stay too long," he said, smothering my neck with kisses.

"Oh, I'm not worried about that," and kissed him on the mouth.

He ended up staying the night.

After an hour of intense raw sex, I fell asleep in his arms with my back cuddled against his chest.

Sometime during the night, I dreamed that Kirk and I were high atop a temple at Angkor Wat. No one was around. I was lying spread-eagled on a flat smooth surface on my stomach, the warm sun radiating on my naked body. I felt his hard member brushing against my behind, and I arched my rear higher, eager for him to enter me. His thumb massaged my sensitive clitoris, slowly at first, teasing, then firmer and more urgent until I couldn't stand it anymore. "Go in me now," I moaned.

I shuddered and climaxed as he rammed like a wild animal, until he, too, collapsed on top of me.

❖

18

I awoke the next morning totally rested and relaxed, feeling better than I'd felt in months. I should be ashamed that orgasms did more for my physical and mental health than jogging and yoga, but I was shameless.

I stretched my arms and opened my eyes to find Kirk sitting on the edge of the bed, grinning down at me.

He saluted me with a cup of coffee. "Morning."

"Good morning. You're up early."

"It's not that early. It's almost eight. I was going to leave at the crack of dawn to beat the heat, but I guess I had too good a time last night. I couldn't drag myself out of bed." He was already dressed.

I sat up and pulled the sheet over my naked breasts. "Why didn't you wake me earlier?"

"You were sleeping so peacefully, I didn't want to disturb you. I was about to leave you a note."

I leaned back on the pillow and smiled. "I had a great time last night, too. I had a weird dream that you and I had sex on top of a temple."

"Well, we did have sex in the wee hours, but it wasn't on top of a temple."

"We did?"

"I was horny for you."

"I must have really been out of it."

"Uh huh, you didn't even wake up."

"Do you really have to go?"

"Yes, I really do. People are expecting me." He got up and planted a kiss on my forehead. "Although I'd much rather get in bed with you."

I patted the bed beside me and smiled at him.

"No, I'll never get out of here."

"I think you should stay."

Even though we had spent the night together and had sex, I suddenly felt a little embarrassed by my nakedness. I grabbed my tank top that was lying on the floor and put it on.

"I have to go. There's a land mine out there waiting for someone to step on, and I have to get to it. I'll see you and Chantrea sometime tomorrow, probably about midday."

"There must be a less dangerous way to make a living."

"You should ask yourself the same thing."

That was a strange remark. "What do you mean?"

"Hunting for art in the backwaters of Southeast Asia has to carry some risk. I ordered breakfast for you. Are you hungry?"

"Actually, I am."

"Stay in bed, I'll get it."

I stared at his back as he got a tray of food that was sitting on a small table. I was still taken back by his comment about my dangerous line of work. And I didn't buy his response. Buying art in the open in Cambodia wasn't inherently dangerous—buying it as an undercover police agent was.

I gave him a big smile as he brought back the tray.

"Wow. Breakfast in bed! How nice."

"I thought you'd like it."

In one basket was an assortment of breads and miniature muffins. Another basket contained jams and butter. Slices of fresh papaya, pineapple, and mangoes were arranged artfully on a small plate. He poured coffee in my cup.

"Eat already?" I asked.

"I'm not a big breakfast eater."

❖

Instead of leaving, he sat down on the bed again. He looked a little pensive and subdued as I spread jam on a piece of bread. Something was on his mind.

"Is anything wrong? You look like you want to tell me something."

He waited a moment before answering. "You should go home."

"Excuse me?"

"I think you—"

"I heard what you said, but why are you saying it?"

He shook his head. "I get the impression that you're not here just for a little R & R and to pick up legally exportable art, the tourist grade stuff. Something in your body language. You're too cautious and careful about what comes out of your mouth, too. Bullock spotted it, that business about not revealing that you were also in the art business."

"He's an ass. I had enough of him in the short time I talked to him on the plane. I didn't want to spend hours chitchatting with him about art."

"I don't blame you there."

"If you don't think I'm here for art—"

"I didn't say that. My concern is that you might try to get an artifact out of the country, thinking you can slip it past customs officers for a few bucks. The customs people are corrupt, but it's not done openly like that. Trying it would guarantee you a one-way ticket to a Cambodian prison."

"Look, I'm here to enjoy myself. So far I've done all the touristy things, the museum, the Royal Palace, eaten Cambodian food. And now I'm going to see Angkor Wat. I don't intend to steal any national treasures."

He didn't say anything.

"Kirk, like everyone else, I came to see Angkor. But I have a personal reason, too. My father was an art teacher who wanted to be Indiana Jones. He talked about Angkor Wat but never saw it. I'm not leaving until I see it."

I paused for a response from him but he was still quiet.

"Is that the real reason you want me to go home? Because you're afraid I'll try to smuggle out something?"

He sighed and said, "I guess I'm just worried about you wandering around and something happening to you. Nom Pen's okay, but not the safest place in the world for a woman alone."

❖

"I wasn't born yesterday, you know. I'm aware of all the perversion and corruption going on around this place and I know better than to be out after dark alone." I grinned. "I even know to carry my purse on the building side of sidewalks and cross streets with monks."

"Wow. I guess that makes you a real pro."

"I had a good teacher."

I pulled him close and kissed him on the lips. "Are you sure you don't want to join me for breakfast in bed."

"Gotta go. Just be careful."

"Hey, a lot of tourists come here and nothing happens to them. I want to see things just like everyone else." I picked up a muffin and took a bite. "It's good."

He glanced at his watch. "Why do I get the feeling you're not taking me seriously?"

"Oh, but I am. It's a dangerous place with dangerous people playing dangerous games." And I wondered if he was one of them.

He kissed me on the forehead. "I'll see you tomorrow." Before he closed the door behind him, he turned and smiled. "Just for the record, I like you better with your top off."

Something told me to hold back the truth from Kirk about what I was doing in the city. My intuition was screaming not to trust him. I liked him but something wasn't right. He was too concerned about me. That made me wonder why . . . unless he knew something I didn't know.

Stopping the purse-snatcher had not been faked. The blow caught the thief entirely by surprise. But that didn't mean it was a coincidence that Kirk had been on the street behind me at that moment. He could have been following me.

I didn't know what to think. I had just made love to the man and would have done it again if he had stayed. Yet I wasn't sure I could trust him.

Something was rotten in Denmark and I think my attraction to the wrong kind of man was part of the stink.

I got up and headed for the shower. It was my day to visit the notorious Killing Fields.

When I passed through the lobby the concierge asked if he could get me a taxi. I lied and told him I'd rather walk. I was afraid I'd be followed to the exhibit and be seen talking to Rim Nol. I decided to grab street transportation.

On Monivong, I bought a straw hat to protect me from the sun and then boarded a motorcycle-rickshaw pulling a small cart that had a canvas-topped seat compartment. Pho had called it a tuk-tuk.

I hoped I chose a driver who was honest. When Kirk was giving me a laundry list of the city's ills, he told about the time he was returning to his hotel one night in a moto when the driver detoured and took him on a side street. The driver stopped and told Kirk he wasn't going to take him back to his hotel until Kirk handed over twenty U.S. dollars. Obviously, the driver picked on the wrong foreigner. He got a beating rather than dollars.

I showed the driver the picture of the Killing Fields monument I'd ripped out of my guidebook. He got the idea.

The Choeung Ek exhibit was only about ten miles out of town but the going was slow, with the streets choked with traffic. By the time we reached the area down a pockmarked road, I was coated with sticky heat and dust. A regular taxi would have been better, but I told myself it was more exciting going native. It just didn't feel like fun.

Small children and an older man with a leg and one hand missing were begging at the entrance. Cambodia's atrocious land mine heritage brought home my mother's admonition not to complain if I have no shoes because some people had no feet.

I spotted Rim Nol as I followed a path toward a tall, pagoda-style tower that had become the symbol of the exhibit.

After a cordial greeting, he walked beside me toward the tower. I didn't see any other large buildings and asked where the prison was located.

"Choeung Ek and other places we call Killing Fields were not prisons, though those existed, too. One of the most brutal prisons, Tuol Sleng, had been a high school. It's now a genocide museum in Phnom Penh. The Killing Fields were places people were brought solely to be murdered. Open fields worked well for the Khmer Rouge because there were so many victims that mass graves were used."

"For political crimes?"

"Few were killed for reasons as commonplace as political crimes or even any violation of law. My wife was killed because she was a schoolteacher and educated. My father was killed because he wore eyeglasses. To the peasants who comprised much of the Khmer army, people who wore glasses were intellectuals." He touched his glasses. "I broke my glasses during the exodus when hundreds of thousands of people in the capital were forced into the countryside. That is why I was not killed as an intellectual."

"That's insane."

"Yes, in a sense people like Pol Pot who belonged in an asylum for the criminally insane were running the asylum. Only in this case, it encompassed an entire country."

He explained that the plan was to take the country back to an agrarian culture in which people grew their own food and made their own clothes. I'd heard some of the horror story before, but pretended it was all new to me.

"You saw our wonderful museum," Nol said. "It was not spared by the Khmer Rouge. The museum was closed and looted, the director and many staff members murdered. Once it took on an abandoned state, not only the exhibits but the building itself degenerated. It was not that long ago that our biggest problem besides faulty electric wiring was bat dung."

The silver-colored central building was tall, perhaps eight or ten stories high. As we came up to it I realized it was more a monument than a building. Inside were tiers of glass cases, rising one above the other, containing thousands of skulls.

You could reach out and touch the skulls.

"Many of them show how the killing was done," Nol said. He pointed at signs of damage to skulls. "That one was smashed by a club, that one, too; this one was shot—"

I spun around and walked out.

He came out behind me and I apologized.

He shook his head. "Many people have the same reaction. To suddenly see thousands of skulls, realizing that these were people, it's a shock."

"Why do they display such things?"

"So that we remember. We did this. Cambodians did it to other Cambodians. We are guilty, even those of us who are victims because we let it happen. To make sure it never happens again, we must never forget it."

❖

We walked toward craterlike depressions with signs indicating they were mass graves. Small mounds of bleached bones were stacked in front of the signs.

"You can find bones almost anywhere around here where you dig," he said. He pointed at small pieces of cloth sticking out from the ground. "Pieces of clothing of people buried."

We paused by a large tree with a sign written in Cambodian and English. It said, "CHANKIRI TREE AGAINST WHICH EXECUTIONERS BEAT CHILDREN."

I could see the heads of rusty old nails. "Jesus. Did they . . . ?"

"Yes. The heads of children were bashed against the tree. The nails helped kill them. If you look closely, you can see the tree bark is scarred from the blows."

"But how could they kill children?"

"Ones that wore glasses or looked intelligent were killed. Those who cried too much because they were separated from their mothers were killed. At Tuol Sleng the guards kept a meticulous record of the prisoners murdered. If you visit it, you will see posted on the walls the pictures of those interrogated, tortured, and then murdered. It includes the pictures of children."

I felt a welling up in my throat and couldn't speak. To read about this insanity in a guidebook didn't carry the impact that his voice did.

He gave a sad smile. "You have to understand. The madness knew no bounds. People were told to do evil things and knew that they would be killed if they didn't do them."

I walked away, unable to speak.

Catching up with me, he said, "Perhaps I should not have asked you here. Many of my own people won't visit the Killing Fields. They believe the spirits of the victims are unsettled because of the way they died."

"I'm only a visitor. I know it's personal to you, but it's new and shocking to me."

"Yes. Very personal. I come here to visit my family."

I wondered if he came here thinking he could find the bones of his wife and father. I changed the subject.

"I am really puzzled by a couple of things. Maybe you can explain. Don't you find it strange that the Siva was chosen to be duplicated? I mean, why a major piece like that?"

❖

He shrugged. "Perhaps it would sell for so much more than other pieces. Few pieces are of the caliber of the Siva. And I understand that it was mostly an accident that the piece was exposed as a forgery. The pieces in our museum are not as well known as those in the large museums in places like Paris and New York."

"True, but there's still a much higher risk of exposure because it *is* a museum piece. It just doesn't make sense to me. The forger would have had to work months on the piece. There must be an organization in place to market something this valuable."

"I don't have an explanation for you. Perhaps there is as much madness among art criminals as the Khmer Rouge."

I hadn't come out and said expressly that I was investigating the looting of Khmer art, but I was certain Nol had reached that assumption when we first spoke at the museum. Some things were better left unsaid.

"Nol, there's another point, too, one that you must have some knowledge of. A forger could not have made a precise duplicate of the Siva from photographs."

He met my statement with an impassive face.

"You know what I mean?" I asked. "It's not possible for someone to make an exact duplicate that would get by experts without examining the real Siva at great length. Don't you agree? The forgery had to be perfect, not varying in even the tiniest detail."

No change in his stoic features. I hated backing him into a corner.

"Nol, I don't see how the piece could be duplicated without the forger having access to the piece in the museum. I can't see the person just working from photographs or dropping by once in a while to get a passing look. Unless someone in the museum is the forger."

That thought just struck me, but I had no reason to say it.

He pursed his lips as we walked in silence to the main gate.

When we stopped in front of the entrance, I gave him a hug. "I'm sorry. I think I've inadvertently brought some bad things into your life."

"Your intent is to help my country. I understand that." He looked around again before he spoke. "I can recommend a guide for your visit to Angkor."

"That would be nice."

"Bourey." He spelled it for me and pronounced it *boo ree.*

❖

"It would be better if you did not mention this to others. It would not be proper for a museum employee to recommend a guide. You understand? Mention it to no one."

I understood from his confidential tone that keeping the name to myself had nothing to do with museum rules, but I kept my face blank.

As I was walking away, he spoke my name softly.

"Do you recall seeing a sword in a glass case in the museum?"

"Yes, I think so."

"It's an executioner's sword," he said. "Do you know about *srangapen?*"

I shook my head. "I've never heard the word."

"The traditional Khmer execution involved a ceremonial dance performed by the executioner. We call it *srangapen.* The victim would be blindfolded and forced to kneel beside an open pit. The executioner would dance beside him, shuffling his feet so that the victim knew exactly where he was at and knew that as long as the dance went on, he would not be killed. As the victim followed the movements with his ears, believing he was safe for the moment because the dance was still going on, another executioner chopped off his head."

The curator gave me a sad, lonely look.

That is often how it is in my country. The blow often comes from an unexpected direction when you believe things are safe."

I nodded my thanks and left.

The story gave me the willies. And I felt sorry for Nol. I lived in a country where I could travel over three thousand miles coast to coast and not have to worry about anything except the price of gas and whether the nearest fast-food restaurant still used trans fats. He probably didn't know when he arrived at work that morning whether there would be political upheaval by lunchtime.

The story about the sword had been a warning, of course. A warning about whom? Chantrea had introduced us. Nol might know that Prince Ranar had me watched. He might also have been ordered to report our museum discussion to Ranar. And Nol had more to say. He just wasn't ready to say it.

I wondered what piece Bourey would add to the puzzle.

❖

19

❖

I took a quick shower to wash off some of the day's heat, then had something to eat. Too antsy to sit still, I decided to pay a visit to the city's most famous location for forgeries.

I felt pressured to get information for Ranar. So far all I had gotten from him was money to cover my expenses. Time was running out and I needed some solid facts and a progress payment.

The Russian Market, properly called the Toul Tom Pong, was located away from usual tourist areas but still attracted plenty of tourists. At least that's what my guidebook said.

I got instructions from Pho, the concierge. It turned out Sinn's wasn't in the market, but nearby. He offered to get a regular taxi for me. This time I let him do it. I'd already told Ranar I was going to check out the market.

I slipped a twenty-dollar bill into his hand. "Tell the taxi driver to let me off at the main entrance to the market. I'll get to Sinn's myself. Pho, when I take a taxi, I want to make sure that the driver is reliable and discreet. Sometimes business competitors like to know where I go and I don't want them to."

Pho gave me a knowing nod as I followed him outside. Three taxi drivers were waiting. He bypassed the first two and took me to the third one.

"This driver is more honest than those two," he whispered. "His name is Samnang. He speaks some English."

He spoke to Samnang in Cambodian, then said to me, "I have made sure the fare is arranged. You can pay him as little as two dollars, but if you feel he warrants it, give him more."

My driver seemed like a likable fellow with a nice smile as he weaved through the heavily congested traffic of cars, motos, and bicycles with more caution than other drivers I'd seen.

We headed south on Monivong Boulevard away from the downtown business area and into more residential and industrial parts of the city. He took a turn on Mao Tse-tung Boulevard and down a dusty, potholed street to the market.

The main building was an exotic temple-looking dome with lower wings extending out. An array of open shops under umbrellas near the main entrance crowded the street like jungle foliage.

I asked Samnang if he wouldn't mind picking me up in an hour. I figured that would give me plenty of time to check out the market. To make sure he came back, I gave him ten dollars and told him he'd get another ten.

The covered market was larger than I expected. The interior had long rows of stalls, easily over a hundred. The plan of organization appeared to be planned chaos, though major merchandise categories—food, motorcycle parts, clothes, stoneware, and porcelain—were generally grouped together.

Kirk was right about the variety. You could find everything there: electronic goods, clothes, shoes, jewelry, silks, handbags, woodcarvings, CDs, DVDs, antiques, pottery. Some stalls sold fake items but you could also find real designer brand names that cost a fraction of what you'd pay in department stores because the items had flaws, some very minor.

I passed by one stall that had jars and jars of weird-looking liquids with unidentifiable objects in them, no doubt some medicinal herb concoctions, some of which looked pretty disgusting. Strange odors hit my nostrils as I walked by the place.

Tourists crowded everywhere, bargaining on everything. It was considered a mandatory thing to do at the stalls. You never paid the full price for anything and the people who were good at it were usually more vocal and persuasive. The thought of culture-ugly Bullock haggling with these poor people was a disgusting image.

I passed through several antiquity stalls that sold fakes. It was obvious tourist junk, nothing good enough to tempt me to leave my name and hotel number. At the last stall, the finishes on several of the pieces still looked fresh and too clean, as if they had recently been painted despite the sign that said "Antiquities." Trying to be discreet, I picked up a Buddha and carefully scratched my fingernail on the finish when the shopkeeper wasn't looking. The paint came right off.

Amazing how easily you could fool an unsuspecting tourist who didn't know anything about art. They could buy what was presented as a five-hundred-year-old sandstone Buddha, with a written guarantee of authenticity, only to find out later it had been made only weeks before.

The shopkeeper gave me several "hellos" when he finished selling a Buddha to a tourist.

"I'm looking for a real antique, not tourist stuff."

He stared at me as if I had said something insulting. "All pieces real," he said in broken English.

"Do you have something really special?"

He bobbed his head and picked up a bronze statue with a greenish-brown patina. "This special. Very old."

I controlled myself from telling him it was an obvious fake. He was lying, of course, thinking I was just an innocent tourist who knew nothing about antiques, but it was all a game and it would be rude for me to have said so.

He had picked up the piece I'd scratched.

"For you, two hundred."

"No, I'd like something *really* old."

He had some good copies of Khmer antiquities, but nothing that pinged real to me. I was just testing the waters, to see if he'd reach behind the counter and pull out an authentic artifact.

He shook his head and insisted that the item he had in his hand was a genuine antiquity.

I had read that art dealers in Cambodia were starting to be prosecuted by the government and the police, so some of them were being more careful of what they sold and to whom. Or maybe he didn't really have any real valuable pieces.

I thanked him and moved on. I went out an exit and onto the street. According to Pho's instructions, Sinn's shop should be across the street and down less than a block. Ahead I saw two familiar figures. I quickly veered around a shop that sold necklaces made out of wood. Hiding behind a corner of the canvas overhang, I took another look.

Kirk and Bullock. My new lover and a scummy crook. They were standing on the sidewalk in front of a shop. I could see faded green paint on a sign advertising the shop as Sinn's.

My nerves went on fire. That miserable bastard. Kirk told me that he had to leave town early to disarm a land mine halfway to Angkor.

What a fraud. He'd shown contempt for Bullock at the Foreign Correspondents' Club but here they were, chatting away like old pals.

Bullock walked away, going down the street away from me, while Kirk got into a big white SUV parked at the curb and drove off.

I waited a moment, shaking my head at the old woman running the shop. I left her a dollar for taking up space for a moment and headed for Sinn's shop under the theory that the best time to visit the shop was right now when I knew people I didn't want to run into weren't there.

My intuition was right about Kirk. I couldn't trust him. My temper was high enough that I must have had steam coming out my ears as I thought about Kirk. What kind of game was he playing? I knew it had to be dirty if it involved Bullock.

Was it bad karma or what? I wasn't a bad person but lately it seemed like I was attracting the wrong people. Maybe I deserved it, like water seeking its own level, but I couldn't think of a reason why.

Sinn's store looked like the other storefront shops—a big front window too dusty and too buggy to see into the dimly lit interior. I entered, setting off a jangling bell attached to the door. The place had the distinctive smell of burnt marijuana.

A woman making thumping noises as she walked came out of the curtained opening to the back, smoking a cigar.

Sinn, I presumed, an observation aided by the fact a black and white picture of her standing next to a Cambodian notable—politician, king, or whoever—was prominently displayed on the counter.

❖

She had stumps ending at the knees with prostheses for legs. A land mine victim.

The "cigar," which looked like an awkwardly rolled wad of pot, added to the pot smell in the room. Hopefully the marijuana helped whatever pain she endured.

Her English was as nonexistent as my Cambodian but we found common ground with hand signals and facial signals. I noticed her French was slightly better than mine.

She thought I was a tourist and immediately began showing me souvenirs. I kept trying to convey the impression that I was a clueless American with too much money and it seemed to work because she finally brought something from under the counter that pinged as the real McCoy.

She laid a pretty battered, chipped, and broken sandstone Buddha about four inches tall on the counter. I examined it. I had a feeling that it was real, centuries old, but not a very valuable piece. It was neither in good condition nor did it demonstrate fine craftsmanship. The only thing it had going for it was old age. I wouldn't have paid more than a couple hundred for the piece even if I could have gotten it out of the country. But I had established a major point: she dealt with antiquities. Now the question was whether she had something of museum quality.

I shook my head and got across again that I wanted a finer piece. Finally, I cut to the chase. Taking a hotel notepad out of my handbag, I wrote down $10,000.

She looked at the figure and back at me and disappeared into the back room much faster than anyone on poor quality prosthetics should have been able to move.

She came back with a small bundle wrapped in newspaper. She laid it on the counter and carefully unwrapped a small piece of sandstone. I froze. Like the piece Sammy showed me, it was a bas-relief of a scene from Hindu mythology—the god Vishnu with the celestial nymphs called Apsarases.

"Twenty thousand American."

That came from her in perfect English.

I took the magnifying glass from my purse. "I need to look at it."

The lighting was bad, but I was only looking for one thing and I found it. The half moon mark.

❖

The piece was a fraud, made by the same artist who had made the Apsaras piece Sammy had in New York and who was suspected of making the Siva that went for millions at auction.

"Twenty thousand American," she said, again.

"Yes, I heard you." I knew she would take ten, probably even less. She had to know it was a fake. A marvelous one, but a reproduction nonetheless.

I looked up at the woman. She saw through my facade and read me right—I wasn't really a buyer. I had been putting her on. Her eyes narrowed, her lips had tightened. She looked meaner than a Rottweiler whose bone I'd just grabbed.

Panic hit me. What was I doing? I finally stumbled onto something important, something I could report to Ranar, and I felt like a scared kid. I had to get out of there.

I hurried out the door. I stopped and snapped back at her, "It's a fake."

"Of course it is," a voice behind me said.

I gasped and spun around.

Bullock.

WHAT A SHIT. I woke in the middle of the night and laid in bed thinking about that jerk. Kirk, not Bullock. Bullock wasn't human enough to be called a shit. I nearly passed out when I ran into Bullock holding a cup of iced coffee outside the shop. I left him leering—not grinning—at me as I dashed around him.

No, it was Kirk on my mind. Damn him. I thought I had found an ally, someone I could trust and who was tough and street-smart and was good-looking and sexy on top of that.

Should I I tell Ranar about the fake piece at the shop? I realized the woman wasn't violating any laws—there was no law against selling a fake as a fake and I suppose in Cambodia it's buyer beware—no one's going to have sympathy if you buy a fake thinking you're robbing the country of a priceless antiquity. But there certainly was a connection to the New York sale.

I decided to keep the information under wraps until I had resolved in my mind that Ranar could be trusted.

It would be nice to find someone in the country who I could trust.

❖

20

❖

An official car with two Culture Ministry security officers was waiting for Rim Nol when he came out of the Killing Fields main gate after his shift.

He kept his features inexpressive as he obeyed the officer's command and got in the back of the car.

"Where am I being taken?" he asked.

"Shut up."

The command was spoken without malice or even irritation and he accepted it without anger, just as he accepted without complaint what he thought to be his detainment, if not arrest.

When they were near the river on the outskirts of the capital, Nol realized where he was being taken and confirmed his suspicion of who had commanded his presence. He had attended a reception at the sprawling palatial mansion and on several occasions had delivered museum documents.

It was the home of Prince Ranar. He had an official office at the ministry building but preferred working out of the comfortable, climate-controlled atmosphere of his home.

The two officers escorted Nol into the house and to the reception area outside Ranar's office. Nol sat for an hour until the prince was ready to see him. It occurred to him that the wait might have been designed to make him nervous and more eager to please when questioned.

When he entered the office, Ranar gestured at a cold pitcher of mango juice, but Nol smiled politely and shook his head. His mouth was dry but he was afraid his hands would shake if he held a glass.

"Tell me everything you and the American woman discussed at the museum," Ranar said.

Nol started to speak and Ranar held up his hand to stop him.

"Also tell me why she met you at Choeung Ek. And what was said there."

CHANTREA ENJOYED HERSELF IN the pool at Ranar's villa while Nol was being questioned. She swam naked, bathing in the cool, sweet waters in the atrium courtyard. She loved the tropical paradise Ranar had constructed in the center of his residential compound—with a domed, glass roof and temperature-controlled climate, the atmosphere was pure, bugless, and serenely pleasant. Best of all, Ranar's wife stayed in another section of the residence.

When she saw Ranar come into the atrium Chantrea leisurely swam to him. She stepped out of the pool, unashamed of her nakedness. Almost forty years old, her body was still firm and sensuous.

Ranar had seen her naked before but his eyes still feasted on her body. He pulled her toward him and kissed her on the mouth, tenderly at first, then with fiery passion.

"You have a very beautiful body. You know that, don't you?" he said huskily.

"Yes, I do." She lightly toweled off as Ranar got out of his expensive clothes, dropping them at his feet for the servants to pick up later. "So what did Rim Nol have to say?"

"The woman was curious. She asked some interesting questions."

"Like?"

"Why was the Siva chosen when it's a museum piece? How did the artist duplicate it without being able to examine it at length? I already knew these issues puzzled her."

"Good questions," Chantrea said. "I hope he didn't answer any of them."

"He says he didn't."

"Do you believe him?"

"I believe him. But he's weak. And idealistic. Two bad traits for someone to keep their mouth shut."

Ranar gave her nipples a squeeze before he waded naked into the pool. Good living was putting a ridge around his waist, still only bicycle tire size, but noticeable.

The door opened and a girl entered.

The first thing Chantrea noticed was her age—she was young, probably no more than eighteen.

Chantrea wasn't surprised that another person was joining them. Or that Ranar came out of the pond with an erection. He picked up a towel and patted himself, not bothering to hide his engorged organ.

The girl was a younger sister of Ranar's. Their father had been married four times and produced a brood that left big age differences between the half-blood siblings.

The old man had neither the power nor the money that Ranar had accumulated. Chantrea heard that Ranar and his father were not on good terms.

"My sister wants to go to a fine arts university in Paris. She needs money and a letter of recommendation from the Ministry of Culture."

Ranar looked at the girl and nodded at the pool. She dutifully took off her clothes and went into the water.

Chantrea knew her own body gave a man much more pleasure than a young girl's. "Young stuff" was a psychological titillation for men, not so much a pleasurable physical one. It made men feel younger and more virile, but like the affects of liquor, it was a form of false courage. She lay on the soft grass and was already starting to get wet from the anticipation as she waited for the young girl.

Ranar motioned his head toward Chantrea as the girl came out of the water. He had long ago become bored with having sex in a way that was considered customary.

Chantrea went along with his sexual deviations not because Ranar told her to, but the truth was she found the experience of sex with two people titillating. Having another woman touch her while being stroked by a man aroused her much more than a single sex mate. And having sex with another woman was definitely more erotic.

She also knew that she wasn't that much unlike the girl who was fucking for a French education. Not having the education and career opportunities granted upperclass men, Chantrea and the girl both chose to feed a wealthy, powerful man's ego and lust in exchange for the opportunity to live richer lives themselves.

Chantrea slowly spread her legs apart and drew them back. The girl came toward her and knelt between her legs. She was hesitant at first, so Chantrea leaned up and took the girl's head and pushed it down between her legs. "Lick me with your tongue."

Awkward at first, the girl got the idea. She flicked the lips of Chantrea's vulva, then took Chantrea's clit in her mouth and started sucking.

Chantrea moved up and down with the rhythm of the girl, then brought the girl's head up and had her suck on Chantrea's nipples.

Ranar's phallus was enlarged and throbbing as he watched the two of them. He positioned himself behind the girl's buttocks and pushed his cock inside her. She was tight and he had to work his cock in despite the wetness. He began to pump, shoving back and forth in a rhythm.

Chantrea looked at the girl's face. Her eyes were wide. She was no longer nervous. The expression on her face was one of wide-eyed glee. *She likes it*, Chantrea thought. This was probably the first time she had done it both ways. Chantrea pushed the girl's head back down between her legs.

Ready to orgasm, Chantrea pictured Madison Dupree on top of her instead of the young girl.

21

❖

I spent the rest of the day in my room reading up on Khmer art and Angkor Wat and Angkor Thom. And slept. It gave me a chance to rest my body and mind. I needed it after realizing that Kirk was flat-out lying to me.

Thinking about the road trip to Angkor, I almost decided to call it off. I took their word that it was a safe trip . . . but was it safe for me? Could this Cambodian art mafia or whatever they were ambush us on the road and murder me?

With cheerful thoughts like that, I was already waiting in the lobby the following morning when Chantrea arrived to pick me up for our trip to Angkor Wat. When we were a few blocks from the hotel, she pulled over and bought some roasted crickets from a sidewalk street cart.

"I thought you might like to try them."

Uh huh. The thought of eating a jumping insect didn't quite appeal to me but they seemed to be sold all over the place and a part of me wanted to find out what they tasted like.

Wrapped in a green lotus leaf, the brown, glazed crickets smelled of smoked sweet wood.

Chantrea downed them like candy.

❖

"Sure, I'll try it." I took a small bite and started chewing.

"How do you like them?"

"They're . . . interesting." I gave her a scrunched-up face.

She laughed. "They're addictive. You can't have just one."

"They taste a little like salty burnt nuts."

"It's good protein. Have another?"

"No, thanks. One's enough for me." It wasn't high on my list of exotic treats. "What time are we supposed to meet with Kirk on the road?"

"He didn't give me an exact time. I guess it depends on how things go with his crew in removing the land mine. But we'll reach Siem Reap well before dark."

The answer seemed a little vague to me. I decided not to mention that I'd seen Kirk yesterday with Bullock at the Russian Market. He may well have left for a land mine excursion after that. I wasn't sure what was involved in disarming a land mine since I really hadn't gone into any deep discussion about the subject with him.

My intuition was starting to kick in again, telling me that maybe I shouldn't totally trust Chantrea. She was conveniently at the Foreign Correspondents' Club where both Kirk and Bullock hung out. She had taken me to the museum but basically assigned Nol to deal with me—maybe even watch me—and now was chaperoning my Angkor trip.

Even though she had called Bullock disgusting, I wondered if it was an act on her part? Were the three of them a team? Maybe they were involved in some big-time antiquities scam? Maybe I was in the way and they planned to get rid of me in some deserted place?

Too many maybe's and questions swirled in my head. The tension was slowly creeping into my neck. I recognized the symptoms and quickly popped two aspirins in my mouth with the bottled water that I always carried with me. If I didn't take them now, I knew it would just get worse and turn into a migraine.

"Not feeling well?"

"Just a little headache," I said. "It'll go away."

We were on the outskirts of the city heading north in the direction of Siem Reap when she asked, "Do you mind if we make a quick stop? I have to drop a package off to someone."

"No," I said.

She drove us into a street with shabby tenements. The street was unpaved and had rubbish strewn all about. I'd seen a hundred like it in the city.

Pulling up to a building, she said, "I won't be long."

She took a cardboard carton off the backseat and went to the ground-floor window of an apartment. The curtain was moved aside as she approached and a young girl slid open the window to take the box.

I winced when I saw the girl's face. I tried not to stare but I couldn't help it. She had terrible raw, red lesions and blotches. I quickly turned away, not bearing to look at her.

Chantrea came back after a short discussion at the window.

I waited until we were back on the road and Chantrea hadn't volunteered an explanation before opening my mouth. "That poor girl. What happened to her?"

Chantrea didn't speak for a moment. I realized she was holding back her emotions. Finally she said, "Acid."

"Acid? Someone did it deliberately?"

"A jealous wife drenched her with acid. Walked into the bar where the girl worked and threw acid in her face." She gave me a grim look. "It's not the first time it's happened to a pretty young girl who's become the lover of a married man. You can't blame the women. Most of the people alive today have lived through not only some of the most horrific violence, but almost continuous war, civil war, political turmoil, and atrocities. We're all shaped by the violent atmosphere we were nurtured in."

I didn't know what to say.

She looked over at me. "There's nothing to say," Chantrea said, reading my feelings. "What happened in the past doesn't excuse the brutality of the wife. But in a way, this girl was lucky. She didn't get blinded by the acid. Some do."

"Throwing acid in someone's face is pure evil and vicious. What about the police? What happened to the wife?"

"The wives are usually married to prominent officials or businessmen. The police rarely dare to arrest them. And when the police do make an arrest, justice is a matter of how much money passes under the table."

"Aren't there any laws?"

"Laws?" She laughed. "We've been a civilized culture for a couple thousand years and we still don't have a modern court system capable of truly expending justice. Key figures of the Khmer Rouge, people who were involved in the murder of a million people over thirty years ago, still haven't been brought to justice."

I shook my head back and forth, more in disgust than disbelief. Thinking about the scarred girl made we wonder about Chantrea's background and family. I really didn't know that much about her.

"Do you have any family?"

"My family is mostly gone. That girl you saw is a distant relative. A cousin, second or third, maybe even more distant. A lot younger than me, not someone I even know well, but still family. I drop off money and special cream for her to relieve the pain. She will always bear the scars. She'll never have the money to go to Hong Kong or Tokyo where they can be repaired. I don't have it, either."

"Your family, what happened to them, if you don't mind my asking?"

She took a deep breath. "I was five years old when the Khmer Rouge took over Cambodia. They killed my father because he was a teacher and they wanted to get rid of anyone educated. My mother was killed because she pleaded with the soldiers not to take her children away. Family units were no longer permitted. My two brothers and I were separated and sent to different camps when they evacuated the city. I never saw them again."

There was no anger, no outrage in her voice, just a plain statement of fact about the atrocities committed to her family.

"It must have been horrible to lose your family like that."

"For a five-year-old, it's scary and frightening to be separated from your family. To see your parents killed and not understand why . . . that falls beyond frightening and into the realm of the macabre."

"What about other relatives?"

"Most of the older ones died from starvation or illness. A few of the younger ones managed to survive, barely. If you were sick, they left you by the roadside; if you couldn't walk any farther, the soldiers killed you."

"I can't imagine—"

"No, you can't imagine what it's like to work twelve to fourteen hours a day, every day, to be fed one bowl of thin soup a day, to see your friends and family die from starvation or torture, to be in constant fear of being murdered over doing some little thing wrong, for not working hard enough, for looking at them cross-eyed, for showing sympathy to someone . . . they didn't need a reason to kill you."

Bitterness was creeping into her voice. "They took everything away from us. Our homes, our families, our dignities, our very humanity. Some of us who weren't beaten to death or shot or starved just died inside."

"Why didn't the people rebel?"

"What good would it have done? People were hungry, worn down, scared. They tortured and killed anyone who showed the slightest resistance, even the slightest disapproval of anything they said."

"You must have hated the Khmer Rouge."

"I was too young to understand what was happening. But I learned to hate them. I hated them for taking my family away from me. I hated them for the cruelty they inflicted. But I was lucky. I survived. The question I always have is: Why? Why did it happen to us?"

She took her eyes off the road and turned to me. "Do you know that Cambodia is the only country in the world that has a Day of Hate? A day to remember the atrocities and hate those who committed them?"

❖

U.S. Department of State
Bureau of Consular Affairs
Washington, D.C. 20520

Consular Information Sheet: **CAMBODIA**

TRAVELING IN CAMBODIA

Safety of Public Transportation: Poor
Urban Road Conditions/Maintenance: Poor
Rural Road Conditions/Maintenance: Poor
Availability of Roadside Assistance: Nonexistent

Driving at night in Cambodia is strongly discouraged. Cambodian drivers routinely ignore traffic laws and vehicles are frequently poorly maintained. Intoxicated drivers are commonplace, particularly during the evening hours, and penalties for DWI offenses vary greatly. Even on heavily traveled roads, banditry occurs, so all travel should be done in daylight between the hours of 7:00 A.M. and 5:00 P.M.

The U.S. Embassy advises Embassy personnel not to travel by train because of low safety standards and the high risk of banditry. Travel by boat should be avoided because boats are often overcrowded and lack adequate safety equipment.

Moto-taxis and cyclos (passenger-carrying bicycles) are widely available; however, the Embassy does not recommend using them due to safety concerns and because personal belongings can be easily stolen. Organized emergency services for victims of traffic accidents are nonexistent outside of major urban areas, and those that are available are inadequate.

22

❖

As we drove I occasionally took a subtle look behind us. There was nothing to see, of course, except other cars on the road. I don't know what I expected to see—thugs in black cars following us?

The farther north we drove, the more I got to see the "real" Cambodia with tropical foliage, rice fields, and gentle, thin, smiling people with warm eyes. I also saw people with missing limbs from land mines and empty bomb casings used by the people as pig troughs, benches, and fence posts.

As we passed through villages, I noticed that most of the houses were clustered around a monastery or wat. That was typical of towns in Europe and Latin America, too.

"How many people live in the rural areas compared to living in the city?"

"About eighty percent. Their principal occupation is subsistence farming on family-operated holdings."

It was obvious people possessed little in terms of material goods. "I imagine we Americans spend more money on medical treatment for our pets than these people do for themselves and their children."

"And I'm sure your pets eat better, too."

❖

She was probably right. It was a depressing thought.

We drove in silence for a while before I brought up a question that I was dying to ask.

"You never did tell me what Bullock is really famous for."

"You may regret asking that question. At the Stung Meanchey garbage dump hundreds of the poorest of the poor, including many small children, swarm over the refuse hoping to find something of value."

I had a disgusting feeling why he went there. "He doesn't go there for the trash."

She nodded. "Bullock goes to the dump to buy children. Renting them perhaps is a better definition."

"That is sick. Really sick. Why don't the authorities do anything? You can't tell me that they turn their heads when it comes to molesting children."

"They do if the evidence isn't rubbed in their faces. Cambodia is a corrupt country, as you know. Like most underdeveloped countries, corruption is a way of life for these government officials and they often can't survive without participating in it. It's not something people do because they're bad. Often it's expected. They do it to survive. You can't open up a shoe store without paying off government officials, from the licensing department to the inspectors. And you can't get a job in the government without paying someone."

"Felony ugly," I said, more to myself.

"Felony ugly?"

"Sorry. I was thinking out loud. It's a lawyer's expression in the States. When a criminal looks like he could commit the crime he's accused of, they call it felony ugly. Bullock could easily pass for a child molester to a jury."

I was curious as to how she managed to get a good government position in a corrupt society, and once again she read my mind.

"I was lucky," Chantrea said. "I got an education in France. That opened doors."

The explanation came across as inadequate to me, but I kept my mouth shut. Whatever it took, no one on earth who didn't walk in her shoes could question her actions.

"Oh, fuck it," Chantrea said.

I looked at her in surprise.

❖

"Kirk is right about Cambodia. It's a hellhole. Few places in the world can rival Phnom Penh's traffic in illegal weapons, heroin, child prostitution, and money-laundering. I'm sure he told you about the local English-language newspapers carrying ads for companies that help foreigners negotiate with kidnappers."

"He did."

She gave me an angry glance. "Thailand and Vietnam are making ventures into information technology and manufacturing. Here, the hottest new business is a black-market trade in human organs for medical transplants."

"It doesn't surprise me. That's hot in other countries, too."

Thinking about all the daily corruption and injustices of life that Chantrea had to put up with made me appreciate that I lived in a civilized, rational country more or less. It reminded me again of my mother's comment: Don't complain about not having shoes when some people don't have feet. Chantrea and the people of Cambodia were cut off at the knees.

I wanted to know how well Kirk and Bullock knew each other, so I asked, "Kirk doesn't seem to like Bullock all that much."

"I really don't know."

She obviously didn't take the bait to gossip about them, so I decided to drop it.

The region that unfolded as we drove remained pretty much the same—plenty of rice fields, sugar palm trees, and jungle. Every so often we would pass a small village. On the road we saw people carrying loads on the backs of their bicycles and wagons and trucks; one motorcyclist even managed to drive with a dead pig tied behind him.

At one point she left the main road and drove me to the Tonle Sap Lake to see a floating village.

"For these people, life revolves around water. Very often the houses change according to the rise of water and the season."

"I can't imagine what it's like for them during the monsoon and heavy rains."

"Some of them don't survive."

The houses were on floats or flat boats. Some were connected to the road by a wooden runway but a lot of them were just sitting in the water.

"If they stay on the water, how do they get their supplies?"

"They have merchants in boats that go from house to house to sell their products. Their fresh water is stored in the earthenware jars like the ones in the villages in front of each house."

People in small boats were bringing in their fishing nets with the catch of the day.

We passed an old plantation house and she said it dated from the days when Cambodia and the rest of Indochina were part of the French colonial empire.

"The finest collection of Southeast Asian art isn't here but in France," she said. "Taken from us by our colonial masters."

I didn't bring up the old controversy about whether the collections of cultural treasures from Africa and Asia sitting in museums in Europe and America had actually preserved the artifacts from destruction.

"The turnoff to where Kirk is at is just up the road. We'll have to stop and ask for directions after that."

We left the main road and went onto dirt roads that were little more than paths through dense foliage to get to Kirk's location. After we had driven for half an hour, Chantrea stopped at a village to ask specific directions to the field where Kirk and his team were working. Most of the roads were unmarked. I didn't know how she found her way that far without some local guidance.

A village boy about twelve years old climbed on the hood of the car with his feet dangling over the front end. He pointed straight ahead and jabbered to her in Cambodian.

"He's going to show us the way," she said.

As we got going another boy climbed onto the roof and leaned over the side on his belly, grinning at me through my side window. He laughed as he struggled to hang on while Chantrea moved the car over ruts and bumps. I couldn't help but laugh myself.

Every so often the boy riding in front would shout an instruction and signal with his hands.

"He says we're getting close."

"Are we okay to drive on this road? I mean, are there any mines?"

"There are no mines on this road." She glanced at me. "Now."

"So this is land mine country that we're in right now."

"Yes. Most of the mines are found in rural areas and especially in the north and west provinces of the country. So you definitely don't want to walk in dry rice paddies or forested areas without a guide with you. Hopefully you're not the one who steps on the wrong spot first."

"How do they find them? Like the one Kirk's working with."

"One of the villagers was picking bananas where he came upon an old temple site. There are thousands of sites scattered around, mostly overgrown with jungle. He broke off a piece of artwork." She gave me a look. "I am horrified at the destruction of my people's cultural heritage, but at the same time I don't have the heart to lay blame on poor peasants who live short lives with little besides the shirts on their backs and the dirt between their toes. Finding a small piece of old stone, which is what it is to them, can mean a great difference in their lives."

She left a pause for me to fill in but I didn't. It was all too much for me. I'd heard of people who engendered pathos but the whole country seemed to provoke it.

"Anyway, he stepped on a land mine on his way back. He crawled back to the village with no legs and died. The villagers found more mines and Kirk was called in to take care of them."

Hearing that didn't leave me with a good feeling in my stomach.

"How many land mines are out there?" I asked as I held on to the hand support above me as we went over the uneven ground. I didn't know how the boy above me was staying on top of the car. I would have fallen off a long time ago.

"I've heard an estimate that eighty million mines lay buried in more than sixty countries. Each day fifty people, many of them children, are killed or injured. Here in Cambodia?" She shrugged. "Most estimates are in the millions. We have more land mines and unexploded bombs than people. They're left over from decades of war and civil wars, troubles along the border with Thailand and Vietnam, plus warlords and drug lords staking out their territory."

"Drug lords plant land mines?"

"Oh, yes, just like the warlords, they use them to define and protect their territories."

Jesus. I was beginning to wish that Scotty had beamed me up and put me back down in my Manhattan walk-up. "What about the ones Kirk's working on?"

"He thinks it's probably from one of the civil wars. They've de-mined a lot of the suspected and known minefield areas so far but there's always places that they miss."

"What a horrible thing it must be to know that if you step out to pick fruit you might get blown up by something planted decades ago."

"It's not a pretty sight. Over thirty five thousand amputees and many deaths have occurred since the war ended. I suppose knowing about land mines isn't a big thing in your country."

"A nonexistent thing. We don't have them, period. I mean, I know they're used for military purposes and that they maim and kill people. How does he find and disarm them?"

"Kirk hasn't told you about his work?"

"Not how it's actually done."

"You'll have to get him to tell you about it. It's really quite fascinating. And dangerous. Being a bounty hunter for land mines must be one of those unique jobs in the world, almost macabre—like being a wild animal trainer or leading mountaineers up Mount Everest. He'll never be tamed, you know."

I laughed. "I don't have any plans for housebreaking him."

"Good, because he will ultimately self-destruct."

"Why do you say that?"

"I don't mean suicide. It's just that there are people in this world who aren't destined to live to a ripe old age. Dangerous explosives have mesmerized him. He can't walk away from them. If he left Cambodia, he'd go to Rwanda or the Sudan or somewhere else where life is lived on the edge."

That was about the same deduction I had made about him.

She took her eyes off the bumpy road for a second and met my eye, her features cynical, her smile bitter. "But there are no guarantees for any of us, are there? I don't expect I will see old age, either."

"Why do you say that?"

"Because that's the way my life is written. You Westerners believe that you have control over your own destinies. We of the East believe differently. Our fates are sealed by our karma. Good and bad actions in this life or in a previous one determines our fate."

"Are you saying that you've been predestined for a bad ending? Or at least an abrupt one? What a negative thought that is."

She shook her head. "You don't understand. It's not a negative thought. It's my cosmic destiny."

"I see. And have you seen this destiny in a crystal ball?"

"I see my destiny in the past lives I've led and the one I'm leading now." She glanced at me again. "Do you think you will see old age?"

I shrugged and mumbled something to the effect of "I hope so." Her voice and demeanor had grown melancholy. Talking about the old days—old horrors—had brought back bad memories.

I remained silent to give her space to struggle with her demons.

"*Chap teuv*," she said, out of the blue.

"What?"

"*Chap teuv*. It means 'taken away.' During the Khmer Rouge rule it came to mean never to be seen again."

I didn't get it.

"That's how I feel about my life. Family, love, happiness—it's all been taken away. Never to be seen again."

U.S. Department of State
Bureau of Consular Affairs
Washington, D.C. 20520

Consular Information Sheet: **CAMBODIA**

LAND MINES

Land mines and unexploded ordnance can be found in rural areas throughout Cambodia, but especially in Battambang, Banteay Meanchey, Pursat, Siem Reap (the region where Angkor is located), and Kampong Thom provinces.

At no time should travelers walk in forested areas or even in dry rice paddies without a local guide. Areas around small bridges on secondary roads are particularly dangerous.

Travelers who observe anything that resembles a mine or unexploded ordnance should not touch it.

They should notify the Cambodia Mine Action Center at 023-368-841/981-083 or 084.

23

❖

Kirk never took his eyes off the ground as he walked on the well-worn path that led to where a man had stepped on a land mine. He had a metal detector on wheels and a long rod in front of him. The suspected minefield was off the path but Kirk didn't want to take any chances.

The man accompanying him, a French missionary-schoolteacher who came to the rural area of Cambodia to teach near where the mine was found, had asked to watch the land mine procedure.

The schoolteacher's presence was a nuisance. Not in regard to land mines, but smuggling. The village headman told Kirk that he had something "special" for him. It wasn't hard to figure out what it was. The peasant who stepped on the land mine had looted an antiquity site in the jungle. He was carrying the looted piece at the time.

It wouldn't be the first time Kirk had bought an artifact with blood on it.

"I'm curious about how land mines are found in the ground," he said.

"Unfortunately, they're often found by stepping on them. The government has a program to sweep known minefield areas but the job's too big and the money to pay for it is too small. So, all too often the first word of a minefield is someone stepping on one. And it usually means there's more unless it's an orphan left from a prior sweep of a field."

"It's sad how people have to live with this terror. Worse than having a forest full of wild animals. At least an animal can be heard or seen."

"Sad, but we have to deal with it."

"What do you do once you are advised there's a minefield?"

"That depends a lot on the terrain. Sometimes mines can be spotted; usually they've been in the ground for so long they're covered with dirt or overgrown with vegetation. We have to find the mines and decide whether they can be removed or have to be exploded on the spot." Kirk grinned at the Frenchman. "My personal preference is exploding them but that can be hazardous, too. I have a steel roller I call a sweeper that can be extended from the front of a bulldozer. It can be used to set off small devices called APLs, antipersonnel land mines. The APLs can kill but often maim, taking off feet or legs. The ones with smaller charges amputate your foot up to the ankle, the bigger charges take off your leg. These don't damage my sweeper, but if I hit a mine designed to take out a tank, the explosion and shrapnel could take me out, too. Sometimes they planted tank and antipersonnel mines in the same field. So I have to know what's what. And that means going into the minefield and seeing what I'm up against."

The Frenchman shook his head. "Insanity."

"Once a minefield is spotted, you can't just walk up to it. Older APLs are usually set off by pressure—stepping on the detonator on top. But sometimes they go off just touching them, or by vibrations around them; some have trick triggers that go off when you try to disarm them; some are booby-trapped with a trip wire. Sometimes they're so damn old they just go off from pure meanness." He grinned at the schoolteacher. "Some clever bastard invented mines made out of plastic so a metal detector won't sound off over it."

"You must be commended for the valuable job you do."

Kirk shook his head. "Unlike you I'm not out here for humanitarian reasons. I came to Cambodia to do a job, and I'm still doing that job. That's all there is to it. I won't be winning any humanitarian awards."

At forty-two, Kirk knew he was too old for the dangerous games he played—hunting down land mines and smuggling antiquities. Like most people who had a dishonest income, trying to change and do something else was wishful thinking. He liked the danger, he liked the big money. He saw himself as a little guy taking on a corrupt government that was permitting the destruction of priceless artifacts.

Kirk had seen the destruction hundreds of times—poor Cambodian peasants destroying big pieces of their cultural heritage to break off a little piece that they could sell, or an army commander using his troops to steal pieces so he could pay them with the proceeds.

He knew that until an honest government had tight reins on the country, the police, army, and customs officials could be bought and the cultural slaughter, the "genocide" of the relics of ancient empires, would continue.

He didn't kid himself into believing that in a way he was saving the nation's cultural treasures from ruin by getting them out of the country and into the hands of wealthy museums and collectors. In his mind, the "owners" of the art had been dead for a thousand years . . . what they left behind was up for grabs to those who were the toughest and the smartest.

If he had to define exactly why he dealt in contraband art he would say it was for the money and the excitement.

"This is not my personal technique," Kirk said, "but I've seen mine-clearing personnel go into a field wearing big, pillowlike pads strapped to the bottom of their boots. When they hit a mine, the pad spreads the force of the explosion. The theory is sometimes better than the result."

The Frenchman shook his head. "I find it amazing how many ways humans have devised to kill their fellow man. Thank God there are people like you who are willing to go into the danger and defuse it."

"You can thank the rats and dogs and bees, too."

"I've heard of dogs being trained to sniff out explosives just as they sniff out drugs, but what's this about rats and bees? The only thing I know about rats is they carry the plague and poor people eat them."

"The giant pouch rat from Africa gets to the size of a cat, over two feet long including its tail. It's the largest rat in the world. In some countries it's a source of red meat."

"Are they like little kangaroos with pouches?"

Kirk shook his head. "They have these hamsterlike pouches in their cheeks. They stuff their pouches so full of date palm nuts, they can hardly squeeze through the entrance of their burrows. These rats are intelligent, social animals." He glanced sideways at the schoolteacher. "Smarter and kinder than some of the two-legged animals I've dealt with."

"For a certainty. And you use these creatures like dogs to sniff out the land mines?"

"Yes. Like dogs, they have a superior sense of smell. They can be trained reliably with food-reward incentives—you associate the smell of the explosive with a food award like a peanut. And they're typically too small to set off the mines."

"So how does a rat actually find a mine?"

"We put a bunch of them on long leashes with handlers holding the reins and have them sweep back and forth. The rats will stop and sniff and scratch when they detect a mine. We mark the spot on a grid and come back with a metal detector. Depending on the terrain, sometimes we just run my bulldozer sweeper over. But I won't do that unless I'm sure there are no tank mines in the field."

"As a teacher, I would be fascinated to know what it takes to train a rat?"

"Rats begin training at the age of five weeks when the kids are weaned from their mothers. A positive reinforcement method known as clicker training is used. When the animal does something right, the trainer clicks a small, handheld noisemaker before giving the rat a piece of banana or peanut as a reward."

"Like Pavlov's behavioral experiments with dogs."

"Exactly. Behavioral conditioning. It's similar to how dogs are trained in obedience schools. We also use bees."

"Bees as in . . . honeybees?"

"Yes. Bees have a very sophisticated sense of smell. They're cheaper than dogs and rats and I'm tired of losing animals. They have a ninety-eight percent success rate and they can be trained in a few hours. A hive of fifty thousand bees costs less than a hundred dollars. The giant rats cost a couple thousand each. Dogs are much more expensive."

"Certainly bees can't be trained to locate land mines with peanuts and a clicker noise."

"No, but they're also conditioned with food. Most land mines leak explosives into the environment and the bees are conditioned to associate the smell of explosives with food. A sugar-water feeder and traces of explosives are set up near a bee colony. As the bees feed, they associate the explosives' odor with the food source and will swarm an area where they detect the explosives. They'll search for hours, or even days, with appropriate reinforcement. Another good thing about them, they also train each other. If multiple hives are needed in a large area, only one hive needs to be trained."

"All this work, danger, and misery because of war."

"Not just war. A lot of mines came after the wars and the Khmer Rouge. Even after the Khmer Rouge fell, some of the generals kept their armies and their territories. They laid mines around their gem quarries, valuable timber stands, and munitions dumps to protect them. Drug dealers use minefields to protect their crops and hoards. The bastards who bury these things don't just kill humans, but animals. Work elephants step on them. If they survive, their handlers will outfit them with metal shoes so they can continue working."

"It's so sad," the schoolteacher said, shaking his head. "Land mines being planted to protect criminal activities. People hobbling around with feet blown off. Elephants wearing steel shoes so they can continue working on stumps. Sometimes I wake up in the middle of the night and wonder if I am still on the planet I was born on."

24

❖

"I see Kirk's SUV up ahead," Chantrea said.

Finally. I was getting a little paranoid driving in land mine country. The two boys on top of the car had jumped off earlier.

A battered white Land Rover with a faded U.N. insignia was in the clearing along with a truck and trailer. A bulldozer was on the trailer.

"Is that Kirk's SUV?"

"Yes. Something he picked up after it was stolen or maybe abandoned by the U.N. Looks like they're finished." She pointed to a group of men off to my right down a path cut through the dense growth. "I'll get the lunch I packed out of the back."

Kirk waved to us as Chantrea parked the car to the left of his Land Rover.

I couldn't help but notice as I got out of the car a small object inside Kirk's vehicle. Crudely wrapped with newspaper and tied with string, it reminded me of wrapping I saw at the Russian Market. Some of the stalls there had boxes full of small relics that were unwrapped and visible to the eye, while other pieces were still wrapped in newspaper. My paranoid brain interpreted the wrapped package as booty from temple looting.

I looked around while I waited for Chantrea to get the food. She had told me the area that Kirk and his men were working on used to be a fertile rice field but abandoned decades ago during the civil war. Several mines had recently been discovered here.

The whole area was overgrown and heavily forested with trees and brush. As I gazed at the dense overgrowth to my left, something caught my eye. The longer I looked the more I was certain it was a temple, hidden behind the growth of the thick brushes and trees.

"Here." Chantrea handed me a small baguette with slices of spicy chicken and pork wrapped in foil.

"Thanks. Look over there," I said excitedly, pointing to the area. "I think it's a temple."

I wondered how many of these treasures were hiding in Cambodia, camouflaged by vegetation and jungle, still undiscovered.

"It is," she said as she took a bite of her sandwich. "There are thousands of relic sites in Cambodia, most of them covered by jungle or brush just like this one."

"Makes for open season for looters, doesn't it?"

"Exactly."

I moved closer to the area to get a better look. "Can we get to it? Has Kirk cleared it for mines?"

"I wouldn't go there even if he did. This area is filled with snakes."

I stopped in my tracks. She gave the answer so quickly, I wondered whether she was telling me the truth or if there was another reason she didn't want me to see it. My gut feeling said it was the latter but I remembered my guidebook saying that the country had many varieties of poisonous snakes.

"We'll find more accessible temples to look at."

So far on the trip we hadn't stopped at any.

It occurred to me that Kirk had the perfect job for obtaining and smuggling antiquities. He went to places where no one else did and his missions were not questioned because they were sanctioned by the government. Even better, no one looked over his shoulder since what he was doing was too damn dangerous.

"Let's go talk to Kirk," she said.

My feelings about Kirk were still mixed. I was definitely attracted to him but he had also lied to me. I was determined to find out what he and his pal Bullock were up to. I was sure he hadn't seen me spying on them at the market, but by now Bullock could have told him he saw me there.

Kirk finished his business with the crew by the time we reached him.

"I see you two made it safely. Enjoy the ride so far?" Kirk directed his question to me with a grin. He had a pistol in a shoulder holster.

"Absolutely. I feel like a real urban adventurer. I've seen lots of rice fields, people, animals . . . and bad roads."

"There are worse, believe me. You definitely stay off them at night."

"Speaking of roads, I think we should head out for Siem Reap now," Chantrea said, "before it gets too dark."

"You're right. Let's plan on having a nice Khmer dinner in Siem Reap. On me. I'll follow you two," Kirk said.

"**We're more than halfway** to Siem Reap," Chantrea told me when we got back into her car. "It'll still be daylight when we get there. None of us likes to travel rural roads at night. Along with the banditry, there are all kinds of animals, kids, and motos with no lights that pop out in front of you."

So much for the road trip being safer than flying. Now I was sure it was arranged to keep an eye on me. "I take it we'll go to Angkor Wat tomorrow morning."

"Actually, I've arranged for both you and Kirk to stay at the site. We'll go there after dinner. It's just a few minutes from town."

I didn't question why we were staying on the temple grounds instead of at a hotel in Siem Reap. Who wouldn't want to stay at one of the most incredible places in the world? But I was curious about the sleeping arrangements.

"Is there a hotel at the site?"

"Only the kind with a canvas ceiling."

"A tent?"

Chantrea laughed. "We've been experimenting with offering a camping experience to visitors. Many foreigners, especially the Australians and New Zealanders, prefer roughing it. Not exactly luxurious accommodations but you'll have a great view, especially at sunset and sunrise."

"I'll love it."

It certainly helped to know the right people. An offer like that didn't come along every day. My father probably would've given his right arm to stay the night at Angkor Wat.

I just hoped the accommodations came with a modern bathroom, a wet bar, and a swimming pool to cool off in after seeing the ruins.

U.S. Department of State
Bureau of Consular Affairs
Washington, D.C. 20520

Consular Information Sheet: **CAMBODIA**

ANGKOR WAT: The town of Siem Reap and the vicinity of the Angkor Wat temple complex remain officially open to tourists. The Embassy advises U.S. citizens to travel to these locations by air or to exercise caution if traveling by road or boat and to limit their movements to the city of Siem Reap, the main Angkor Wat temple complexes, and the main national auto routes.

25

❖

The ancient temples and ruins of the vast Angkor site, the "Pyramids of Asia," were located north of the Tonle Sap Lake and Siem Reap, about five miles from the town. We had traveled about two hundred miles north of the capital, most of it with the enormous lake some miles off to the left.

The region—forests and farms—looked pretty much like what I'd seen during the drive from the capital. But nothing prepared me for being waved past the front gate and seeing the ageless edifices of Angkor Wat in the distance, its towers inspired by the shape of the exotic lotus plant.

We arrived at sunset and Chantrea drove me to a spot where I could see the eerie, shadowy temple spires in the fading light. It was magical and otherworldly.

I felt every bit as excited, awed, and mystified as the first time I saw the Sphinx and pyramids outside Cairo.

Chantrea turned me over to Kirk and went off on administration business. She told me she'd take some time tomorrow to show me the complex and suggested I take in the Apsaras performance at the site that evening.

❖

I told her not to bother, that I would rather see them by myself. I didn't tell her I already had a guide in mind.

"We'll have dinner about nine," Kirk said. "It'll be cooler then."

That worked out good for me. While Angkor was usually closed after dark, the Apsaras show under lights was scheduled for that evening. I hoped I'd run into Nol's friend, Bourey, when I went over for the show.

Chantrea hadn't been kidding about the tent—that's what was waiting for me at the Angkor site. The actual Angkor conservation park was enormous, miles in every direction. The experimental campsite for tourists wasn't set up next to the temple complex but in a grove of trees several hundred yards away. Strings of bare lightbulbs ran from tree to tree.

A golf cart was parked outside each tent. "For going back and forth," Kirk said. He showed me a can of mosquito repellant. "The mosquitoes are thirsty at dawn and dusk."

Five tents, each representing a hotel room I supposed, were lined up in a row. A young couple with backpacks and Aussie accents said hello after they came out of their tent to head for the antiquity site. That's what this tent city was geared for—backpackers, young people who stayed at hostels when they traveled. I was definitely the five-star hotel traveler.

"This is terrific," Kirk said when he saw the look on my face. "You'll be able to experience the real Cambodia up close. Isn't this much more exciting than staying in a sanitized room in a luxury hotel?" he said, laughing.

"I can't tell you how thrilled I am that I came halfway around the world to camp in a jungle with mosquitoes as roommates. Are there snakes around here?"

Chantrea had assured me there was only a "slight chance" that I'd get bitten by a deadly snake while walking among the ruins at night. After checking my guidebook and discovering that Cambodia wildlife included panthers, tigers, bears, and elephants, along with "numerous poisonous snakes," her definition of "slight chance" wouldn't make me take a walk by myself at night without a powerful flashlight and some kind of weapon. Too bad I didn't have a gun like the one Kirk carried in a shoulder holster.

"There are snakes everywhere in the world, especially in the tropics. You're much more likely to be annoyed by bugs that—"

"A simple 'no' would have done nicely. I hope those things aren't what I think they are."

"Those things" were small, square canvas shelters that looked suspiciously like they were meant to be a tropical version of an outhouse.

"Toilets and showers."

"No roofs. What do you do when it rains?"

He grinned and shrugged. "You can shit and shower at the same time."

I was afraid he'd say that. And after ten hours of a hot, sweaty trip, I was in desperate need of a shower.

"I suppose there's no hot water in those showers?"

"I think you'll get what you expect. Nice cool water. You'll love it. Just don't lick your lips while you're in the shower."

"Why?"

"There's bottled water in your tent. The water used for showers is clean enough to bathe in, but I doubt if it's drinkable. My stomach's used to the local micros, yours will rebel."

I estimated it would take three days for me to see Angkor Wat and Thom. One night in a tent was fine, but tomorrow I'd be checking into the Siem Reap version of the Ritz.

Kirk got on the phone to make arrangements for a meeting later while I went into the tent to change. I wondered what the "meeting" was about.

The tent was a double—two small "army" cots with a folding canvas end table between them, two racks for hanging clothes, and two bamboo benches for holding luggage. A reed mat covered most of the floor—but not under the beds. That made me wonder what kind of nasty crawling critters might be lurking there. Foot-long scorpions and fist-size hairy black spiders came to mind.

I put on my short robe, grabbed a bar of soap, and flip-flopped over to the row of canvas showers in my rubber thongs. The floor of the shower stall was a wood pallet made up of strips of wood. I looked carefully at the inch-wide cracks to see if anything like a snake or scorpion raised its ugly head. I knew I was being a pansy, but I was not an outdoor girl.

I took off my robe and hung it on the hook. It took a second to get used to the cool water but surprisingly it felt good on my sweaty body. I soaped down, getting ready to wash my hair, when I heard the shower start up next to me. Kirk hadn't said anything about taking a shower so I was curious as to who was next door.

As I washed my hair I heard a tearing noise in the canvas. I looked over and suddenly froze. I saw the knife slitting a hole down the canvas. I just stared at it, unable to move. This was not happening, I thought.

Just as I was about to let out a bloodcurdling scream, Kirk's head appeared through the hole.

"Hello." He had a big grin on this face.

"Jesus, you scared me. I was just about to yell bloody murder."

"Sorry. I wanted to surprise you."

"Well, you did. You're going to get us into trouble for damaging the place."

"Chantrea will take care of it. I'm just making sure we don't offend the sensitivities of Cambodians when I fuck you."

"You sure know how to have fun."

"Especially with a beautiful woman."

I had to admit it was exciting to have a man rip through your shower tent to have illicit sex with you.

Kirk easily slipped through the tear. He pulled me against his wet glistening body and kissed me on the mouth, then worked his way down to my nipples, devouring each one with this mouth.

"You are crazy, you know that."

"That's what makes it exciting."

Damn. Why was I so weak? I knew he was wrong for me, probably a tomb raider and smuggler, but he had that strong masculine appeal and slightly dangerous vibe that turned me on.

I gave in to my need for sexual gratification. I grabbed his limp cock and squeezed, feeling it come alive in my hand. I couldn't deny it; I was horny for him.

"God, it's hard already."

"That's what you want," he said huskily.

His erect cock slipped out of my hand as he moved his way down my abdomen and to the mound between my legs. His tongue found my sweet spot and I pulled his face harder against it, spreading my legs for him.

"Feel good?"

His tongue stroked my clit and I started to tremble inside. "Yes," I groaned with pleasure.

"You want more," he teased.

"Yes."

"What do you want. Say it."

I was about to come any moment. "I want you inside me."

I wrapped my arms around his neck as he grabbed my buttocks and lifted me up. He shuddered and held me tight. A minute later, I started giggling uncontrollably . . .

We hadn't heard the elderly Japanese couple in the tent next to us until we stepped out of the shower. The man avoided my eye but the woman gave me a big smirk.

Maybe she figured she would get lucky tonight, too.

❖

Looting History—and Destroying It

In Angkor Wat . . . almost all the Buddhist statues have been beheaded. Looters and dealers prefer to take mainly heads. . . . [O]ut of the thousands of statues that once stood at Angkor Wat, only twenty-six are left.

—MASHA LAFONT, *PILLAGING CAMBODIA: THE ILLICIT TRAFFIC IN KHMER ART*

Looting has caused even more destruction than war. At Angkor Wat scarcely a freestanding statue retains its head, while many statues have disappeared entirely. In the 1980s the Cambodian government removed most freestanding sculptures and stored them in a guarded warehouse in Siem Reap. Even so, armed bandits attacked the warehouse and made off with priceless works. Today the worst pillaging has shifted to hundreds of outlying temples, such as Banteay Chhmar.

It takes no special insight to see why looting would be endemic to Cambodia, one of the poorest countries in the world, still swept by periodic famine. A poor farmer who finds a sculpture in his fields or a soldier who plucks one from a temple at night knows that if he sells it to a smuggler, he will be able to feed his family for several years.

—DOUGLAS PRESTON, "CLOSE ENCOUNTERS AT A KHMER TEMPLE,"
NATIONAL GEOGRAPHIC, AUGUST, 2000

26

❖

I left my golf cart near the causeway entrance to the temple complex. Since we were camped inside the park, I didn't have to go through the main gate and buy a ticket. The front of the buildings were lit for the evening show. I wouldn't have minded seeing the show, but I preferred to meet up with Bourey the guide.

I was sure the curator had a reason for referring me to the guide besides getting a good tour of the temples. I felt as if I was being tested . . . as if Rim Nol knew something, wanted to share it with me, but was still cautious to do so because he didn't know if I could be trusted.

The gate where tour guides hung out was at the entrance. I wasn't even sure if there were guides on duty this late. I was about to head for the front gate when a man slowly approached me.

He appeared older than Nol. To my Westerner's eye, he was a venerable *ancient* yet ageless relic. His hair was snow white, his features resembling the classical majesty of the faces of Angkor kings on the Bayan temples on the cover of guidebooks. Like Rim Nol, he was rail-thin, not an ounce of excess flesh on him. He wore casual, loose-fitting clothes typical of Cambodian men, sandals, and a clipped-on laminated ID that identified him as an Angkor guide.

Also like Rim Nol, he oozed honesty, reliability, and sincerity. I liked him immediately.

He met me with the traditional Cambodian *wai* greeting, a small bow with his hands clasped together in a prayer position. "I am Bourey."

"How do you know who I am?" I asked.

He smiled and nodded again. "Nol said you were an exceptionally beautiful woman."

I liked this man a lot. I offered my hand and he shook it. "After a comment like that, I am your faithful servant for life. Nol's, too."

We walked together toward the temple.

"Nol says you are an art expert," he said. "Is Khmer art your expertise?"

I shook my head. "I'm afraid not. My expertise is Mediterranean—Greek, Roman, Egyptian, Babylonian, and other civilizations."

"We of the East are as blind about your Western civilizations as you are about ours. I know little of the Mediterranean antiquity sites."

We headed toward the western entrance of the temple where the evening show was being presented.

Gesturing at the structure in front of us, he said, "I am told that Angkor is the largest religious center in the world. Our temples here number over a thousand, spread over a great area, but some of them have been turned into little more than rubble in rice paddies by the ravages of time.

"Angkor means city and it was the capital of the great Khmer emperors, from about the ninth to the fifteenth centuries. The empire held dominance over much of Southeast Asia. The temples you see here were built of stone and brick. Most tourists don't realize that the buildings were religious shrines and not intended for public use. Only the gods and those chosen by them were permitted to live in buildings of stone or brick. The king and his court lived inside the temple walls."

"Where did the common people live?" I asked.

"In the wooden huts found around the central temple compound."

Our conversation continued as we walked across the causeway toward the temple entrance.

"Angkor Wat is a twelfth-century complex inspired by Hindu mythology while Bayon nearby in Angkor Thom is a Buddhist temple completed about a century later. Each of the complexes have their own monuments, canals, and reservoirs. The designs represent the shape of the universe according to mythological beliefs and the entire complex is walled and surrounded by a moat that represents the primordial ocean. Four causeways run across it. Carvings of nagas, half human, half serpent, were put on the causeways to defend them." His voice was calm and melodious as he described the ancient site.

"I've heard that Cambodia has a problem with temple looters," I said. That was an understatement but I decided I should proceed politely and test the waters early.

"Antiquity sites around the world have the same problem as we do. But yes, it is something we must deal with. The site is protected by a police force who the French assisted in training. French police agencies and even the French Foreign Legion are still involved in protecting the sites, but besides Angkor, there are thousands of more sites and we lack the resources to protect them all."

Nothing he said so far signaled me that he was anything more than a guide taking me on a tour.

"There are three levels containing galleries and courtyards with the five towers atop the third. The tallest tower rises nearly to the height of a twenty-story building. It represents the peak of Mount Meru where the gods reside. The other four represent peaks of adjoining mountains."

He gestured at the walled compound. "All sandstone, plus an earth material that acts as a mortar. The blocks were cut from a quarry far from here and brought by boat near where the Siem Reap ferry landing now is. From there they were brought by oxen cart and elephants to the site."

"I imagine that like the pyramids of Egypt, it took decades and thousands of slaves to build this temple?"

"A million slaves toiled forty years just to build Angkor Wat. As you will see when you examine the carvings yourself, it is not just the power of the backs of people that were used to build this Khmer wonder, but the power of their minds and the artistic skills of hand and eye. Many of the surfaces in the complex have relief carvings depicting characters and legends from our mythology. The wat has the longest relief carvings in the world."

We arrived at a raised terrace with giant stone lions guarding each side and climbed up the steps. In front of us was a long causeway leading to the interior. Inside, a courtyard theater had been created with rows of folding chairs.

"Would you like to see the show?"

"Yes, I would."

Bourey said I could get a better view if I didn't mind standing and I followed him up a stairway to a wood platform.

"You are familiar with the dancers we call Apsarases?" he asked.

"Oh, yes."

"They were a favorite subject of ancient artists and are featured throughout the site. These heavenly nymphs were born to dance for the ancient gods and tonight they will dance for the new gods—tourists who pay."

He chuckled at his joke.

Torchlights scattered along the outer walls and through the courtyard gave the whole place an unearthly feeling. Every seat was taken now and it had suddenly gotten quiet. The dancers began appearing, one by one.

Bourey whispered, "The performance tonight is a tale we call the Nymph and the Sage. The Apsarases were playful and seductive and were often used to distract a spiritual master from his meditation. Menaka, the main dancer tonight, was considered to be one of the most beautiful of the nymphs. She was sent by Indra, King of the Devas, to break the concentration of the great sage, Vishwamitra.

"When the sage sees her beautiful naked body, he is filled with sexual desire and the two become lovers. After many years of having Menaka as his lover, Vishwamitra finds out he has been tricked. He becomes angry and returns to his meditations. Menaka has his child and leaves the baby by a river. The child is found later in the forest surrounded and protected by birds. She is named Shakuntala."

Four apsaras dancers were now onstage. Dressed in brightly colored tunics and skirts, each of them had on elaborate headdresses, as well as glistening jewelry on their head, arms, wrists, and ankles.

"They're beautiful," I whispered.

To one side of the dancers an orchestra played drums, gongs, and xylophones.

I was mesmerized by the slow hand gestures and sensuous body movements. Bourey explained their graceful hand movements were a language.

"A finger to the sky means 'today,' arms crossed over the chest 'very happy,' a hand up means 'dead,' one down 'alive.' Other movements depict birth, aging, sickness, and death."

They danced so exquisitely, as if they were born to dance. "How long does it take them to learn to dance?"

"They start when they are very young. Dancers must be trained while the bones are still flexible."

I noticed that their fingers were extraordinarily elastic. The dancers could bend their fingers backward almost to the wrist.

After the performance, he took me to a spot where all five towers were visible in the bright light of a full moon.

We returned to the center of the terrace and continued our path on the stone causeway.

Bourey said, "Angkor was not just a temple complex, but was a city in and of itself."

"Yes, the capital of an empire."

"I understand that the pyramids of Egypt were built not just as resting places after death, but passageways to eternity for the pharaohs. Likewise, Angkor Wat was built by King Suryavarman II as a temple of immortality in which he would become one with the great god Vishnu.

"Among the beautiful sculptures here are bas-reliefs running for hundreds of meters depicting scenes from Hindu mythology, the *Mahabharata,* and the *Ramayana.* Also carvings of Suryavarman holding court." He chuckled shyly. "For most men the beautiful carvings of Apsarases are the favorite scenes, next to war, of course. Did you know that the nymphs are said to be able to change their shapes at will . . . and that they rule over the luck of people, especially in gaming and gambling?"

"How is the restoration coming?" I asked.

"Much improvement has been made, but in some ways we have only scratched the surface. An American satellite that scanned the area with radar revealed many buried structures that we did not know about. So much work needs to be done, so little resources are available; many buried treasures of our culture will not be found during my lifetime."

I felt like I had taken a journey to another world, a journey back to a place and time that must have been truly magnificent. It also made me think of my father and what a mistake he made in not fulfilling his dream.

Bourey said something.

"I'm sorry?"

He smiled shyly. "Your mind flew away from here to another time and place."

"It did. I was thinking about my father. His dream was to see Angkor Wat. He never got here."

"Perhaps he will in his next life."

That was a nice thought.

"Tomorrow by the light of day I will show you much more of the temple. There are three levels that tourists can enter. But if you are up to climbing, I will take you up into the main temple." He pointed up at the temple that was two hundred feet high. "From there you can see much of the site. Even the vestiges of Angkor Thom. You must visit it, too. At Bayon, the central temple about a mile from here, four enormous heads are carved into the top of the tower. You have no doubt seen pictures of the heads, but you must see them in person. Over fifty smaller towers surround the central tower and have carved heads facing the four directions."

He held up his index finger to make a point. "Yes, you definitely want to see the huge stone faces, but you'll be a little disappointed at the sculpture and relief. They are inferior to those of Angkor Wat. Now, would you like to see the Churning of the Ocean of Milk?"

"I've read about it. I'd like to see it."

"It's at the east side, opposite to where we entered. Lights were set up there earlier to show important diplomats the relief. I can show them to you, also, and let you examine them closer by flashlight. Tomorrow you can see them by the light of day. The different effects of night and day are quite striking."

As we walked in the darkness, Bourey asked, "Do you believe in ghosts?"

"Well, I've never seen one, but . . ." I shrugged. I didn't *disbelieve* in ghosts.

"Some monks claim they have seen aberrations of ancient princes and princesses walking in the corridors here."

❖

"Wonderful. I love ghost stories when I'm wandering around dark places at night."

Bourey chuckled. He had a nice sense of humor.

"Are you familiar with the stories of secret treasure?"

I wasn't. "No."

"It is said that when the empire was invaded, the royals and nobles would throw their jewels and treasure into the ponds, that today there are untold riches buried in the mud."

"Has anyone ever found anything?"

"Some artifacts have been found, but if it was great treasure, the finders did not reveal it. There is a sacred chamber in the central core of the temple. It was walled up in the mid-fifteenth century. Five hundred years later, in the 1930s, I believe, a French curator discovered a vertical shaft about ninety feet deep with some jewels at the bottom. The curator died a few months later. It is said he killed himself. As with whatever was taken out of the ponds, the gems disappeared. Many people who have worked here at Angkor believe that there are many secret depositories of treasures."

"Why?"

"Because it is true; treasure had to be hidden from invaders. But we have not excavated below the temples. We have spent our resources working to clear the sites and protecting them from looters."

"Wasn't it the French who started preserving the monuments?"

"Yes. After the monarchy moved farther south in 1430, Angkor was deserted. When the French came here five hundred years later they found it overgrown with jungle vegetation. For the last century the temples have been alternately cleared and looted." He paused and looked at me. "I understand you are friends with a land mine hunter."

"Yes." I wondered how he knew about Kirk.

"As strange as it sounds, the land mines placed in this area by warring factions helped reduce the looting because it kept many thieves away."

We reached the galley containing the churning sculpture. He told me the story as he shined light on the stone carving. The relief depicted gods and demons churning the milky sea by pulling a line of rope back and forth like a tug-of-war.

"This is one version of the tale. Once upon a time," he said, smiling, "the ocean flooded the land and one of the precious treasures that the gods lost was the elixir of immortality. To retrieve it, the gods thought they could churn the water like they churned milk to make butter. But they needed the demons to help them with the churning. The churning pole they used was a mountain that rested on the bottom of the water. For the churning rope, they stretched out the giant man-serpent Vasuki.

"The demons pulled on one side of the rope and the gods pulled on the other. Slowly their lost treasures began to appear but a poison also came out, which the god Shiva swallowed. When the elixir appeared, the demons and gods fought for it and—"

"And the gods win in the end," I finished for him. "The good guys always win."

"Not always."

I decided to plunge in. "The people of Cambodia haven't been winning when it comes to looting of Khmer art, have they? Did Rim Nol tell you that I'm investigating the international smuggling of your art?"

I assumed that was the conclusion Nol had come to from the questions I had asked him.

His expression didn't change. "Perhaps it will be safer if I showed you the galleries in the morning."

I was being shooed. He brought me back to my golf cart. I had screwed up. I forgot I was in a country with a corrupt government and that I might be putting the poor man into jeopardy.

As I climbed into the cart, Bourey said, "I sometimes wonder whether countries are subject to karma like people."

"Come again?"

"My country has had many rebirths. In my lifetime I have seen wars and the tragic, violent era of the Khmer Rouge. Now it has another life and is struggling to be reborn again. It can have a bad rebirth . . . or it can be reborn with some of the greatness that created these wondrous monuments."

He smiled, a little sadly. As with Rim Nol, it was a smile that had weathered decades of hardships.

"Some of us are working to make the rebirth into one which our people will achieve their inherent greatness again," he said.

"I wish you luck," I said. "And I only want to help."

"Yes, I understand. If you wish my services again, we will talk more tomorrow about the subject you have raised. All great things have small starts. Perhaps together we can create a spark that will raise a flame that burns away the corrupt emanations that bring bad karma."

We agreed to meet an hour after sunrise.

I drove my cart away feeling a little better about my progress. Maybe I was getting somewhere.

27

❖

Dinner was sour soup and a concoction of steamed fish with coconut and spices wrapped in banana leaves. I passed on the snake salad. I was tired after the long trip and short tour of Angkor and even a little disturbed by my discussion with Bourey.

Chantrea hadn't shown up and I wasn't exactly good company for Kirk, but he didn't need me—most of the men and women in the place came to our table with beers to talk to Kirk. He was a local celebrity to the other expats—or sexpats, drugpats, whatever they were. Fortunately, Bullock wasn't among them.

When I finally made it back to my tent, I was physically and mentally exhausted. I wanted another shower but I was afraid to go out in the dark and take one, though I was forced to take a flashlight and visit the canvas outhouse where the portable potty roasted in the heat all day long, waiting for someone to lift the lid.

I definitely planned to go to a hotel tomorrow.

Kirk was lying on his cot dressed only in baby blue boxer shorts. The flap was a little open, hinting at an invitation. I was tempted, but too tired to accept. He didn't say anything so I assumed he was sleeping. I undressed and slept only in a short tank top and underwear.

❖

I wasn't asleep when Kirk woke up sometime later. He did it quietly, slipping out of the tent like a wraith. Waking up after two or three hours of sleep and having my problems run through my mind had become a habit.

After he left, I crept to the tent opening and opened it a crack to peek through. Kirk had the rear door of his SUV open. He gathered up a bundle in his arms and set it on the ground. He carefully shut the back to avoid making noise, then picked up the bundle and walked away.

I quickly put on my jogging pants and shoes and grabbed the flashlight Chanthrea had given me earlier and headed out to follow him. Had I been thinking straight, I would have realized it was dangerous to go creeping out at night.

At first I didn't see anything, but then I saw a shadow moving in the distance. I wasn't sure what I planned to do if I encountered any jungle beasts. Flash the light in their eyes hoping that would scare them away? What if I stepped on a snake?

The moon was bright so I didn't really need the flashlight but I carried it anyway for security. What worried me more were land mines. Even though most of them had been cleared around the ancient grounds, they still warned you not to stray off the beaten paths. Warning signs were posted to remind you. I figured as long as I stayed behind Kirk, I'd be safe.

I followed him down a dirt road and through the bushes. I came up to a land mine warning sign but Kirk continued walking even without a flashlight, so I just kept following his lead.

When he came to a clearing in the brush, I remained hidden. I couldn't see it, but I heard the sound of a car coming. No lights appeared anywhere on the car. I had a sneaking suspicion of who would be behind the wheel. My hunch was right.

Bullock.

As I watched him get out of the car, I suddenly felt something crawl up my leg. Instead of screaming, which I wanted to do, I quietly tried to squash whatever it was with my flashlight. I shook my pants leg afterward to make sure it was out.

Kirk and Bullock stood there for several minutes when a third car arrived, a white official Apsara pickup truck. Two men got out of the truck. Even in the dim light I could see that they wore park police uniforms.

❖

Kirk gave the package he was carrying to the two men. After examining it briefly, they put it in Bullock's car. From my vantage point I couldn't see what it contained. The two men then unloaded something bigger from their car. It appeared to be something wrapped like a mummy in a cloth with ropes around it, approximately three feet long and maybe a foot wide. It wasn't light because the two men were straining to put it into Bullock's car.

It was obvious that the pieces were stolen antiquities. Bullock was leaving the complex grounds with the antiquities, driving on a back route that was closed due to land mines. Kirk had no doubt cleared the mines already, but the signs would be enough to keep everyone out. In a country where tens of thousands have died and hundreds of thousands have been mutilated, a land mine sign was more effective in keeping people away than a chemical spill.

I left them and made my way back to my tent. Luckily it hadn't been that far. I took off my shoes and lay my jogging pants on top of my cot.

Thoughts began swirling in my head. Was Chantrea involved? She was the one who arranged to let Kirk camp inside the temple area. The idea of staying at the temple grounds instead of Siem Reap still bothered me. It wasn't that far from town. A nice experience, sure, but certainly not necessary.

It came down to one thing: It was easier to make an exchange at night instead of during the day.

I heard the light crunch of footsteps outside the tent. Kirk was back. I closed my eyes and pretended to be asleep. He came in and kissed me on the forehead.

"Can't sleep?" I asked him, opening my eyes.

"No. How about you? Looks like you can't either."

"I think I must have dozed off for a while. I heard you come in."

"I know what might help." He took off my top and panties and spread the blanket on the floor.

I wanted to resist him, but my body controlled my mind again. I didn't want to make love with him since I would be sleeping with the enemy. But I was still attracted to him, and when it came to sex, great sex, I was a weak person. Maybe I was the one that had a problem.

Damn it. Why did he have to turn out to be a rat?

❖

28

❖

Bourey lived two miles from the Angkor site in a small two-room house with conventional wood walls and a bamboo roof. The house had electricity but no plumbing or phone. A bicycle was his only means of transportation.

Like most older Cambodians, his loss during the horrific Khmer Rouge years had been tragic, losing both his wife and child in 1976 to the excesses of the brutal regime. He remarried ten years later but lost his second wife to cancer.

He lived a simple life of guiding and chatting with tourists at Angkor, working the vegetable garden in his backyard, and once a week playing cards and drinking a homemade brew with old friends. Most of his life had been spent associated with the antiquity site. When he was younger he worked to clear the monuments from centuries of jungle growth. As he grew too old for hard labor, he worked with the restoration group that did more delicate work with the ancient images. Because of his familiarity with the temples, becoming a guide was a natural evolution for him.

Late in life, he went through another evolution of spirit and purpose.

❖

Rather than be a passive observer of the damage done by avaricious looters to his nation's cultural treasures, he became an active participant in stopping the genocide of Cambodia art.

Like his friend Rim Nol in Phnom Penh, whom he shared fear and misery with in a Khmer Rouge camp during the insane days when Pol Pot ran the country, he was a patriot of his country. Both men recognized that only a great people could have built a temple complex recognized as one of the great wonders of mankind. They wanted those wonders preserved for future generations and not taken by rapacious thieves of culture.

It was Nol who had first approached Bourey about making a contribution to the protection of artifacts. Nol had made contact with an administrator in the Ministry of Culture who was also concerned with the looting. He had gone to the man with suspicions about thievery at the National Museum. With the administrator's encouragement, Nol recruited his friend at Angkor Wat, another at Angkor Thom and other key antiquities sites. They were an unarmed, unauthorized, unofficial group who lacked everything but courage and resolve.

The morning after he showed the American Madison Dupre some of the wonders of Angkor by night, he rode his bicycle to the local marketplace where a phone in the back of a fish shop could be used for a small fee. He called Rim Nol in Phnom Penh to tell him of his meeting with the woman and to ask his advice as to whether she should be told their suspicions about what was actually happening to the finest Khmer art in the country.

"I agree with you that she is a sincere person," Bourey told his friend over the telephone. "But we must move cautiously. She doesn't understand the political dynamics of our country. She may say something innocently that will reveal our investigation."

Rim Nol concurred but didn't want her to stop from progressing with her own investigation. "As a foreigner, she has more protection in asking questions than we do, but even a foreigner is not immune to disappearing, never to be seen again. I have let her know that something is amiss and that those she socializes with are not her friends. I think she realizes the power of the forces that she is offending, but we must let her know just how much danger she is in."

❖

BOUREY ARRIVED EARLY AT Angkor the next morning. Early risers were already taking photographs of the complex in the rising sun, but hordes of tourists arriving like tsunami waves would not begin until later. He skipped his morning exercise group because he had received a message to report to the supervisor of guides. It wasn't the first time he had been instructed to report early to the supervisor. Sometimes it was for instructions on changes in procedures, but usually it was to give a special tour to a VIP. He didn't like giving tours to important people because the tourists were much more generous than VIPs, most of whom never bothered to reward him with a gratuity. Important people lived in a different universe than those who had to earn their rice.

The supervisor said, "You have a special assignment this morning. An important American art expert. He wants to get started before the gates open."

"I already have a customer, also an American art expert. I gave her a tour last night and made arrangements to guide her again today."

The supervisor waved away his objection. "Another guide can serve her. You have been requested by this American. You should be pleased that your worth as a guide is recognized."

"But I promised the woman—"

The supervisor pointed up. "The instruction that you serve this American man came from the gods atop Mount Meru. Now go, he's waiting outside. He wants to get started before the tourists begin arriving. Perhaps he will only need a short tour and then you can still serve your tourist."

There was no arguing with the supervisor. When the orders came from Mount Meru—meaning a high-ranking Angkor executive—refusal was not an option. He had no faith in the supervisor's prediction that the art expert would want a quick tour. Art experts took much more time that ordinary tourists.

His customer was waiting outside. About fifty years old, the man was unhealthy from what Bourey called a form of food poisoning—eating rich foods to excess. His skin was as pallid as a fish's belly.

Everything about the man offended Bourey's sense of peace, tranquility, and spiritual path. People who led bad lives suffered negative rebirths. This man was the product of a bad past life and a bad current one.

Bourey had seen him before at the site a number of times, but he had never used a guide. The man had once rebuked one of their guides claiming that he knew more about Khmer art than the Angkor guides.

Bourey introduced himself.

"Bullock," the man replied. "I won't be taking up much of your time. I just need an interpretation of a relief near the top of the main tower. Let's get going. I want this done before the great unwashed masses arrive."

As they walked, Bourey noticed that two off-duty park officers followed behind them.

❖

29

❖

The rising sun was spectacular over Angkor, but the red tint made me wonder again about my karma. Red sky in the morning, sailor take warning. Not a good sign from the heavens.

No sign of Bourey was the first indication that all was not right. I wondered if I had misjudged him. As with Rim Nol, I had been reading between the lines of his remarks. I was positive that Bourey was planning to share a confidence with me.

I shook my head and told myself that he had to have a good reason for not being there. Flat tire, dead battery, stomachache. Anything could be possible. But my excuses didn't work because my gut told me something was wrong.

My paranoia spiked earlier when Kirk sneaked out before dawn. He knew I was getting up early, too, to see the sunrise, but he had left without waking me. I pretended to be asleep as I watched him gather up his stuff. He hadn't left anything . . . which meant he didn't plan on coming back. It seemed odd that he left no note, either.

He had left like a thief in the night. He knew I was planning on checking into a hotel in Siem Reap later today. If he cared about me, wouldn't he want to know where I'd be staying or recommend a place where I should stay?

After what I witnessed in the brush last night, a thief in the night pretty well summed up his character, anyway.

I told myself I should be happy he'd cut out. It wouldn't be long before I would have to accuse him of being a looter. I refused to think of what would happen to him when I did that. Or what he would do to me.

I waited half an hour at the foot of the causeway and then went to the hut where the supervisor of guides held court.

"Not available today. Special assignment. I will get you the best guide in all Angkor."

I turned down the best guide in Angkor and made my way to the temple complex hoping I would see Bourey. My paranoia was running high. "Special assignment" didn't set right with me. He had promised to meet with me. It sounded too much like somebody high up had jerked him out of my reach.

The only somebody I knew who could do that was Chantrea.

Kirk was a temple looter. Chantrea was a temple administrator. The two really didn't mix, not unless they were working together.

Jesus. What a complicated mess! Cambodia had more intrigues than the *Sopranos*.

I wandered in, looking for Bourey. It was a big complex. What had he said? The biggest religious monument in the world. Even if he was here, I might not see him. And I wasn't sure he was still at Angkor Wat. The wat was just a small part of an archaeological site that ran miles in every direction. If the motive was to keep him away from me, they could have sent him miles away to any one of a dozen areas in the park.

He could be anywhere. Which at the moment left me nowhere.

I could go on and enjoy one of the great archaeological monuments on the planet, except that I couldn't think of anything but the fact that I seemed to do nothing but screw up. I had been in Phnom Penh and now Angkor Wat and I had accomplished nothing.

I could spend days roaming Angkor, but I was undecided as to whether to turn around and take a taxi to the airport and go back to New York and hole up in my apartment . . . or go back to Phnom Penh and start all over.

I decided not to give up until I made sure nothing had happened to

Bourey. Besides, I was a weak person when it came to antiquities. I was in the midst of a cornucopia of some of the world's best art. There were a million things I wanted to see. I wanted to see everything. I opened my guidebook and started reading about a relief that related the tales of the *Ramayana,* the epic account of Rama's search for his wife, Sita. The wife, Sita, had been kidnapped by a demon king. There were wars and intrigue and—

I heard a shout, more like a cry of fear, and looked up to the great central tower, the same tower that Bourey was planning to take me up. In one of the doorlike openings a man stood, pausing as if in slow motion. I don't know why but it reminded me of someone getting ready to jump. I just stared at him, mentally telling him not to do it.

Then he came out, all the way, over the edge, flying off the temple like a giant heavenly bird.

I heard the thump as he hit the ground. I ran over to the crumpled body. It was Bourey. His mouth opened to take a breath, then collapsed. It was his last gasp.

I LEFT THE SITE immediately and checked into a hotel in Siem Reap. I tried to call Rim Nol at the National Museum to tell him about his friend but was told he was out sick.

I didn't tell the person who answered the museum phone who I was out of fear that I would compromise Nol. Nol would know soon enough anyway.

I was sick and scared. Sick for poor Bourey. Frightened for myself.

An accident was the reason put out by the Angkor authorities. The hotel concierge heard radio news reporting Bourey stumbled and fell when he was showing a customer the upper level of the central tower.

Accidents happen.

But I didn't believe it was an accident. Bourey was too competent a guide.

He also fell from where he had planned to take me.

It didn't take long for me to figure out my next move: get out of the country as fast as I could.

I had the concierge make a reservation for me on a flight to Hong Kong from the Angkor airport. He claimed it was a busy and safe airport.

So much for my road trip to avoid the dangers of third world flying.

My excuse for going to Hong Kong was to follow the money. A good reason. I needed a fresh lead, but more than anything else I needed to get away and clear my head and recharge my courage.

I felt I'd worn out my welcome in Cambodia, fallen from grace with the country. So much greatness, so much gentleness, a land that could produce the likes of ancient Angkor and modern men like Nol and Bourey. But so much savageness.

I called Michelangelo in New York. I wanted to talk to someone in authority who knew where I was in Cambodia and could help me if I suddenly became a statistic.

I didn't tell him everything. In New York he said he was cooperating with Ranar and the Cambodian authorities investigating the looting and smuggling. He could very well say something that could get back to people in the government who were in league with the criminals. Ranar himself could be that person. That meant I couldn't relate my suspicions about Bourey's death. Too much chance that it would bring trouble to Rim Nol and myself.

"What do you think of Cambodia?" he asked.

"The people here are gracious and wonderful, but the corruption is incredible. Even the innocent have to keep their mouths shut because there's no protection against retribution. There are ads in the local paper by people who negotiate with kidnappers for the families of victims. If you don't hear from me every couple of days, send the Marines."

"They wouldn't be too welcome. The last time the American military went to Cambodia they dropped about a million bombs. Have you made any progress?"

I told him about the piece with the half-moon on it in Sinn's shop. "There's a disreputable art dealer named Bullock from San Francisco living here. From what I hear, he's also what they call a sexpat instead of expatriate. He specializes in molesting children when he's not dealing in contraband art."

Michelangelo said he would check him out.

As usual, I didn't have any problem throwing Bullock to the wolves. I was almost angry enough at Kirk to include him, but I opted out at the last moment.

❖

"Actually, I called to get some information about the woman who sold the Siva at the New York auction."

"Nadia Novikov. Was a top Russian model. Poor girl who worked her way up in a tough industry on the casting-room couch. Hooked up with a former KGB thug named Illya Daveydenko. He got to the top by fucking people, too, but the screw jobs he gave were considerably more violent. When Russia went capitalistic and the whole country turned into a free-for-all in which whatever you could grab and defend was yours, Illya was one of the guys who got rich quick. With bribes and murder, whichever worked best, he took a bite out of the old Soviet oil industry. Probably a big enough mouthful to make him a billionaire."

"You told me he was murdered."

"Thoroughly. He'd moved his operation to Hong Kong when Putin's boys started cracking down on the ruthless thugs who had taken over Russian industries in the violent business atmosphere of the early nineties. They called Russia the Wild Wild East because the guy with the fastest gun—or checkbook—would grab ownership of a bank or a factory or, in Illya's case, an oil company, with no down payment, and gut it before the next robber baron came on the scene to bribe government officials to let him have it. Illya left the country following Putin's crackdown on business fraud and tax invasion and ended up buying the farm on foreign turf."

"I take it Comrade Daveydenko ran afoul of another big gun?"

"Two of them. Hired, the kind of Russian *mafiya* wiseguys who used to break heads for the KGB and now hire out as enforcers for the new cadre of the country's billionaires. After leaving Russia one step ahead of a criminal indictment, he came to the Far East to work some oil deals and got nailed by two hired guns as he came out of a nightclub in Hong Kong."

"And Nadia managed to dodge the bullets?"

"She did, but the girl with Illya that night didn't. There were some nasty rumors that Nadia herself set up the hit because Illya was dumping her."

"How does the Siva fit in?"

"If you're asking whether Illya knew it was fake when he bought it, I wouldn't know that from a rat's ass. The Hong Kong police tell us Nadia cleaned out Illya's place minutes after he was shot. She told the police the art was a gift from him. Some of the pieces are worth millions. His body was still warm when she put out the word she had merchandise to sell."

"That was sentimental of her. Is she still in Hong Kong?"

"That's what I've been told."

"I'd like to talk to her."

"She told the police Illya bought the stuff from a dealer but she never knew the dealer's name."

"That's convenient. But she might open up to me."

"Don't bet on it just because you're a woman. Nadia Novikov doesn't relate to other women. She's the type of manhunter who considers women competition."

"Detective Michelangelo, you are underestimating this woman's ability to deal with other people. If there's anything I've come to understand after years in the art business, it's that the common trait of just about everyone with a whole bunch of money is greed. They all want *more*—money, power, status, envy. Remember the scene in *Key Largo* when the gangster Rocco who had everything told Humphrey Bogart that he wanted more. *Rocco wants more*, he said. Or something like that. Well, that's how people are. Nadia the model got millions from the sale of that Siva. And she's sitting on other pieces that can get her plenty more if she can figure out a way to get around the scandal of the Siva being a fake."

"You have the perfect background to approach someone about dealing in contraband art . . . is that it?"

Bastard. "What's Nadia's address?"

He didn't have an address for Nadia but gave me the name of the Hong Kong art gallery that arranged the New York sale of the Siva—Cheung Dragon Antiques. "They told the Hong Kong police Daveydenko lied to them about how he got the Siva."

I called Bolger and asked to him to check out Nadia and the art dealer who handled the New York sale. I told him I'd talk to him on my cell phone when I hit Hong Kong.

When I came into the lobby to check out, the clerk had a message for me from Kirk. *Call me*. He had tracked me down.

I trashed the message and headed to the Angkor airport.

❖

Who Owns History?

Many countries have rich cultural histories, producing objets d'art over the eons that are today considered priceless museum pieces.

Egypt, Iraq, Turkey, Greece, Italy, Mexico, Peru, China, and Cambodia are just a few of the countries that have amazingly rich pasts that produced fine statues, vases, weapons, ceramics, and hundreds of other items that today are considered "museum pieces."

Many of these magnificent relics of the past were produced over the eons by long-gone empires. And are often located in "third world countries" which lack the resources to properly protect them from looters and the wear and tear of time.

Some people argue not only that the "history" of long-gone empires belongs to the world at large, but that the museums and collectors in the rich industrialized nations of the world have a right and duty to keep and preserve artifacts that are part of the cultural history of less fortunate nations.

There's some merit to the argument. Of course, it ignores what would happen if the Iraqis suddenly started dismantling pre-Columbian native American buildings in the southwest to ship to Baghdad . . . if the Turks suddenly started taking down Britain's Hadrian's Wall to ship it to Istanbul . . . if the Cambodians suddenly started digging for Jomon pottery in Tokyo.

In other words, what if the shoe was on the other foot?

30

❖

Hong Kong

I chose the Peninsula Hotel in the Kowloon District. The hotel had old snob appeal and was famous for its white-gloved doormen who attended a line of Roll-Royce "taxis." My budget called for Motel 6, but if I had to give Nadia or the art dealer the name of my hotel, I wanted it to be one that fit my profile of a woman who could talk millions. Even if I was a buyer's agent, which is how I planned to pass myself off, I still had to have the smell of money.

Hong Kong wasn't very big, basically a whole lot of islands and a large peninsula, but it had many geographical and governmental divisions. As the name of the hotel revealed, it was on the peninsula—in this case Kowloon. The south end of Kowloon was separated from the central government and business district on Hong Kong Island by Victoria Harbor. The district spilled across the harbor and spread into Kowloon's Tsim Sha Tsui district and adjoining areas.

The Peninsula had an enormous colonnaded lobby, fancy restaurants, a shopping arcade, and high tea in the lobby bar. Flipping through the description in the guidebook, it had only one feature besides snob appeal that appealed to me: body massages. My body and soul needed some TLC.

❖

It was hard to imagine that this bustling postage-stamp commercial entity filled with hurrying people, predatory business types, and concrete towers for more than a decade had been a special administrative region of China. Red China.

I took a walk around the area after I checked into the hotel. It wasn't long before people edged closer to me and whispered, "Handbag?"

Shades of Chinatown.

The art dealer who set up the New York sale for the Siva would be my first stop. Regardless of what he told the police, he would know who sold Daveydenko the pieces in the first place. Probably not a good chance he would tell me but it was worth a try on my part. I also wanted the dealer's insight about Nadia.

Getting information would not be easy. Art dealers were more secretive than magicians. And just as tricky when it came to sleight of hand.

In the taxi to the hotel, I called Bolger to find out what he had discovered about the dealer and let him know I was in Hong Kong . . . just in case one day I mysteriously fell off the radar and my body—sans identification—was later found floating facedown in the harbor. After my discussion with Detective Anthony in which he had expressed no concern for me, I wanted to make sure someone who cared knew where I was.

Whenever I had these thoughts of my premature demise, I reminded myself that just months ago I didn't think this way and someday my life would be back to normal.

"I read that Hong Kong has more than two hundred stores selling Chinese antiques," I said, showing off my guidebook knowledge. "So maybe I'll bring home a tea set that belonged to a Ming emperor."

"Your guidebook won't help if you're caught doing it. China doesn't allow it's priceless cultural treasures to be slipped into Hong Kong and sold to the world at large. But don't worry about that—your chances of getting a genuine Chinese antique ceramic in hand are about nil."

I knew that and I knew the process for authenticating a ceramic, but as usual, I let Bolger talk to see what else I could glean.

"You probably remember we use a thermoluminescence test to check authenticity," he went on. "It involves drilling a small sample. By measuring the amount of light emitted from the sample when it's heated, it tells the amount of time that has passed since it was fired. But fakers can inject radioactive material to fool the TL test. That's why you look at other factors: the shape, the color, the consistency with the period in question, the weight, the chop."

The "chop" was an intricate signature of Chinese characters.

I changed the subject. "I thought this place would remind me of a big Chinatown, but it's got a life of its own. Like a mini-world. It's part Chinatown, part Wall Street with Fifth Avenue and Times Square thrown in."

"You do know that the Brits held Hong Kong for over a hundred and fifty years before the Reds took it back."

It really wasn't a question but Bolger's erudite way of leading into a subject so he could show off his knowledge—at my expense.

"Of course. I do know something about world history beyond London, Paris, and other points west. You always make it sound like I learned all my history from guidebooks I buy at the airport." Which, I didn't add, was the source of my knowledge about Hong Kong—other than what I already knew, that they made men's suits cheap and it was a merchandise pirate's paradise.

"Then you know all about the Opium Wars."

I'd heard the phrase but couldn't remember the history.

Bolger snorted his intellectual contempt for my ignorance. "The Brits and other Westerners made big bucks selling opium to the Chinese. The Chinese government tried to put a stop to it and seized opium warehouses in China. The Brits outgunned them and the Chinese not only had to permit the opium trade, but conceded Hong Kong Island and eventually Kowloon Peninsula and the rest of what we call Hong Kong to the British."

"Thanks for sharing." I loved these charming stories of how Americans and Europeans screwed over the rest of the world, especially when I was traveling in the places that took the beating.

Even though Hong Kong was civilized territory in comparison to Cambodia, it was also home for some of the infamous Chinese gangs called triads, not to mention where Daveydenko bought the farm.

"Bought the farm" was a nice old expression for death. I asked Bolger about it.

"I think it has something to do with fighter pilots talking about buying a farm to retire on," he said. "So their pals say they bought the farm when they're shot down. I can look it up for you."

"That's okay, the less I know about ways of getting killed, the better. What about the Hong Kong dealer?"

"Your cop friend is correct," Bolger told me, "Cheung Dragon Antiques arranged the transfer of the Siva from Nadia to the New York auction house. I spoke to an appraiser for the auction house. He said the Cheung firm claimed it wasn't involved in Daveydenko originally acquiring the piece. They said it was a transaction between Daveydenko and a private collector."

"They'd hardly fess up to helping him acquire a piece that later turned out to be a fake," I said. "What's the reputation of the dealer?"

"Outstanding. Run by Albert Cheung for decades. I recall examining some pieces he sold to the Met. All were as represented. But Albert retired and his nephew took over and doesn't have the old man's pristine reputation. Hong Kong is one of the world centers of fake art and Jimmy Cheung has joined the not-too-exclusive club of peddling things off as genuine if it means a big price tag."

"You think he made the Siva's phony provenance for Daveydenko?"

"Maybe. But Russia's as violent today as Al Capone's Chicago was in the thirties. In a country where you can buy suitcase A-bombs at flea markets and become a billionaire overnight by starting a bank and stealing the deposits, he could have had a provenance made that tracked the ownership history back to Genghis Khan."

He gave me the phone number and address of the store on Cat Street. He'd been to Hong Kong antique dealers in the past, but not to the Cheung store.

"Cat Street is off Hollywood Road, the city's antiques row. It's probably the place where the expression 'caveat emptor' was born. *Let the buyer beware* should be printed on the shop doors along with the hours of operation. Hollywood Road, by the way, got its name from a colonial administrator's English manor house. It used to have more brothels than antique shops."

"Maybe I'll rummage around the stalls and pick up a rare treasure for you for a buck," I kidded.

"Yeah, and maybe you should use the dollar to buy a hundred-million-to-one lottery ticket—we'd have a better chance at making a profit. If you decide to buy anything and shake on the deal, count your fingers afterward. Jimmy Cheung isn't the only dealer in Hong Kong who isn't particular about what he sells. I'll bet you don't know how Cat Street got its name."

"Enlighten me."

"Like the Thieves Market in Bangkok, it was once an alley where crooks unloaded their loot. The thieves were called rats and the shopkeepers who bought their stuff were called cats."

"This anything goes attitude must be contagious in the Far East. I saw it in Cambodia."

"It's a worldwide pandemic. We close our eyes here and pretend we're not as crooked. We are. We're just holier than thou about it."

"Were you able to come up with an address for Nadia the model?" I asked.

"In a manner of speaking."

"Which means?"

"I couldn't get a home address, but I got a business one—sort of."

"Sort of what?"

"She's got a booth at the Epicurean Fair."

"Come again?"

Bolger chuckled. He loved to make me dig for an answer.

"You've heard of the trade shows held for rich people in different countries around the world?"

"Sure. They rent an auditorium at a five-star hotel and rent booths to high-end vendors. People with too much money come to buy the costliest things on the planet—like hundred-thousand-dollar mink shower curtains."

"You got it. Besides mink shower curtains, you can buy the finest sheets for the most comfortable mattresses on the planet, a million-dollar car and a hundred-thousand-dollar entertainment system for it, or a baby elephant for your kids to play with. Luxury items from all over the world gathered in one place."

I knew what he meant. The rich gone wild. A vulgar display of materialistic items for people with money to buy—things that the rest of us couldn't afford—so they could be envied by other people. Right now, I'd give anything to be one of those ostentatious people with enough money to pamper myself.

❖

"So what has this got to do with Nadia?" I asked.

"She's started her own line of perfume . . . ten thousand dollars an ounce."

"You've got to be kidding. Nothing smells good enough to sell for that much."

"People don't pay for its smell, but its effect. She claims it's an aphrodisiac."

"Wow. What a pitch for a scent. What's in it?"

"That's a secret that keeps her from selling it in many countries. She's not telling because it's supposed to have some banned substances in it."

"What kind of banned substances?"

"Rumor mill blogs on the Internet claim it has stuff like ground tiger penis and the drug ecstasy in it."

I howled. "Tiger penis!"

"Don't laugh. In the Far East, tiger penis sells for a lot more than ten grand an ounce. It's been a Chinese Viagra for a couple thousand years. Which is part of the reason tigers are on the endangered species list."

"Does it work?"

"How the hell would I know? Some Chinaman emperor probably got a hard-on after nibbling on one and the rest is history."

I could see the use of the party drug ecstasy. I'd never taken it but friends who had claimed it made them feel really uninhibited and ready to try about anything. Even if it didn't make you horny, I suppose making you more amiable toward the idea of sex made it something of an aphrodisiac.

Besides being a pedantic collector of miscellaneous information, Bolger had tons of common sense, so I asked his take on the perfume.

"Bullshit for the mink shower curtain crowd. There are plenty of rich men who will give their lovers an ounce of the stuff just to show off . . . and who knows, they might get lucky and not get a faked orgasm for once. Consider this—at that price, a gallon of the stuff would bring in over a million dollars. That lady has a sweet little racket."

Racket was right. "I bet Nadia planted the tiger penis and ecstasy rumors on the Internet."

I collected the address for the luxury fair and signed off with Bolger.

My next call was to the antique dealer. Jimmy Cheung wasn't in, but would be back later . . . hopefully he'd call me back if I passed the acid test of being a big enough buyer to impress him. I told his assistant that I was representing an American collector who wanted a Chinese museum-quality piece for which an export permit could be obtained.

I gave the assistant information about my credentials in the antiquities trade to impress her boss. I left out the part about having once bought a fifty-five-million-dollar fake. But I knew they'd check me out in minutes on the Internet and find out enough to wet the whistle of any self-respecting art dealer who pushed fakes. The Hong Kong art market was closely affiliated with the New York and London markets and my connection to the biggest art scandal in modern history roared through the art world like a tsunami.

Since I was representing someone else, it was my credibility rather than my line of credit that counted. Jimmy Cheung would assume that we spoke the same language after he heard my comment about needing a Chinese museum piece with an export permit: You couldn't get a museum piece out of the country without an export permit—and it would be a cold day in hell before you got a permit because China didn't permit its antiquities to be smuggled into Hong Kong and sold to foreigners.

It just wasn't done, not unless you were in a venue where officials could be bribed—and bribery wasn't something to attempt in a country where there was a death penalty for just about everything.

Basically my message implied I had a buyer but something would have to be arranged under the table. And it amounted to an open invitation to sell me a superior fake I could pass off to my collector as the real McCoy—even the best replicas didn't need an export permit.

CHEUNG'S SHOP WAS OFF the street in a short alley that could only be entered by ringing a gate buzzer and being observed through a barred window.

I passed inspection and was admitted inside.

Jimmy was a nephew, but wasn't a kid. Thin, short, probably fifty, he talked fast in hard-to-understand English. Since my Chinese was limited to saying "Nî hâo" (I pronounced it knee how)—my attempt at saying hello in Mandarin—he was light-years ahead of me in terms of international communications.

I explained I wanted a museum-quality piece of Chinese origin.

"Much problem with export," he said. This was the third time he explained that he couldn't sell me something that required an export permit. It was a game we both knew and he knew better than me. He had to give the spiel that he only dealt with aboveboard transactions, but it was all just opening moves in game playing—required before we got down to what it was really all about: money. "No export license approved."

So tell me something I didn't know. "Mr. Cheung, what do you have that will please my client?"

That gave him an open invitation to offer me something under the table. He'd sell me Chairman Mao's eyeteeth and let me figure out how to get it out of the country if there was a big fee in it for him.

"A piece was sold at auction in New York recently," I said. "A Siva. My client loved the piece. He wants something similar." The Siva wasn't Chinese. There wouldn't be an export license problem.

"Genuine piece," Cheung said, waving his arms. "Many lies about it. Not a fake."

Yeah. Sure. I smiled sweetly. "My client is not extremely discriminating if it's something he likes. And he liked the workmanship on the Siva. You have more?"

"No more Siva."

"My client is one of those really anxious types who thinks money can buy anything . . . and is willing to pay for what he wants. If you don't have a Siva, he would be interested in something by the same artist."

He shook his head with real regret. "Taksin is gone."

That sent a quiver through me. I'd found out something important: The name of the artist. "He's gone?"

Cheung shook his head. I saw real regret. He wasn't acting. Obviously Taksin had helped the bottom line.

"Taksin make the best pieces," he said. "As good as thousand-year-old. No one can tell difference, not even museum curators. Then . . . poof." He threw up his hands. "Gone."

"Dead? Missing?"

"Fish food."

"Fish food?"

❖

"Gone."

"Dead?"

He shrugged. "Gone. Dead. Fish food."

"Why?"

"Why?" He threw his hands in the air. Obviously it was a stupid question. "To make into fish food, someone no like. Maybe someone pay too much. Now fish food."

"Yes, well, uh, I'm sure that here in Hong Kong—"

Cheung shook his head almost off his shoulders. "Bangkok. Taksin not in Hong Kong."

"Bangkok? Thailand? Taksin's in—"

"Fish food."

"Yes, of course. Thai fish food. Do you have any more of his pieces?"

His expression turned sly. "Very fine piece."

"Ah . . . good. I'm looking for a very fine piece. Money's no problem. My client is a very eager collector. May I see the piece?"

He went into a back room and I pretended to examine a jade Buddha. Nice piece, but not old. My mind was reeling. An artist named Taksin in Bangkok was making the pieces. Now he was missing . . . maybe dead. Daveydenko was dead. This Taksin had started something that'd gotten out of control.

Jimmy came back with the piece. A statuette of Ganesha. I remembered the elephant-headed god from my college days studying art. He was the son of Siva and his wife Parvati, two of the most important Hindu gods. Parvati created him from the rubbings of her own body so he could stand guard at her door while she bathed. When Siva came to visit, he saw Ganesha. Enraged with jealousy because he didn't know it was Parvati's son, he had Ganesha's head cut off.

When he found out it was Parvati's son, Siva promised that he would replace Ganesha's head with the head of the first animal that came along. And along came an elephant . . .

Ganesha was the god of wisdom, able to overcome obstacles, but he didn't look like much. Short, fat, with a big belly and broken tusk, the small statue Jimmy Cheung sat before me had four arms, respectively holding a noose, an ax, a book, and his broken tusk.

It was a fake. Not a bad one, it would fool most collectors and even some acquiring agents, but I had spent too much time as a museum curator examining pieces for authenticity to be fooled by a common fake. For sure it wasn't made by the Thai named Taksin. Not only did it lack his exquisite artistry, but the sandstone didn't have the same color as the Khmer pieces I'd seen. It was from a different quarry than the other Khmer pieces. I guessed it was a modern fake made somewhere in China—for the upscale tourist market.

"Ten thousand U.S.," Cheung said. "Bargain."

I smiled and set the piece down. "Very nice. I'm sure a tourist would pay as much as five hundred U.S. dollars for something this nice."

He gave me a smile back and bobbed his head in a bow. "Yes, yes, very nice piece."

"Mr. Cheung, perhaps you could arrange a meeting between me and Nadia Novikov that would be profitable for both of us."

His eyes lit up with black fire—and it wasn't friendly fire. He looked at me as if I were a poacher.

"No meeting."

"Have a nice day."

As I turned to leave, he said, "Wait."

He pulled a handkerchief-wrapped object out of his side coat pocket. He unwrapped a jade piece several inches in height and width and handed it to me.

A small Buddha sitting in a lotus flower. I knew it was real, the Met had pieces like it when I worked there. A very nice piece, probably about three hundred years old, Ch'ing dynasty. It wasn't an extremely rare piece, I'd see a number of similar ones, but it was a high-quality piece—a museum piece, one that no doubt made its way to the colony via mainland China.

"Very valuable," he said. "For you, a thousand American dollars."

I hoped I hadn't flinched when he quoted the price. A thousand dollars was ridiculous. The jade content alone was worth more than that. If it was genuine—and I was certain it was—the piece was worth twenty times what Jimmy Cheung was asking.

I met his eyes. Dark pools revealing nothing. But the slightest closure of his already narrow eyelids told me that he was hiding something.

I looked the piece over again, turning it over in my hand. And mind. No question . . . it was real. No question . . . I wouldn't have a snowball's chance in hell of getting it out of the country without an export permit . . . and no chance of getting a permit.

"This comes with an export permit?"

He shrugged. "Very small. Fit in luggage."

In other words, I could smuggle it out he was saying. I handed it back to him and he accepted it in the handkerchief. Did he think I had the plague?

"Handling another piece for Nadia Novikov?" I asked.

He turned and walked away without answering. I took his cold shoulder to mean our session was over. So much for my plan to get some insight into the Russian model.

I left the shop in a brown study and completely puzzled.

Now what was all that about?

First the man tries to pass an overpriced fake off on me at an outrageous price, then offers me a museum piece I couldn't get out of the country without risking arrest—and asks a fraction of its value.

Jimmy Cheung wasn't crazy—so why all the bullshit? Had he been testing me to see if I really could recognize art?

His motives were beyond me, but the session had left me with an eerie sense of free-floating anxiety. I couldn't put my finger on why I was so disturbed, but I had a feeling that there was malice in Cheung's act. A malicious intent that didn't bode well for me.

Shit.

Why wasn't anything in life simple?

What did I do to deserve all the crazies in the world coming into my life?

Maybe I did a few things a woman shouldn't do . . . at least, what a man would say a woman shouldn't do, but I definitely wasn't a bad person.

Not that bad, anyway.

❖

31

❖

I grabbed a taxi to the convention hall where rich people bought things that I couldn't afford but would love to have.

En route I called Detective Anthony and told him about Taksin the Thai. I was excited that I not only got the name on my own, but found out he was fish food.

"He's the artist who's been making the fakes," I said. "He's Thai. And he's disappeared."

The New York detective seemed singularly unimpressed with my startling revelations.

"I'll check him out," he said.

That sounded a lot like he'd send a memo to whoever was in charge in whatever American agency that interfaced with Thai police and ask that they contact whichever Thai police agency and ask . . . whatever. In other words, it would get lost in a bureaucratic morass.

I told him about the strange session with Jimmy Cheung. "First he tries to unload a tourist fake, then he offers me a museum piece for a fraction of the price . . . knowing I'd get arrested for trying to get it out of the country."

He didn't say anything, just listened. I wasn't exactly getting any rip-roaring enthusiasm or sympathy from him.

"You realize what would happen to me if I got caught at the airport with that piece?"

His lack of shock and anger at Jimmy Cheung trying to set me up left me with an empty feeling once again. I needed some enthusiasm; I was in a foreign country and up to my rear in alligators or crocodiles or whatever they had in the Far East.

My free-floating anxiety was swirling around my head by the time I reached the Epicurean Fair. Nothing I could put my finger on—just a strange day in a strange place had revved up my feeling of insecurity.

My feeling of unease was soon replaced with one of horror—a ticket to the rich people's fair cost five hundred dollars. With some Vegas shows costing half that and championship fights and football games costing more, I suppose I shouldn't have been surprised. Besides, even if you didn't buy anything, a five-hundred-dollar ticket that lets you see things you can't afford and mingle with people who think they're superior should be worth some bragging rights back home.

As I made my way down a red carpet, passing gold-plated bathtubs and a real estate firm that specialized in private islands, I hoped I displayed the same disdain that wealthy people did when they walked by the booths.

Nadia's tiger penis scent booth was wedged in between a Bugatti sports car that called itself the fastest street-legal car in the world—it got 3 miles to the gallon at 250 miles per hour and had a price tag of 1.5 million—and a lingerie display featuring live models and champagne. From what little the models were wearing, the manufacturer—a Chinese silk merchant—seemed to be advertising more flesh than silk.

Nadia wasn't hard to find—she was the only person in the small booth. She definitely had Hollywood looks, the type of glamorous female villain who would try to kill James Bond after fucking him. With high Slavic cheekbones and startling cornflower blue eyes—contact lenses, no doubt—her exposed breasts seemed to be so perfect that the plastic surgeon who crafted them probably could have faked the *Venus de Milo.*

Her seductive, diamond-sequined, and strapless dress, something I had seen in Saks Fifth Avenue with a price tag of $4,000, fell just to the limits of indecency, leaving almost as little to the imagination as the lingerie next door. The whole ensemble—clothes, shoes, hair, makeup—spelled hot-hot-hot.

It went without saying that her perfect lips could also only have been crafted by a master surgeon. What he didn't hide was the hard edge—that characteristic quality of doing whatever it took—to whomever—that some women got when they had to walk a hard road in life.

Boldly sensual, exotically sexual, runway fashionable, and a very, very high-maintenance appearance, she gave off an aura of challenge that told men *come fuck me if you're rich enough.*

She was the kind of woman that women like me loved to hate.

Even as I got near the booth and made contact with those startling blue store-bought eyes, I couldn't decide how to approach her. For sure, she'd be gun-shy about discussing anything about the fake art she'd sold and the pieces she still planned to sell. No doubt the Hong Kong police had been at her door at the bequest of the New York and Interpol authorities.

I realized my plea to this sexpot would have to be an appeal to a universal human aspect, one of those inborn cultural qualities that separated us from the lower beasts.

Greed.

She tensed, eyes narrowing, as she saw me come directly at her in a frontal assault. I could see her claws dig in, ready to defend her territory. Not all women were aggressively territorial—this one was. I don't think she would have backed off if a tiger had come back looking for its penis.

"Ms. Novikov, I'm Madison Dupre, an art buyer from New York. I've handled pieces valued over fifty million dollars and I want to talk to you about your collection." It was a mouthful, but to the point. "I just spoke to Jimmy Cheung. He was unhelpful after I told him I was in the market for very rare pieces—Khmer pieces—like the kind you have in your collection." I needed a reason for not having Cheung's blessing, so I gave one. "He tried to sell me something else."

A man suddenly appeared from behind the booth wall. Big, wide-shouldered, blond-haired, gray eyes, and square-jawed handsome in a brutal way, he could have played a movie villain. My immediate impressions of him were bodybuilder, personal trainer, bodyguard-lover.

Nadia ignored me and spoke to him in Russian. Then they both looked back at me.

"I know who you are," she said. Her English was good, but underlined with a Russian accent.

"You do?"

She shrugged. "I follow New York and London art news. You were headlines in both."

"My friends call me Maddy." I offered my hand.

She ignored it.

I smiled. "You can call me Ms. Dupre."

"What do you want?"

I raised my eyebrows and shrugged. "To make money, of course. But I'll do it with someone else."

I spun on my heel and walked off.

Halfway to the front doors, the big guy caught up with me. "Mad-ee my name is Lav." His English was more heavily accented than the model's. "Nadia wishes to talk to you."

I pursed my lips, pretending to take my time about whether I was willing to give her the time of day.

"About making money." He grinned. He reminded me of a tiger—an albino one. "You must pardon her. She is still in mourning about poor Illya."

Uh huh. No doubt she wept crocodile tears all the way to the bank. And into bed with this stud. But I wasn't in a position to be choosy.

I took my time walking back to her booth.

Nadia eyed me more neutrally this time, letting me know that she still had claws but was willing to talk.

"What can you do for me that a hundred other dealers can't do?"

It was a good question.

"I have access to just about every major dealer capable of making bank transfers in millions. I can create a buzz about your pieces that will get worldwide attention, do the paperwork you need to make the deal, take care of where the money should go when the deal is closed. And know how to get the best price."

"I expect those things from every dealer. Cheung is local and he did all that for the Siva."

"Cheung also got you the scrutiny of major police agencies all over the world—FBI, Interpol, NYPD, Hong Kong PD, and the Chinese police."

I had no idea whether the government of China had any interest at all in her pieces—they were not Chinese cultural art—but threw them in because they were the most threatening of the bunch.

"The difference between Cheung and me is that he has to bring in other dealers in New York and London to find a buyer. That gets a spotlight on you. I deal directly with collectors. That puts me into a position to offer you something priceless."

"What?"

"Secrecy. I'm not the only one who has made headlines in the art world. The Siva got you a starring role, too. If you want to cut a deal for other items, it has to be done discreetly. Cheung is the kind of dealer who'll put a picture of your pieces in his Internet catalog."

More Russian talk erupted between Nadia and her bodyguard, lover, or whatever he was. They definitely were a number—he wasn't arguing like an employee.

I checked out her bottles of tiger penis juice. Gold-plated bottles with thin black lines. She certainly wasn't into trying to be subtle with the U.N. or whoever came down on people who kill endangered species for fun and profit.

A couple entered behind me. A skinny, older Chinese man who looked like he was with his granddaughter—or a lap dancer at a hostess bar. I could see why he came in—Grandpa was going to need some tiger penis if he planned to have the girl ride his jade stalk.

Nadia looked at them, then back at me, dollar signs rolling in her eyes like the spinning symbols on a slot machine. They were a quick ten-thousand-dollar-an-ounce sale. Money in the bank. I was a question mark.

I quickly relieved her of the need to make a decision.

"I can meet at your convenience, but it has to be tonight. I have to get back to New York to close a deal. I'll need to see the pieces."

"There's a party at my house tonight. We can talk there and you can examine my art."

"I didn't bring a dress for a party."

She raised her eyebrows. "There are many designer booths in this place. I'm sure you'll find something."

❖

Yeah . . . I could only imagine what they would cost per ounce.

She rattled off something more in Russian to the big guy and left me.

"Let me have your card," Lav said.

He reminded me of Kirk, only bigger, a cross between Kirk and Arnold Schwarzenegger.

I gave him the card. "You can check me out on the Internet."

He raised his eyebrows. "What will I find?"

"Besides the piece that caused an uproar, I've handled many other valuable pieces, probably much bigger than anything in Nadia's collection. Sometimes the provenances weren't right, but I managed to get them sold."

The last remark inferred that I was a crook, but I was finding out that passing myself off as someone from the dark side of art deals came natural to me.

I had only stubbed my toe once—more like cutting off my feet, actually—and it had been an accident. But I deliberately painted myself as a little shady to him.

Nadia not only had a shaky past herself, she was from a country where corruption had become a fine art during the repressive Soviet days and a way of life when the wall and Iron Curtain crumbled. I was certain she'd feel more comfortable with someone like herself. As my father used to say, water seeks its own level.

He gave me the address for the party. "It starts at ten o'clock."

"I can come earlier and examine the pieces—"

"Ten o'clock. Nadia wants to get to know you before she lets you look at her collection. Give me the name of your hotel. We'll send a car."

I gave him the address.

He walked away leaving me in a feminine quandary. I had nothing to wear to the party and I certainly couldn't afford anything being sold here. I casually walked around to leave the impression I was planning to buy something, then decided it just wasn't good enough for me.

While I wandered around looking at five-thousand-dollar dresses, I called Bolger in New York.

"I need to know where the least expensive high-fashion faux clothing and accessories are in Hong Kong. The merchandise has to be good enough to fool a professional model like Nadia."

The Internet was truly a remarkable window on the world. Bolger would not only get me the name of a store, he'd probably find a blog that gave customer opinions of the store, pinpoint its exact location on a map with GPS, get driving instructions, mileage, and current weather conditions, do a virtual tour if the store had a Website . . . and see the exterior of the building with a camera from a satellite in space.

32

❖

The limo that pulled to the curb to pick me up was sheer opulence. Besides the usual wet bar, computer, phones, and adjustable rear seats with warmers and coolers, the best part was the massage features. I could have spent hours in it, days. It was only slightly smaller than my walk-up.

It looked a little like a big Mercedes but I didn't recognize the front emblem.

"What kind of car is this?" I asked.

"Maybach," Lav said. "German. If you decide to buy one, you can go to the factory in Germany to decide on the million or so design features. It's like ordering a custom-built yacht or a personal jet. No two cars are exactly alike."

"Like fingerprints."

That one flew right over his head. Mine, too. I didn't ask him the price. I knew it had to be in the hundreds of thousands.

I wondered if Lav was going to search me before he let me into Nadia's villa. If I was lucky, maybe he'd be thorough and give me a full body cavity search.

❖

Lav was pumped and glowed with masculine power. I had a fantasy that he waxed everything below the neck. As far as I was concerned, he could have swept me into his arms and taken off into the sunset, ripping off my clothes as soon as we got to his castle.

I knew it was hypercritical for a woman who cherished and fought for her independence to be fantasizing about a man's protection, but sometimes the only solution to a problem was brute force applied by someone very big.

I'd found a good knockoff of a Valentino cocktail dress at a designer boutique store for three hundred dollars. Having paid ten times that much in New York, it would have been worth the airfare to Hong Kong just for a shopping trip. I knew it was a pirated copy, but I was too poor and desperate to care. Dealing with murderers and thieves had numbed me to mere clothing fraud.

The drive took us up the mountain and to the Victoria Peak district on top. An almost vertical tourist tram could be taken to the peak itself. As we drove around curves on a high road I got some good views. Victoria Harbor to the north was a bustling seaway, but the south end of the island was a surprise. Hundreds of small boats, mostly sampans and junks, crowded a bay. Sampans were fishing boats tipped up at both ends and with a small enclosure roofed with reed mats. Junks, which had square sails spread by battens and a high stern, were larger and often housed several generations of a family.

The villa overlooked Hong Kong harbor. The view alone had to be worth millions. I wondered if she'd inherited the estate from Illya . . . or had simply taken squatter's rights when word came that he had been terminated with prejudice.

Nadia left her other guests and floated over to greet me. "What a lovely dress. They make such good knockoffs in Hong Kong, don't they?"

Bitch.

The only way to handle a biting dog was with a kick, so I raised my eyebrows and smiled innocently. "Dresses, antiquities, boobs, lips, asses, you can buy anything fake here. Maybe even good manners."

Lav chuckled at my remark, but Nadia just smiled and went off to greet another arrival. It didn't faze her one bit.

I let Lav lead me down to the courtyard. It was surrounded on three sides by wings of the house and was elevated above the level of a swimming pool. Standing on the tiled floor, I had a view of the lights on the harbor and Kowloon beyond.

The effect was stunning. So was the guest list.

The crowd in the courtyard could have been selected from the United Nations—every color, race, and culture was represented. Lav pointed out an oil rich sheikh, an Indian film producer, an African statesman, and a British dot.com auction house founder who looked so young he was still fighting acne.

The only thing these people seemed to have in common was their age—mostly mid-thirties but made up to look even younger, and rich.

The women wore more jewelry than clothing. The men dressed out of magazine ads but lacked the smug, chic Euro-trash look of those thin, dark, unshaven male models that magazine advertisers always preferred. Mostly they looked like accountants and computer nerds dressing like male models.

A hot crowd: Yuppies, Generation X or Y or whatever they were calling them . . . young, ambitious, well educated . . . all with money or faking it. Many of them had that smug look of prep school types whose biggest accomplishment in life was cashing checks from the family trust.

The party quickly got interesting as the courtyard got darker and the touching got more personal.

Lav took me to the edge of the partygoers and introduced me to a skinny young man who was a CEO of a nanotech firm—whatever that was. The guy looked way too young for me unless he was looking for a one-night stand. I must have aroused his motherly instincts because he quickly melted away with a young woman wearing glittering jewels.

I did a double take at her outfit. *Just jewels—no clothing.* The lights in the courtyard had gone down, the music was way up, people in the darkness were becoming a blur around me, but the young woman's platinum blond hair and bare white flesh glowed in the dark.

As I looked around, I noticed there were more glows in the dark. It was funny to see the servants scrambling to collect all the clothes being tossed.

Women and men . . . naked . . . dancing bare ass.

A naked couple brushed by me, dancing. His feet were on the floor, but her legs were wrapped around his hips. They were conjoined at more than the hip.

❖

Okay. I was a modern woman. I'd seen men and women without their clothes on before. It wasn't new. I'd explored a few naked bodies of both sexes of my own in my short time on Earth. But I'd never been to a party like this where everyone took off their clothes.

I seemed to be one of the few people who hadn't stripped.

The party scene seemed so . . . sixties . . . flower children, sexual revolution, daisy chains, wife swapping, group sex, swingers, UC Berkeley students protesting the war and their hypercritical parents by having sex in the streets.

Things had apparently changed over the past decade as I ran with an older, moneyed crowd that could afford seven-figure art. Lust and perversion in my social milieu was private . . . or at least exhibited with no more than three or four getting together to swing.

Nadia's party scene was into open and obvious perversion. From the embraces I saw, people weren't being particular about who—or what—they nibbled on.

The music picked up a beat—electronic dance music with a persistent, repetitive beat. Psytrance music—morphing, throbbing melody, a succession of single tones that sucked you in physically and mentally.

A rave party. That's how I thought of it. The music was a little different, the people a little older and a lot richer, but the effect was the same except that the sex was more overt than when I went to college.

Lav was suddenly by my side. He handed me a drink.

"Nice party," he said.

"Looks more like an orgy to me."

He shrugged. I wasn't sure if he understood or just didn't care.

Glow sticks and fire pois came alive. The glow sticks looked like the swords used in *Star Wars* movies. They weren't much different than what I remembered from college. The fire poi were pots of fire on short chains. A flammable material like cotton soaked in kerosene or lighter fluid was used for the fire. When the pois were swung, startling fire images were created.

The drink Lav gave me was also giving me a glow. It went down smoothly, but I soon felt its effect from head to toe. People around me seemed to be moving faster, the shapes were becoming more of a blur in the darkness that was only broken by the swinging lights and fire.

The psychedelic images of light and fire helped focus your mind away from other people, the visual images capturing the mind so it could relax and not think about anything as the music hypnotized you.

Despite the strange surroundings, I felt myself relaxing into a euphoric bliss.

I was in a strange house, strange city, and among strangers who were acting out their sexual passions and perversions in public darkness and I was totally content. Apprehensions and anxiety about Jimmy Cheung and international art fakery melted away in the euphoric fires created by the psychedelic music and whatever was in the drink.

Seeing all the naked flesh around me made my clothes feel cumbersome. I had this terrible urge to take it all off.

Good God, where had my inhibitions gone?

It occurred to me that my drink had been spiked, but at the moment I didn't care. I swayed to the music, feeling completely at peace with the world.

Lav's voice came from behind me and I felt his presence as his arms went around me. He whispered in my ear, "You're flowing with it, that's good."

His warm breath on my neck gave me goose bumps.

"You put something in my drink," I said.

"We all go through life afraid of what people will think. Now you can be your real self."

Then it hit me. Ecstasy. The "secret" ingredient in her perfume—along with tiger penis—that got it banned. Ecstasy made you feel more in harmony with other people, welcoming whatever they did. And that included their sexual preferences. Pleasing others was part of it. Not only arousing passions, but having a love and unity that connected you with others.

I leaned back against him, feeling his strong arms wrap around me.

"You've got the glow," he said.

Yes, I had the glow.

My mind left my body and floated above the party. With the swirling light I could see everyone had now shed their clothes and their inhibitions.

Some guy once told me as we were making love that human beings were the only animals who had sex face-to-face. I'm sure there were positions here tonight that animals hadn't even attempted.

❖

A fire poi dancer appeared in front of me creating psychedelic images with swinging fire chains.

I couldn't move as my clothes started coming off. I wasn't physically paralyzed, my body still swayed with the music, but I was enraptured by a sense of well-being. I didn't stop Lav as he took off my clothing. If this big handsome Russian wanted to take off my clothes, if it gave him pleasure, then I wanted to do whatever pleased him.

My bra came off and he lifted me in the air and pulled off my panties.

The fire poi whirled around and around, leaving a fantastic trail of fire in its wake that seemed to stand still in midair.

Lav's huge hands were warm as they cupped my breasts. He pressed his bare skin against mine. Somewhere along the line he had taken off his clothes.

I felt his hard erection slip in between my legs from behind. I started giggling. Tiger cock.

Someone stepped in between me and the swirling fire display.

Nadia.

Like the other women, she was only wearing jewelry. She squeezed my breasts and kissed me on the mouth, pushing her tongue in, eager and hungry.

I rode the sensuous wave after wave of pleasure as her tongue started moving between my mouth and my nipples. With Nadia sucking me and Lav now pumping his cock inside me, my body exploded in sexual ecstasy.

❖

33

❖

I woke up naked in bed the following morning. Alone. But I knew I'd had company: A white Egyptian cotton robe, my purse, and clothes—freshly laundered—were laid out for me, along with a pot of hot coffee, croissants, butter and jams.

I struggled out of bed, showered, and dressed, then grabbed a cup of coffee and went hunting for Nadia and Lav. Before I left the room, I called a taxi. I didn't want to be at their mercy for a ride back to my hotel.

They were having breakfast and Bloody Marys by the pool. Naturally there was no mention of last night's activities. Like the Mafia dons say when they order a hit on an old family friend, it's just business.

"The pieces are in there," Nadia said. "I figured you'd want some privacy."

She pointed to a small poolside tent put up to keep the sun off of food items during pool parties. So much for privacy—the entire front of the tent was open.

I could see artifacts on a table.

One thing she could rely on—with a tiny clutch bag and skintight dress, I wasn't likely to walk off with anything.

❖

"Where did Illya get the pieces?"

She shrugged. "I don't know. From a man."

"A dealer? At auction or a private sale?"

"I don't know. Private. Illya did nothing public. He would have killed me for selling the Siva at a public auction in New York. Never let anyone know what you're doing, he always said."

"You have no idea at all?" I asked.

"Why is it so important? I have the pieces. You say you have a buyer. Do we have a deal or not?"

I almost broke out laughing.

"Nadia, I know you want to sell and I want to make money, but my buyer isn't a fool. With the scandal over the Siva, we have to come up with an ownership history so I can give the buyer a provenance that satisfies him even if we all know it's bullshit. Can you tell me anything about how Illya got the pieces?"

I shot Lav a glance, hoping he could add something to the conversation, but his face remained impassive.

She pursed her fat collagen lips. Blower's lips, a friend of mine would call her type—and he wasn't referring to blowing up balloons.

"Petrol," she said.

"Petrol? As in oil and gas?"

"Illya made money in petrol. Developing fields. The pieces had something to do with that."

"I don't understand. What's the connection between a business deal in petrol and art?"

"Illya wasn't an ordinary businessman," Lav said. "What he did was not only secret to the rest of the world, but to those around him. If competitors found out he was making a deal that would make him big money, they would kill him and do the deal themselves."

"What kind of deal was it?"

"Petrol," Nadia said. "That's all we know. He was working something with petrol. Making a revolution."

"A revolution? Where?"

"I don't know." Nadia flapped her hand in the direction of the world at large. "Out there somewhere."

All I got from Lav was a shake of his head.

I assumed that Illya's "secret" development deals with petrol probably involved bribing government officials to get oil rights—the kind of corruption that was rampant in third world countries. But why would someone give Illya art? Bribes work the other way.

"What do you think the pieces represented in the deal?" I asked Lav.

"Who knows? Illya knew how to make money. That's all he knew how to do. The only art he cared about was the shape of a woman's body and even that took second place to the figures printed on money. He wasn't a collector, he didn't care about art. He wanted to make money."

It was about as clear in my head as what happened last night when I was making psytrance love.

"Undeveloped," Nadia said.

"Come again?"

"I remember hearing Illya talking to someone about petrol and the pieces. They were talking about a petrol field that hadn't been developed yet." She raised a hand to block my next question. "That's all I know. None of it matters. I have the pieces, you have a buyer. Look at the pieces. Make an offer."

I walked over to examine the artifacts. It didn't surprise me that all three were images from Hindu mythology. Or that one was an obvious fake.

The fake was a statue of the god Hari-Hara. Unlike the Roman god Janus, which had duplicate faces on the same head, Hari-Hara had two different faces: Vishnu, also called Hari, and Siva, called Hara. The effect was called syncretic in art because it was a union of opposing personalities—Vishnu's visage was peaceful and mild because he was worshipped as the protector and preserver of the world and the restorer of moral order, while Siva's countenance was more dynamic because he could be a destroyer and wrathful avenger.

Made of sandstone, about thirty inches high and also mounted on a slab of sandstone, the Hari-Hara had two arms and a broken foot. Despite the typical breakage, it was a magnificent piece that predated the high Angkor period by several centuries, much rarer than an Apsaras or Siva. But I knew instantly it was a fake: I'd seen the original in the Royal Museum in Phnom Penh.

Taksin's work was astonishing. I was surprised though that I couldn't find what I had come to think of as his signature, the little half-moon shape.

Was it possible that this one wasn't made by Taksin . . . that there were two art fraud geniuses working the same turf? It didn't seem likely, considering that the Thai forger's quality of work wasn't the sort that came along too often. Maybe this was made before he started marking them with his signature. Or maybe Illya or whoever sold it to him had somehow managed to get the signature off so only microscopic examination would reveal that the mark had been there.

The second piece was a Brahma. Said to have been born from a golden egg, he created the Earth and all things on it.

Wearing a *sampot,* the distinctive Cambodian sarong, the Brahma sandstone piece had four faces, four arms (one hand missing), and was mounted on a swan.

It pinged legitimate to me. Then I found Taksin's signature.

The third sandstone piece was a bas-relief of Mount Meru, the golden mountain that stood in the center of the universe and was the axis of the world. The home of the gods, an Eastern Mount Olympus, mythical Mount Meru was so high its foothills were the Himalayas. Angkor Wat itself was a representation of the Mount Meru story.

This version, a piece about two feet long and half that wide, could well have been broken off from a long relief over a doorway or along a wall of Angkor.

Again, I found Taksin's signature.

I leaned back and sighed. Poor Taksin—had he been born in the age of kings, he would have been considered a master artist instead of a master criminal.

I left the pieces and took a walk around the pool. Nadia and Lav followed me with their eyes. I wasn't sure what my status would be once I told her that all her artifacts were fakes. Nadia was the claw-out-the-eyes type . . . while Lav would strangle me with piano wire and stuff me into a fifty-gallon barrel to be dumped at the local landfill.

With such pleasant thoughts, I decided not to tell Nadia that all three were fakes.

"Two of the pieces are fakes, but they're so good, I can get you a good price from a collector who doesn't mind buying a fake."

That was the truth—but that meant selling them for thousands of dollars rather than millions.

❖

Nadia's eyes narrowed. "They are all real museum pieces. That's where Illya got them, from a museum. He told me so."

A minute ago she knew nothing about where Illya got them.

"The Brahma and the Mount Meru relief bear the signature of Taksin."

"Taksin? What's Taksin?"

I was disappointed that she didn't recognize the name. "He's a Thai craftsman who's noted for creating museum-quality pieces. He leaves a distinctive mark on his creations."

"How long has he been dead?"

That from Lav. A strange way to approach the subject, but no doubt a reasonable question from the nature of his employers.

"I don't know if he's dead. He's not from the ancient world, if that's what you mean. He lived and worked in Bangkok and has dropped out of sight recently. Maybe terminally."

I had a feeling that if he wasn't already dead, Lav would give him a helping hand to hell.

I gave them a bright smile. "The good news is that the Hari-Hara doesn't have Taksin's signature." This wasn't the time to tell them it was also a fake.

"How much?" Nadia asked.

"It's extremely rare, so rare that I don't think another one like it has been on the market in years."

"We can check on the Internet here."

"I can't surf the Internet. I have to call museums and collectors all over the world." A partial truth—I had to call the museum in Cambodia to find out if the Hari-Hara still was on display. "It's going to take me a few days and I'm flying back to New York tonight. I'll get an offer from my collector on the other two Taksin items and get back to you as to how we should handle the Hari-Hara once I verify its authenticity."

"You mean, museum pieces," Nadia said.

"Right. I'll be in touch. I think my taxi's outside."

I fled, hoping the taxi was waiting.

❖

34

❖

Forged art. Oil billions. Revolution. Cheung's strange offers. None of it made any sense as I mulled it over in the taxi on my way back to the hotel.

I called Detective Anthony and gave him an update, including what I learned about Taksin and his signature. "When I get back to the hotel, I'll have the concierge help me call the Royal Museum in Phnom Penh. I need to get ahold of that curator named Rim Nol and have him check to see if the Hari-Hara is still there."

"It'll be hell getting through. I'll call Ranar and have him check it and give you a call back. You can bet it's there. The word would be out if a piece that valuable got stolen."

"Then there must be another master artist out there making these things."

"Maybe Taksin was paid not to put his signature on it."

He didn't sound impressed with Nadia's connection of art, oil, and political upheaval.

"Just talk," he said. "Probably Illya boasting to his girlfriend that he'd buy her a country."

It took less time for the detective to call Ranar and get back to me than it did for my taxi to crawl through Hong Kong traffic and reach my hotel.

"The Hari-Hara's at the museum. His highness was in the building and personally checked it. Call me when you get back to New York."

I still liked my second artist theory and was curious about what I'd learn if I checked out Taksin for myself in Bangkok.

By the time I reached my hotel, I'd already decided I was going to book a flight to the Thai capital rather than go home with my tail between my legs—or back to Phnom Penh empty-handed.

THE WOMAN AT THE concierge desk assisted me in arranging a flight to Bangkok. She pretended not to notice that I was wearing a cocktail dress before noon.

I put my carry-on, my sole piece of luggage, on the bed and started cramming everything in, pressing down to get in the new things I'd bought, when I felt something hard. An object was wedged in the layers of the soft material of the carry-on.

A short line of stitching looked different than the regular, obviously machine-made stitching on the luggage. I used a fingernail file to open it up, reached in, and pulled out something and gasped—the jade Buddha Jimmy Cheung had tried to literally give away.

A piece of paper was there, too: a bill of sale from Cheung Dragon Antiques. U.S. $20,000.00. Cash. Stamped onto the receipt in bloodred ink was "REGULATED ANTIQUITY—NOT FOR UNLICENSED EXPORT."

My heart jackhammered.

The jade Buddha came with Chinese prison stripes.

No way would it have gotten by airport security. I would have been taken out of the security line, turned over to the police, and not seen the light of day till I was old and gray. My hands shook as I held it.

Son of a bitch. That little prick Cheung. He had set me up.

But why?

I shook my head. Why didn't matter at the moment. I had to get rid of the jade—fast. The Red Chinese didn't have a sense of humor about Westerners smuggling out their cultural history. Thoughts like no right to an attorney, wasting away in jail awaiting trial, sharing a cell with criminals who I couldn't even communicate with, flew through my head.

I put the piece in a plastic bag and went into the hallway intending to drop it into the trash bag hanging on a maid's cart, but I hesitated outside my door. The maid had come out of a room and looked askance at me. I smiled and shook my head and stepped back inside.

I couldn't trash the jade Buddha. The little guy had survived centuries of war and storm and manhandling and it was still exquisite. Besides, it was a revered religious object. It would be a crime for it to be crushed in a landfill. I couldn't take it with me and couldn't leave it in my room to be found.

The obvious thing to do was turn it over to the police. Anonymously, of course.

I got the address of police headquarters in the phone book, then stuck the Buddha in my purse and headed for the elevators and checkout.

At the concierge's desk, I waited while she dug up a manila envelope and what I estimated was enough stamps. I retreated into a ladies room, addressed the envelope to the police, wiping my fingerprints off the envelope and statuette, and went out onto the street and grabbed a taxi to the airport. At the airport, I picked up my ticket and boarding pass for Bangkok and deposited the Buddha in a mailbox.

As I sat in the waiting area for my plane, I tapped the floor with a nervous foot, wishing it was Jimmy Cheung's face. The reasons for his strange mannerisms were apparent: Someone had hired him to set me up. Or maybe he did it because I was getting too close to some rich and dirty scheme he was engineering. I opted for the first reason. I had a list of candidates wanting to screw me, and number one on the list was Bullock. It would be right up the alley of a man who set up phony robberies. And Cheung had handled the jade with a handkerchief so my fingerprints wouldn't be smeared.

Obviously, someone thought I knew something . . . or was getting close to finding out. I just wished I knew what it was.

I didn't breathe a sigh of relief until we were in the air and miles high.

I wondered what new challenges faced me in Bangkok.

❖

35

❖

Bangkok, Thailand

People . . . motorcycles . . . cars . . . buses . . . chaos . . . turmoil . . . noise . . . engine exhaust. I felt as if I were back in Phnom Penh, but the Thai capital was much bigger and vibrated even more with rich and poor, monks and Mercedes, ancient temples and modern skyscrapers.

It was everything I imagined and nothing I expected.

The city was dirty, crowded, violent—but with rare beauty, infinitely more interesting than America or Europe.

My guidebook said the official name of the city was "City of Angels." Not unlike the infamous city on California's coast, it was huge—seven or fourteen million, depending on who was counting.

Like Phnom Penh, the people were beautiful in form and essence. Physically attractive—copper-toned skin, large walnut eyes, slender, firm muscles. It was rare to see anyone obese as I took a taxi in from the airport.

And there was pathos. The children weren't just too skinny, they were mature in ways that no child should be. Kids ten or twelve years old were already responsible for their own survival. What a terrible thing, I thought. A child shouldn't have to survive by their wits.

I had to admit that despite the third world qualities of Bangkok and Phnom Penh, there was cultural magic to both of them that I loved. I was a diehard romantic when it came to exotic locales.

Learning about the fascinating art and experiencing the cultures of the Far East was an exciting new encounter that would prove useful in the future when I dealt with Asian art.

Now . . . if I could just keep my head above water financially and stay alive long enough to use some of this exciting new knowledge.

To find Taksin, the King of Art Forgery, the most obvious place to start would be with art dealers. Like Hong Kong, the Thai capital was a world-class venue for tourist junk and antiquities. With thousands of dealers I could spend weeks or months before I got a hit. And after being framed by a dealer in Hong Kong, I was in no mood to mentally arm wrestle with another dealer.

A cop who dealt with art fraud would be another choice, but finding one in a country where art fraud wasn't necessarily illegal—as long as it was practiced on foreigners—would not be easy. And I wouldn't trust a cop any more than an art dealer.

I quickly eliminated museum curators. I had become a curator after earning my stripes through buying, selling, and appraising art, but most curators were university types who knew little about how the market really operated. They were too scholarly, had too much of an esoteric relationship with their museum pieces to give me a tip about where to buy forgeries.

That boiled down to the real experts on the underbelly of just about everything in a city: taxi drivers and hotel concierges. Between them, most were able to direct you to a fine dinner, a good play, an "escort" service . . . and hopefully the best place to buy art fakes.

After checking into a tourist-class hotel because I didn't have to impress anyone, I made the rounds of concierges at the best hotels where the high-roller art collectors would stay.

I hit pay dirt at my third stop and got the name of a taxi driver who spoke English and an appointment to have him pick me up and take me to dealers.

"I'm not a tourist," I told the cabbie after he picked me up. "I'm looking for a particular person. Find his shop and I'll pay you well."

It took all day with the cabbie getting out and talking to dealers, but he finally found it. I couldn't read the name written in Thai but I knew right off this was the right place: A small symbol, the half-circle I called Taksin's signature, was also on the sign.

The only person in the shop was a rather forlorn old woman. I used the driver to ask her questions. We started by letting her know I would pay her for information.

Taksin was gone, that much came out in a burst of Thai immediately. Not just gone, but taken, leaving behind a dead friend, several weeks ago. Coming back from a festival, she had seen him being taken to a van and had found his friend's body.

"She says Cambodians came and took the shop owner and killed his friend. The police were paid to look the other way."

She rattled off something else and he said, "An American or European, too."

"Helped the Cambodians?"

"He was the boss man, but she doesn't know what he was, just that he was a white foreigner."

I had two immediate candidates. Kirk and Bullock.

I tapped my hair. "What color hair did the foreigner have? Dark like mine and yours or blond?"

Blond was the response. My heart sank. Kirk had blond hair. I tried to pin down more description but all she said was that the "boss man" was a white foreigner with light-colored hair.

"She hasn't heard from or seen Taksin since?"

"Not since that night."

I asked whether she knew which art dealers Taksin made pieces for.

After querying her, the driver shook his head. "For a long time he worked for Bangkok dealers, but lately worked only for Cambodians."

"Do the Cambodians have a local shop?"

No shop that she knew of; the only thing the woman seemed to know was that they were Cambodians. As traditional enemies of Thais, she had a few choice words for them that the driver told me he couldn't translate.

I pointed up at the "signature" on the sign. "Ask her what that means."

"It's a begging bowl. Taksin had been a monk."

❖

A begging bowl. How appropriate for a Buddhist monk.

"She says that his work was so good, that if he didn't sign them, no one could tell that they weren't real."

Unfortunately, his work was so "real" it may have cost him his life.

I paid off the driver and the old woman and meandered in a brown study through the Thieves Market, shaking my head at hustlers as I made my way in the direction of my hotel.

When I witnessed Kirk smuggling Khmer artifacts, I felt like someone had kicked me in the stomach. Now that he might be involved in murder . . .

I wondered if Taksin was still alive. Good chance that he was. They could have killed him when they killed his friend. Instead they had grabbed him because he had something they wanted. Maybe nothing more than his talent. A man who could create a multimillion-dollar piece of art from a chunk of cheap stone with a hammer and chisel would be an asset for crooks who could market the pieces.

Who "they" were was still a puzzle to me, but Kirk had too many strikes against him: a blond-haired foreigner with connections to Khmer art smuggling, he was a perfect fit for the "boss man." I just wished I had had a picture to show the woman.

I tried fitting the pieces together.

Kirk, Bullock, and some unnamed Cambodians were stealing Khmer art and smuggling it out of the country. At some point they realized Taksin was capable of making pieces that were much more valuable than the ones they stole. And not only more valuable, but far less risky than smuggling them.

It made sense and no sense at all.

What bothered me was that I couldn't see Kirk involved in both smuggling and dealing with Illya's faked pieces. It took two different talents. Hacking through the jungle to rob Khmer tombs fit Kirk's soldier of fortune personality. Working with the Jimmy Cheungs in Hong Kong, New York, and London was more of a ruthless gentleman's game played by people who spoke art. Bullock, scum that he was, spoke the right language.

Kirk and Bullock. They would make a perfect pair. Kirk the acquisition man—and enforcer when necessary—Bullock the marketer.

I felt I had put more pieces of the puzzle together, even though there were still a lot of empty spaces on the board. I needed to know more about Bullock and what he did in the Russian Market. And I still had some questions for Rim Nol, the curator. I believed he knew a great deal more than he had revealed. I kept thinking about a forger needing to closely examine museum pieces besides photographing them. You couldn't fake a great work of art from a snapshot.

I had to get back to Phnom Penh—and this time not let anyone know I was coming.

Bourey's horrible death lay heavy on my mind as I bought a ticket back to the Cambodian capital. I didn't think his spirit would rest while his killers remained free and unnamed.

Phnom Penh

36

❖

I checked back into the Raffles Le Royal. I liked the hotel because it wasn't in the heart of the government area where Kirk and Bullock's favorite drinking hole—the Foreign Correspondents' Club—was located. And I felt safe there.

Now that I was back in the fire from the frying pan, I needed a plan.

Nol was in a position to give access to the Siva. Or knew who did. But he didn't strike me as the type to take a leading role in an art conspiracy. For sure, something was bothering him. Maybe he was feeling guilty. That was my impression—a guy who had done something he regretted but had no control over it.

My instincts screamed that he was a reluctant participant. Someone who had been ordered to let Taksin copy the piece or at least told to look the other way.

Ranar also had the power and position to get the Siva into Taksin's hands for duplicating. He was a high official in a small country noted for its political corruption. The Killing Fields were history, but police and military corruption were still rampant. If I found out he was involved, I'd get back to New York fast and make my accusations from there.

❖

I obviously couldn't just waltz into the Royal Museum and start cross-examining Nol.

I decided on a little deception.

THE NEXT MORNING I arranged with the concierge to join a tour group going to the museum. Wearing dark glasses, an oversized sun hat, and a poncho, I carried an umbrella for both protection from the merciless sun and to hide under. I felt confident that I blended into the group of teachers from Iowa.

Once I was in the museum, I slipped the tour guide a twenty-dollar bill and asked her to find Rim Nol for me.

While I waited I walked over to the Hari-Hara. A beautiful piece. And completely indistinguishable from the knockoff Nadia had in her possession. I'd need a magnifying glass and more time to make a real comparison, but I had to shake my head in amazement at the work of two great master artists: Taksin, a modern forger, and a craftsman whose name we didn't know and the one who had created the museum piece a thousand years ago. Both were geniuses.

The tour guide came back and reported that Rim Nol had not reported to work that morning. "He's out sick."

My gut told me something was wrong. And it scared the hell out of me. I suddenly felt alone and vulnerable. And paranoid.

I left the building.

Getting sick when I was about to use him to expose a multimillion-dollar art fraud ring was too convenient. I felt sick myself. My stomach curled into a hard tight knot.

How bloody stupid of me to come here alone! Did I really think I could come back here and set the country on its head? A country with an unparalleled modern history of violence? Was I that naïve?

As I hurried out to the street from the museum to grab a taxi, a policeman suddenly appeared on each side of me.

"What do you want?" I asked.

Their response was in Cambodian, gibberish to me as they grabbed my arms and steered me to a car at the curb. They opened the rear door and pushed me inside.

Bullock was in the backseat.

"Please don't scream or try to jump out and get run over by other cars." He pulled a gun out of a side pocket just to show me he had it. "I shot a water buffalo once, you know."

"That was very brave of you. I hear you pick on small children, too. Did you ever look in the mirror and wonder if the existence of a creature like you isn't a good argument for the nonexistence of God?"

He twisted in the seat and jabbed his gun under my ear.

"Don't confuse me with someone who you can bandy words with. I'd like to blow your fuckin' stupid brains out—and I'll do so as soon as I find out what you know."

He was right—I had stupid brains and a stupid mouth to go with them. I'm lucky he didn't permanently shut my mouth by shoving a gun in between my teeth and pulling the trigger. But that might still be in the cards.

The car took us to the back of Sinn's shop near the Russian Market. Bullock hustled me inside the shop and into a dark room. A little light came from a crack in the wooden shutters.

He left the room, but I knew he would come back. He wanted answers from me. And then he'd kill me. Getting a preamble that I'd be murdered after I talked implied one thing—fessing up and dying would be less painful and more welcome than what he planned to do to me if I didn't cooperate. He enjoyed inflicting pain, and would enjoy hearing me beg for him to stop. And I'd probably fill all his expectations as he applied pain.

I'm going to die.

The realization got me on my feet as I felt around in the dark for a weapon. I found nothing, but cut my finger on a piece of cracked glass on a display case. I used my shoe to knock off a bigger piece of glass, then wrapped my handkerchief around a wedge of glass with a sharp point. Not much of a weapon against a man with a gun, but it was all I had.

Hours later, Bullock came in with no gun in hand, but he was a man, bigger and stronger than me. He probably enjoyed thinking that he was giving me a sporting chance to fight back before he strangled me or whatever he had in mind.

He came close and I backed up. His thin purple lips spread in an ugly grin of power and contempt as he pulled a pair of pliers out of his pocket and slowly opened and closed them in front of my face.

"I have questions to ask you. Don't give answers I don't like." He put his free hand on my breast and I jerked back, hitting the wall behind me—He snapped the pliers at eye level again. "You'd be surprised what these will pull off. Eyes, nose, teeth—"

"You sick bastard."

My hand shot up and jammed the jagged glass into the flesh of his throat under his chin. He screamed and staggered back, blood spurting out and onto me from his jugular vein. I ran past him and through the door that led into the shop and out to the marketplace.

It was dark and a downpour had erupted. Most of the shops were closed and I didn't dare run into an open one screaming that they call 911. I not only couldn't speak the language, but the men who had helped kidnap me were policemen.

I hurried through the marketplace, buttoning my poncho and pulling the hood over my head, hoping the rain was washing away the blood.

My most pressing thought right now was getting to the airport and taking the next plane out of here, no matter where it went. But first I had to get to the hotel and check out so I could get my passport back from the front desk.

I grabbed a ride on a moto until I saw that the police had blocked the street. I quickly got off and went inside the first place available.

❖

37

❖

Half an hour later

A damaged person. That described me perfectly as I lay in a whorehouse with a naked masseuse hovering over me.

I hadn't bothered reading the sign that offered "exotic massages." And paid twice over for one.

In a strange city, a strange country, terrified of murderers and no where to turn . . . when the girl caressed my nipple, it got hard.

I was truly a damaged person.

She came down and kissed me on the lips, cupping her hand against my breast. I gently pushed her back and sat up.

"Sweetie, you're a nice person, but it's time for me to go."

She stared at me with sad eyes.

Poor thing. She lived a cruel life, knowing nothing but poverty, misery, and abuse her entire young life. She was probably lucky to be even alive—in many poor Asian countries, girl babies were murdered at birth because they weren't considered as valuable as males. When girls her age in the West were worrying about whether they'd get breast enhancements for high school graduation and what to wear for college, she had to worry about getting food and shelter.

Thoughts of not casting the first stone, knowing that but for the grace of God go any of us, and never complaining about having no shoes because there are people with no feet—homey little adages my mother was fond of saying anytime she saw me wasting something when I was a teenager—flew through my head as I dug in my wallet after I got dressed.

I calculated how much I'd need to get out of Dodge, including paying the madam, and gave the girl ten twenties. I gave her a quick hug.

She stared at me in complete puzzlement.

"Take care."

I paused at the door. She had rolled up the bills and was inserting them into her vagina, no doubt to hide them from the bitch outside.

THE MADAM WAS STANDING at the end of the corridor as I stepped out of the room. Two policemen were talking with her.

She pointed at me.

They were the same ones who had grabbed me at the museum for Bullock.

38

❖

The officers also didn't speak English, but I didn't need a Berlitz course in Cambodian to tell me I was in extreme danger. And helpless. They had guns and badges.

I was strangely calm as I sat in the backseat of a police car moving through heavy traffic. Maybe calm was the wrong word. More like dazed.

The rain had stopped. Oppressive heat sneaked back in.

The backseat smelled of piss and vomit, fermented by the hot-wet climate. Under ordinary circumstances, I'd be imaging all kinds of nasty critters crawling on me, but I was too numb to get excited about that, either.

I had tried to cleverly press the recall button on my cell phone to contact Detective Anthony almost the moment I was in the backseat, but an officer heard the telltale beep and took it from me.

Resting my head back on the seat, I closed my eyes and prayed. *God help me!* It's not the first time I prayed when I had problems. I was one of those people who forgot about religion unless I was in dire need of divine intervention. I didn't think I was a bad person. For sure, I had screwed up my life royally, but not by trying to hurt anyone. I only killed one person and he was a pervert who hurt children and animals. My only regret was that someone else hadn't killed Bullock long before he laid hands on his first victim. I hoped he was reborn a worm in a boiling cesspool in hell.

The clouds thinned out. I squinted out the window and saw water. We were on a road that paralleled the river. Heading north, I thought, upriver, though with several rivers coming into the city I wasn't sure what the waterway was called at this point. Chantrea and I had headed north out of the city for the Angkor trip, but this road didn't look familiar.

"Where are you taking me?" I asked.

The cop in the front passenger seat turned and gave me a deadpan look but said nothing.

I tried the door handle and it moved loosely but didn't open the door. "Take me to the American embassy."

The passenger said something to the driver and I caught the word American. They laughed. He understood my request, all right.

Panic started mounting in me. Why weren't they taking me to a police station? Were they taking me out to a deserted area to shoot me?

The police car turned off the paved road and went down a dirt track that brought us closer to the river. My imagination went wild and I saw myself being murdered, my body weighed down and dumped in the river.

The driver flashed his lights on and off three times and then flicked the high beam three times. A spotlight from a boat flashed back three times. I made out the boat in the car's headlight. It was large and military-looking—a *gunboat*, the kind I'd seen on tropical rivers in movies. The boat dwarfed the small fisherman's pier it was beside.

A small shack with an abandoned appearance was nearby. No lights showed from the open doorway and glassless window.

Through the window on the left side of the car I could see dim lights on the hillside that bordered the road. The terrain rose steeply from the road. What I assumed were houses or a single very large house was several hundred yards away. Too far away for me to shout to for help even if I wasn't terrified that the cops would beat me to death with their clubs.

The police car pulled up next to the pier where two men waited. The men wore military field uniforms, the mottled camouflage pattern in greens and browns called battle dress. I didn't see any military insignia on the uniforms or the boat; it was too dark to make out details. One thing I did notice—the soldiers or sailors, if they were in fact military, wore sloppy, ill-fitting uniforms. They didn't have the sharp appearance of the soldiers I'd seen on the streets. One of them had a pistol in his waistband. I would have expected a military person to carry a pistol in a holster.

The gunboat had the same mottled color as the uniforms.

The two policemen got out of the car and left me sitting inside. The four men stood together, passed around cigarettes and a bottle, and talked, once in a while looking at me and laughing. Jesus. Why did I come back to this country? I should have stayed out and communicated my suspicions long distance.

Finally the officer who had been in the passenger seat opened my door.

"Get out."

Perfect English. And I'd bet he knew much more.

One of the men in military dress propelled me toward the boat. Were they going to take me out onto the deep part of the river and dump me with weights?

"Let me go! I've called the American Embassy—"

He pulled a pistol from his waistband and shoved it in my face and said something in Cambodian. I didn't need an interpreter. He led me down the short pier and to the side of the boat and indicated I was to climb up the ladder and onto the boat. Three men lined up on the boat stared down at me.

As I went up the ladder he grabbed my rear end with both hands and squeezed, setting off howls of laughter from all of them.

I lost it completely. I screamed and kicked him in the face with the heel of my shoe. He cursed as I scooted up the ladder and onto the boat.

A crewman grabbed my arm and led me to a companionway leading down inside the boat while another man went ahead of me. As I came down, he grabbed my body and ran his hands over my breasts. I hit him as hard as I could with my fist but he pulled me in close and started lifting up my dress.

The second man came down and pulled him away from me, an argument quickly ensuing. The masher, who had a big grin with a wide gap of missing teeth, found it all very funny. He was drunk and stunk of alcohol and nastier things.

I was pushed through an open hatch and into a small cabin. The watertight bulkhead door was shut behind me, leaving me in the dark. I felt the wall next to the door with my fingers and turned on a light switch. The light barely took the edge off the darkness, but it was enough for me to see that I'd been put into a small cabin that was being used as a storeroom.

Wood crates with writing in a foreign language that looked like Russian were stacked inside. The stamped-on picture of a weapon, the type they call AK47s, was on the crates. I lifted the lid of a crate. It was filled with canned food, not rifles.

A small, one-person built-in bunk with a soiled blanket and no mattress occupied almost half of the tiny cabin's space. With crates stacked up against the other wall, I barely had room to stand.

The walls of the cabin were metal but thin enough for me to hear laughing and shouting. I turned the handle to the door slowly and opened it an inch. The group of men were gathered around a table playing cards and drinking and howling with laughter.

My fear level soared when it occurred to me that they were probably wagering to see who was going to rape me first. Rape and then murder me. I wondered if these men had AIDS. I read it was common in third world countries where store-bought sex was readily available. But what did it matter if they were going to kill me anyway?

There was no way out of the room. The porthole was too small to even put my head through. It was open and let in a tiny bit of night air, but not enough to cool down the oven of a cabin.

The door had to be pushed open into the room for anyone to enter. I needed to jam the handle and block the door. The crates of cans could block the door if they were in line one after the other rather than piled on top of each other.

I tried to lift the top crate but it was too heavy. I frantically unloaded the crate and set it empty against the door and refilled it. I unloaded half of the next one and slid it off the top and onto the floor, against the first one. By the time I got the third one in place the laughter outside had become a howl.

I emptied the final crate and wedged it up under the door handle. I had just gotten it into place when someone pounded on the door and yelled. It sounded like Toothless to me, no doubt announcing he had come to claim his prize.

The door handle jiggled and someone banged against it. It held.

The laughter stopped and the pounding and cursing became violent. Toothless wasn't too happy about not being able to get in. Soon I had the impression that more than one person was putting their weight against the door.

After more pounding and kicking and grumbling, the men appeared to get tired of their game because the noise stopped.

I didn't know how good Russian rifles were, but for sure, the heavy wood crates were built like Sherman tanks. Filled with canned foods, the door was not going to budge. The only way the men were going to get in was to blow the door down. Or shoot off the hinges?

I was pretty sure that whoever had arranged for my kidnapping was planning to have me murdered. It looked like the preliminaries were going to be pretty brutal, too.

I moved the dirty blanket off the bunk and sat down. The walls were wet from the humidity. The room smelled . . . not from human stink, but river smells baked by the tropical sun into the boat's metal-like paint—river water polluted for an eon by rotting vegetation, dead and live fish, and the excretions of man and beast, come together to suffocate me in the oven-hot cabin.

Sweat rolled off me. The country was so hot and wet, I had to wonder if wood even rusted.

The boat rocked and knocked and scraped against the pier. The motion of the boat and the stale, stinking air got me queasy.

I heard a noise on the outside of the boat and a body came into view and then a leering face at my porthole. Toothless had been lowered down to porthole level. He shoved a leather sack through the porthole. The sack fell to the floor.

Something in the sack wiggled as I stared down at it. A green head came out, followed by a long, slithering body. *Snake!*

I screamed and grabbed the empty crate blocking the door handle and threw it open side down over the snake. I jumped on the crate and came face-to-face with the toothless seaman who howled with laughter as he was pulled back up.

❖

Squatting on the crate, my heart jackhammering, my breath barely coming, I had to think about what to do, but my thinking wasn't coming out straight.

It was a joke, I told myself, they were just laughing and having fun. Cruel fun. If they had wanted to kill me, they could have done it right away. Unless they had put me in the room to take turns—

I had to stop it. If I gave in to panic and fear, I was doomed. I stood up on the crate and took in gulps of air through the porthole. *It's okay*, I told myself. *I can handle it.* Whatever happens, I can handle it. They're just drunk and playing grab-ass with a helpless woman.

I knew they were not the ones who had ordered me to be kidnapped. That had to be Ranar. That only made sense. He had the power.

I leaned back, trying to get my heart and breathing under control. For now I was safe from the snake.

Snug as a bug in a rug, my mother would say as she tucked me into bed when I was little.

"Snug as a bug in a rug," I whispered.

But what would happen when they made me open the door? It was inevitable that at some point I would have to open the door. If Toothless was lowered back down to my porthole with a gun in hand, I'd have no choice.

At the moment though, I was more concerned about the snake under the crate.

39

❖

Kirk was at the Foreign Correspondents' Club exchanging war stories about the Cambodian jungle with a *National Geographic* photographer when he received a message from Bullock to come to Sinn's store near the Russian Market. The message had nothing more than the numbers 911 and a scrawled letter B.

That meant Bullock and trouble. They used 911 as a code whenever there was trouble. Trouble in their business usually meant that an honest police official had seized one of their "exports" or, much more likely, a dishonest one was demanding much more money than he was worth.

There was another possibility and it disturbed him. The FCC bartender had told him that when he was coming onto his shift earlier he had seen Maddy on the street.

Maddy was supposed to be gone, back to New York, anywhere but Cambodia where she had stirred up trouble for herself. He hoped Bullock's message didn't concern her.

Kirk finished his drink, trying to wash down the bad taste in his mouth with the alcohol. He hated dealing with Bullock. Not because they were coconspirators in a smuggling ring—Kirk was a realist not to judge himself any less culpable than other crooks—but because Bullock was a slime.

Foreigners hung around Cambodia for different reasons—most to make money, legal or illegally, a few humanitarian types to help the poor and sick. But Bullock hadn't come just to make a dishonest buck; he took advantage of the loose enforcement of sex laws. Even at that, if the creep had stuck to adults, Kirk would have found him more amusing than repulsive.

He left the bar and boarded a moto for the trip to the market.

Even though Kirk was Swedish, he was born in Dutch Amsterdam where his mother had been a prostitute. He wasn't sure if the Swede listed on his birth certificate was actually his father. Kirk tried to find the man once, but discovered he had a criminal record and had dropped out of sight years earlier.

Amsterdam wasn't a town filled with Dutch people wearing funny hats and wood shoes. It was an international city, vibrating with people from the former far-flung Dutch colonial empire; a sex and drug capital of Europe, its citizens were both morally conservative but socially liberal and worked hard to regulate both industries. It was a place where growing up on the streets gave him an education about people, places, sin, and survival.

When Kirk was nineteen, he moved to Sweden and joined the Swedish army to escape a problem he got himself into in Amsterdam. He had stabbed a drug dealer who was beating up a woman. The woman was a druggie, but since his own mother had spent much of her life abused by men, Kirk instinctively rose to the defense of women.

Punching the thief who grabbed Maddy's purse had not been planned—he acted as he always did with women. People who got to know him—and very few did—quickly understood that he had an old fashioned, chivalrous attitude toward women. And he never paid for sex.

KIRK FOUND BULLOCK LYING on his back. He stood by the cot and stared down at the antiques dealer. The man's face was wet from sweat and pasty white, his breathing shallow. Bullock's neck was heavily bandaged.

"You look like death warmed over."

Bullock's eyes fluttered open. "The fuckin' cunt. She tried to kill me."

"Where's Maddy?"

"Ranar's got her. General Chep's camp. Ranar will dispose of her after he checks out a couple things."

"Checks out what?"

"She told the cops who picked her up that she'd called the American embassy. Ranar doesn't buy it, but he needs to wait to see if the embassy asks about her." He touched the bandage around his neck. "Fucking bitch. If I had the strength I'd get my pliers red hot and pinch off every fucking piece of flesh on her body. I'd—"

Kirk cut him off. "What else does Ranar want from her?"

"She's been talking to that curator, Rim. Ranar doesn't trust him. Thinks he snoops around too much. He wants to know what the two of them know. And who they've talked to."

"What'd you do to her?"

"Nothing, I was just getting started when the bitch cut my throat with a piece of glass. We caught her at the museum trying to contact Rim."

"Where's Rim?"

"Crocodile meat by now, probably."

"You killed him?"

"Ranar's got him."

"Why the 911 message?"

Bullock tried to get up, but fell back down with a cry of pain.

"You have to get me out. Help me into your car and take me across the border. An American woman can't go missing without questions being asked. People in New York will know why she came here."

"That's *your* problem."

"*Our* problem. Ranar isn't going to kill an American woman and a museum curator without cleaning house afterward. He'll make sure there's no leaks back to him and that means we'll join Rim and the woman in a croc's belly."

He reached up and grabbed hold of Kirk's shirt.

"He'll get you, don't think he won't. Ranar will have his military and police friends kill us both and frame us for the woman's death. We have to get out of the country. Now. Help me up."

"Why should I help you?"

"Because I'll have your ass burned. I make a call to Ranar and you'll be the first to go."

Kirk shook his head as he drew the knife from his hip sheath. "I can stand working with a thief, maybe even a murderer, but you're a sick pervert. I've always wanted to strap a land mine to your ass and set it off."

Bullock croaked. "Too late to cut my throat, your fucking bitch did it already. Look, I have more pieces, better ones than you know about. I kept some aside, I'll share them with you. You don't want to kill me. I'll make you rich. I have money—"

"I'm just going to make sure you don't bother any more kids."

The scream was smothered by a group of chanting Buddhist monks walking outside with their clanging cymbals.

40

❖

I woke up when I fell off the crate sideways and the crate skidded on the floor and moved away from me. I quickly got back on the crate, breathless.

It was dark in the cabin, too damn dark to see a dark green snake but I didn't see anything moving. In a low voice, I asked, "Are you still in there?"

I almost went off again, this time falling forward as the boat started moving. I looked out the porthole. Dawn was breaking and we were moving away from land, heading upriver. The sound of the engines and horns of other boats came through the porthole.

From what Kirk had told me, the river had sandbars and floating hazards. That was probably why we didn't move last night.

Morning and I was still alive. My watch had stopped working. It couldn't take the heat and humidity, either.

The cabin was unbearably hot and stifling. Little air came through the small porthole. Ironically, my skin felt dry and inflamed. I had sweated all night but had nothing to replenish the moisture. I'd drink river water if I had it. Or at least soak in it.

I hung on to the porthole to keep my balance. A queasy feeling hit me again as the boat rocked. I sucked in gulps of air hoping that would help but I couldn't stay upright. I was going to pass out.

I sat back down on the crate but I couldn't take that either. When the boat rolled in the wakes of other boats, I swayed back and forth, ready to fade. My throat and body were parched. What I needed was fresh cool air and water.

I managed to get myself off the crate and collapse on the bunk. I didn't care about the dirty blanket or the damn snake. If the snake was strong enough to lift the crate, it would still have to climb up to the bunk. I wondered if snakes could climb. Did they go up trees? I didn't know and couldn't figure it out.

As I lay feeling miserable, it finally occurred to me that there might be liquids in the tin cans.

I willed myself upright and looked down. The empty crate was still upside down. I guess the snake was still under there since I didn't see it wiggling around anywhere.

I rummaged through a case of cans. Damn. Leave it up to the Russians. Not a single lid with a pop top. And no can opener.

I picked a can that showed small potatoes on the label. They had to be canned in water. I banged the lid on the corner of a crate until I popped a hole and liquid shot out. Just like breaking a hole in a coconut.

Pretty starchy liquid, but it tasted like chilled Dom Pérignon champagne to me.

Juice from a can of peas was next. Then diced carrots.

I felt a little revitalized, but still miserable.

Looking out the window as the hours passed, I saw mostly brown water and green foliage. We passed an occasional fishing boat and larger boats that I took to be ferries, and houses on stilts near the riverbank. Finally I couldn't see a shoreline and I assumed we had been on the river called Tonle Sab and now were on the big lake called Tonle Sap. Chantrea had said the lake was huge, the largest in Southeast Asia. When it's so wide you can't see a shoreline, it might as well be an ocean.

The ferry landing for Siem Reap and the Angkor site was near the north end of the lake.

Was I being taken back to Angkor?

❖

Heat and stifling air in the cabin put me in a stupor. I lay in a daze, dragging myself up occasionally to break a hole in a can for the liquid, then lying back down, hot and miserable. It was late afternoon when I felt the boat slowing down.

We were heading for land. All I could see was a shoreline of green foliage. At first I thought I saw logs lying on shore, but I realized they were crocs. Common enough on TV and in movies, but up close in real life they were savage, brutal, prehistoric-looking creatures. My line of vision out the porthole was limited. When the boat stopped, it rubbed against what I assumed was a pier.

I knew some of my questions were about to be answered. And also some of my fears. I had no weapons and no way out. Resigned that the devil would soon be knocking on my door, I sat back on the bunk with my arms wrapped around my knees.

I WAS DOZING AGAIN when I heard the knock on the door.

"Open the door." The command was in English with a heavy Cambodian accent. "Miss, open the door or I will put tear gas through the porthole." He spoke the words slowly.

I could close the porthole, but the glass could be easily broken.

Pushing aside the crates, I opened the door. The man confronting me wore a neatly pressed military uniform. As I stepped out, I started to black out and the man gave me his arm to steady me.

He let me sit on a chair and gave me a drink from a plastic bottle. I downed it eagerly.

"Can you walk?"

I nodded.

He helped me up. I was in the galley and dining area. He guided me to a sink and I washed my face and soaked my head with cold water. I'm sure I looked like hell and I felt even worse.

When the officer led me to the companionway ladder to the top, the toothless bastard who tortured me came down and grinned at me as I stepped by him.

"He tried to kill me with a snake," I said.

The officer shrugged. "It belongs to the boat. Eats rats. It is just a little poisonous."

"Oh, good, then I'd only be a little dead if it had bitten me."

Out on deck I stopped to get my balance. I was still faint and queasy, but the fresh air, as hot and wet as it was, felt like a cool breeze after life in a hot tin can. Clouds were roiling overhead, getting ready to dump an impromptu downpour.

A makeshift pier of bamboo poles strapped to empty fifty-gallon petrol cans ran a hundred feet to the shore. I saw nothing on shore except a small opening in dense jungle foliage. An army truck was backed up to the pier. Cases of supplies were already being unloaded.

"Where are you taking me?"

"To the general."

"What general?"

"General Chep."

"What's he general of?"

The officer waved at the jungle.

"All this. Very powerful."

Which told me nothing. "You're not regular army."

"We are patriotic army."

"Why has your general kidnapped me?"

He took my arm. "We go now."

"I called the American embassy."

I wanted to threaten them with something and that flew out of my mouth.

He ignored me.

We crossed the pier and made our way around the truck to a jeep. The rain started by the time he got the jeep moving. It didn't have a top and the downpour soaked us, mercifully giving me a drenching that my hot, sticky body and stinking clothes sorely needed.

Warlord was the first thing that came to my mind about General Chep. Both Kirk and Chantrea said generals, most of whom were once officers going back to the days of the Khmer Rouge, were still entrenched in rural areas, ruling the regions like old-time warlords.

The warlords were involved in the smuggling trade of both Khmer art and drugs. It gave them cash for arms and for paying their armies. But what did one want with me?

In my own mind, I had thought of Ranar as a white-collar criminal, the type of wealthy bastard who could buy himself out of a mess or spend a short time in prison for having ripped off tens of millions. Now that I had fought to the death with Bullock and had been kidnapped by a Khmer warlord and transported to a jungle realm by thugs in uniforms, I realized I had stepped on some very dangerous toes. I needed to reappraise my image of Ranar and the situation.

The downpour stopped Cambodian style after a brief deluge but it had felt good. I was strangely calm.

I wondered whether this general might be Bullock's supplier and if so, was he going to burn my feet over a hot fire for killing the bastard.

There were many possibilities and all were bad.

We came into an armed camp and what drew my attention at first wasn't the soldiers and equipment but an incredible structure from the great age of Khmer art: an enormous temple.

Chantrea had said there were thousands of temples and other sites of antiquity in Cambodia, many of them still covered by jungle. The one before me was a behemoth, an enormous edifice erupting from the jungle floor and soaring up to the height of a four- or five-story building and half the length of a football field.

A great stone face, like the dramatic faces at Bayon, the temple complex with Mount Rushmore–type faces, peered solemnly from the structure. The temple had been battered, corroded, and blackened by time, with vines and roots breaking and cracking sections.

The face had the grave countenance of a Buddhist priest rather than the commanding presence of a king.

Unlike the main structures at Angkor, this temple was still mostly covered by the invading jungle. Even the face was partly covered by vines. Only the lower third had been cleared of choking growth. A great strangler fig, similar to the one at Ta Prohm, was mounted at the top of the structure, its canopy top spread over the stonework like an umbrella.

The ancient temple would be hard to spot from an airplane. No doubt the warlord Chep knew that.

The army camp finally drew my attention: bamboo huts, tents, stoves made from split fifty-gallon petrol drums, generators producing electricity with cables running to tents shouldering the bottom of the temple.

Jeeps, civilian cars and compact pickups, artillery pieces, tarps over piles of supplies and equipment, stacks of crates . . . and the soldiers, some old, some young, wearing mismatched uniforms but all in battle dress, some with boots, others wearing sandals, some with ancient faces, boys packing guns that actually kill people when they shouldn't be handling anything more serious than a computer game.

I stared fascinated at the young boys. It was one thing to see grinning twelve- and fourteen-year-olds packing murderous rifles on TV news about terrible events in faraway places and another to have them staring at me as I was driven into the camp.

Once again there was an ambiance about the men, their irregularity of uniforms and lack of discipline that inferred the soldiers were not part of an official army.

I expected to pull up in front of the big tent set against the temple but we drove by it and continued on through the camp and onto a dirt path cut out under a canopy of vines and trees.

A couple hundred yards down the road we came into a clearing. A large, rambling old house that looked half French and half traditional Cambodian sat on a hillock next to a small lake. The house, falling into ruin from age and neglect, was one story with a high-peaked roof and a wide covered porch that appeared to wrap around the entire structure. It looked similar to an old plantation house Chanthra pointed out during our trip to Angkor.

Poles with flags hung from the porch.

The officer pointed at trees. "Rubber when French was here." What was once a rubber plantation was now the headquarters for a warlord.

I thought about Nadia's comment that Illya had acquired his art pieces as part of a deal to finance a revolution. The twenty-two million that the Siva sold for in New York would certainly buy a load of weapons for a rebel group in a small country like Cambodia.

As we pulled up in front of the house, Prince Ranar and a man in a military uniform came out on the porch. The military man was short and well fed with a wrinkled face and some gray in his hair. His uniform appeared much more elaborate than the officer who had driven me. He had a fat cigar in his mouth and small, piercing black eyes. Definitely not an empathetic-looking type.

"General Chep," the officer said, snapping to attention and saluting.

Other than eyes that bore into you, the general's features remained deadpan. Ranar, however, looked like he had eaten something that didn't agree with him.

I pursed my lips and gave Ranar an ugly look. He stared at me like he'd never seen me before.

The officer hurried around and took my arm to steer me toward the porch. It wasn't necessary—I was too mad and scared to keep my mouth shut.

"I'll have you know I called the American embassy and asked for their protection. I've called my contacts in New York. All you're doing by kidnapping me is digging a deeper hole for yourself."

"American embassy?" the general said. He gave Ranar a questioning look.

I didn't know how much English the general understood, but like most educated Cambodians he had probably picked up some out of necessity.

Ranar rattled off something in Cambodian but the general still didn't look happy. I heard him say "American embassy" again. No doubt whatever truce the general had with the government didn't include him offending any foreign governments that were a prime source of economic and military aid to the country.

"The American embassy is going to have you arrested," I said.

"You're a liar. You've called no one," Ranar answered.

True, but the general again ragged on Ranar. The prince was patently uncomfortable with whatever questions were being thrown at him. Some sort of accord seemed to have been reached between the two of them because Ranar directed his attention back to me.

"You should have gone back to New York. You were warned not to come back here, but you had to put your nose into our affairs."

"I was invited here. Remember? Your poor country was being robbed of its national treasures."

"You have gotten yourself involved in matters that don't concern you. Now you will have to pay the penalty."

"So will you. Has he told you that his plans for the revolution aren't much of a secret?" I directed the comment to General Chep but I might as well have slapped him on the face. His hand went to his holstered pistol.

I froze—expecting to be murdered.

❖

I knew immediately I had gone too far and had dug a hole for myself, but I had to give them a reason to keep me alive.

Ranar came off the porch and faced me.

"Tell me what you know—what you *think* you know."

"I know about the Russian and the oil deal. Oil for guns." I was deliberately vague, just throwing out rumor and innuendo in the hopes something stuck. Something did.

"Who else knows this?"

"No one . . . not in person, at least. I sent an e-mail to a friend in New York with an attachment. I told him not to open the attachment unless something happened to me."

The lie rolled off my tongue smoothly, but I wasn't sure if Ranar believed me. Regardless of what he thought, the general must have picked up on what I said because the words "e-mail" and "attachment" got tossed between them. And I heard the name of my hotel spoken.

"We shall check out your story here and in New York," Ranar said.

"I didn't send it from my hotel," I said.

"Where did you send it from?"

"I'm not telling you."

"I don't think you sent an e-mail. Once we verify that, I will deal with you."

"In other words, you're going to murder me at your first opportunity. You are really a despicable traitor—"

His right hand came up and caught me on the side of the face, sending me sprawling as I hit the ground. He didn't stop there. He kicked me in the thigh and I cried out in pain, "You're a filthy pig."

"You're being held for smuggling cultural treasures. I'm shocked that you betrayed my trust and have engaged in criminal activities, but considering your past history, I erred in trusting you."

Ranar stared down at me, calm, sounding as though he had just paid me a compliment about how well I had taken his beating. He turned to the general. I didn't understand the words, but I could tell he was addressing the warlord with his diplomatic self.

More jabbering spewed from the general's mouth, but something Ranar said seemed to satisfy him. I heard again the words American embassy, New York, and the name of my hotel.

A smile appeared on the general's face. Ranar probably told him I'd be shot after they checked my story about calling the American embassy. From the looks of the general, I was sure he'd rather roast my feet over a hot fire. Maybe I was wrong about his concern over the embassy—out in a jungle, he probably could care less about a foreign embassy.

Ranar, on the other hand, with links to the U.N. and residences in New York, Paris, and London, had much more to lose.

The general cracked orders to the officer in Cambodian and the man grabbed my arm and jerked me to my feet. Holding me by the arm, he steered me up the stairs and down the porch at a fast pace. I was barely able to keep my feet under me as he hurried me along. My head was spinning and the side of my face hurt worse than my leg.

He took me around back and off the porch to a hut that had shuttered windows and a door held closed by an steel bar set between large metal supports. He took off the bar, opened the door, and gave me a push through the doorway and slammed the door behind me.

Most of the room was dark, but there was light from a lamp on a table on the other side of the room.

A man seated at the table stared at me, his mouth open in surprise, his eyes wide. He had been working a piece of sandstone with chisel and hammer in hand. He was Thai or certainly Southeast Asian, slender, about thirty.

I stood for a moment, looking at the man and getting used to the light, when I heard the sound of the steel bar being reinserted.

My sudden appearance in the room and the door being barred again signaling that I was obviously a fellow prisoner had left him wide-eyed and speechless.

I had looked for this man in Bangkok and was sure he had been taken to Cambodia.

"Mr. Taksin, I presume."

❖

41

❖

Taksin got up, excitedly jabbering in what I supposed was Thai. I didn't know if he thought I had been sent in to question him . . . or pleasure him.

I held up my hand to stop. "Do you know any English?" Like any good American, I assumed everyone else in the world spoke some English if for no other reason than they heard it so often from movies, television, and songs.

He stopped his outburst and stared at me. Finally he sat back down and gave me a good once-over.

I repeated my question.

"English? Little bit."

"We can go slow."

He stood up as I came to the table.

"You are Taksin?"

He nodded.

"My name is Madison Dupre. I'm an American art investigator. Like you, I'm a prisoner."

"American? Prisoner?" He looked past me to the barred door and then back at me, raising his eyebrows.

American and being held prisoner didn't connect in his world vision, I guess.

"Yes, I'm a prisoner, too. I came to Cambodia to investigate the Siva. You know what I'm talking about? A Siva was sold in New York for a great deal of money. The Siva you made."

He shook his head and rattled off something in Thai.

I got the idea. His English only stretched to things *he* wanted to talk about.

I touched the side of my face. I was already swelling. I didn't need a mirror to know my face was red. "You see this? It's only the beginning. They are going to kill me. *They are going to kill you*." I let that sink in. I knew he understood. "You comprehend kill, murder, don't you? They murdered your friend back in Bangkok. They murdered him when they kidnapped you and brought you here." I nodded down at the sandstone he was working. "They haven't killed you yet because they still need you. But when you are through giving them what they want, you know what they are going to do, don't you?"

He stared down at the table.

He understood.

"Taksin . . . listen to me. They want something from you. I guess that piece you're working on. Once you're through with that, they plan to kill you because you could testify against them."

As I talked, I looked closer at the piece he was working on. There were actually two pieces on the table—he was making a copy of a yaksha, an ill-tempered demigod. The original sat next to his copy. I had seen the original at the National Museum.

I had been right when I told Rim Nol that the forger had to see and handle the actual museum piece. Here it was happening in the flesh. The real artifact had been removed from the museum and brought to a warlord's encampment to be duplicated.

Staring at the artifact and the fake, I had an epiphany. What a dummy I had been! I thought I was the world's greatest art expert and all along I had been fooled by sleight of hand.

My leg hurt and my head felt like someone had used it as a punching bag. A chair was against the wall. I sat down on it.

"I've been wrong all along," I told Taksin. "The art fraud scheme isn't about duplicating museum pieces and passing them off as originals."

He said nothing. His features molded into that deadpan expression that people in the Far East seem able to accomplish. I knew I was hitting a cord. He retreated into our language differences when he didn't want to share information.

"The scheme is infinitely more clever than simple forgery, isn't it? The idea isn't to produce a forgery and sell it, is it?"

Taksin's face told me he was pondering an answer, but before he expressed himself we heard the steel bar being removed. The door flew open and guards shoved an almost naked man into the room. The man took only a step before collapsing on the floor.

I recognized him.

42

❖

I knelt beside Rim Nol. "My God. Who did this to you?" I realized it was a stupid question after I said it.

Dressed only in his underwear, he was bruised and bleeding in a dozen places.

"Khmer Rouge," he said. "They like to torture before they kill. They want me to tell them who else knows what they are up to."

"The Khmer Rouge did this to you?"

He nodded his head as he tried to get up. Taksin helped me get him into a sitting position against a wall.

"Not old reds," he said, "but they're the same. They want to take over the country and kill anyone who doesn't think like they do."

Taksin had a bottle of water on his table. I got it and brought it back to Nol. He held up his hands but couldn't take the bottle—his nails had been ripped off and his fingers were bloody, black, and swollen.

Trying to control my own shaking hands, I held the bottle to let him drink. He took a sip and choked, water and blood coming out of his mouth, down his chin, and onto his chest. He had massive bleeding bruises on his chest and abdomen. I wondered if his internal organs were damaged. The animals who did this to him had tortured him all over. And I knew why they threw him in with us—to scare me. It wasn't necessary, I was already sick from fright. And barely able to keep from breaking down as I stared at poor Nol.

I wanted to comfort and hold him, but I would only hurt him more if I did. I wondered if I was the cause of all this. I tried to hold back my tears but couldn't. "I did this to you! I'm so sorry."

Nol's breathing was labored. He shook his head. "No, no, not you. You don't understand. I knew the museum was being looted." He coughed and it broke into a choke and more blood spilled from his mouth. It took him a moment to recover enough to continue.

"Pieces like the Siva were being taken from the museum by Ranar's command. They would be gone for weeks at a time. I went to the Minister of Culture and told him my suspicions. He instructed me to keep my eyes open and report back to him on everything Ranar did."

I tried to give him water but he choked again. He didn't have to say any more about what happened at the museum. However it happened, Ranar found out Nol was spying. And now the poor man was paying a terrible price for protecting his country's treasures.

Taksin looked at me and shook his head, indicating that Nol would not make it. I didn't know whether Buddhist monks were like Christian religious cadre in terms of caring for the sick and dying, but I suppose he saw death in Nol's injuries. As a Westerner from a rich country, I saw injuries that a triage team at an ER could fix.

Nol got control of himself. "But it has been a mystery to me."

"What's been a mystery?"

"Why," he choked, "steal a museum piece when selling it would expose it as stolen?"

"Oil for guns," I said. "A Russian billionaire was financing a revolution for Ranar. He put up the money for Ranar's revolt in return for getting the concession on oil discoveries that have been made in the Cambodian part of the Gulf of Thailand. But the Russian wasn't certain Ranar's revolt would be successful so he demanded security for his advances."

Nol and Taksin both stared at me. I don't think "security" to them translated as collateral for a loan.

"The Russian gave Ranar money for guns, probably for this General Chep's army."

“Chep was a young Khmer Rouge officer back in the seventies,” Nol said.

I had guessed that. I’d been told the Khmer Rouge was still powerful in rural areas. “But the Russian wanted a guarantee that he would get his money back if he didn’t get the oil concessions. He asked for the most valuable thing Ranar could get his hands on—Khmer antiquities. It had to be only the finest ones because tens of millions of dollars was being advanced. And that meant high-end museum pieces.”

I wasn’t sure they were following my story, but I went on because I was laying it out for myself.

“To get them out of the museum, Ranar had to have them duplicated. That’s where Taksin came in.” I nodded at the former monk. “Ranar had him make duplicates that were good enough to take the place of the originals at the museum. Then Ranar gave the originals to the Russian billionaire, along with some of Taksin’s fakes, obviously represented as real artifacts. But they weren’t given to the Russian to sell. They were just collateral, to hold in case the revolt didn’t work.

“But the Russian was killed and his girlfriend got the museum pieces. She probably knew little about the deal since she had no interest in revolutions and oil. She wanted money and selling the pieces was her way to get it.”

I stopped and stared at them. “We have to get out of here or we’ll all be murdered.”

Taksin shook his head. “Jungle. Snakes. Swamps. No way out. We try, they kill us.”

“They’re going to kill us anyway!”

Nol met my eye and I realized how stupid my statement must have sounded to him. He was already dead and he knew it—he wouldn’t be able to run even if we got out of the room.

I realized how Ranar would do it. Rim Nol would be his fall guy. Ranar would “discover” the crimes at the museum and put the blame on the curator, who would be conveniently dead or, more likely, simply missing.

I leaned back against the wall. It was hopeless. We were prisoners of a warlord with an entire army. The thought exhausted me. All three of us were about to die.

Taksin met my eyes and nodded, sweat dripping off his chin. “Fucked,” he said.

❖

I almost laughed. "Exactly the way I feel."

It began to rain again, Cambodian style . . . a torrent as if an ocean in the sky just opened up.

The downpour hit the roof and found many holes. I was under one of them. I didn't move. I stayed next to Nol as he shut his eyes and put back his head.

I shut my own eyes and tried to focus on listening to the falling rain.

I WOKE UP AND saw Taksin kneeling beside Nol, giving him something.

"What's going on?" I asked, rubbing my eyes.

The sound of the door being unbarred cut off a response. I froze in sudden terror. Were they coming for me?

Two guards came in shouting. I couldn't understand what they said but they went for Nol, not me.

My good sense snapped and I got to my feet and pushed at them, screaming, "Leave him alone. Leave him alone."

They grabbed me, each by one arm, and flung me back, slamming me against the wall. The air burst from my lungs and I stood stock-still, stunned.

Nol rolled over from his sitting position against the wall onto his chest. As he did he gave out a cry. His whole body trembled, his legs shaking violently, pounding the floor. He suddenly gave a great sigh, then his body went limp.

A guard grabbed him and rolled him over.

The wood handle of a steel chisel protruded from his chest.

43

❖

The guards didn't bother washing the blood off the floor after they took away Nol's body.

I sat on the floor and stared at it until Taksin came over and helped me to my feet. He led me across the room to a mattress on the floor and told me to lay down.

"He asked you for the chisel," I said.

Taksin nodded. "So much pain. He sought peace."

I laid down and closed my eyes again. The rains came back, this time with wind that lashed the deluge against the hut. I stared up at the dark ceiling and listened to the rain and the gentle tapping of Taksin's hammer on a chisel as he worked a piece of sandstone.

I hoped that Nol did find peace and would be reunited with his family.

I thought again about what a strange world it was. Most of us were caring and humane people, but there were always two-legged beasts living among us that were sick and cruel.

I was still on the mattress, dozing off and on, when I heard the explosions and jerked awake. Taksin had fallen asleep with his head down and his arms folded on the table. He propped his head up and looked at me.

We just stared at each other. Nothing we could do. We couldn't see out or get out. Rain was still coming down.

"Sounded like it came from the camp area where the soldiers are," I said.

The bar rattled again and both Taksin and I stood up as the door swung open. A woman wearing a dark raincoat came in.

"Hurry."

"Chantrea! What—what's going on?" I stammered.

"I'm getting you out of here. Come on."

Another explosion sounded.

"That's Kirk setting off explosions to divert Chep's men. Come on, both of you, before we're spotted."

I hustled Taksin out with me. For a moment I thought of grabbing the museum piece on the table but left it behind, deciding I should keep both hands free.

Chantrea's station wagon was outside, lights off, its motor running. I got in the passenger side and Taksin slipped into the backseat.

She drove us away from the plantation house, staying on the dirt road that led in the opposite direction from the encampment.

The rain was violent. Lightning cracked and lit up the guard shack as we drove by. I didn't see anyone in it. My mind was spinning. I was confused, a state I had been in now for days.

"How did you know we were here?"

"Kirk found out from Bullock."

"Bullock's alive? The bastard!"

Chantrea shot me a look. "Not anymore. Kirk finished what you had started."

"Where's Kirk?"

"He'll meet us later. He started explosions on the other side of the camp and he's going to set land mines up on the road behind us in case we're pursued."

Random thoughts seemed to collide in my head. How could Chantrea just breeze into the warlord's lair and whisk us away?

"How did you get us out so easily?"

She shot me another look. "You're out, aren't you?"

❖

Taksin was quiet in the backseat. I wondered what was going on in his head, too.

I looked back and caught his eye. His facial features were passive but his dark eyes were alive. He had the same thought that I had: We were not out of the woods yet.

She put on the headlights. The rain turned the road into a shallow river. She drove mostly with her headlights off, turning them on just for a second occasionally when she couldn't see. To be able to see through the rain and dark night, she must have had the eyes of a cat.

"Where are we going?" I asked.

"The main road's up ahead, the same one we took to Siem Reap. Kirk left a car there. I'll use it to go back to Phnom Penh. You and Taksin take this car and go onto the airport at Siem Reap. It's not that far, less than an hour's drive."

"If it's not that far, can't we just drive there with you? I don't know how Taksin and I will—"

"I can't go with you. I may be followed. Or they might call ahead and have my car stopped on the road. I can't go to Angkor. I have to get back to the capital where I can get protection from the Minister of Culture."

"I know how they did it," I said. "Taksin's forgeries aren't all being sold. Some are in the Royal Museum, being substituted for the real pieces."

"I learned that, too."

"How did you find out?"

"Kirk. He's been involved in it."

I hesitated. "Chantrea . . . some things don't make sense to me. Have you been involved, too? In the art scheme?"

She didn't react to the question, at least not that I could see. She drove on for a moment before she answered.

"No. Ranar wanted me to be involved because of my position at Angkor. I knew something was wrong, but not exactly what was going on."

"Ranar is financing a revolution with his scheme."

"You learned a great deal," she said.

"He's Khmer Rouge, some sort of modern version of it."

She shook her head. "No, the Khmer Rouge tried to turn back the clock. Ranar's an idealist. He believes the country needs a strong hand to bring it into the modern world." She glanced at me. "I'm sympathetic to Ranar's plan for a revolution that would reform our corrupt government. We're a poor country and what wealth we have doesn't reach most of the people. Neither does political power. We're working for the good of the people."

"But isn't Ranar part of the problem? Rich and privileged?"

"He has money because he has a connection to royalty, but he's always been left out of real power. His father was a distant cousin to the king but the royals look down on him because of his mother. They say she came from an old French plantation family, but there are claims she was a just a bar girl, a prostitute. He hates the royals and wants to bring them down."

Ranar didn't strike me as a democratic idealist.

I still wasn't satisfied with her answers. "The night I was at Angkor, you arranged for us to sleep in tents. That made it very convenient for Kirk and Bullock to steal Angkor pieces." I didn't add that those antiquities were part of her job to protect.

So far Taksin hadn't said a word since we got into the car. I didn't know how much of this he was following.

"I admit I haven't been perfect," she said. "I've never forgotten what happened to my family during Pol Pot's era. I've never forgotten that the leaders who were supposed to protect us didn't." She took her eyes off the road to meet my eyes. "The Khmer Rouge leaders haven't controlled the central government for about three decades, yet they still haven't been brought to justice. Does that tell you who is really in power?

"So, yes. Khmer artifacts have been taken and used to raise money for a political movement to change the government so the Khmer Rouge leaders would be brought to justice. Kirk's work with land mines gave him freedom to travel anywhere in the country and made him a familiar face everywhere. He was able to transport the pieces."

"And Bullock marketed them."

"Yes." She grinned. "Kirk said you did a good job of cutting up Bullock. You should be happy he finished the job."

I didn't know what to say. Not about Bullock, the bastard could rot in hell as far as I was concerned. It was her story that was leaving me confused.

❖

Was she admitting to being part of Ranar's plot? Sometimes it sounded like she was . . . other times it almost sounded like she was making excuses for being involved.

She stared intensely into the rearview mirror and then twisted in the seat and looked to the rear.

"What's the matter?" I asked. I turned and followed her look.

"I thought I saw a car back there."

"I don't see headlights. Maybe it was lightning flashing."

What I did see was Taksin's face. He looked like he wanted to tell me something, that he was alarmed at what was coming down. But he either didn't have the words or wasn't sure of his thoughts. I understood completely. I was also suffering a sense of dread—the sense of the other shoe dropping after something bad had already happened.

"Rim Nol is dead," I said.

No reaction.

"He killed himself because he was being tortured."

She nodded. "Yes, so many of us wanted to end our lives because of what we suffered. It's really not right under our beliefs, you know. Suicide. One is not to end their life to escape agony, but must find inner peace in order to carry harmony into the next life."

"He left in harmony," I said. "He beat the bastards torturing him. They wanted him to reveal who else knew what they were doing."

"If he left this life in harmony," she said, "he'll find peace in his next life."

She was just rambling on. And I was getting more worried. What was going on? I didn't want to keep talking. We had been rescued. Grabbed from the jaws of death. I didn't want to open my mouth and create some sort of bad karma and run into a roadblock of General Chep's thugs. But my mouth often didn't obey my brain, so it kept going.

"Why are you helping us?"

"You're a friend."

"But I know things."

What a big mouth I have.

She glanced at me again.

"I trust you. As they say in your movies, you wouldn't rat out a friend." She giggled.

She appeared hyper. I didn't know if she was frightened, or on something. Nothing she was saying sounded like the woman I'd driven a couple hundred miles with. Chantrea was a very cultured Cambodian with a little French education thrown in . . . not someone who would quote a dumb line from American gangster movies. It struck me as role playing . . . or a cover for nervousness. Of course, she had good reason for being nervous. She had just roared into a military encampment, thrown open a barred door, rescued two prisoners, and calmly driven out.

My right knee began to shake.

She turned off the dirt road we were on and onto another unpaved road. "This leads to the Siem Reap highway. The car for me is up ahead. We're about a mile from the main road. When you get there, you turn left and stay on it until Seim Reap and the airport. Take the first flight out, wherever it's going." She giggled again.

Chantrea pulled to the side of the road across from a parked car. She squeezed my arm. "Good luck."

I stared at her through the blurred passenger side window as she ran to the parked car. She got in the passenger side. So someone had not just dropped off a car for her . . . they were waiting.

Why had she bothered to lie? Was she so high on something that she didn't even realize she had lied?

Who was in the car? Kirk? But he was supposed to be back at the army camp. Or behind us if he had finished creating the diversion at the camp.

Taksin babbled something in Thai and then said, "I am scared. No trust her."

"*Srangapen,*" I said. He didn't understand and kept talking, but I tuned him out as I stared hypnotically ahead. When I met Nol that first time at the museum, he had told me about *srangapen,* the Cambodian method of execution during which the killing blow comes from an unexpected source.

Chantrea had introduced me to Nol.

She was the one that Nol had been trying to warn me about.

That hard fist of fear in my gut that had been there so long started aching.

I couldn't just sit there and wait for the next shoe to drop. I scooted over and got behind the wheel. She left the car running with the lights off. I couldn't see a thing in front of me with rain blurring the windshield and darkness. I reached to turn on the headlights and stopped, remembering she had kept the headlights off so we wouldn't be followed.

Lightning flashed and I saw something in the road ahead. I strained to see what it was through the blur of water washing out my vision through the windshield. It looked like a flat metallic piece that extended most of the way across the narrow road.

The horn blared in the car next to me and my foot hit the gas, the tires spinning in the mud. The rear of the car moved sideways, but we didn't go forward more than a foot.

Something was terribly wrong but my mind wasn't functioning properly. Then it struck me—the car waiting for Chantrea was the same sports car Ranar drove when he had picked me up at the airport.

The road suddenly lit up as a vehicle coming from the rear turned on its headlights. It came by me in a flash, a big white SUV with a heavy black push bar mounted in front of the grill. The SUV struck the rear of the sports car Chantrea had gotten in, pushing it ahead.

When the sports car's front tires hit the object lying across the road, an explosion erupted, lifting the car from the road. The SUV reversed and shot backward as a second explosion erupted when flames hit the sports car's gas tank.

The SUV pulled up beside me and I could see the faded lettering of a United Nations emblem on the side of the door.

❖

“Plan to stay at the Hanoi Hilton?” Kirk asked.

We were at the airport in Siem Reap waiting to board a plane for Ho Chi Minh City. Taksin and I got tickets for the first plane out. Just as I had at the Phnom Penh whorehouse, I kept looking down the corridor expecting police officers to come charging for me in any moment.

Kirk was amazingly calm. I guess I shouldn’t have been surprised. What would it take to make a guy who defuses land mines and bombs nervous?

“Is it a good hotel?” I asked.

Both Kirk and Taksin cracked up. An American businessman who overheard the question and answer walked away, shaking his head. Okay, the joke was on me, but at the moment I was more worried about being arrested than some stupid witticism.

“Very funny.” I didn’t want to appear not to get the joke. Maybe it had something to do with Paris Hilton.

“You keep looking down the corridor as if you expect to see the police at any moment. Stop worrying.”

I sighed. “Stop worrying” had been Kirk’s mantra ever since we got into his SUV after he blew up the sports car. Ranar had been the one behind the driver's wheel.

Two human beings had died and I was cold inside about their passing. I wasn't glad they were dead. I was just happy I wasn't.

Kirk had not caused a "diversion" at General Chep's camp. He had set off the explosions, but they had been made with Ranar and Chep's cooperation. The explosions had been a ploy to back up Chantrea's story that she was rescuing us.

The "rescue" had been set up so Taksin and I would be killed when we ran over a strip land mine that Kirk had laid across the road at Ranar's request. Ranar thought Kirk would kill me to protect himself. He was wrong. Kirk killed Ranar and protected both of us.

Killing two foreigners would cause infinitely more political and investigative heat than the death of Rim Nol. For Taksin and I to join the thousands of victims of land mines was pure genius. Getting lost on a back road and hitting a land mine while driving toward Angkor would be an easy sell to foreign embassies, especially with an inference that Taksin and I would have been looting artifacts, considering our reputations.

Rim Nol was also part of the scenario.

Kirk told me his body had been put in the trunk of the car that Taksin and I were in. He never mentioned Bullock's name. I didn't bring him up, either. He promised to give Nol a proper burial. I asked him to scatter Nol's ashes on the Killing Fields so he could be with his family.

Kirk had been battered and bruised and got some facial cuts after he rammed the sports car with his SUV so their tires tripped the land mine. The facial injuries only added to his sexy masculine appeal.

We survived because Kirk was simply an old-fashioned soldier of fortune. He didn't want to be king like Ranar, wasn't a fanatic like Chantrea, wasn't impossibly greedy and perverted like Bullock, wasn't a murderer. He was also much too independent to take orders from Ranar that went against his grain.

I was eternally grateful to Kirk. Someday I would repay him, but right now I just wanted to get out of this damn country before I was stuck here for the rest of my life—literally.

❖

During the drive to the airport Kirk had told me not to worry. "Ranar has fallen. It's a small country, news spreads fast. Right now anyone who had anything to do with Ranar is taking cover. General Chep is on the phone making deals and distributing some of his ill-gotten gains to politicians to make sure he doesn't have repercussions from the fallout.

"Tomorrow it will be the talk of the capital. Rumor and innuendo will rage, conspiracies hinted at. In a week it won't even be coffee break talk. Ranar and his plot will fade away because the next political plot will take its place."

I glanced down the corridor again. No SWAT team was storming toward me in battle gear. Yet.

An announcement came across the PA system that it was time for boarding. I hugged Kirk and kissed him good-bye.

"What are you going to do?" I asked. "You'll be in danger."

He grinned and shook his head. "Not really. Land mine hunters are hard to come by. It's not a real popular job. Or one with a future and a pension check. Besides, I'm a foreigner. No one will care about me. I'll spread a little money around and just keep doing what I do."

What he did included smuggling antiquities, but it wasn't the right time to give him a lecture.

"I'll never forget what you did for me and Taksin," I said.

His grin widened. "Yes, you will. Everything will be back to normal when you get back to New York and—"

"No, you're wrong. You don't understand. It's not just Cambodia and Bangkok. It all goes back to New York." I grimaced. "It's not over, Kirk. There's a big score to settle back home."

❖

VIETNAM

45

❖

Ho Chi Minh City

I checked into the Caravelle Hotel in the Vietnamese capital. No flights were available for several hours for a connection to New York for me or to Bangkok for Taksin, which actually worked to our advantage because we both needed to clean up and rest.

The tickets and hotel rooms came in just under the limit on my charge card, so I would arrive home broke with no priceless treasures or even a finder's fee. It would be a cold day in hell before I got compensated for anything I'd done for Cambodia. I would be lucky if they didn't try to extradite me for high crimes and misdemeanors.

Both of us were exhausted. A few hours of rest at a hotel would be reviving. Taksin grinned and told me he could find a place where he could treat me to a cobra cocktail but I turned down the offer. I couldn't even imagine what snake blood tasted like. Or why someone would drink it. Or, as he inferred rather graphically, why it would be an aphrodisiac.

I ordered separate rooms.

Out of curiosity, I asked at the front desk about the Hanoi Hilton and just got a blank stare. I'd have to check out the joke after I got home. I was still sure it must have something to do with Paris Hilton.

It's not over until it's over, ran through my head as I lay on the bed.

❖

It had started in New York and it had to end there. Not just because it was home but to finish what had begun there with a knock on my door from Sammy, the delivery guy.

A piece to the puzzle was still missing and it wasn't in Southeast Asia.

Chantrea had been on my mind since I crossed the border. I felt sorry for her. I don't think she really ever had a chance. Things were just too messed up during her lifetime in Cambodia for her to think straight. I believed that she really was trying to help her people. Even when she tried to kill me.

Ranar could rot in hell as far as I was concerned for what he did to me, to Chantrea, and to the deserving people of his country.

Rim Nol was different. I would light a candle for him when I got home. The Cambodians were great human beings because only people with incredible courage and resolve could have survived all the horrors and deprivations that they had to endure. Nol was of that caliber. A light went out in the world when he died.

Leaving Kirk at the Siem Reap airport had been emotional for me. We had been lovers, if only for a short time. He had saved my life. But, of course, he was still a bastard. I was certain he didn't come with us because he had some nefarious dealings to conclude and/or get his loot out. We would not ride off into the sunset together; he was still a smuggler, drawn to the dark side of the art world. Maybe he saved me because he simply drew the line at murdering people he liked.

I had to wonder about my luck with men. Did I automatically gravitate to nice bastards . . . or was the supply of available men in the world for my age so low that I had to scrape bottom? I wanted to think of it as just bad luck rather than a genetic defect or poor karma on my part.

I had hopes of getting an outstanding fake on credit from Taksin that I could sell to a rich buyer who didn't mind buying a fake, but he was all smiles and evasive commitments when I asked. I guess nearly getting murdered together was not enough for Taksin to trust my credit. I wished I had grabbed that museum piece on the table in the cell I shared with Taksin. Hopefully it would make its way back to the museum, but I seriously doubted it.

During the flight, Taksin had taken out a packet of pictures and showed me his reproductions like a proud father showing off his children. I recognized a piece I'd seen in New York and it stunned me.

Taksin had just given me the final piece to the puzzle. It was to end in New York, as I thought. And that weighed heavily on my mind and nerves as I waited for my flight because I had to wonder whether I would get home just to end up as a statistic as my body washed up on the shore of the East River.

Kirk wasn't the the blond foreigner who kidnapped Taksin and killed his friend. After we crossed the border, Taksin gave me an emphatic no—in Thai and shake of his head—when I asked if Kirk was the bad guy who kidnapped him and killed his friend.

That left a few million other blond foreigners as potential candidates but I had one particularly in mind. When we reached the hotel in Saigon—aka Ho Chi Minh City—I sat down with the hotel concierge and had her guide me through an Internet search that brought up a picture of my prime suspect.

I didn't need an interpreter to translate what Taksin was saying when the picture popped up of the blond-haired man who had had him kidnapped in Bangkok and had his friend killed.

Before we parted I had asked Kirk about the New York connection but he either knew nothing or refused to share the information with me. I wasn't sure he was even involved in the museum scheme, anyway. He only fessed up to looting antiquity sites, or more accurately buying stolen pieces and smuggling them out of the country.

I should have realized that a New York connection had been necessary for the sale of the Siva.

That person wasn't just part of a plot to sell the Siva in New York that Ranar had taken from the museum and replaced with Taksin's fake. He was also a coconspirator for looting, forgery, theft, and murder in Thailand and Cambodia.

Boarding my plane for Newark with a changeover in Tokyo, I hoped I was right about a lot of things.

❖

New York

46

❖

Being back in a city of skyscrapers, cold rain, and organized chaos, I rather missed the warm tropical atmosphere, warm smiling people, and quaint disorder in Phnom Penh. I didn't miss being on the hit list of the Cambodian mafia, but I had to admit that the country had an exotic charm that the steel and concrete jungles of New York lacked.

I felt like I had been gone an eon rather than just days. Nothing had really changed. Except I had become harder. I always considered myself strong enough to compete with other women and men in a tough business, but I drew the line at being so ruthless that winning was everything. It was okay in this world for a man to be a bastard—it fit male biology, contact sports, machismo—but women were nurturers biologically and hardness wasn't nurturing.

Right now though I felt angry and betrayed.

I was not a believer in redemption, rehabilitation, or even a little mercy toward violent offenders. My mentality ran more toward an eye for an eye, a tooth for a tooth. I wouldn't condone cutting off a thief's hand, but whacking a rapist's dick was all right with me. And it was time for someone to pay.

Time also for what the French called the denouement. Or as we would call it, the denouncement. The victims deserved closure even if I had to be their stand-in.

That was why I had come back to Chelsea. In a way, it had started here. For certain, it had to end here.

I stopped by the small sign that simply said "Bolger's" and looked down to his basement apartment. I felt my courage melting, my resolve getting mushy. It was easier to think brave thoughts than act them out.

The blinds were drawn for the two wrought-iron barred windows and only a hint of light showed on the blinds. His lights were off in the living room, which meant he was probably in his kitchen.

I went down the steps slowly, feeling a little cold and numb in my stomach. A line from the lyrics of a sixties folk song played in my head: *Where have all the flowers gone* . . . I couldn't remember the next line. *Gone to graveyards everyone*?

I rang his doorbell and waited. Then rang it again. The light never went on in the living room-bookstore, but I saw a window blind move. There was enough light from the streetlights for him to see it was me.

He opened the door. "Maddy. I couldn't believe my eyes. Where did you come from?"

"A cold day in hell."

I entered and deliberately hit the light switch next to the door.

"I've been worried about you. You should have given me a call and told me you were back."

I picked up the linga, the phallic fertility piece from his shelf, and turned around to face him.

"This is an interesting piece of art. You indicated it was Hindu, but this one was produced as a Khmer piece."

He shrugged. "Not really. It's a fake."

"What's interesting about it is that I've seen it before."

"Running around the antique stores in Hong Kong, Bangkok, and Phnom Penh, I'm sure you've seen many fakes."

"True, but this is a very unique fake. Taksin made it. I'm sure if I examined it with a magnifying glass, I'd find his trademark. I should have recognized the sandstone in the first place. It's Angkor stuff."

He raised his eyebrows. "What are saying? All those pieces on that wall are fakes. I couldn't afford to own a museum-quality piece."

"No, you couldn't. But I bet you thought you did. I imagine that the

Thai smugglers represented this piece as real. I wouldn't have known it was a fake if Taksin hadn't showed me pictures of his work."

"And I just accepted that representation? I'm an expert on Southeast Asian art and I let smugglers unload a fake on me? Come on, Maddy."

"Oh, but Taksin's work is so good not even experts can really tell the difference. You told me so yourself. I imagine you didn't check this piece for his mark until after I told you I'd seen it on the Apsarases piece. You probably took it to be just a tool mark from an ancient craftsman, if you saw it at all. I was lucky I saw it on the piece Sammy gave me. You know, it was the Sammy connection that should have turned me onto your connection earlier."

"The Sammy connection? Are you now accusing me of being in league with your Thai deliveryman?"

"Not personally, he's just a delivery guy, but that Thai group he works for is Ranar's smuggling source. And if you're involved with Ranar, which I know you are, then you're involved with them. Actually, I should have stumbled onto your connection to Sammy's group before Ranar even came into the picture."

"And why is that?"

"You called me. Here I was, in need of an expert to help me authenticate a Khmer piece and who calls out of the blue? You. An expert on the subject."

"Have you forgotten that you'd sent me your card?"

"I sent you my card a couple months ago—you and everyone else I ever dealt with in the business. But I didn't get your call until Sammy had been there."

"I had a referral for you."

"No, you didn't. You said you had recommended me to someone else. That was convenient. That way I couldn't check. And if no one ever called, that's not your fault, right?"

"I find it very interesting that a woman who was involved in the most egregious art scandal in history would accuse me of wrongdoing."

"That won't work, Bolger. The Thai smugglers needed someone to authenticate pieces. Did they pay you cash or were you getting pieces like this one in exchange?"

"My God, Maddy, have the tropics fried your brains? Do you realize what you're accusing me of?"

"Smuggling, fraud . . . murder."

He laughed. "And who exactly did I murder?"

Seeing him joke about it sent my adrenaline and anger up a notch.

"A young Thai named Phitsanu, a Cambodian museum curator named Rim Nol, and an Angkor guide named Bourey. There was also the attempt to kill me and Taksin."

"You are amazing, old girl. And delusional. You really think I've been racing around the world killing people?"

"No, I suspect you only directly participated in Phitsanu's murder. But you're as guilty of the other killings as Ranar."

I looked down at the linga as I spoke. Sandstone was hard and heavy. I'd need this as a weapon if he decided to harm me.

"It was the blond hair that tripped you up," I said.

"Really? Am I the only blond in the world?"

"Actually, I ran into an overabundance of blonds—you, Kirk, even Michelangelo could pass for blond. But you were the blond who had Phitsanu killed."

"I suppose you have some proof for these wild accusations."

"How about an eyewitness? Will that do?"

"Who? God?"

"Taksin. He was there when his friend was killed. On our stopover in Saigon, I had the hotel concierge log onto the Website advertising your services as an art authenticator. Taksin recognized your picture."

"And you think the word of an admitted art forger who lives halfway around the world will be taken against mine? Are you really so naïve about the way the justice system works that you think I'll be extradited to a third world country on the word of a criminal?"

"You know what I find interesting about that statement, Bolger? It sounds too pat. I'll bet you've already thought it out, haven't you, just in case the law came knocking on your door. You probably thought about it before you allowed yourself to be seen in Bangkok by Taksin. Of course, you figured that didn't matter, did you. Taksin would end up dead anyway. It's only a fluke that he's not."

He moved toward me, casually, not in a threatening manner, but I veered away anyway getting a table of books between us. When it came time to run, the place would be an obstacle course for both of us, especially for him with his cane.

❖

He held out his hand. "Please give me back my phallic symbol. If you're planning on braining me with it as I attack you, I can assure you it won't be necessary. The only aggression you'll see from me is to try to get you medical help for your poor, sick mind. Perhaps a long vacation would help? Someplace in the tropics?"

He threw back his head and laughed.

Bastard.

He kept a wide grin on his face as he edged toward me and I moved away. "There's not a damn thing you can prove—and the unsupported word of a disgraced art curator and a foreign art forger aren't going to mean anything. Now give me back my piece and get out of here."

I felt something against my leg. Morty was brushing up against me.

"This is the key, isn't it?" I said, holding up the linga. "The accusations aren't unsupported. This piece has Taksin's signature on it, his monk's begging bowl symbol. You won't be able to claim you bought it because there won't be a record of the transaction. The only way you could have gotten it is if the smugglers gave it to you. Which puts you in league with them."

We both bolted at the same time, me for the door, him for me. Bolger cursed as he stumbled over Morty and the cat let out a screech.

I went around a pile of books but spun into another pile as he reached for me and found myself stumbling over books underfoot.

He moved faster than I thought he could, getting a hold of the back of my coat. He jerked me against him and his arm went around my throat. I dropped the linga and grabbed his arm with both hands, kicking back against his shins with my heels as he lifted me off the ground. I screamed and twisted and kicked, trying to break his hold.

His hold tightened and I lost myself to panic, kicking and reaching blindly back with my hand, trying to claw his eyes. My eyes went blurry as I felt a crushing pressure against my windpipe—

Suddenly he released his hold and went backward, with me going back with him.

Strong hands pulled me off of him.

"You all right?"

I pushed Michelangelo away and fell back onto my knees, choking and coughing. "Bastard."

"It's okay, we have him."

❖

Two uniformed police officers had Bolger pinned to the floor.

"Not him, you. What took you so long?"

"I'm calling for an ambulance—"

I shook my head. "Don't do that, no medical insurance. You'll cost me thousands I don't have. I'm okay."

I picked up Morty on my way out the door. I needed air.

I was sitting on the stoop of the building next door hugging Morty for dear life when Michelangelo came out. I had wiped the tears away but I'm sure he could see that I'd been crying.

"I'll take that wire off of you."

I held Morty off to the side while the detective removed the radio transmitter from inside my coat.

"You waited long enough. You were supposed to come in when I got the linga and confirmed his ownership."

"We needed to let you run with it to see if he would incriminate himself more. We have enough for a conviction now."

"Oh, hell, you know it will drag around the courts forever and then some lazy prosecutor will plea bargain him down to a traffic ticket so he can get out and come back and murder me."

"I'll see to it that—"

"See to what? Thanks to you, another couple seconds and he would have choked the life out of me. Morty saved my life by delaying that maniac a second or two."

He reached out to comfort me with his hand and I pushed it aside and stood up, clutching Morty to me again. The cat had become my security blanket.

"I know what you've been through. You were brave to go in there."

"No, you don't. You won't know until a killer has a grip on your neck and you're seconds from death. I should never have let you talk me into going in there to record him. First you send me off to get murdered in Cambodia, then you send me in to get murdered here. What am I? Some sort of sacrificial lamb for the police?"

"Maddy—"

"No, I'm out of here."

I left, taking my only friend in the world with me.

I had the worst luck with men.

Except for Morty.

❖

The secret to life is honesty and fair dealing. If you can fake that, you've got it made.

—GROUCHO MARX

47

❖

Rainy days and Mondays . . . It felt like both even though it was Wednesday and the Manhattan evening had clear skies and a cool breeze. Standing by my apartment window, staring down at the little piece of third world below, I felt melancholy . . . wondering about human nature . . . thinking about when I was rich and famous . . . or at least fairly well off and reasonably well known in my profession.

Now I was more infamous than famous and, unfortunately, better known for being involved in the dark side of art despite the fact I was always struggling to do the right thing and it wasn't my fault that the world was full of people whose driving force was greed.

I felt like James Garner in those old *Maverick* and *Rockford Files* TV shows he did—the ones where he beat the bad guys but never got the money or the girl at the end.

I was feeling sorry for myself, wondering how I was going to pay the rent, thinking about splurging on a Zen Butter cone from the Chinatown Ice Cream Factory and a foot rub when I got a call from the grave.

"When I tell you who this is, you have to promise you won't scream."

I didn't recognize the voice.

"Am I allowed to curse and hang up?"

❖

"I'm looking for something," he said. "It's two thousand years old and was buried with Jesus."

Okay. As soon as I found out who my caller was, my next question had to be . . . what's in it for me?

I heard a tapping at my door.

It was either Poe's Raven come to collect my soul or my landlord collecting the overdue rent.

❖

Life Imitating Fiction

The government of China is as serious about protecting their antiquities as their food exports.

The fact that the head of the equivalent of China's Food and Drug Administration had been shot after tainted food exports made worldwide headlines is well known.

What received less publicity is that the government also shot the head of security for a city's museum.

His crime: replacing museum pieces with reproductions and smuggling the bona fide antiquities out of the country to be sold.

He was caught when authorities discovered that an antiquity that appeared to be at the museum was sold at auction.

❖